WITHDRAWN

LANDSLIDE

LANDSLIDE

3 4028 09429 6143
HARRIS COUNTY PUBLIC LIBRARY

Leet
Leet, Melissa
Landslide : a novel

$16.95
on1019843275

First edition.

A NOVEL

by Melissa Leet

Antrim House
Simsbury, Connecticut

Copyright © 2018 by Melissa Leet

Except for short selections reprinted for purposes of
book review, all reproduction rights are reserved.
Requests for permission to replicate should
be addressed to the publisher.

Library of Congress Control Number: 2017944128

ISBN (paperback): 978-1-943826-33-9
ISBN (cloth-bound): 978-1-943826-32-2
ISBN (e-book): 978-1-943826-39-1

First Edition, 2018

Printed & bound by Ingram Content Group, LLC

Book design by Rennie McQuilkin

Front cover artwork:
"Labyrinth. Green Birds" by Vizerskaya
courtesy of Getty Images

Map by Diane Goodman

Author photograph by Kenneth Leet

Antrim House
860.217.0023
AntrimHouse@comcast.net
www.AntrimHouseBooks.com
21 Goodrich Road, Simsbury, CT 06070

In memory of
my brilliant mother, Helen Ashton Coult Chamberlain
and my remarkable mother-in-law, Judith Heins Leet

ACKNOWLEDGMENTS

Thank you to my publisher Robert Rennie McQuilkin at Antrim House. Rennie, your edits and insights have been indispensable. Your energy, enthusiasm and intelligence have encouraged me every step of the way.

Thank you to Wally Swist. Without you, I would have never have brought *Landslide* to fruition.

I also thank the team at Cornerstones, including Ayisha Malik, Kathryn Price, Kylie Fitzpatrick, Laura Wilkinson and Dinah Ceely. Your early readings gave the manuscript much direction.

Thank you to Susan Elderkin for sharing with me your craft of story writing, and to my friends Ashley Dartnell, Diana Clark, Carol Grose, Sharon Ali, Susan Chan, Virginie Gueroult, Susan Madison, Anna Yang, Noelle Doumar, Jas Bancil, Vera Meislin, Grace Tsao-Wu, Katherine Conover, Elizabeth Collier, Anna Marshi, Katie Sunley, Katy Kingsolving, and Christine Fisher. When I wrote for myself only, you kept me company along the way. Many times I shared with you my own private pleasure of a page well done, and you were so pleased for me. Thanks, too, to Elise Paschen: your delight with *Landslide* spurred me on when I was flagging.

A special thanks to my illustrator, Diane Goodman. You were so patient as we worked to translate my fragmented images into your wonderful drawing.

Thanks as always to my Dad, Jack Tuttle Chamberlain, and my step-mom, Peggy Chamberlain. Your unremitting excitement about the novel has been incredibly lovely.

To my ineffable husband, Ken, and my brightest stars, Christopher, Dillon, William and James: you are my loves and my joy.

CONTENTS

Map of The Garden   x - xi

1. Garden   3
2. A Plan   12
3. Mom   15
4. Business   20
5. Jay   21
6. Date   34
7. The News   41
8. Trouble   45
9. Rain   56
10. Changes   59
11. Charlie   64
12. Tide Pool Trail   72
13. Fruit Loops   79
14. Lunch   83
15. Garden   87
16. Baby   95
17. Business   100
18. Mom   103
19. Charlie   106
20. Parents   108
21. Fire   119
22. Fight   126
23. John Jay   132
24. Giovanni   138
25. Shadow   145
26. Giovanni   150
27. New Day   153
28. Hospital   156
29. Sad   159
30. Giovanni   174
31. Dream   181
32. Charlie   183
33. John Jay's Room   188

34. The Mountain Surprise   194
35. Married   198
36. Engaged   201
37. Waterfront   204
38. Not There   211
39. Wedding Shopping   215
40. Periods   221
41. Bob and Susie   227
42. Jay   230
43. Mom   233
44. Jay   238
45. Sad   242
46. Wedding   245
47. Mountain   254
48. Accident   263
49. Surprise   266
50. Pregnant   274
51. Missing Mom   277
52. Business   281
53. Sailing   285
54. Birthday Cake   290
55. Married   296
56. Children   300
57. Mom's Room   303
58. Children   305
59. Didn't Know   312
60. At Least Try   316
61. Anniversary   319
62. Mom   325
63. Business   327
64. Technicality   330
65. Pregnant   338
66. Giovanni   342
67. Garden   345
68. Charlie   348
69. Jay   355
70. Not Ready   358

71. Landslide   362
72. Maria and Fernando   365
73. Father   367
74. Garden   370
75. Mother   375
76. Animals   378
77. Jay and Jake   380
78. Mountain   388
79. Skull Fire   393
80. Family   395
81. Hacking All the Seasons   398

About the Author   401
About the Book   402

GARDEN

Oh, mirror in the sky what is love?
Can the child within my heart rise above?

Stevie Nicks

LANDSLIDE

1

GARDEN

"Jill," Mom called. "Breakfast!"

I stepped into the chilly air, carrying Lionel. When I was four, Jay had given Lionel to me to look after me while he was away. When we were little, I would push Lionel in carriages, and dress him in baby clothes. Now that we were ten, Lionel was my equal, and he stood guard when he was needed. Mom said whoever loved me must also love Lionel, as he would be getting a twofer when he got married. I didn't want to get married. If I could, I'd stay here in our Garden forever.

When I found Mom, she was by the Scented Beds. Her long auburn hair shined copper where it was free from her hat's darkening shadow. On the nearby mosaic table, my favourite French toast waited warm. Mom had cookie-cut the toast into lion shapes decorated with brown and yellow icing manes, iced blue eyes, and brown, sprinkled sugar noses. Our glass house strawberries ringed the plate like a frame. In a mug, mini marshmallows floated atop steaming chocolate.

"Happy birthday dear Jill, happy birthday to you." I blew on the chocolate's top while Mom sang, pooling the marshmallows. Then I caught them up, frog-like with my tongue.

Mom eyed me with disapproval. She was strict about manners. "If it weren't your birthday…"

"But it is!" I shot back happily.

"Are you intending to eat like a savage at your party?"

"I was thinking more green space alien."

Mom laughed. "Give me strength."

"What about me?"

"*You* could use a fork and a knife," indicating the French toast in my fingers.

"What fun is that?" I asked, leaning in close to nestle. She smelt of mint, dirt and vanilla lotion.

"What are you snuffling at?" she asked.

"You smell like mint."

"The mint has jumped the bed again," Mom admonished. "It's such a weed!"

I laughed. Mint was so not a weed.

"I thought we could use the clippings to make jugs of mint lemonade for your party."

"Yes!" Mint lemonade was my favourite.

"But first we have to finish your cake."

For my birthday, we always made cakes – lady birds, horses, pirate ships. This year it was a lion. We had lion napkins and plates. Toys and sweets filled a lion piñata. Helium balloons waited to be changed into floating lion balloons with streamer legs and tissue paper faces. After the balloon lions were made, we would play who could pop theirs first, throwing real darts from behind a masking-taped line. The best party game, though, would be Hide and Seek. The Garden was great for hiding!

Our Garden was in the foothills of the mountains. From its edge we could see far out into the rocky scrub that Jay said was caused by the mountain's rain shadow. Our Garden would have been dry as well, but high mountain springs fell through it in wandering brooks.

"We should close the fabrics," Mom said, pushing back her hat. "It's going to be hot."

The fabrics were our awnings. Mom used them to cover the flower beds most vulnerable to fierce sun. Mom had collected the cloth traveling with Jay when they were first married. Her first textiles were from Morocco. She had bought them back when she was still at school, and didn't have money. Mom was bargaining for the cloths, when Jay cut in, speaking in Arabic. Mom was about to get cross at him, when Jay turned to tell her that the stall seller would sell Mom all five fabrics for the money she had been offering. At tea after, Mom said talking with Jay was as if she had known Jay all her life even though they had just met. After that first tea, they were together every day until Mom had to return to England to school.

"Mom, how did Jay learn Arabic?" It was a new question.

"Arabic?" Mom asked, helping herself to lion French toast.

"When you met Jay in Morocco."

"Oh," Mom said, smiling. "Dad has a way with languages. He can go to a country, and just pick them up."

"Really?"

"Kind of how you picked up Spanish by listening to Maria and Fernando talk." Fernando and Maria helped Mom with her Garden business, and were part of our family now.

* * * *

"Perfect," Mom said, standing back to look at our cake. "He's real enough to roar. Let's take a picture to add him to our Hall of Fame Cake Book."

"I think he's our best cake yet," I told her, pleased.

"You might be right," Mom allowed.

After the Polaroid, Mom gave me my birthday present. She had made a sky-blue, beaded dress that was soft and slippery in my hands.

Mom beaded the way grandmas knit. She could make anything – wall art, bed spreads, Halloween costumes. Some of her beads were so small that when strung, they blended like carpets, where a hundred thousand knots became a single design. Mom kept many of her very first necklaces in an ancient mariner's chest Jay had brought us from Chile. I loved playing with these necklaces, and not just for dress up. I made them into snakes and eels, stepping stones and paths. At Christmas, they strung across our tree, glistening like jeweled ropes.

Mom always beaded in front of the fire. On those nights that were too warm, we were in the Garden and her box stayed shut. Mom could string almost without looking. She would bead like the winter rain that falls all day long without stopping once. Sometimes I would try too, but I always got tired. Mom said she could keep on and on because she had dancing hands. I had wished for dancing hands too, but Mom said no. "Your hands are beautiful," Mom said, "because they are still."

"So do you like your dress?"

"Oh yes," I breathed. Its soft weight felt nice on my shoulders. "And listen!" I swayed. The dress swirled around my knees. "It chinkles!"

Mom laughed. "Cow principle."

I paused. "What do you mean?"

"In Switzerland, they tie bells around the cows so they can hear them wander. This way, during Hide and Seek…"

"Mom!"

She laughed, her green almond eyes glinting.

"No one will find me, beads or not, except maybe Susie." Susie lived down the Mountain from us, and had been my best friend since I was three. She was half-American Indian. As if on cue, the doorbell sounded. I knew it was Susie even before I started for the door.

"Wow!" Susie exclaimed at my sky-blue bead dress. Mom came up beside us.

"That must have taken forever," Susie said to Mom.

"It took a while," Mom agreed.

"Come see my lion cake," I said, pulling her inside.

"Can I try it after the party?" Susie asked, skipping along with me. Although Susie was almost two years older, we were close in size.

While we were in the kitchen, the doorbell rang again. "I bet that's Chad," said Susie. "He said he would come early." We rushed down the hall together, my beads tink-tinkling as we raced.

****

"Throw!" I screamed at Susie. The party was in full swing. Now our girls' team raced to pop our lion balloons before the boys. We had three lions to the boys' two. We had all thrown wildly, quickly, but Susie was not being rushed. She spread her feet, aimed with one eye. Chad was opposite. Pop! Chad now had one lion balloon left.

"Throw!" we cried.

Susie flung the dart. Pop! Then rapid-fast her next! Pop! Chad looked over as they both lined up their last shot. Susie smiled, and her black eyes had that look. Chad's dart bounced off his red balloon, but ours went Pop! We shrieked! Susie grinned at Chad, who was not pleased.

"Cake time!" Mom called.

"We'll win next game," I heard Chad say to Susie as we made our way to the picnic table.

"Next game is Hide and Seek," Susie told him. "You don't stand a chance."

****

That night, I opened my presents before a crackling fire. Susie had given me a silver and turquoise bracelet. In her card, she said she had one too, and that once on, we must never take them off. Maria and Fernando had given me a pink present with a big pink bow. Inside, were more Maria-made animal clothes. Lionel might be grown up, but Michael Marmot, Red Rabbit, Daisy Deer, Harry Hedgehog, Squirrel, and Rascal Raccoon were all still young.

My last presents were from Jay. Two were books: *Shackleton's Antarctic Adventure* and *Buddhism for Children*. He also gave me a rectangular moving machine. It tilted side to side. Blue, black, white and green liquid sand swirled inside like crashing waves. Each crash created a new shade of blue, a different colour of green. I wondered about Jay in Antarctica where the wind screamed instead of blowing. Was he thinking about me?

"What's Jay doing right now?"

Mom set down her beads. Her mouth turned down, but she caught herself, and her voice stayed light. "If I know Dad, he's probably out there taking pictures of penguins."

"Or icebergs."

Mom smiled. "Or icebergs."

Jay's photos covered the walls on each side of our fireplace. In one, Jay was on Everest; in another, he was kayaking down the Amazon. Amongst these and his pictures of deserts, seas and trees were photos of monasteries. Jay collected monasteries in the same way Mom gathered mint. There was also a snap of Mom taken the day they had first met. She was wearing a yellow sun dress and a large, flappy straw hat.

"How come you don't still travel with Jay?"

Jay was famous for his photos the way Mom was famous for her gardens. When they first married, Mom had gone everywhere with Jay. They had even been to Varanasi together, where holy cows wandered ancient streets, and pilgrims bathed in the Ganges at breaking dawn.

Mom said what made Jay such a good photographer was that he was exceptionally patient. When he sensed a shot, he waited, sometimes for days. Mom said she couldn't count how many times she had watched with him while the clouds came and went, while morning turned to night. Just when she had been looking at the same tree or village or road for so long that there was nothing left to see, the sun would come or go, or the clouds would shift just right. That was when Jay took his shots.

"I had you, for one," Mom said, starting to bead again. She was making another wall art. On one wall in our living room she displayed these hangings, changing them out as mood took. I also had a place in my room where I could put them up. I could choose any one I liked and swap them as often as I wished.

"We could travel together," I offered. I had often tried to imagine how it would be to travel faraway.

"Most of the places Dad goes are no place for a child," she answered, her voice hardening as it did when she was firm.

"Like the war in Rwanda."

"Like Rwanda," Mom agreed.

"But couldn't Jay photograph things that weren't so dangerous?" Mom smiled gently. "I also have my Garden."

"But Fernando could look after it," I persisted.

"And my clients?" she reminded.

"He could look after them too."

Mom's eyes smiled. She cascaded another vial of black into her beading bowl. "Poor Fernando. Can you imagine him alone to tackle Mrs. Lewis?" Mrs. Lewis always changed her mind. "Or Mr. Hawk?" His name wasn't really Mr. Hawk, but he rescued hurt birds, so we called him that.

"I bet he could handle it."

"I know he could too," Mom agreed. "But that's not the point. Following Jay wasn't right." Her eyes flickered, narrowed. She had said more than she had meant.

"What do you mean?" I pushed. I still wanted to know.

In her eyes I could see Mom collect her thoughts. After a bit she said, "It was hard for me to do nothing for myself when I traveled with Jay. Always, Jay would find places to just sit and watch, and the more he watched, the more it seemed he had always been wherever we happened to be. Within no time, he would be getting by in the local language, slipping into their habits. It made me feel left out, even though I would try to stay occupied."

I had never thought about how hard it would have been for Mom to wait while Jay took pictures. Everyone knew that Mom was busy like bees.

"Beading helped. It gave my hands something to do so the rest of me could be steady," she said, searching Jay's photos. Still, when I found our Garden, it felt as if I had finally found the place where I really belonged." Her eyes came back to me. "Gardens are what I love."

"But I thought you loved Jay."

"I do love Jay, and he loves us."

"Then why is he gone so much?"

One of the fire's logs burnt in half, falling forward. Mom picked up the old piece of wrought iron fence that was our poker and pushed the wood back. She stayed squatting a moment, while firelight danced on her face. Mom had quick emotions that could alight like dry tinder. She was practiced at being still until her emotions quieted. "His work makes Jay feel whole," she said finally, turning toward me.

I nodded slowly, trying to understand. "Like you feel in our Garden."

"That's right."

"Doesn't he get lonely?" Jay often went where there was no one at all.

"Growing up with Grandpop in Montana got him used to looking after himself," she told me.

"Do you think he missed his mom?"

Mom came close to me on the couch, taking her beading back up. "It's hard to miss someone you never knew."

"Oh, but I'd miss you," I told her with certainty. "Even if you left the day I was born."

Mom's smile was warm.

"Still," I said, "I don't see why that means he has to be gone now."

"Jay can seem quiet," she told me, swirling her fingers through her beads as she talked, "but underneath he has powerful feelings. One way he finds peace is to go to places that accommodate these feelings."

I looked at the photo of him on top of Everest.

"We let him be happy, and he loves us more because we allow him to be free."

"Like the rabbit."

"That's right. When his leg was better, we let him go."

"Because he was wild."

"Exactly."

"Is Jay wild?"

Mom laughed. "In part, I guess he is."

"Do you miss him when he's gone?"

"Do you?" Mom asked.

I hesitated, watching the flames jump. "Not all the time," I admitted. "Is that bad?"

Mom touched her foot with mine. "No."

"I get used to not seeing him, I mean, when he is gone a long time," I confessed.

Mom's eyes softened. "You see my beads?" Mom spread out the half-completed hanging on her lap so I could see it better. "After you are in bed, I try to imagine what Jay's doing, and all this imagining goes into my beads."

"It's like the Antarctic!" I said, really noticing the blue, white, grey, yellow design for the very first time.

"And the green one, of the forest? Where was Dad?"

"In the Congo! You're following him with your beads!"

Mom laughed, but then her face quieted. "I don't miss him all the time either," she told me.

"You don't?"

"Most of the time, I'm just too busy. Between you, the Garden, work – the day just flies."

It was true. Time went fast a lot. I thought some more. "But don't you get mad that he's gone away?"

Mom's smile was like a puzzle. "No one is without flaws, Sweet

Pea," Mom said gently. "Jay has fewer than almost anyone I know except maybe Maria and Fernando."

I thought about how when Jay was last here, our school was about to tear down the big kids' playground, because it was unsafe, and there was no money to fix it. Jay organized a drive, and saved the playground.

"I'm sorry he missed your birthday."

On the coffee table, I watched the coloured waves mix black with white which swirled with green.

"But we had fun, didn't we?"

I nodded.

"Did you really like it?"

"So much!" I breathed

Her green eyes glinted elf-like. "Me too," she agreed.

2

A PLAN

Next to me, my business plan waited ready for the bank meeting. In their time, Mom's gardens had been famous. Now I had my own garden idea. Glossy sketches of garden furniture gleamed amongst the growth forecasts. At home, my actual financials were not so rosy. I desperately needed some working capital.

Now, though, I risked being late. I should have waited until after the bank meeting to look at the photos. Seeing them had caused my feelings to course through me like spring runoff, and I had lost track of time. Rising quickly, I hurried toward Café Alfredo's exit, shoving the pictures back into their envelope as I rushed.

"No!" exclaimed a guy, springing back. My elbow had knocked his coffee hard. Coffee stains made brown slashes across his white shirt. My photos sprawled on the floor.

"Unbelievable!" he cried. His anger escalated, carried. People stared. "Just look!" His eyes rose from his shirt to my face. Our eyes linked. My cheeks burned. His handsomeness embarrassed me even more.

"I'm so sorry," I stammered. My eyes caught Café Alfredo's large wall clock. My heart quickened. I knelt to collect my pictures. Images of Himalayan peaks and glistening rice fields were scattered on the floor. There was the Nepalese village where I had passed nights, medieval in its rhythms, musical with chiming prayer bells and bleating goats. With my pictures hastily collected, I stood to go past. I kept my eyes down, hoping he would not say more.

"Wait!" he called after I was already by. He held out a snap of me at Camp Three. I took its end, but he did not let go. Instead, he looked from photo to me, and again our eyes locked. His were deep brown, magnetic.

"I'm really sorry," I said again, tugging to free the picture from his hand, pulling my eyes from his. Once I was outside, I felt anger surge at my images, which made no sense at all. The truth was that the photos had sat months, trapped in their film canisters, as I worked on my business plan. Yet not developing them had begun to niggle. Now that my business plan was finally done, I had thought that I was ready to see them, but they had hurt more than I had expected. The photos of the base camp had been the hardest. Blue and red tents dotted the snow like coloured igloos. Vivid prayer flags flapped. I remembered my excitement, my hope, but a picture of me at 21,000 feet showed me worn down and worn out; I should have known. I had tried to push through it. This was when the mental replaced the physical; it was the mental that got you to the top. That was what mountaineers did, what Jay did. I had so wanted to be tough.

That day I had tried focusing on my mantra as I took step by difficult step. My mantra was the names of all our Garden's places – Scented Beds, John Jay's room, the Glass House. Like a slideshow clicking by, I saw Colonnade heavy with grapes and Silver Tree's whispery leaves. I was really there, going through Arabian Room, by Southwest's skulls and cactuses, slipping through the Concealed Door. The sun still seeped on Pine Path which skirted Babbling Brook which always called.

That day, I had longed for Mom more than I had wanted to scale this mountain; I wanted to be home. My longing had made my memories of the Garden waver. I slowed down my mind. If only I could smell the dusky scent of Lavender or hear the Poplars stir. Like a ghost, Mom had appeared again by the Lilacs, but as quickly as I had imagined her, she was gone. I was so devastated to lose her that I squandered the Garden too, and I became aware again only of cold and snow, that smelled of nothing but water and rock.

My team had summited. I had not. Disappointment still singed. Even more, though, if I couldn't push through then, would I have what it takes to build my business now? Certain challenges were more than the things themselves; they were omens of how to rise when push came to pull.

I touched my turquoise bracelet, protective like a talisman, as I checked the time. Thirteen minutes until my bank meeting. I picked up my pace. My heels clacked fast against the pavement. My satchel bumped uncomfortably against my side.

3

MOM

"What's the capital of Michigan?" I asked Mom, looking up from my homework. Around me, my animals gathered, impatient. I had promised them a play in the Olive Trees as soon as I was done.

Mom was bent over the mint, tying new shoots to a bamboo-framed hideaway, which the herb covered like a blanket. I often went into the hideaway to study, since I thought well in its cool green shade. Mom said that was because mint is a good stimulant.

Mom leaned back on her heels. "Lansing, why?"

I showed her my map. "I've got to learn all the capitals by Friday."

"That's a good one," Mom said approvingly.

"Boring," I countered.

"When I was your age..." Mom started.

"You walked a mile each way to school," I mimicked, cutting her off. This she had told me at least a thousand times.

Mom laughed. "I wasn't going to say that."

"You were at the top of your class then," I continued. This she hadn't told me, but I was sure she was. Mom was really smart. Everyone said so.

Mom's smile became droll. "Actually, at your age, I tried *not* to get good grades."

"What?"

Mom's eyes softened at my surprise. "When I was your age, it wasn't cool for girls to be smart. Even though I always knew the answers, I had to pretend I didn't, so school became boring because I didn't have to try."

In our hallway, by the kitchen, hung black and white photos Jay had taken of Mom's hometown. Once, there had been an automotive seat factory where Grandpa worked. Our photo showed the factory now all boarded up. Another photo showed the little house where Mom grew up, paint peeling from its porch. Grandma now lived in Florida, but we didn't see her much.

"Grandma let you?"

"She didn't really know."

"How could she not know?" Mom knew everything about my school work.

"It was just different. She didn't think school mattered so much. When I got out of high school, she thought I'd marry a local boy as she did."

"Not go to college?" Mom talked about college all the time.

Mom's smile pinched her eyes. "Truth was, I never really belonged."

Here Mom was the center of everything. I had never thought of her otherwise. "What?" I asked. Her eyes held a secret now.

Her smile softened. "For a while anyway, I got into a mess of trouble," she confessed,

"Trouble?"

She took a long sip from her tea as a careless breeze caught her hair. Recently, grey strands sometimes streaked across her copper. When she saw them, she plucked them out. "For a while, I stole candy to share so kids would like me better."

I couldn't believe it. Mom returned to a store if she realized she hadn't been charged enough. If she didn't get something done, she didn't make excuses; she apologized.

"Then one day I got caught. It was awful." Mom had shifted her weight from her heels to her bottom, both hands circling her tea. "What was worse, everyone knew. In a small town, everyone finds out everything."

"What did Grandma do?"

"Came down on me like a ton of bricks. You might not be able to say a lot for my mother, but one thing's certain, she's dead honest."

Mom didn't get along with Grandma. The few times we had seen her, it wasn't long before they started fighting. Their fighting made me not like Grandma very much.

"After that, I stopped trying to fit in. Instead, I'd sneak off to the library. I started reading about faraway places, because I knew, one way or other, I had to get out. It was at my hometown library that I found *English Garden Mazes of the 1800s*."

I knew that book. We had a copy of it, and it had the pride of place on Mom's Garden bookshelf. Sometimes we looked through it together. The book was the one that had led Mom into gardening.

Her green eyes flashed. When they gleamed like that, I thought they looked just like an elf's. "*That's* when I started coming *top of my class*," she said, emphasizing each of the last four words. "I made a plan right then and there to study horticulture in England. I also started working at every job I could get."

"Weren't you scared?" I asked. "I mean to go to England alone?"

Mom reached forward and pulled off a dead mint leaf. "Petrified."

"I could never do that."

"That's because you haven't yet discovered your dreams," she said, her voice certain. "Once you know those, you'll be able to do anything you want."

* * * *

In the kitchen, Mom quizzed me on capitals while my animals scaled my knees as I sprawled on the floor. We hadn't had time for the Olive Trees, so I was making myself into the jungle. The doorbell rang. Susie often came to hitch a ride. I rushed down the hallway, just missing Fernando and Maria who were heading into the office.

"Careful Niña," Maria chided, holding her tea cup from her chest.

"Sorry Maria. Morning Fernando," I called, not breaking stride. Five feet away, I stopped running and leaned back, sliding on socked feet to arrive perfectly at the door.

Susie had on the same t-shirt as yesterday; stains splotched its front. Dark shadows ringed her eyes. She had recently bobbed her hair. I still wasn't used to it, as before it had been past her bottom. It was all mussed up.

"How's your mom?" I whispered.

"Still drinking," she said, scratching her head. "And there's nothing in the fridge."

"We're just having breakfast. Want some?"

"Do you think your mom would mind?"

Susie ate quickly, hungrily. Without even asking, Mom refilled her plate with eggs, adding sliced apples and bananas. I drank a large glass of milk. Susie had two.

"Spelling today," I said conversationally as we ate.

Susie's eyes shot up. I could tell that she had forgotten. Even though we were in different grades, Spelling Tuesdays were school-wide. She scratched her head again.

"Susie," Mom said gently. "I think we'd better check your hair."

"What do you mean?" Susie asked, looking at her, and then the penny dropped. It had been a big problem in the school lately so we had all gotten fliers about it. "I don't have lice."

"I think you might, sweetie. You keep scratching your head."

Susie's cheeks went red. I could tell she was trying not to cry. "That's ok," she mumbled, looking down, pushing back her chair. "I'll have my mom do it." I could see she was going to scratch again, but she caught herself.

Mom came to the table, kneeling low so she could see Susie's down-turned face. "If you go home now, your Mom really won't be able to help, will she?

How had Mom known?

Mom turned to me. "If Susie has them, chances are you do too."

"But I washed my hair yesterday," I protested.

"It has nothing to do with clean hair," she insisted. She widened her eyes at me purposefully. "Both you and Susie stay very clean."

"Actually, maybe I have been a little itchy," I pretended.

"How about it?" Mom asked Susie.

Susie hesitated.

"Come on," I said. "We can be late, and Mom has to excuse us."

"I'll blame it on my old truck again," Mom promised.

* * * *

After, as we waited for our hair to dry in the quickly heating sun, the mail arrived. Jay had sent me photos of Antarctica. Penguins huddled in colonies and waddled among chunks of ice, leaping into and out of the dark green sea. Ice reared in strange white-blue shapes. The last photo showed Jay in outdoor gear, his face just visible under his fur-lined hood. On the back was written: "All going well. Miss you. Love you. Jay."

Susie admired the photos over my shoulder. "Look how cool all that ice looks," Susie said, laughing.

"Ha ha," I mimicked, although it actually was funny.

"I'd love to be like Jay."

"A photographer?" I said, surprised.

"Not a photographer," Susie said. "But a journalist maybe, like for *National Geographic.*"

Susie had collected every used issue of *National Geographic* she could find. She often bought back issues from our used book store.

"Susie," Mom called. "Backpack."

As Susie went to get her knapsack, I replaced the photos in the envelope, except for the one of a baby penguin nestled between its parents. Using the glue stick from my pencil case, I stuck it to the inside of my English binder. I lingered over the little chick whose parents bent their head toward it like a hug. Mom called again, this time for me. I looked to her voice and saw my reflection in the patio window. I had Jay's blue eyes, his blond hair. Everyone said I was his image. But I wasn't like him, not at all. I wanted to be like Mom.

4

BUSINESS

Grey permeated the morning like sadness, but I pulsed with my own secluded sunshine. It had taken another six weeks of meetings, but the bank had finally agreed to finance Garden Architecture. I examined the loan documents as I pushed open Alfredo's tall wooden door with the side of my hip.

"Watch out!"

I looked up.

"It's you!"

"You're..."

"The one you dumped coffee on."

The memory made my face grow hot.

"Do you have some pathological need to dump coffee on me?" he asked, waving his take-away cup.

"No. Sorry, I..."

His brown eyes softened, crinkled. "Because if you do, we should talk."

My smile was tentative.

"I'm sorry about getting so mad," he offered. "I had a big meeting that day."

"Oh God. Were you able to change?"

"No."

I cringed.

"It turned out ok," he said kindly.

His wavy brown hair was unkempt. He wore a faded green t-shirt, jeans and sandals. A dark blue fleece dropped over his shoulder, hooked on his thumb. With his foot he held open the door. Uncertain what else to do, I shifted forward. He stood back so I could come in.

"I think you should buy me coffee."

"What?" I asked, turning.

"You've got to do penance somehow." His whole face lit up when he smiled.

I tapped my pockets. I only had a fiver.

"Lucky I've already got mine then," he responded cheerfully, waving his cup again. "You get yours and I'll find us a table."

He was gone before I could protest. I watched him as I queued. He smiled up at me as he cleared an emptied table. I smiled back, then quickly looked away. But I watched again as he wiped it down and as he tossed the napkin into the refuse bin when he was done. When he sat facing my direction, I pretended to be caught up placing my order. The whirr of the espresso machine and the coffee orders shouted by the baristas muffled Alfredo's classical music that assuaged us in the background.

"I'm Charlie," he introduced himself, standing as I came back. His palm was calloused, his grip strong. "So what brings you to Alfredo's on a Saturday?"

"I live close by," I told him, sitting down.

"Devastate anyone with coffee recently?"

"You're my one and only."

"Should I feel honoured or persecuted?"

I laughed. "Honoured, of course."

"Well then, I am," he said, raising his cup.

I touched my ceramic mug against his paper, but I jostled the cup as I pulled back and latte sloshed over its brim.

We both reached for the spare napkins piled in the table's center, but Charlie's hand was there first. It brushed against mine as he wiped up the spill.

"Thanks," I said as he finished. He shot and again binned the napkin into the refuse container on our right. My eyes stayed on the napkin as I scrambled in my mind to think of what next to say. In my peripheral vision, I could see Charlie leaning back in his chair. I could feel his eyes on my face like a touch.

"Looks like you are also working," Charlie said, indicating my loan documents.

"You're working, too?"

"My office is just down the road."

"What do you do?"

"I have a company that designs wind turbines. The day of the coffee I was pitching to a consortium from Denmark and Sweden."

"Oh God."

"That's ok. I made the sale," he said, beaming.

Vivaldi's *Four Seasons* came on. Susie and I had heard it repeatedly when I had visited her in Venice the year before.

"Vivaldi," Charlie said, as if he could read my mind. Susie said with a guy, you should never look away first, but there was something about Charlie that was daunting. I stirred my coffee, watching the foam turn brown.

"Tell me about your climbing."

"My what?"

Charlie smiled. "You dropped your photos the day you splashed coffee on me."

I had forgotten. I felt embarrassment rise, then burn.

"That was Nepal, right?"

How did he know?

"What were you climbing?"

"I didn't summit," I blurted, then regretted it instantly. I looked down at my lap. Between my legs my hands crushed a napkin into a ball.

"Last summer one of my buddies lost several of his toes when we were climbing in Peru, because he convinced everyone to push through a storm when we all wanted to turn back. What matters is keeping yourself and your partners safe. My friend put us all at real risk because his feet became so frostbitten that we barely got him down," offered Charlie, clearly delineating the lesson learned.

"Gosh."

"Not good," Charlie agreed.

Suddenly I wanted to tell him more – about the snow storm, about my cough, but Charlie was looking at his watch.

"I've got to run," he said, his eyes on mine again. "My team's meeting in five. We have clients in on Monday, and there is still a lot of work that has to be done."

I felt taken aback. I didn't want him to go.

"Thanks for sharing coffee with me," Charlie said, reaching to touch my arm before pushing back his chair. His hand felt warm even after it was gone. "Don't work too hard," he said, nodding at my documents.

"You neither."

He was half-way across the café when my mobile vibrated.

"What you doing?" Susie asked by way of greeting.

"Watching an incredibly good looking ass," I told her.

"Does this ass have a name?"

"Charlie."

"You haven't mentioned any Charlies."

"I've only just met him."

"Where are you?"

"Alfredo's."

"And he just started talking to you?"

At the door, Charlie turned and waved. I waved back, and then he was gone.

"Remember the guy I dumped coffee all over?"

"That's Charlie?"

"Yeah. I just bumped into him…"

"Literally…"

"Ha ha." Leaning back, I slipped my feet up onto the chair that Charlie had vacated. "We just had coffee together."

"Is he cute?"

"Very."

"Did he get a number?"

"He didn't ask," I said, feeling unexpectedly disappointed.

"Did you get his number?"

"I'm not going to ask for his number!"

"Why not?" Susie challenged.

"Because I'm not some hussy journalist." The line crackled with static. "Where are you anyway?"

"At the Berlin airport. I am waiting to board for Istanbul."

I became aware of airport noises in the background.

"Did you get the loan?" Susie asked.

"Yes!"

"Yes!" she echoed, and in my mind I could see her punching the air.

"You know what that means don't you?"

"What?"

"Your climbing photos weren't bad luck after all. In fact, their karma was probably what got you the yes."

"Right," I said sarcastically.

"Seriously," Susie insisted. "They're great pictures. If you won't hang them in your office, then at least put some up in the apartment. The hallways are so bare it makes a whore look dressed." We had moved into our new apartment two weeks before. "Besides," she said, her voice softening. "There are a lot of summits, Jill."

An airport intercom broke through our conversation.

"That's last call," she said. "I'll phone back from the plane."

I had barely hung up before my phone vibrated again. "I'm not saying I'm agreeing," I said by way of greeting. Already though, I thought that hanging some of the photos in the apartment wasn't a half bad idea.

"But I haven't even asked yet," protested a man's voice.

"Who is this?"

"Charlie."

Charlie! I shifted forward, my feet back on the ground. "How did you get my number?"

"Your name and address were on the loan documents."

I was impressed.

"Are you free tonight?"

In my head I heard Susie telling me to say I had plans, but I liked this guy.

"Do you like the Blues?" he asked.

After we hung up, I immediately called Susie. "Charlie just asked me out for tonight!"

"You didn't say yes, did you?"

I laughed. "I knew you were going to say that!"

"He's going to think you're a total loser."

"It's not like he had plans either."

Susie didn't answer. I could hear her talking in the background.

"They want me off," she told me. "But I'll call you from Istanbul. I want the blow-by-blow."

"Be safe," I said, suddenly emotional.

"Stop already with your constant worry."

"I'll kill you if something kills you."

Susie laughed. "I'll remember that."

5

JAY

I stalked lizards. Yesterday in science Steven had brought in an eight- incher. I had boasted that our Garden had bigger. He said he didn't believe me, so I was proving it. As I searched in the crannies of the earliest sunspots where the lizard first crept out of the night's cold, I heard the throaty sound of a motor. Mom heard the approaching engine too, and she sat back on her heels in front of a vegetable bed to look in its direction. A worn pale-blue pick-up crested our driveway in a swirl of dust. Mom cried out. I ran towards it, but Mom was quicker, and Jay was out, and they were in each other's arms, kissing.

"But what are you doing here?" I heard Mom ask as I stole behind a gazebo.

"There was an evacuation plane," Jay began.

"Did something happen to the Research Center?"

"One of the mechanics fell ill." He was kissing her again. "Oh God, I've missed you."

"Your hands," Mom said. I noticed now that they were both wrapped in thick white gauze.

"It's nothing," Jay said. "They are almost healed." I retreated, not waiting to hear more.

In my hideaway, knees to chest, I stroked Lionel's paws with my fingertips. Jay was supposed to be spending the whole winter in Antarctica. What was he doing back? I heard him coming; his feet crunched scattered stones. I saw the toes of his battered, blue canvas shoes, then his blue-jean covered knee.

"Can I join you?" he asked, peering in.

At the sight of him, tears stung like traitors. I wiped at them harshly, but they wouldn't stop, so I rose to push through Mint and out the other side.

"Wait!"

"You weren't supposed to be back," I accused, my anger suddenly big.

"One of the mechanics came down with bad pneumonia that wasn't getting better, so they had to evacuate him. I caught a ride."

"What about your pictures?"

"I had finished," he said, gesturing. His bandages looked like mittens except that his fingertips were showing. Patches of skin were peeling off his face.

"What happened?" I asked, indicating his hands.

"Frostbite."

"Are you going to lose your hands?" I had read about people having to cut off fingers, toes, and even whole feet because of frostbite.

"No," he reassured. "They're almost better."

"Do they hurt?"

"Not anymore," he said. "I'm just about ready to remove the bandages."

I imagined red, peeling skin underneath. "What happened?"

"I got caught out while photographing the penguins."

His eyes had that tired-out look he sometimes had when he came back from an assignment that was especially hard.

"I have something for you," he offered.

I watched as he took out a dark box from his knapsack. Whales, icebergs and seals were beautifully carved on its wooden surface. I took the box carefully. Admiring it, I traced my fingers over the engravings.

"Open it."

Inside, a necklace of sea glass coiled like an eel. Each small piece was a different colour of green, an unlikely shade of blue. The glass shined on a silver chain. Gently, I lifted it out.

"I thought of you as soon as I saw it."

It was beautiful. I couldn't wait to show Susie.

"Would you like me to put it on you?"

I nodded.

He fastened the clasp behind my neck. "It suits you," he complimented.

I touched the necklace with my fingers.

"The blue is like the colour of your eyes."

Blue made me think of the wave machine. "You missed my birthday." My voice came out meaner than I had meant.

"I'm sorry."

"And other things."

"I'm sorry." Jay's eyes didn't flinch.

"Sometimes I think you won't come back."

He nodded again.

It wasn't good enough. "I've wished you'd never come back."

The expression in his eyes pulled back, as if it had been pushed.

"What you do is dangerous," I said angrily.

"It can be," he said finally. "I am very, very careful, but it can still be dangerous."

"But why?"

"Why?" he asked

"Why are you doing it then?"

His eyes shifted to the mint behind me. He was quiet so long that I thought he wasn't going to answer. "Taking pictures is what I do," he said finally.

"You could take pictures of the desert or Mom's gardens. It's not just because of the pictures that you go away."

"That's true."

I waited.

Jay shifted, setting his backpack on the ground, turning so that he was facing me more fully. "We are destroying so much," his voice in turns took on an edge and exposed a sadness. "By documenting what's left, I bring it to people's awareness. I document conditions so that people with resources can better visualize the problems. Hopefully, this will help them to fix them. Can you see this?"

I wanted to say: But you missed Father-Daughter Day at school. You missed last month's running race where I came in second. Instead I said yes, because I did see, at least in a way.

A large lizard scuttled through the mint, leaving a scratchy trail in the soil. I lunged for it. Jay was quicker, catching the lizard's tail.

He leapfrogged his other hand up, gripping below the reptile's head. The lizard whipped his caught head side to side, trying to bite.

"I bet he's bigger than eight inches!"

Jay eyed him. "Tip to tail I'd say nine, nine and a half."

"Excellent!"

"Why is that excellent?"

I didn't say about bragging to Steven. "It's science today at school, and I want to bring in the biggest lizard I can find."

"I've seen bigger than this where I laid all those rocks by the back fence last year."

"Do you think they're still there?"

"No harm looking," he said with a smile. "Let's put this fellow in your box until we find another." The scared lizard scrambled quickly into the dark interior.

"Jill! Jay!" Mom called. It was breakfast.

"We better hurry," he said, indicating Mom's voice with his head. He offered his bound hand. I was careful not to grip too tightly, but he closed his hand firmly on mine.

* * * *

Back from school, I found Jay with a pickaxe. "What are you doing?" I asked.

He set the pickaxe down, and mopped sweat from his forehead with the back of his worn leather glove. His t-shirt was soaked. Dirt and perspiration marbled his knees and calves like the handmade Italian paper Maria had given Mom after her Italy trip.

"Expanding the irrigation ditch."

"Doesn't it hurt your hand?"

"Not with the gloves."

"You look hot."

"After Antarctica, hot is feeling pretty good right now. How was school?"

"Fine."

"Did they like the lizard?"

"A lot." Steven had been really mad I had beaten him out.

"There you are," Mom called. Jay watched as she approached.

Her hair, which she almost always wore in a pony-tail mid-day, was loose along her face.

"What's homework?" she asked, handing me a glass from the tray she carried. The lemonade felt cold on my inside, all the way down.

"Math and history reading."

"Jill has been put in advanced maths," Mom told Jay.

Jay nodded, acknowledging.

"Why not do your homework now, so we can relax after dinner?" Mom suggested.

"Will you play chess with me?" I asked Jay.

"I'd like that."

"I've gotten better."

"At many things, I'm noticing."

I felt lifted up by his praise, but I just looked at the ground, shrugging.

Mom returned to the kitchen with the emptied tray. I settled on the ground near Jay, my back against a rock that cast long shade while Jay started digging again. His pickaxe swung in easy arcs, swiftly ripping up the dry clay soil. Rivulets of sweat seeped from his temples, yet he didn't look tired. The ditch got bigger quickly. Already he was looking more like himself, not all used up as he had looked this morning. Our Garden was like that, making you feel better and stronger when you were really tired.

* * * *

"What are you reading?" Jay asked. Lights should have been out a while earlier, but Mom and Jay had been talking all evening about people they knew. I flipped closed the cover of *Buddhism for Children* cover so Jay could see. It showed a red and black monastery up on a hill, its gold roof sparkling.

"That's in Shangri-la," he said.

"Shangri-la?"

"It's in China, but mainly Tibetans live there. The Tibetans are good people."

I studied the faces of two robed monks standing at the foot

of the monastery's stairs. They looked happy. I tried to imagine Jay standing with them, his favourite brown pack slung over his shoulders.

"I see the penguins have replaced the gorillas," he said, looking at my new picture collage.

"Except for that guy," I said, pointing. Above my desk a gorilla hung upside down, his mouth open as if he was smiling.

"Henry."

"Is that his name?"

"A real rascal that one," said Jay fondly. He snatched my blue backpack when I wasn't looking."

I laughed. "Really?"

"Luckily, I had just put both my cameras around my shoulders, but I lost a couple of lenses."

I looked at Henry again, this time seeing him up a tree, Jay's backpack in his hairy hands.

"It seems to me it is way past your bed time," Jay said, eyeing my bedside clock. Taking my book to set on the night-side table, he kissed me lightly on the forehead, touching Lionel's nose, which poked out from under the duvet. All my other animals were already asleep, tucked under a small, Maria-made duvet on my window bay. Jay snuggled my old baby blanket more tightly around my shoulders. Mom had wrapped me in it when I was born, and when I was little, I couldn't sleep without it.

"Jay?" I asked, as he was getting up to leave. "Could you teach me how to take pictures?"

"Sure," he said.

"And Jay?" He was at the door now. "Could you get Mom?"

Mom was laughing as she entered my room. I could smell the wild rose perfume I had gotten her for Christmas. "You should have been asleep an hour ago."

"You didn't come to turn off my light," I reproached.

"You don't need me to turn off your light," Mom countered firmly.

"And to say good night."

"Jill."

"I was waiting for you," I said, my voice catching.

She sat next to me on my bed, and although I rolled away from her, I could feel her watching me. From the kitchen, I could hear the tea kettle singing. "So how's it seeing Jay?" she asked, her voice softer.

"OK, I guess," I said to the wall.

"You guess?"

I rolled so that I could see her, but I placed Lionel between us. "When he's here, you act like I'm not even around."

Mom laughed. "That's not fair and you know it."

"It is!" Mom even walked funny when he was here, as if she were moving in slow motion. Usually she was fast when she went about.

"It's not always easy having Jay pop back into our lives, is it?" Mom offered.

"It doesn't seem hard for you."

Mom pressed her lips together in a line, but then her lips eased. "I also have to untie all the missing."

I pulled Lionel in closer so that my chin rested on his head. "What do you mean?"

"When Jay's away, sometimes I feel as if I tie up all my missing in a box inside of me," she said, her hands mimicking knotting as she spoke. "When Jay comes back, it takes a while to unknot all my feelings, especially if it has been a while."

I always thought of putting Jay up on a shelf, like all the stuff we kept in the pantry.

"Besides, we three are always changing," Mom continued, "so we all also have to get to know the new parts of us."

She reached over and ran a finger affectionately down what she liked to call Lionel's prominent snout. "And you're changing the most because you're growing so quickly."

I did feel different from the last time with Jay. Then, I was only nine. "But what about your beading?"

Mom smiled, but it was a sad smile. "I guess that part of the missing I don't put away so easily."

I wondered if that meant that Mom was sad when she was beading. I had always thought that beading was a happy thing for her. Maybe she was like those shamans in Africa that we had learned about in social studies. Maybe her beading was her trick to keep all the bad stuff away. "Maybe he should just stay gone," I said.

"Have Jay never come home?" Fear skirted her eyes, gone as quickly as it had come. Maybe Jay's bandaged hand had worried her too. It occurred to me then that Mom must worry a lot about Jay when he was away, although she never said so.

"Why not?" I pressed.

"Jill!" Mom reprimanded. "I know you didn't mean that." Mom thought saying such things brought on bad luck. That was the elf in her.

"Didn't I?"

Mom's eyes flashed. She didn't tolerate back talking. "You're tired," she said carefully. "You need some sleep."

"I'm not tired!" I said, my voice rising. "In fact, now that I am ten, I should be allowed to stay up later."

"When you start acting ten, we can talk about it."

"I am acting ten!"

"You're not. You're acting like a…" She caught herself before finishing the sentence. "Goodnight Jill."

I rolled back to face the wall, taking Lionel with me.

I could feel her hovering. She reached out to touch my hair, but I wriggled further away. Yet, when the door eased shut, I realized we had not hugged. We always hugged, kissed, and hugged again for what Mom called love and luck. How was that not more bad luck than anything I had said?

6

DATE

In a rough part of town where I had never been, Charlie took me down grimy steps. The steps led into a dark basement where beer, greasy food, and sweat smells swirled in the close air. The main illumination came from the stage lights which burned on an abandoned drum set. Three bare bulbs dangled above the bar. Tea candles flickered like moving dots on the round, crowded tables. A busty black woman in a tight, red-sequined dress was moving toward the door. When she saw Charlie, her face lit up. He raised a hand in reply. She snaked rapidly through the crowd with an agility that belied her bulk, and struck Charlie like a cobra, whipping her arms around him hard and tight. Her large hips swayed against him in a slow dance. Charlie rocked back.

"Damn, you feel good, Charlie," she boomed, pulling back at last.

"You feel pretty good yourself, Angel," Charlie returned, his eyes crinkling.

His arm still entwined halfway round Angel's waist, Charlie turned to me. "This is Jill."

Her smile broke big and wide. "So this is the girl you told me about."

He's been talking about me? Before I could say anything, Angel's enormous breasts were squashing against mine like mounds of soft jelly.

"She's skinny as a rail," she tutted when she released me.

Charlie was laughing.

"Let's go get you food before you faint," she told me sternly.

We took a table that hugged the stage. She snapped her fingers at a gay, Latin-looking waiter who scurried over to us, his full tray balanced easily above his head. From the tray, Angel slapped down two brimming glasses along with peanuts and white paper napkins. "Mojitos tonight," she told Charlie. To me, "I'll get your hamburgers out right quick." She scowled at the waiter who was already turning.

"And bring extra fries," she called to his retreating back. "You just relax, honey," she said, turning back to me. "I'll make sure Ramon gets your food in no time."

Before I could even say thanks, she was off, and within seconds she was striking a tall black guy at the door with the same force she hit Charlie.

I looked at Charlie incredulously. He was chuckling. "I hope you're not a vegetarian," he called over the crowd's noise.

"Does she always order for everyone?" I asked, still watching her over Charlie's head.

"Only the people she likes."

"You come here a lot?"

"As much as I can," he said. He raised his glass to me. We clinked. The drink was strong. Before I could say as much, the lights dimmed. The band washed onto the stage. Clapping was silenced before its crescendo by a vocalist with a gravelly, raw voice who sang of pain and work, reality and dreams. Horns blew like soft cries. Drums pulsed. The base throbbed. A piano played like a second voice. Everyone froze, mesmerized.

"You tell it, Ray," Angel called out, her voice shattered with emotion. Charlie's face had also changed with the sound. He leaned in, as if his ears were reaching, and under the table, his foot kept easy time.

It was late when we left. The fog that earlier had been spilling into the city like liquid cotton now covered everything like a shroud. From the bay, foghorns called.

"It's like Sherlock Holmes!" I breathed.

"I haven't seen fog this thick in a long time," Charlie said happily. "Want to walk for a while?"

There was something exciting about a densely foggy night. "Let's!" I agreed. Actually, it felt good to be outside.

Charlie took my hand for the first time. It felt right, and I pushed mine deep in. He was different this Charlie. I had thought the music was great, but Charlie's response was entirely unexpected. When it bopped, Charlie's feet tapped. When it wept, it was as if he felt the pain viscerally. But it wasn't just the way he had responded to the music that made him seem different. He also had this comfortable-in-his-skin way that was hard to describe. When Ramon had squeezed Charlie's ass, and then snatched his hand back as if it had been burnt, crying, "Ay, caliente!" Charlie had laughed appreciatively. None of the other guys I knew would have found that funny.

The strange glow of the fog-shrouded lamp posts reminded me of Bill Brandt's Blitz photos. I asked Charlie if he knew him. "He photographed during the War," I explained. "All his night-time Blitz photos have this same, queer other-world quality," I said, indicating the fog.

As we followed the street downhill, the fog thickened. Charlie hugged us to the buildings as we walked.

"Sure glad I'm not out on my boat in this," Charlie said.

"You have a boat?"

"A sail boat. I share her with my buddy Tim. He's my business partner."

"Have you had it long?"

"Since I was thirteen."

"Thirteen?" I was surprised.

"Tim's dad owns a Marina in Maine. It had an abandoned boat that Tim and I used to use as a fort. When Tim's dad decided to sell it for scrap, we talked him into selling it to us for a hundred bucks instead. Tim and I worked a paper route for five years to earn enough to pay her off."

"It took you five years to earn a hundred dollars?"

Charlie laughed. "It took a lot more than a hundred to make her sea worthy. But once we got her on the water, it was magic," he said. "She was quite the hangout during high school."

"Is that how you became interested in wind? Because of your boat?"

"That's how both of us did."

We were going uphill again. My breath quickened as we crested.

"I don't live far from here," Charlie said. "Want to come up?"

* * * *

A large piano sat in its center of Charlie's apartment like a big black dog. Black and white posters hung above it – a lighthouse perched above crashing waves, a dappled forest path, and a mountain lake where sunlight pooled. On his piano, a photo caught Charlie on his sailboat, swinging forward on a rope. The other photo had to be his parents; the resemblance was strong.

"Can I get you something?" Charlie asked. The kitchen connected to an open-planned living room. Charlie was behind the kitchen counter, his hand on the fridge. "Wine? Beer?"

"No thanks." Already my head was clearing; my mouth felt parched. "I'd love some water actually."

"Or tea?" Charlie offered. "I have green tea, peppermint or Lipton."

"Peppermint would be amazing."

"Peppermint it is," he said, flicking on the kettle.

I moved toward the counter and eased myself onto a stool across from him. The stool swivelled.

"Do you play," I said, asking the obvious.

"As much as I can. What about you?"

"I don't have a musical bone in my body."

"I don't believe that," said Charlie.

"Trust me," I insisted, turning my stool back to face him. "What kind of music do you play?"

"Pretty much everything," he said, pulling cups from the cupboard.

"Are you in a band?"

"I've been in bands, but I'm not right now."

Blue chairs and couch grouped around a large TV which hung on the wall.

"What's that?" Below the TV was a large plastic pad with squares.

Charlie followed my gaze. He smiled. "My dance pad."

"Your what?"

His face lit up. "You haven't seen a dance pad?"

I shook my head no.

"You've got to check this out!" he said animatedly, walking to the living room to collect the remote. He pulled up a *Dance Extreme* game on the TV. He chose advanced, and stood loosely on the mat. Mimicking the indicating arrows, Charlie's feet flew. Even more than how well he moved, what astonished me most was that he didn't seem remotely embarrassed.

"You try," he said.

"No way."

Switching the program from advanced to easy, he came to the stool, and pulled my hands toward the mat. I tried to resist by hooking my legs around the stool, but it flipped, spilling me out.

"Come on," he encouraged. "It's a blast."

Dubious, and feeling awkward, I stood on the plastic squares. The arrows started slowly, first one foot than the other and I found that I could keep up easily. By the end of the song, my feet were moving with respectable dexterity.

"That was awesome," Charlie encouraged. "Now try it faster." After three more songs, I dropped to the couch, panting and laughing. Charlie got me my steamed tea and I drank it gratefully. From the blanket chest he used as a coffee table, Charlie took out two microphones. He switched the program from dance to singing. His voice was magical.

"You're amazing."

"Thanks."

"I mean really."

"Let's sing a duet."

"I can't sing."

"That's what you said about the dancing, and you were great."

"Yeah, but this time, I really mean it."

"I don't believe you," he said. He sang first. When it was my turn, not one of my notes hit the indicated bar. Tomatoes pelted my graphic image by the song's end. I hid my face in my hands. Charlie pried them loose.

"You weren't so bad."

I cocked my head.

"All right, maybe a little bad," he admitted, laughing.

I became aware of Charlie's hands, and then it was as if Charlie became aware too. When we kissed, I felt it everywhere. His fingers traced my skin like sparks. His palms whispered across my breasts. I did not resist him when he eased me back. When his hand slipped in my shirt, I arched to meet it. I saw his whole face alter with desire. I thought – I really want this, and then – I'm really going to, and then – while I still had thought – finally!

"You are so beautiful," Charlie told me, his hand trailing down. I felt on fire, as he explored, as he lingered. His voice was husky, "Look at me." I opened my eyes as he began to move. I felt pain, then tensed, and closed my eyes tight.

"Are you ok?"

I grabbed his bottom. "Don't stop." It hurt, then it hurt less, and when he came, I felt his flood even through the protective condom.

"Wow," said Charlie. We lay there delicious with sensation. He brushed hair from my face, ran his thumb across my lips. When I finally opened my eyes to look at him, his expression was intent. "Can I ask you a question?"

My eyes shifted from one of his to the other.

"That wasn't your first..."

I nodded yes.

He looked at me, taken aback. Indecipherable thoughts passed across his eyes like a ticker tape. It occurred to me that this news might make him feel obligated.

"It's not a big deal," I tried to assure him.

"It is. I mean it's wonderful. I mean thank you."

I laughed. "It's me who should really be thanking you."

Charlie was still looking curious; it was hard to know what he was thinking.

"It's not a big deal," I tried again.

"It is. I mean..."

"What?"

"How does an amazing, beautiful woman like you get this far

without, well…"

"It just never seemed right," I said, cutting him off.

"So why…"

"With you?"

"Tonight?"

I looked past his shoulder to the waves in the black-framed poster. I answered him with the only thought that came to me: "It just felt right," I told him. I didn't know why it had, with him, but it was right.

7

THE NEWS

"You had sex with him?" Susie shrieked down the receiver. "I don't believe it!"

Sitting in our kitchen looking out at a slice of the Bay, I told her everything as I watched slow freighters pass by regally, while sailboats careened and chased around them.

"He's actually got one of those teenage dance pads?"

I told her about my awful singing.

Susie was laughing. "And he still slept with you?"

I told her that we made love again in the morning, and I had come. He had made me breakfast in bed, and I had been famished. Right before I was going to leave, we did it again, against the wall.

"You tramp!"

I squealed. "Each time was better than the last."

"That's wonderful!" Susie said.

"Guess what else?"

"I couldn't."

"About ten minutes after I got home, he called."

"Did he?"

"We were on the phone for over an hour, and then he asked me out again for Saturday.

"Good man!" Susie said approvingly.

"I really like this guy."

"I can tell."

"It makes me afraid how much I like him."

"It's good that you like someone," Susie said, soothing my concern. "That's not wrong at all."

"But…" I was trying to explain that liking Charlie made me feel all opened up, vulnerable.

"You had fun with him last night right?"

Fun didn't even begin to describe it.

"And you want to see him again, right?"

Without a doubt.

"So that's all you need to know for right now. Just step by step, all right?"

What Susie said next was garbled by something nearby blaring.

"What's that noise?" I asked.

"My room's right by a mosque. They're calling prayers," she said in a loud voice.

"How's Istanbul?"

"Beautiful," she shouted.

"Who's your photographer?"

"Bob Brennan."

"The guy you used for Lebanon?"

The crying of the mosque subsided. "One and only," said Susie in a normal voice. "He's quite the eye candy."

"Susie! You haven't…"

"No."

"Seriously, remember Columbia."

A year and a half ago, Susie had been sent to Columbia to cover a spate of kidnappings. All the other reporters and photographers were guys. Early on, she had slept with one of the reporters. Five weeks later, she ended up getting together with her photographer. It had turned out, however, that he had gotten all the other guys to set up a fuck kitty, proceeds going to whoever could fuck Susie next. When she found out, she had called me in tears, vowing never again to sleep with any of her colleagues.

Yet Susie loved sex. Her work was forever taking her off, sometimes for months. It was hard for her not to engage in short term relationships, as she was never anywhere long enough to make a more permanent commitment.

"I have not slept with any guys."

There was something in her voice that didn't sound right. In the background, I heard a stifled laugh.

"There is a guy with you! I hear him!" I accused.

"I'm telling you there's no guy," she said, her voice gay with amusement.

I heard the background laughter grow louder, then muffled conversation. When she got back on the line, mirth still reverberated in her voice.

"That wasn't a guy," she told me brightly, "that was a girl."

It took me a minute to cotton on to what she was saying. "You didn't!"

"I did." The smugness in her voice was ringing.

I shrieked. "Who?"

"Diana. She works for Associated Press."

"I know Diana! You were in Paris with her."

"Exactly."

"And you picked her up?"

She laughed. "No I didn't pick her up. If anything, she picked me up."

"Details," I insisted, both excited and a little shocked.

"Well, we were out drinking last night," she began.

That was how almost all Susie's stories began.

"And we started talking about how guys can fuck with impunity, but if we girls do, we get slandered. Diana said that women should just bypass guys altogether. I said that I'd drink to that. She looked me straight in the eye and said: 'Is that all you do to it, drink?'"

I gasped; I couldn't help myself.

"To make a long story short, we ended up back here."

"And you actually did it?"

"Every bit."

"How was it?"

"Nice, actually."

"Are you gay?"

Susie laughed. "You are so black and white."

"Well are you bi, then?"

"I still like guys if that's what you mean."

"Are you going to sleep with her again?"

"Probably not. We're just friends really. This morning, I think we both felt a bit embarrassed."

"You're incorrigible."

"And you are no longer a 24-year-old virgin!"

I saw Charlie's face, changed with desire. "Finally," I sighed.

A high-pitched beep signaled, the sound of Susie's pager.

"That's Bob. He says there's action on the street. In fact, I can hear it," she said, excitement growing in her voice. "It's some kind of protest. Oh look, and they've just started burning the American flag. What fun!"

"Susie! Be careful."

"I am being very careful," she answered in her best, pathetic French accent.

"Susie, I'm serious."

"Don't worry so much."

Her pager sounded again. "Gotta run. Call me tomorrow."

"I love you."

"I love you too," she said, and she was gone.

The line went silent, hollow and crackly with distance; then it disconnected. I waited until it beeped loudly before I finally replaced the receiver. It seemed most of our life was conducted now over telephone lines, with Susie always calling from someplace far away. I had gotten used to reading all the tones and silences of her voice, in the way that I would have read her expressions. She had learned to stay close, no matter how distant her travels.

8

TROUBLE

The hot afternoon sun stippled into shadow under the cherry tree where I rested, crumbling shortbread cookies. The crumbs made expanded rings on our Fish Pond's glassy surface. It was my game to see how big the water circles would become before being broken by my gobbling fish. To have any chance at all, I had to sneak the crumbs over the Pond's edge before Sierra and Nevada saw me. Today, they got there fast, vacuuming up the cookie. I laughed as Sierra slapped his tail at me before returning, opened-mouth, to beg.

A loud whisper came from the bushes. I startled, turned. Susie crouched, half hidden.

"Where are your Mom and Jay?"

"Have you been crying?"

"Where are they?" There was an edge to her voice that was scaring me.

"Susie, tell me what's the matter!"

"They can't see me," she insisted.

I pushed my purple binder and my half completed worksheet back into my backpack. "Let's go to the Gazebo. If they come, you can get away while I distract them."

Keeping low, we cut along a shady path lined with white Impatiens, past Baby Lamb, through a gap in the hedge which led to the Lavender Beds.

"Lavender will help," I said, and we pulled handfuls of the purple flowers as we ran, their heavy smell releasing in our grips. Susie and I were expert harvesters of scent; scent had power and healing. Through the Red Flower Room, we skipped down Circle Steps into a sun-baked part of the hill where Olive Trees grew. The white-latticed Olive Gazebo stood at the far end of our Olive Tree Orchard. At mid-day, the sun cast a checkerboard on its floor. Susie and I often played chess on its light, using chess pieces we gathered anew each time – rocks, flower buds, seed pods. We believed that how well we picked our pieces would help decide whether we lost or won.

"My parents are getting divorced," Susie blurted. Inside the gazebo, we faced each other crossed-legged, Indian style.

"What?"

"Mom's still drunk, and Dad and she had this huge fight, and Dad said he wanted a divorce. Since my birthday three months before, Susie's mom had been drunk more often than not.

I grabbed her hand. She pulled it away. She was furious. "I'm sure he didn't mean it," I tried.

"She's ruining everything," she said. Suddenly she slumped as if her bones were rubber, tears falling. "First, my brother, now Dad," she cried. Since Jed had joined the army, Susie had only seen him once in two years.

"But what about you?"

"He won't stick around for me."

"You don't know that."

"I do, and so does she."

I thought Susie's Dad was mean. He was almost never around, and when he was, he was usually mad about something. "Still, being gone for good…," I said.

"I'll have to stay alone with her. I won't be able to stand it," she said, wiping her nose with the back of her wrist.

I took a tissue from the packet Mom always kept in my backpack. Susie blew her nose loudly.

"The worst is that I am afraid that she is making herself sick."

"What do you mean?"

"You know when I went to the bookstore last week?"

The mall was a twenty minute walk down the dirt trail off our mountain. Even though she wasn't allowed, Susie sometimes went there alone when her mom drank. Sometimes she went to get food. Sometimes she just looked around. To pay for things, she took money from her mom's purse. I never thought of it as stealing. Sometimes there was so little food in her house that if she didn't go to the store, she'd be starving.

"There was this book about drinking. It had a test in back that ranked drinking by severity with 15 being dead. I scored Mom at 14."

"That can't be right."

"I'm telling you."

"But she always stops."

Mom called for dinner, her voice coming from what sounded like the patio.

Susie's face tightened.

"Stay for supper."

Susie shook her head. "I have to get back. I'll call later, all right?" But as I watched her jog down the mountain back home, I knew it wasn't all right, not right at all.

I found Mom looking for me by Herb Beds. She put her arm around me as we walked toward the kitchen.

"When's Jay going?" I asked.

"Jay?" she asked, looking down at me.

"When's his next assignment?"

"He has a short piece to shoot in a few weeks. That should only take a few days."

"After that?"

"His next long one will be in about eleven weeks. He'll be in Siberia for about two months, and then he's here until he leaves again for Antarctica for the final winter."

I nodded.

"Not so bad," she said.

I shrugged.

"We do pretty well together when he's away, don't you think?" she asked, squeezing my shoulder.

"Yes."

"But it's nice to have him home too, isn't it?"

"Yes," I said emphatically, and in my mind I thought this hard – how good it was to have Jay with us.

****

When Susie called later, I was so upset that I became scared all over again. Even though she hadn't asked, I just knew that I had to get to her. Still, I hovered at the edge of Olive Trees, hesitating. It wasn't just because Susie was older that she was allowed to come and go alone between our houses, and I wasn't. Mrs. Smith didn't worry in the same way that Mom did. Crossing my fingers and then my toes, I counted backwards from ten. At zero, I ran. Quickly, the Garden gave way, and a sage-like, dusty smell snuffed out its aromas. Rocks, ground and the shrubby brushes on each side of the trail were all becoming black as I rushed past, the coming night stealing their colour from the dying day. A rock caught my foot, and before I could catch myself, I fell, sliding on knees and hands. I rolled onto my bottom. Red blood polka-dotted the inside of my palm where the gravel stuck to the skin. It stung, but I pushed myself up, barely pausing. If anything, I ran faster, the unfamiliar mountain sounds urging me onward.

Susie's rusted chain-metal gate squeaked on its hinges as I eased it open. The house's brown-leaf curtains were drawn, so I couldn't see inside. I tried to steady my breath as I crept across the gravel to the back door, which was always open. I manoeuvred carefully past its torn screen. Inside, a new red stain splotched the olive shag carpet. Dirty clothes spilled over the hall chair. From the kitchen, I could hear Susie's raised voice. I crept toward her down the darkened hall.

Mrs. Smith had a spatula in one hand, while the other held the counter. As she raised the spatula, she swayed slightly. Susie was right. Mer mom did look sick. I had never seen her drunk before. It was as if something else had invaded her body.

"Go on, I dare you," Susie taunted. Her mother made as if she'd swing. Instinctively, I moved forward. Both heads turned in my direction. Mrs. Smith's face tried to change from anger into a smile, but she still had the spatula raised. Susie became even more furious, although deep down I could also tell she was glad to see me.

"Hello Mrs. Smith," I uttered, as my heart throbbed. I grabbed my turquoise bracelet with one hand; the other bent across my stomach.

Mrs. Smith lowered the spatula, her smile uneven.

"My mom asked me to ask if Susie might please spend the night," I blurted. "She's been helping me with my history project."

"How niceth," she slurred, her expression smudged. I could see a large bruise on the hand that gripped the counter. She swayed again, and for a moment I thought she would fall. "But Susie's staying here." There was another smaller bruise on her cheek.

"You can't tell me what to do," Susie spat.

"I know this is last-moment," I broke in quickly. "But I'm really stuck."

Mrs. Smith considered me. I knew she would have helped me herself, if she hadn't been drinking.

"Please," I begged. "It would be a real lifesaver."

She smiled and for a moment, I caught a glimpse of the normal Mrs. Smith, the one I loved. This faded when she turned to Susie. "I expecth you to help Jill, until she is completely finished. Do you hear me?"

Susie didn't answer.

"She will, won't you Susie?" I said, pulling at her arm as she came closer. I could tell Susie was tempted to fight. If she did, I was scared she'd do something really bad. We had to get out of there. In her room, I filled a duffle bag with what clothes I could find. I shoved books into her backpack. In less than five minutes we were on the trail, heading upward.

Susie turned on me as we climbed. "What's this bullshit?"

I was glad she was with me. It had gotten darker. "I had to say something."

"I told you I don't want to see your mom," she said. I knew Susie was embarrassed about her mother's drinking. I was the only person who knew outside her family. At school, she never, ever said anything.

"She doesn't even know I'm here."

Susie snapped her eyes on me. It was just dawning on her now what I had done. "You shouldn't have come."

I felt proud. "You can hide in my closet."

"I hate her," said Susie, but the coldness of the kitchen had drained from her voice like bath water from the tub.

"I know," I said, even though I knew it wasn't true, not for either of us.

* * * *

I smelled the Garden before I saw the twisted forms of the Olive Trees. I sped up to leap over the imaginary line which marked our boundary. Susie came more slowly.

"We need to be careful now," I whispered. I reached into the duffle to pull out flashlights packed from her drawer. "We'll use this as a signal," I said, holding it up to her. "Two flashes if I see someone, one for all clear." I flashed the light in demonstration.

"It should be the other way," Susie said. "If you see your Mom, you'll only have time to single once."

I smiled a little. It was a good point. Susie wiped her nose on her wrist. Her mood was shifting. She liked spying games.

Leaving Susie with the bag, I slipped through Olive Trees as Susie concealed herself inside Gazebo. Two flashes at the Hedges. Two flashes at the Fish Pond.

"There you are," Mom said.

I jumped. "You scared me." One flash. Had Susie seen it?

"Where have you been?" She was cross. "I've been calling."

Behind my back, I flashed again. Had Susie seen the warning?

"What is that?"

I brought the flashlight around so she could see it. She studied it and then me. It was good it was dark. If it had been light, she would have known something was up.

"It's bath time," she said, the irritation in her voice easing. "If you hurry, I might let you and Jay have a quick game of chess."

Susie was already in my room by the time I got there. She had climbed through my open window.

"Jill," Mom called, almost immediately. I could tell she was a bit fed up again, which was hardly fair.

"Go ahead," Susie said, grabbing a pillow and a throw from my bed and disappearing into the closet.

I hesitated. "Maybe we should tell my mom," I said. It didn't feel right leaving Mrs. Smith like that.

"No!" Susie's eyes were adamant, pleading.

"Jill! Come *now*!"

"Go," insisted Susie. "Before she comes looking."

****

The fire's heat felt good as I lay on my belly studying the chess board. I had started out all right, capturing several of Jay's pawns, a castle, and a knight. Now, I was on the defensive, and I was having trouble concentrating. I kept remembering Susie's mom. I moved my bishop forward, my finger still on as I tried to see danger. Jay's expression was thoughtful, neutral, and showed no sign of what he liked to call "sighted opportunity."

"Good play," Jay complimented, as I released my bishop.

"Look who I found." Susie stood by Mom, pale-faced. Instantly, my cheeks burned.

"Perhaps you girls will join me in the kitchen?"

I looked at Jay. "I'll save the game," he offered.

In the kitchen, Mom turned on us, her green eyes flashing. "Susie, does your mother know where you are?"

"Yes," she answered, not looking up.

"She gave permission for Susie to spend the night," I said.

Mom turned on me, her eyes narrowing. "And why did you not extend the same courtesy to me?"

I tried to defend myself. "It wasn't as if she was bothering anyone. We weren't even playing."

"That's not the point and you know it."

"Please," Susie said, her eyes welling. "It's my fault. I'll go home right now so you don't have to be mad at Jill."

Mom's voice caught.

"It's not that I want you to go home. That's not the point either."

"But I want to go home," said Susie, her voice catching. She was fighting back tears. "Can't I go?"

I felt my heart quicken. If Mom took her home now, Mrs. Smith and Mom would both know I had lied.

"Of course you can," Mom told her gently. "But you can't walk home by yourself. It's dark out now."

Susie looked trapped, like the tiger at the zoo.

"Couldn't we have hot chocolate first?" Mom asked gently.

Susie was looking at the ground.

"Please Susie?" I begged, getting her to look at me. With my eyes I tried to tell her how it would be if Mom went down there.

She looked from Mom then back to me. I opened my eyes wider, touching her feet with mine under the table.

"All right," Susie agreed.

We said nothing as gas flame burst under the pot filled with milk. Mom put out a plate of oatmeal cookies and nectarine slices.

"The question is," Mom began, after placing hot mugs of cocoa before us, without marshmallows, "what if being a friend means breaking house rules? What should you have done in the first place?"

"You mean the questions are…"

"What?"

"That was two questions," I said, more confident now that Mom wasn't so angry.

Mom smiled, changing the room's feeling.

"It's my fault," Susie said again.

"Do you want to talk about it?"

Susie looked into her cocoa. I could see her considering. In my mind, I pleaded for her to tell Mom what was happening. "My mom's been drinking," she said softly, her cheeks reddening.

"Oh, sweetheart."

"My dad's left for good. I came to see Jill, but I just didn't feel like seeing anyone else."

Mom came and joined us at the table, sitting across from Susie. "What's important for you to know is that you are always welcome. I'll understand if you just want to curl up with a book and not talk to anyone. But for safety reasons, it's important that we know where you girls are. OK?"

"She's scaring me," Susie answered, her voice barely a whisper.

Mom's face clouded. "When you girls are in school tomorrow, how about I go see how she's doing?" she said gently.

Anxiety creased Susie's face.

"I won't say anything about tonight," Mom reassured. "But she's my friend too, and if she's not well, then I want to help her."

Susie looked uncertain.

"You'd do the same for Jill wouldn't you?"

She nodded.

"Let's try then."

Susie was quiet as we made our way back to my room and slipped under the covers. I rolled toward her in the dark. Her tears spilled.

"It's good Mom knows," I whispered. "She'll help make her better. I'm sure of it."

* * * *

"Susie's right," I heard Mom tell Jay as I came from the bathroom. "When I saw her last week, her stomach was all puffed out like she was pregnant. I don't want Jill being around her like that. I don't want her at Susie's."

"It sounds like her liver's going."

"If Tom has really left her, then there isn't anyone to look after her or Susie. As it is, half the time Susie's starving."

"Does she have any relatives?"

"She has a sister who lives down south."

Scraping back his chair, I listened as Jay called information, then a number.

"She's going to drive up tomorrow morning," Jay told Mom after finishing the call.

Slipping out from behind the grandfather clock, I tiptoed back to my room, but at my door, I rushed, diving back into bed. In a low voice, I told Susie what I had heard, except for the part about my not being allowed at her house.

"I knew I shouldn't have said anything." Susie whispered back, agitated.

"What are you talking about?" I asked, pushing Blankie further under my head to better prop it up.

"My aunt will just make things worse. She totally stresses Mom out."

"But we can't just leave her. If your aunt or anyone can help," I told her, "they have to come before she gets sicker."

* * * *

The smell of garlic, old socks, and bad breath was suffocating. The drawn curtains blocked out air and light. Susie's mom swayed drunkenly. She had even more bruises – on her neck, on her arm and a faded yellow one darkening the side of her mouth across her lips. Her blood-shot eyes glared furiously as she screamed about my lying.

I awoke, my heart hammering. Even awake, fear still gripped as if it was the approaching drop of a towering roller coaster. I shifted in my bed, trying to shove away the feeling. I hugged Lionel tightly.

* * * *

The next day, Mom collected us from school. Something was up. Susie sensed it too. "Did you see my mom?" she asked.

Mom shifted in her seat so that she faced us fully. "Your mom's gone to a hospital that will help her get better from her drinking. She'll be there six weeks," she answered Susie gently.

"Won't I see her?" I heard panic in Susie's voice.

"You can visit her every weekend," Mom reassured Susie. "Your aunt is happy to have you move in with her while your mom gets better."

"But what about school?" Susie questioned.

"You'd have to enroll in the school close to your Aunt's for the time your mom's in the hospital."

Susie's face fell like a tumbling tower of wooden blocks.

"Or you could stay with us during the week, and with your Aunt on the weekends."

I could tell Susie didn't know what to say.

"The hospital is very good," Mom continued. "I think if she finishes the treatment, there is a good chance she will get completely better. Particularly as it was your mom who asked to go."

"She did?"

"She did," Mom confirmed. "She loves you very much. She knows that if she keeps drinking, she won't be able to keep taking care of you the way she wants."

"She said that?"

"She did."

Susie was quiet. I could see her thinking.

"You have to stay with us," I pleaded. Six whole weeks of sleepovers!

"Can we stop at mine so I can get my things?" Susie asked.

"I thought I'd drop Jill off first, and then you and I can go down together."

"Wouldn't it be easier to just stop on the way?"

Mom hesitated. I realized she was fudging it.

"I just need to make a quick call," she said. "I'll take you down as soon as I'm done."

9

RAIN

The noise slipped through my sleep – patter, patter patter. My eyes sprang open – rain! By the time I got to the living room, the French doors were already thrown open. Mom stood on their inside edge. I slipped between her arms, my back to her stomach. I felt the storm's cold like metal on my bare skin.

Flash! Lightning – one thousand four... Boom! I jumped. Lightning! One thousand one... Crack! Mom held me close. The rain pounded like a river surging over a cliff. Crackle! One thousand three... Scratch! We watched until the downpour's violence depleted, until a steady rain fell in its place. The wet released pungent fragrances – geranium, pine, rock, rose, soil. I breathed deeply in their fresh-spun smells.

Chocolate mingled with buttered sourdough toast and wood smoke. We were now before the fire, and I sat especially close so that its heat could prickle my back. Occasionally, I rocked forward when the hotness began to scorch.

"Careful, you'll spill," warned Mom as flames reflected in her happy eyes that were all washed through. Mom loved a good rain. Mom had picked our Garden for its large underground aquifer that bubbled to the surface in babbling streams. But while it had water, it was not often that we had rain. Rainstorms were mostly caught in the mountains, or came just briefly. This particular rain, though, had staying power. It would blanket the peaks in snow. It would soak our soil.

"You are going to be tired for school tomorrow," Mom said.

"School! It's a rain day. Oh, please..." On the first day of a steady rain, I was always allowed to stay home. Mom would not work. Instead, we would be cozy and slow in front of the fire, or join in the kitchen to make cookies and soups, always with the windows open, always listening to the water fall.

"It might not have staying power," Mom said half-heartedly.

"Oh, it does." I knew my rain. "I'm sure of it."

"Well, then," said Mom.

"Susie too, right?"

I could tell Mom hadn't thought about what to do with Susie, whose mother did not subscribe to rain days.

"There's no way you can make Susie eat vegetables, do homework before TV, shower each day and then still make her go to school. That would be hypocritical," I argued. Hypocritical was one of last week's vocab words.

Mom laughed. "I suppose that's right."

"Wait until she hears!"

"I can't believe she's still asleep," Mom said, reaching across the table to take a slice of toast. Susie slept like a log.

"She's getting better, right?" I asked.

"Mrs. Smith is definitely better than she was," Mom said carefully, "but she's still very, very sick."

Again, I saw Susie's mother trying to smile that night in the kitchen. It was as if only half her mouth was working. "But she will get better, right?"

"We're hoping so, Sweet Pea. That's definitely what we're hoping."

* * * *

Susie was cleaning up at Monopoly. Maria, Fernando, Mom, Susie and I had had a mammoth tournament all day, and in each and every round, Susie had managed to bankrupt us, even when we had all plotted against her. She kept getting fantastic rolls, skipping over our properties, while we hopscotched from one of her building-filled squares to the next.

All day the rain fell. I had never seen it come down so hard for so long. At lunch the radio broadcasted record levels. Some low-lying streets were pooling water. When we stopped for hot chocolate in the late afternoon, the news said that a nearby stream had overflowed its banks.

"No!" Fernando cried. His monopoly roll had landed him on Maria's hotels. Maria raised her hand in triumph.

"Maria, my love," Fernando cajoled. "How can you bankrupt your husband?"

"By taking all his money," she answered, sweeping up his sums.

The game was now just down to Susie and Maria. Defeated, Fernando rose. He went to the French doors and traversed to the window at the far side of the room. All day, Fernando had been pacing periodically. "Fernando, sit down!" Maria complained.

Fernando's face constricted. His eyes narrowed. He hated being caged in. "I'm going out."

"No," Maria said sternly.

"I'm going out," he told her, already in the hall.

"Don't come to me when you get sick," Maria called after him. "Stupid men," she told us when we heard the door close.

Soon, though, Fernando was banging frantically on the French doors. Maria jumped up. Mom came rushing at the noise. "It's gone," he stammered when Mom threw open the door.

"What are you talking about?" Maria cried.

"The Bonsai Room –it's down the cliff!"

We were all running now, but when we reached it, the gash in the land brought us up short. Irrigation pipes were exposed like broken bones. Where our land dropped away most steeply, a large part of the hill had caved away, carrying the Bonsai room with it. Mom gave a little cry. She had been nurturing her Bonsais for years. Susie grabbed my hand. The Bonsai Room was one of our most enchanted spaces, where elves slipped silently in silver slippers.

"I see one," Maria called. "There!" She pointed down the cliff face at a miniature maple. Fernando saw it too and was already easing himself down.

"I see another," he called, having carefully set the first aside. He clawed at dirt and rock with his hands.

"I'm coming," Mom cried.

"I'll get a shovel," Maria shouted, already turning.

I turned to get a shovel, too, racing ahead of Maria. Susie ran with me, still clutching my hand.

10

CHANGES

I set Rascal and Red Rabbit in the potting shed in a time out. They had been quarreling all afternoon and I was fed up with them. My rascally raccoon had even taken to lying, which was something completely new. But even though Red Rabbit was right to be cross, he shouldn't have pummeled Rascal with his powerful feet until Rascal howled.

My animals were separated by four mending Bonsai. Most had severed branches like amputees. One had a long crack in its main trunk and was slowly dying. All its leaves had gone, scattered like litter. It had taken Fernando and his men more than two weeks to repair the irrigation system and rebuild and reinforce the whole hill after the landslide. Instead of waiting for another Bonsai Room to be built, Mom had immediately replanted those Bonsais that were strong enough. Six Bonsai had been lost completely. Sometimes, I thought Mom looked for them without realizing. At different moments I found her by the Landslide, lost in stillness, her green eyes searching in a way that seemed if she did not see at all.

I left the animals in the shed as punishment and returned to my room, where we had been playing. The others were on the window seat in the bay window watching the Garden quietly. I was still cross with them all, so instead of joining them, I went to my desk thinking to do more homework. While looking for a pencil, I found a heart-shaped silver locket in my desk drawer, and underneath papers a photo-booth picture of Susie and me. It would make such a great surprise. I cut our photo to size, imagining giving Susie the locket all wrapped up. Or a treasure hunt – we loved treasure hunts! I'd have her searching everywhere. I'd make it a statue hunt! Excitedly, I began writing clues on shiny fairy paper.

When I was done, I hid her sparkly clues amongst the mice, dogs, deer, rabbits, metal trees, ducks, people, frogs, badgers and porcupines that populated our Garden. The hunt began at the Frogs. Moss-covered and bulbous-eyed, these were bad Frogs. I had often tried to convince Mom to get rid of them. Before befriending Bird Griffin, I had avoided the room entirely. I was scared of the Frogs, whose stone tongues whipped like spined lashes. But now, by climbing a ledge by the door, I could just touch the Griffin's beak. When I did, the watching Frogs feared to flay me, because Griffin would gobble their tongues like delicious snakes.

Susie was even more scared of the Frogs, which was strange, as usually she was the braver one. I put the first clue inside the biggest Frog's mouth, using long barbeque prongs. I wasn't going to tell Susie about the tongs. To find the locket she would need courage as well as ingenuity; otherwise it wouldn't be much of a treasure hunt.

Statue by statue, I wound through the rooms into which our Garden was divided. Jay called these rooms windows into Mom's artistic soul, and when he was home, he always encouraged her to make new ones, happy to do hours of what he called hard labour to create her newest idea. Over time, in my mind, the rooms also marked Jay's comings and leavings. After hard trips, he would spend days resting in their dappled shade until the hurt faded from his eyes.

The treasure hunt ended at Flower Girl, carrying her basket of stone blossoms. She hid in a sheltered cove whose walls were covered with climbing roses. When they flowered, as they were now, their fragrance drifted like perfume. The stone girl walked along a path of wildflowers which Mom always kept blooming even when the roses were gone. I slipped the necklace around her neck, and then I kissed her cheek. I promised to make her a daisy chain more beautiful than any silly metal so she wouldn't be sad that the locket wasn't for keeping.

Mom looked up from her dead-heading as I skipped back.

"All set?"

"Yes!"

"Here then," she said, handing me a pair of clippers.

I frowned.

"You can start the treasure hunt as soon as she's here," Mom assured me. "Just help until she comes."

Actually, I didn't mind snip-snip-snipping dead flowers. It was very satisfying.

At the sound of an engine, I jumped up, and rushed to meet her. Susie's red, raw eyes found mine through the car window.

"What's the matter?"

"I'm God damn moving," she cried, kicking the car door shut hard with her foot.

"Susie!" her aunt admonished, jumping out, but Susie was already gone. Susie was fast, one of the fastest in school, but I was fast too. I found her in the Mint. Clue number six glittered in her hand.

"What's this?" she asked, as I crawled in to join her.

Her face looked angry and crumpled. I was scared to ask if it was really true, because I didn't want to hear the answer. "You were supposed to start with in the Frogs' Lair," I said instead.

"Scents to give you the scent," she read. She guessed. "Of the treasure trail?"

I nodded.

"I knew you meant that."

And that was it. Susie always knew what I meant about everything.

"Are you really moving?"

"My aunt says it will help Mom if I am closer."

I rubbed mint leaves between my fingers. "But what about school?"

"I have to finish school near my aunt's."

"But I thought that you couldn't see her except on the weekends."

"I can't."

"Then why can't you still stay with us?"

"That's what I said, but my aunt just got really upset. She said that I cared more about you than about Mom."

"But that's not fair!"

"None of it is fair!" she hissed, spittle flying from her mouth. Her anger was like a cobra-strike. As quickly, it uncoiled. "I don't want her to die," she lamented.

"She's not going to die. Mom says every day she's getting better."

"I overheard my aunt on the phone saying that Mom has alcoholic hepatitis and cirrhosis of the liver."

"What does that mean?" I asked.

"Basically, her liver might die. If it does, she will."

"But that won't happen."

Susie's fingers raked rows into the dirt as if she were ploughing. "She will if she starts drinking again." I watched her tears splatter like rain over her dry furrows. I couldn't imagine life without Susie close. I pulled off more mint leaves. Ever since I'd been little, there had been hardly a day when I had not seen her.

"You found the mint cool and dark," she read as I looked up. "But you haven't finished on your lark. Going forward by the trees is an elf with moss-covered sleeves." Our Garden had three elves, all of which were by trees.

"The river elf, right?" Susie guessed.

I knew she'd think that one. I kept my eyes down to guard the secret.

"How many clues are there anyway?"

I didn't answer.

"More than six?"

"Way more."

"What's the treasure?"

If I said anything, I'd say it all.

"I'll do it then."

"Really?" I didn't know why but all of a sudden, going on the hunt felt really important.

"But I don't want anyone to see us."

"We'll have to be careful by the Herbs," I said. "But after that we are safe."

At the Frogs, Susie touched Griffon, her eyes closed. I knew she was asking for protection from more than just the toads. When Susie saw the clue sparkling in Gollop's mouth, her eyes widened. I was going to tell her about the tongs, but before I could say anything, she put her hand in and retrieved the paper. When she turned to me, there was no triumph. Suddenly, I was sad I had put the clue in there. At the Rose Alcove, the silver locket shone in the fading light. Gently, she lifted it off Flower Girl. We both cried as we looked down at our picture.

* * * *

"Can't you sleep?" Mom asked when I came into her room late that night. I shook my head. She held open the covers and I cuddled close. Susie had fallen asleep a long time ago.

"Sad news today," she offered, trying to console me.

"Is Mrs. Smith dying?"

"Is that why Susie said she was moving?" Mom asked, stroking my hair back from my face.

"She said Mrs. Smith's liver is dying."

Mom nodded. "It is very run down."

"So she does have heparosis?" I mumbled.

Mom smiled, but her eyes were sad. "Hepatitis and cirrhosis, yes, but she is getting very good care."

My tears brimmed.

"The most important thing right now is that she doesn't start drinking again."

"But I still don't understand why that means that Susie has to move," I began, trying to make my case.

Mom's eyes searched the moon-lit room. "That's not our decision to make, Sweet Pea," she said finally. "Even if we love Susie like family, it is her aunt's decision."

"But what about her dad?" I asked, offering up this last hope.

The sadness in Mom's eyes became wider, like a river on a plain. "No one can find him right now, Sweet Pea. We've tried, but we've had no luck at all."

11

CHARLIE

"He blew me off," I said to Susie, fighting the urge to cry. I hadn't seen Charlie since what Susie and I had taken to calling "The Night," but I had thought about him nearly continually all week.

"What are you talking about?" Susie asked, her voice raised to be heard over the poor telephone connection.

"He was supposed to be here more than forty-five minutes ago. I'm such an idiot." I should have known better than to have set myself up like this. I should have known that this would happen. I slumped to the hallway floor, resting my head on the front door. A little Nepalese girl smiled down at me from her photo. The mountain peak next to her – that I had first thought beautiful and eerie under the rising moon – now had the feel of utter bleakness.

"You're not an idiot," Susie soothed. "I'm sure there's an explanation."

"I just don't need this right now," I groaned. I was in the middle of developing a massive marketing campaign at work. Instead of pathetically stalking my empty front door, I should have been at work now, getting something productive done.

The doorbell buzzed. I jumped to my feet. "Oh god," I said to Susie. "It's him. What am I going to do?"

"You see," she said, but her voice had an edge. She was upset with him, too.

The doorbell sounded again. "I can't do this." I felt too rattled.

"You can't just leave him out there," Susie reasoned.

"I could have already gone out."

"Come on Jill. Give him a chance. He's worth that much."

* * * *

Seeing Charlie made me feel even more flustered than I had before opening the door. He looked fresh, shiny. Upset, I turned away, but Charlie caught my hand. I could smell soap and clean skin. "Hey," he said gently. "Are you ok?"

I kept my eyes turned, my head down. Charlie shifted his body closer. "What's the matter?"

"I didn't think you were coming," I said, and then felt immediately embarrassed.

"Why?" he asked, his surprise real.

I looked at his face, felt pulled by his eyes. I remembered us on the couch.

"You were supposed to have been here almost an hour ago." God, what did I sound like?

He looked at his watch. His eyes crumpled. "I'm so sorry. I was all caught up sketching out this new idea I had for one of our wind turbines and I didn't even realize. I must have misread the time."

How could you misread time?

His thumb was stroking the inside of my palm. His other hand brushed back hair that had fallen forward, clearing my face. His fingertips feathered across my cheek. "I'm so sorry."

I believed him, but I felt suddenly drained, too, by my deflating anxiety. Charlie brushed back my hair again, and this time his thumb whispered across my lips, and I felt sheer want rise. I had thought about our making love all week. His eyes were asking now, and my body wanted it, demanded it, even if my mind was still catching up; and then he was kissing me, and I was opening my lips.

"Where's your bedroom?" His voice had gone rough. We barely made it before our clothes came off. It was all sensation, all so fast, so hard, and I wrapped my legs around him until I cried out. Charlie moaned low and long. After I lay in a state of timelessness, my eyes closed against his beating chest.

"Who's this?" he asked after a time. Opening my eyes, I saw Lionel. I quickly snatched him back, intensely regretting I had not hidden him. I had not expected that we would end up in my bedroom. Amusement played in Charlie's eyes.

"I take it you have had Lionel for a while?"

"Jay gave him to me when I was four."

"And Jay is?"

"My dad."

"You call your dad by his Christian name?" He sounded surprised.

I tried to think about how Jay had become Jay instead of Dad, but I couldn't remember.

"And this?" he asked.

"Blankie," I said, taking her too.

"Given to you?"

"By Mom."

"Mom being Mom?" he asked.

"Yes."

I watched his eyes sweep the room. I felt not at all ready for him to see so much. His eyes stopped on the picture of Susie and me hugging inside a crystal frame. "Your sister?"

"My best friend." Our bracelets were visible from where our arms were thrown over each other's shoulders. "She's back next week. She wants to meet you."

"She knows about me?"

I nodded.

"All about me?"

I was embarrassed.

"Hmmm." He picked up the photo to examine her more closely.

"She hates that picture."

"Why? It's a great picture."

"Because of the glasses. She only wears contacts now."

"I hated wearing glasses too."

"You wear glasses?"

"Wore, up until I was twelve. I spent a lot of my early years being called variations of four eyes."

"Ouch."

"Ruined my image with the girls," he joked.

I smiled, but then wondered, "How many girls?"

"What do you mean?"

"You know…with a lot?"

"A few," he answered vaguely.

"A few?" His voice sounded as if it had a count different from his words.

Charlie laughed uncomfortably. "I don't make notches."

"Don't you know?" This was bad.

"Not exactly."

That must mean there were a lot. "Guess."

I could see him thinking. "Sixteen, maybe seventeen."

"Seventeen!" I felt knocked off balance. "Does that include me?"

"No, I mean…"

"So I am eighteen." This guy was so going to break my heart.

"Hey," he said, turning so that we were face to face on the pillow. "Being with you isn't like anyone else."

"I bet you tell that line to all the girls," I joked, trying to keep my voice light.

"I don't tell girls lines," he said.

"You don't even know me."

"I don't have to know you. I feel you." His eyes softened. "Don't you feel it too?"

* * * *

By the time we left my apartment, the sun was bouncing off surfaces still moist from fog. I was famished. Instead of heading directly to Charlie's boat as was the initial plan, we diverted to Betty's. As he drove, Charlie cranked up the radio. Fleetwood Mac's *Landslide* was on. "Took my love, took it down. Climbed a mountain and I turned around." Charlie's voice was rich and melodious, soft and soulful. "And I saw my reflection in snow-covered hills until a Landslide brought me down." I hummed along in my head, my legs tucked crossed-leg on the seat.

Betty's Café was already brimming when we arrived. We were lucky to get the last table. The Café was housed inside a glass conservatory in which orchids grew. Orchids were Betty's hobby, and she sold them as well as breakfast, lunch and the best take-away sandwiches in the city. Always, bird-themed music played. Her two yellow canaries sang along noisily.

"I'll have Eggs Benedict, the berry bowl, a large orange juice and a latte please. Oh and bacon," I said, looking up from the menu.

Charlie laughed. "Hungry?"

"What?"

"I'll have the same please," Charlie said, returning his menu to the waitress.

"It's not because we..." I said, as the waitress receded.

"Because we what?" His eyes were merry.

I kicked his leg under the table.

"Ouch!"

I just looked at him.

"So she has a temper."

That was so not true.

"I believe you just violently assailed me."

"You're provoking me."

"I didn't mean to," he said, his expression changing, his voice softening. He took my hand. I watched his fingers play upon my wrist. The waitress returned and the coffee smelled of promise. I drank in the first, best sip, the caffeine slipping into my awareness the way daylight infuses darkness before dawn. Our breakfast came as fast, and I tucked in hungrily, taking big bites of egg tangy with Hollandaise, while swiping up the runny yolk with buttery sourdough toast. When I looked up, Charlie was watching me.

"What?"

"Have you ever been sailing?"

"I've never been on a boat."

"No boat at all?"

"No," I said, wiping my mouth with my napkin. "But it feels like I should have."

"What do you mean?"

"Jay has spent a lot of time on boats. He's even sailed the South Pacific Ocean. I feel like I know boats from all his stories."

"He sailed the South Pacific Ocean?" Charlie asked, clearly surprised.

"He's a photographer and it was one of his assignments."

"Your dad's not Jay Tuttle?"

I nodded.

"I know him!" he said enthusiastically. "His photographs are amazing."

"Thanks," I said, pride inflating inside.

"And he's never taken you on a boat?"

In the end, Jay had never taken me anywhere.

"So you don't know whether you get sea sick?"

I paused, mid-bacon bite.

"I have some medicine in my pocket if you want to take it preventatively," Charlie suggested in a way that indicated it was a good idea. "In the afternoon, the bay gets pretty choppy."

I imagined seeing breakfast again, masticated.

"I'm glad," Charlie said, his eyes dropping to my near-empty plate as he unwrapped the pill from its foil packet. "I'd hate for you to have a bad first time out."

* * * *

When we got to the marina, Charlie's white-hulled, wooden boat rested prettily in her mooring. It was smaller than I had imagined. Charlie held my hand as I stepped aboard. As he unfurled sails and pulled on ropes, I slipped into her interior. A miniature kitchen held an equally small brown table and booth-seating. Across, a dark blue, vinyl-padded bench stretched its welcome. Above this, rows of CDs filled racks stacked to the ceiling. Between the racks was a picture of a younger Charlie playing music. The label on a copper plaque read *Dragon Boys*.

"That's your band?" I called up to him.

Charlie popped his head into the cabin to see me studying the picture. He smiled. "In college, yeah."

"The Dragon Boys?"

Charlie winced. "I was out-voted."

Further back was a bunk for sleeping. Lying back on it, I gazed through the large hatch open to the sky. It occurred to me that Charlie had probably made many of his conquests here. I wondered how many, and then, as quickly, realized that I didn't want to know. By the time I returned to the deck, Charlie was pushing us off. He turned winches. The sails caught the wind. He smiled as I sat next to him. "How's she look?"

"Very loved."

"That she is," said Charlie, pulling ropes tight. "That she is."

Close to the Marina's opening, alone on a protruding bay of docks, a group of sea lions basked. Sea lions were not uncommon in the Bay, but I had never seen them up so close.

"We are the only marina to have them," Charlie boasted, slackening the sails so we slowed as we approached. With his sneakers, he lifted the lid off a cooler by his feet. Inside were frozen fish. Not far from where the sea lions lounged, a sign forbid feeding the sea lions on penalty of fine. Charlie rapidly started tossing fish far from the boat. The lions barked and began lumbering and jostling. One slipped into the water and was coming to us fast. Charlie diverted it with three fish flung over its head. Charlie was throwing two-handed now, rapid fire as more and more sea lions were entering the water. When the cooler was empty, he quickly pulled tight the sails and we surged forward.

"Wasn't that dangerous?" I asked, staring at the receding sea lions still searching for stray fish.

"You don't want them to knock you against the rocks," Charlie admitted. The sea lion dock was the last to be enclosed by the harbour wall.

"They got really close," I said.

Charlie laughed. "That's half the fun."

Away from the marina, the wind picked up. He tightened the sails still further and we skipped through the waves. Once he was pleased with our course, he used wipes to clean his hands, throwing the used wipes in the emptied cooler. With his feet, Charlie replaced cooler's lid then put his feet on top. With the hand not on the rudder, he pulled me near. A spray of sea mist cooled my face.

"Want to take the rudder?"

"You mean steer?"

"It's easier than it looks," he encouraged, guiding my hand to the till. "Just pick a point on the horizon and head for it."

I scanned the area ahead of us.

"Like the mountain," he said, pointing.

Each wave seemed to knock "Sierra" off course. As I corrected her, the sails began to flap. Charlie's hand stayed on mine. "Keep the wind taut. You need to feel her. There – where she's locking and pulling, catch her before you have to over-correct."

It took a while, but then it was as if she was alive beneath my hands. The sun had real heat now, warming us underneath the cool sea air, which was salty with adventure. I hadn't been steering long before Charlie moved my hair to kiss my neck. Another hand slipped under my shirt to find my breast. I looked across the water in all directions, but there was no one close. His lips found mine and our tongues touched. Already he was working off my bathing suit bottoms. I lifted my hips. He ripped open a condom with his teeth. I straddled, leaning so that my back was against his stomach. Putting his hand over mine, he took us fuller into the wind so that we angled way over. We bounced fast against the water. The movement of the boat, of Charlie, was unbelievable, unbearable, exquisite.

12

TIDE POOL TRAIL

It had taken her three weeks, but Susie had finally arrived from Turkey, and we were now hiking the Tide Pool Trail with Charlie and her colleague Bob, the photographer. The trail followed the coast for about twelve miles, weaving up and down sheer cliffs until spilling onto the rocks where the sea's raw power sent the crashing saltwater shooting up in vertical sprays. Susie and I hiked this trail whenever we could, loving the wispy fog, the raucously cawing seagulls, and the fishing boats that chugged to and from harbour on white crested waves.

We were on the rocks now, and the tide was coming in fast. Even at high tide, the tide pools were traversable, but they got slick with salt water and kelp, and the sea's closeness felt like a threat. To cross the rocks was to scamper, scramble, leap, and lower oneself over their constantly changing forms. Susie and I were especially good on the rocks. In fact, Susie had been setting a brutal pace all hike; she was enjoying seeing Bob struggle to keep up.

"What I like about Bob," Susie said, breathing heavily as we jumped from rock to rock well ahead of the boys, "is that he's gay."

Incredulously, I said, "Bob's gay?" I turned to look at him over my shoulder. Charlie and Bob were chatting as they made their way around a particularly crevice-filled section. "He doesn't seem gay."

"How many assignments have we done together now?" Susie asked. She was lowering herself down a four-foot rock to a ledge which opened to a large tide pool. "Starfish!" she cried. "Four assignments," Susie continued, answering her own question.

"I thought it was three."

"This one makes four. And not once has he hit on a girl."

"Have there even been any girls to hit on?"

"Sure."

"Like who?"

"In Turkey, there was Diana."

"I thought you were sleeping with Diana."

"Not funny," she said.

"But true."

"There was Syria."

"You were the only girl in Syria, outside of the Syrians," I countered, pulling myself up onto a large boulder with both hands.

"Carla from the Herald," she added.

I rolled my eyes. Carla looked like a Mack Truck. "Has he ever hit on you?"

"Never."

It occurred to me. "Is that why you think he's gay?"

"Don't be stupid."

I looked at her meaningfully.

"Remember Bobby Banks?"

In high school, Bobby Banks was the last person you would have thought to be gay – all-star quarterback, cheerleader girlfriend. Susie had called it during junior year. I thought she was nuts. Yet by his first term in college, he was out. She raised her eyebrows at me.

We were approaching the lighthouse, its yellow orb already flashing in thickening fog, its horn blowing sombre and resolute. My stomach rumbled. It was only about a mile now to Fisherman's Bay and I couldn't wait for calamari.

"Let's make them work for it, shall we?" Susie suggested cheerfully. Before I could reply, she turned and bellowed to the boys, "Last one in is buying drinks."

"All night?" Bob called back, the alarm clear in his voice.

"And I'm drinking," she called back merrily.

"Bloody hell," I heard Bob swear.

Susie laughed, while pulling me along by my sleeve. "Come on," she said. "For a Brit, the guy can move when he wants."

We began to run. The guys had started running too, but it was getting darker now, and we knew these rocks well while they struggled with their route. By the time we were across the sand and up the pier stairs, I was gasping for breath. The boys were now walking towards us at a leisurely pace. We watched them as they approached.

"So?" I said.

Susie looked from the approaching boys to me. "Still reserving judgement."

"First impressions."

"First-class ass."

"Told you!"

"Definitely crazy about you."

I flushed. "Do you really think?"

"Totally."

"So you like him."

"Let's see how he drinks."

"That's no test."

"It is in my book."

"That's not fair. No one drinks like you." There had been a time when I had worried that, given her mother's alcoholism, Susie's drinking was bad. Over and over again she had promised that in journalism, drinking was just a way to fit in and to get information. It was also true that even when she was home for months, she never drank unless I convinced her to do so.

"Bob almost can," Susie countered.

"Bob's had lots of practice."

"Practice makes perfect," she said smiling.

"He's got to like you too, remember."

Susie searched my face.

"What?"

"You *really* like this guy."

I shook my head. Dating Charlie was kind of like dating a pinball – he's late; he's early; firm plans to see a movie morphed into a party over at Tim's without Charlie thinking to check with me first. At times it made me feel completely unbalanced.

Susie smiled. "Was it a good party?"

It had been a great party, but that wasn't the point.

"So, he's spontaneous."

Maybe that was it – Charlie was constantly abrupt, turning unexpectedly depending on what life presented; his constant curiosity meant that he was incessantly uncovering what others had not.

"It's good for you, Jill," she said, catching my eyes even as I rolled mine upward.

Maybe; I mean, I did like him; I mean he was kind of driving me nuts.

"Gentlemen, gentlemen, gentlemen," Susie admonished as the boys came close.

"Did we agree?" Bob argued.

"Did you disagree?" Susie asked, as we began walking towards Pete's. Charlie took my hand.

"Did you even give us a chance?"

"You clarified bet terms," Susie batted back.

"What are you talking about?" Bob protested.

"You said 'All night?'"

"I thought I said bloody hell."

"That too," she said gleefully.

* * * *

The bar teemed with ruddy-faced fishermen. Most clustered around a big screen showing a fight. Many rooted for an Irish fighter who looked as if he was getting badly beaten by a Cuban.

"Let's go in back," Susie called over the noise. We found an empty booth overlooking the fishing fleet. A waitress came quickly, bringing still-warm sourdough, butter and iced water. "Drinks?" she asked, her low t-shirt revealing full, tanned breasts; both guys looked.

"A beer please," I said.

"Make that two," said Charlie.

"Four," Susie chimed in, "and a round of tequila shots."

I looked at her.

"Bob's treat," she said, smiling.

As we munched calamari, sipped beer, and began to buzz from the shots that Susie had us knock back, Charlie asked Susie questions.

"Why journalism?"

"I'm curious. I love to write. I like to travel. I like people's stories," she said, flipping fingers out as she made her list. As Susie talked,

I thought she had never looked more beautiful. Her night-black hair framed cheeks still rosy from our hike; intelligence burned in her oval eyes.

"Susie is one of the best listeners I have ever met," Bob offered.

Surprised, Susie looked at him.

Bob met her eyes, continuing, "She has this way of making people feel completely comfortable. Once people start talking with her, they never want to stop."

Susie blushed. "That's…"

"True!" I interrupted. Bob was exactly right.

She rolled her eyes. "They call me the priest," she joked to Charlie.

The waitress reappeared.

"Shots all around," said Susie, clearly pleased by the distraction.

"She can also drink like a Mongol," Bob said to Charlie.

"Unlike this woman," Susie said, looking at me, "who is a total light weight."

"Tell me the dirt on Jill," Charlie said to Susie.

Susie's smile widened delightedly. "The first boy Jill ever kissed was named Max."

I couldn't believe it. She wouldn't.

"When he put his tongue in her mouth, she was so surprised that she jerked her head back, hitting it so hard against the corner of the pay phone that she needed eight stitches."

I was going to kill her.

Susie proceeded. "The first time she got properly drunk…"

"Don't you dare," I warned.

"The first time she got properly drunk," Charlie encouraged.

"She got up on the table and started dancing. She had her shirt half way off before I could drag her down."

I slammed my foot down on hers, making her cry out.

"You're welcome to reciprocate," said Bob.

Susie narrowed her eyes.

"She cries all the time," I said, leaping in. "At movies, the Olympics, at the comments you guys are always making about her."

"Jill, that's my work you're fucking with," said Susie, suddenly serious.

"I've never seen you cry," Bob said, turning to Susie.

"…like when you saw that dead guy in Africa and told her she should jump it. She laughs like it's funny, but later, she calls me and cries."

"I never said that," Bob said, visibly rattled.

"But you were there."

"I thought it was no big deal."

"That's my point."

"I'm sorry," he said, looking at Susie.

She tried to brush it off as the waitress returned, interrupting us. She was quick to turn tables when the waitress went. "So Charlie, Truth or Dare."

"Truth," said Charlie.

"What's the most embarrassing thing you have ever done?" Susie asked.

I could see Charlie thinking. "Recently? Probably crashing my boat into the dock."

"That doesn't sound so bad," said Susie.

"I was coming in too fast so I leapt to the dock to stop her, but when I pulled on the rope, it wasn't attached. I lost my balance, and fell into the water. The boat hit the dock so hard that it actually splintered wood. Cost me over three grand to repair."

"Ouch," Bob said.

"Truth or Dare," said Susie.

Charlie considered her.

"One more," Susie encouraged.

"Dare."

Susie was thrilled, clapping her hands. "On your knees, hold Jill's hand, and sing her a love song loud enough for everyone to hear."

"You got to be kidding," Charlie said.

"Jill says your voice is amazing."

"No, no, no," I protested.

Charlie looked from one to the other of us, then back to Susie. He knocked back his shot, then mine, and then slid to the floor taking my hand. My cheeks burned. The restaurant went quiet as Charlie's voice easily carried above the noise. Everyone stared, even the waitresses. When he was done, applause erupted. Charlie bowed gallantly before sliding back into the booth beside me.

"You are amazing!" Susie admired.

"I told you," I said.

Charlie shrugged, but it was clear he was pleased.

"So that leaves you Bob," Susie said.

"Since when did I get involved?" he protested.

"Since when you told me to reciprocate," I said, backing Susie up.

He grimaced slightly. Susie laughed delightedly.

"Truth or Dare?" I asked.

"Truth."

"Have you had sex with a colleague?" I asked.

"Not for a very long time."

"Why not?"

"Cause I got burnt by it."

"So if you are always working, and you don't date your colleagues, how do you hook up?"

He smiled. "Oh, I figure it out," he said, evasively.

"Truth or Dare."

"You only told me one thing about Susie."

"Yes but it was a good one," I argued.

"One more."

"Are you gay?"

Susie kicked me under the table.

"Gay?" Bob looked horrified. For that matter, so did Charlie on Bob's behalf. "No, I'm not fucking gay."

I gave Susie an "I-told-you-so" look.

He turned to Susie, "You thought I was gay?"

Susie stuttered.

Bob was going to say something, but smiled instead. "I can absolutely one hundred per cent assure you that I am not gay."

Susie was looking shame-faced at her drink.

"Look at me Susie."

Susie raised her eyes to his.

"I am not gay."

"All right," she said, trying to shrug it off. "So you're not gay."

13

FRUIT LOOPS

"Hey."

I jumped, caught out. In front of me was a bowl of Fruit Loops that I wasn't allowed except as desert, on special evenings. I could feel my cheeks go red, but the only light came from my flash light, so I hoped Jay couldn't see.

"Mind if I join you?" Jay asked.

I jiggled my head no. He took down a large candle from the shelf above the stove, lit it, and then switched off the flashlight. The candle cast ample light across the table. Jay poured himself a large bowl of the cereal, covering it with enough milk so that the loops rose. Quietly, he began eating. Uncertain what else to do, I also picked up my spoon. The sounds of our eating seemed loud in the hush of the kitchen, and I chewed slowly, trying to be as silent as possible. I couldn't figure out what Jay was doing. If he'd been Mom, he would have told me off for being out of bed and for eating Fruit Loops without asking. Jay drank the milk from the bowl. Mom wouldn't have allowed that either.

"I love Fruit Loops," Jay said, sighing happily. "I had them for almost every breakfast when I was little." Mom would never allow them for breakfast. They had way too much sugar. It occurred to me then that Mom must be buying the Fruit Loops for Jay and not for me, which was why, now that I thought about it, we never had them when Jay wasn't here.

"Do you have Fruit Loops a lot?"

"You mean now?"

"Yeah."

Jay smiled, his eyes crinkling. "Most nights," he admitted.

"Is that why you're up?"

"Tonight?"

"Now?"

"I heard you."

"You did?"

Jay smiled. "I never miss the clink of a cereal bowl."

"You knew it was a cereal bowl?" I asked with thorough disbelief.

The smile that spread across Jay's eyes made the sides of his mouth crinkle. "I didn't know for sure, but I was definitely hoping." His eyes changed, softened. "Why aren't you sleeping?"

The truth was that I had been restless all week, ever since Susie had moved in with her aunt. I'd fall asleep all right, but I kept jolting awake; and the thought of Mrs. Smith being sick, or her being drunk, or Susie moving would come at me like a slap in the face, and it was hard to sleep again.

"Are you worried about Mrs. Smith?" Jay asked.

"Is she going to die?" My voice cracked.

"I don't think so," Jay said simply. "She's having a tough time, but I think she's gotten through the worse of it now."

What do you mean?"

Jay shifted his chair forward, so that he was closer to me at the table. "When you stop drinking after having drunk a lot for a long time, your body goes through withdrawals. For a while you feel even sicker than you did when you were drinking."

"Is that why Susie hasn't been able to see her?"

Jay nodded. "By the weekend, though, my guess is she'll be ready for Susie to visit."

"What about her liver?"

"The doctors are treating her liver as well. The most important thing for her liver is that she doesn't start drinking again."

I should have been happy that Mrs. Smith was getting better, although instead, I felt even more miserable. Susie might never come back if her mother recovered.

"I also had a good friend leave school once," Jay said.

I looked up at him.

"Tom came from a ranching family, so I only got to see him when he was at school because after school he always had chores. At sixteen, his Dad made him take the high school equivalency test. Back then, a lot of the ranching kids did."

"Did he want to leave school?"

"No, but his Dad didn't give him a choice."

I touched my finger to the hot wax puddled on the table. It made a light warm film on the tip of my finger. "Weren't you lonely without him?" I asked.

"Really lonely. Tom was my only real friend. I wanted to quit school too after he left, but my dad wouldn't let me. It made me angry. I was angry about a lot of things then."

I tried to imagine Jay angry with his dad. I had seen Jay worn out from his trips, but I had never seen him upset, ever. Even when he was at his most tired, he always had this calmness.

"Like what things?" I asked.

"Oh, I was angry at almost everything, at one point. I guess since I never quite fit in, I never felt right. Everything I thought about didn't seem to matter to anyone else."

I tried to imagine no one talking to Jay when he was walking down the school hall.

"After Tom left school, I felt even more isolated. I also started having a lot of trouble sleeping, like my mind was processing all my wondering why in my dreams, and at some point it would just over-load. I started thinking that if I could just tire myself out enough, then I would sleep, so I started hiking."

So that was how Jay's climbing started.

"One day," he said, his eyes getting a faraway look, "I came across this elk." Jay's eyes filled as if he could see the elk still. "He was all raw muscle and magnificent antlers and when our eyes locked, it was as if he shifted my whole perception, my whole ability to perceive. His beauty – the wonder of it – changed me. It was as if for that moment nothing else in the world existed."

"Is that why you became a photographer?"

"Yes."

"To see beauty?"

"To see beauty, and also because taking pictures keeps me look-ing, even if what I am seeing is difficult. Really seeing is what makes me feel alive. It makes me feel that I'm contributing something to the world."

My eyes watched the flickering flame as I listened.

"Having Susie gone is going to be hard. When Tom left I was really sad. What helped was when I started taking photos for the school paper. It gave me something to engage in, and a way to connect with people again. I was thinking that maybe you could try something new at school too. Maybe that might help with missing Susie."

I twisted my lips uncertainly.

"Maybe you could suggest the same to Susie. She's got it tougher, having to start at a whole new school. If I were her, I'd be feeling pretty scared."

"You'd feel scared?" I never thought of Jay as scared. I didn't think he was scared of anything.

Jay smiled. "Everyone gets scared."

"Are you scared in Antarctica?"

"Sometimes."

"Then why are you going back?"

"It's my last winter." His voice was firm.

But I persisted. "You've already done two winters."

Jay held my gaze. "It is a three-year assignment. There's a lot of important work that I need to finish."

"But it's for such a long time," I said, my sadness turning to anger. I wanted to tell him that he'd miss my eleventh birthday. I wanted to tell him that while Susie couldn't stay, he could. Suddenly, it all felt too much. Why couldn't the world just be still for a while?

14

LUNCH

"Have lunch with me," Charlie said over the phone.

"I can't." Stacked papers demanded action on my desk.

"Let it wait."

"I've got to prep before my sales meeting."

"You also have to eat," he persisted.

"I've already ordered in."

It was as if I could hear Charlie thinking. Charlie never took no easily.

"What are you having?"

"Vegetarian sushi, why?"

"Gina," Charlie called to his secretary, "can you please order me miso soup and the usual?"

"Did you just order Japanese?" I said, swirling in my chair to look out the window.

"I did." He sounded pleased with himself. "Now we can have lunch together."

"What are you talking about?" I asked, looking at the phone.

"Put your phone on speaker."

"You're kidding."

"Just do it."

I pressed the speaker button.

His voice now had a faraway quality. "Now we can eat together while working."

"This is silly," I said, but under the table my feet swished. I could hear Charlie moving papers in the background.

"What are you working on?" Charlie asked.

"The Window Boxes pitch." If I could get Window Boxes to pick up even one of my lines, then finally I'd be safe. I still had working capital left from my bank loan of four months earlier, but we needed even more revenue to really run in the black. My costs were down to the bone. I had even taken to turning off the office lights between 10:00 and 4:00 unless the fog blotted out the light. Reaching profit wasn't going to be about further cost savings. What I needed was just one more slice of revenue. Window Boxes was my best shot.

I had been working for over two weeks on background research and on developing ideas. My Italian metal urns were completely different from anything else they had been selling, but they would complement their other lines perfectly, especially in their southwest urban markets. I had even sketched a couple of urns that they could sell exclusively. I also thought I had a good chance of convincing them to pick up my statuary line made from twisted reeds that looked like baskets.

"Want to go to a movie tonight? There's a 9:00 French film at Cinema Four."

"OK. Meet up at 8:00?"

"Let's meet at 7:00 and eat first."

"It's going to be 8:30 if you don't stop talking! Charlie, we aren't getting anything done."

"I'm working."

I was about to respond, but instead frowned at my mental image of Charlie smirking. I was halfway reading through more market research when I heard Gina bring in Charlie's food.

"I ordered first!"

"We're closer," Charlie said.

"Not that much closer."

"I'll wait," he said gallantly.

"That's silly."

"I'm waiting," he insisted.

A minute later I heard the unmistakable sound of chewing. "You're eating."

"Only ginger."

"You know you can eat."

"Not without you."

After a bit my food arrived too.

"What are you starting with?" Charlie asked.

"Miso."

"OK, I'll have my miso too." We slurped companionably. I returned my attention to pricing. I considered just the right discount to offer to lure Window Boxes in.

"Now what are you eating next?" Charlie asked.

"Avocado sushi."

"Avocado with a dash of soy sauce."

"What are you going to do when you get to the tuna and salmon? I didn't order those."

"You'll have to politely wait until I finish," he said. "Then we can both have dessert."

"I didn't order dessert."

"You have your M&Ms and I have my red bean cake."

"How do you know I have M&Ms?"

"You always have M&Ms."

I laughed because it was true. "It's beautiful outside," I said, sighing. Across the street in the little square, sunshine had drawn the people out.

"Great day for sailing."

"Great day for gardening," I said, reaching into my drawer to pull out my M&Ms.

"Don't eat those yet."

"What are you talking about?"

"I can pick out the rustle of an M&M bag anywhere."

I laughed. "You're totally insane."

"Perhaps, but I'm also almost done."

I circled my chair back to the window again, with the M&Ms on my lap. A silver-painted mime entertained the crowd.

"We could have been there," Charlie said when I told him.

"We could be in Paris," I said to emphasize the pointlessness of it.

"That's a great idea! Let's go at the end of the month."

"We can't just go to Paris."

"For five or six days we can."

Already I had promised Susie to take time off when she was here next week.

"Come on," Charlie encouraged. "What good is being boss if you can't be spontaneous once in a while?"

"I'm spontaneous," I protested.

"Prove it," Charlie persisted. "You, me, Matisse, red wine, walks along the Seine. I'll plan everything."

His enthusiasm was catching. I saw us hand in hand in front of the Notre Dame.

"Even if we live to be one hundred," Charlie argued, "already our life is a quarter over. We've got to go for it, live without a single regret."

I imagined Jay on top of his mountains. "I'll do it," I said, caught up.

Excitement lit up his voice. "An M&M to seal the deal."

"I've got to go."

"Just one," he cajoled.

I had a handful, all at one time.

15

GARDEN

I followed Fernando's voice to the Vegetables. I saw Maria first, her quick hands plucking pea pods. She was humming to Fernando's Spanish song, her black hair secure in its familiar bun.

Fernando's voice soared. He had spotted me over the corn. His hand stretched out theatrically, and as his note rose, his bushy black moustache quivered. Maria scowled to chide Fernando's silliness, although deep down she also thought he was funny. Maria and Fernando had known each other since childhood, and Maria could not remember a time when they had not been in love. No matter how angry Maria became at Fernando, and she was often plenty mad, Fernando always coaxed her out of it. Maria got most mad when Fernando was late. Mom said that nobody was able to get as much done as Fernando in so short a time, so she never worried about it. For Fernando's first time on a new job, though, Maria and Mom always pretended the job started earlier. After that, it wouldn't matter. Once Fernando started working for a client, it was hard to send any of our other gardeners.

When his song ended, Fernando bowed with a flourish. I applauded. Lightning fast, Fernando tossed me a tomato. I caught it, barely. I loved tomatoes still warm from the sun. Its juice squirted in my mouth and on my shirt even though I had leaned forward, caving in my stomach. Maria tutted, her handkerchief already out and wet from her water bottle. She dabbed at my shirt, while I kept eating the tomato over her bent head.

Fernando winked at me. "How was school?" he asked, his deep voice still heavily accented despite all his years away from Mexico.

"Good," I said, stuffing the last of the tomato in my mouth.

Maria stood back to look at her work. A wet mark replaced the red. She swiped at it twice with her hand just for good measure. "Your mama's in the Monastery, Niña. Go say hola, and after we can make cookies."

"Really?"

"We have a church event tonight, so I volunteered to bring them."

No wonder! Mom never said no if it was for Maria.

"We can make enough for your class, too," Maria said, her smile expanding. The truth was Maria liked making cookies as much as I did. She leaned toward me, her voice dropping. "I've got ingredients for chocolate chip, sugar, and lemon."

"Oh, Maria!"

Her eyes glinted, and then, as if she remembered herself, she quickly straightened. "I have my work to finish here. You go see your Mama," she told me.

Fernando was already back behind the corn, singing. As I skipped off, he threw another tomato, quick fast, but I had guessed he would, and I was ready. "What did Mama Tomato say to Little Tomato when he was slow to follow?" Fernando called after me.

"Ketchup!" I cried, spinning in his direction and then back around again, my voice muffled by my tomato-full mouth. Maria was laughing now, even though she had heard the joke at least a thousand times.

* * * *

Crossing under a brick archway, I descended stairs to the Silver Tree so named because of its grey, shimmering, feathery leaves. I followed the path onto the old slate patio into which were cut large beds filled with pink and lavender flowers. Through the beds, the Colonnade wound. Mom had purchased the columns from Rome. Grape vines were trellised to their crowns, and during harvest, fat black bunches of grapes hung down. Fernando, Susie, and I snipped off the grapes when it was time. On top of tall wooden ladders, we filled large wicker baskets, harvesting and eating until our stomachs felt as if they might burst.

The Colonnade ended at the Hedge Maze. When I was little, I was terrified that I would be lost inside. To make me less frightened, Mom brought in our Flamingos. She placed them so that I could always see one, no matter where in the Maze I wandered, their tall necks like beacons in the blinding hedge. Even though they were carved from a stone Mom called green verdite, they didn't feel like rock. They were elfin; their carved feathers were silken soft, and kind, inlaid-black eyes pooled deep and ageless. Touching their large curved wings felt like safety, even when I was in the most hidden part of the maze, where paths spilled deceivingly in all directions. The first time I went alone into the Hedge Maze, the Flamingos called as I weaved and zigzagged:

"You are the most wonderful," the first Flamingo said, bringing me close.

"I am?" I asked, stroking its neck to calm my thumping heart.

"Magnificent actually," called another, singing me onward.

"The loveliest of girls," tinkled a third, as I rounded the bend to where it waited.

"We will always be friends," promised the fourth, its neck curving down in caress.

"Will we?" I asked.

"Always," the flamingo assured, its beak lifted to the green, arched exit.

On the other side, our Maze opened to a stone courtyard. Its large trees cast mottled shadow over our massive, granite Lion Table which rested on four stone lions. When we had to sacrifice, it was on Lion Table that Susie and I sliced open worms and beetles. Just once, we had killed a frog. Its blood had spurted as we cut into it. I screamed, and the wounded frog almost escaped. We then had to stab him over and over with our smuggled kitchen knives. After that, we never again sacrificed something so living and large.

The tree shadows ended at the Arabian Room. Tiny Moroccan mosaic tiles covered the floor and walls. Cut into the floor, flat fountains pooled. Over the large rectangular fountains water arched like see-through rainbows. When the arches caught the light just right, the clear water coloured like prisms. We thought the exact moment of this colouring was enchanted, and if we saw it, then its magic touched us too. The magic faded with the day. Still, if I had something big on at school, I would always try to come on Sunday to see it. Unlike Susie, I believed the teeniest bits of enchantment still clung after the sun had gone down, like glitter still sticking on a just swept floor.

When the sun was hot, Susie and I often splashed in the Arabian Fountains, happy in their cold spray. Afterward, we picked oranges from the room's four citrus trees, and then lay on its large divan, pulling shut its diaphanous net curtain.

The Arabian Room led to the orange and turquoise Southwest Room, its walls covered with cattle skulls. Twenty-four different varieties of cactus filled every bed. Once, when I was little, I had tripped into one of the large cacti. Its spikes had pierced me deeply. After that, I hated every ugly one. On party nights, Mom built a bonfire in Wood Pit at the room's center, and we toasted marshmallows and roasted sausages and bread. Fernando often strummed his guitar and sang in Spanish. If Jay was home, he played along on his wooden flute. I did not like this room, except on nights such as these, when its spooky skulls became part of the magic.

The Concealed Door led out of Southwest Room into a part of the Garden where Mom never took clients. Here, fluffy bamboos, enormous ferns, and oversized palms subdued the sun. Unseen water cascaded. Overhead, the birds chattered their alarm. I pushed past waxy, purple-green leaves to the Hidden Stairs which veered off without notice. I followed these to our little Monastery. As a surprise, Jay had shipped the Monastery to Mom from Romania where the vampires roamed.

"Hi," Mom called. She was at the table in the shade, painting with water colours.

"Can I paint too?" I asked, coming close.

Mom made space between several drying Garden sketches. They were all variations of something simple. From the bucket, she drew a cup of water. My dipped brush streaked it blue as I rinsed.

"How was school?" Mom asked, taking up another sheet. Using a pencil, she quickly sketched. It always amazed me how she could take one concept and change it again and again.

"It was good," I said, my mouth half-full of the apples slices that Mom had passed. Mom gave me the look, and I swallowed before asking, "Who are the designs for?"

"My city clients. I promised to get something to them for to-morrow."

"There's not much going on."

"They want their garden to be a contrast to the city's chaos. It goes on a rooftop ten floors up." Mom was drawing quickly as she talked. When she designed gardens, she worked in waves, drawing ideas in pencil, hardly ever erasing until her thoughts played out. She added the watercolour after. Mom could watercolour any time, but her pencil designs had to be immediate. She said they were fleeting, like changing light, and had to be captured before they escaped. I tufted green grass across the bottom of my page.

"Penny for your thoughts?"

When Susie had visited over the weekend, she had spent Saturday afternoon with Chad. He had asked her to go steady. She hid his ring in her pocket, which seemed stupid, especially as I had overheard Chad hinting at it to a friend on the bus on the way back. I rinsed my paintbrush in the water again. I hadn't promised Susie I wouldn't tell. She had just told me that I was the only one she was telling.

Mom smiled. "Are they?"

I shrugged, compressing my lips between my teeth. I began adding black to the blue I was mixing. I could feel Mom watching me.

"Does that feel weird?"

I shrugged again. More black made the sky look dangerous, like a coming storm.

"Love isn't finite, you know. Susie doesn't love you less just because she likes Chad."

"People do stop caring about each other," I said, looking up at her.

"Not you and Susie."

"Mr. and Mrs. Smith did."

"Ah," said Mom. "But that's different."

"Because of her drinking?"

Mom nodded.

"It makes her seem like a monster," I said, but as soon as the words were out, I wanted to take them back. I kept my eyes down on my painting, hoping they would go unnoticed like bubbles popped before they could float.

In my periphery, I saw Mom set her pencil down. "Did you see her?"

She would know if I lied. She always knew when she was paying attention.

"Susie was so upset," I tried to explain.

Mom's eyes tightened. Like falling dominoes, I could see her making the connections. Mom figured most things out. "The night I found her in the closet?"

I was scared of Mom being angry; but more so, the night at Mrs. Smith's kept bothering me. I kept recalling new things – the stains on her nightgown, her matted hair, dirty dishes piled in the sink. It made me feel bad because I loved Mrs. Smith, but now all I remembered was how horrible she looked.

"She was very ill," Mom said gently, "but she's getting better now."

"But she could have stopped," I accused. That was the bit I couldn't understand.

"She's trying."

"But how could she?" My words felt like betrayal, like betraying a friend by being mean. "She's Susie's mom."

Mom's smile was sad. She reached to stroke a strand of hair from my eyes. "Even moms get ill sometimes."

"Then I won't be a mom." My voice came out off. It wasn't what I meant. Moms were supposed to make the world safe, not more scary.

"It can take a person a really long time to see just how sick they are with alcoholism," Mom answered. "Until they realize they are sick, they have no chance of getting better."

I thought again about Mrs. Smith's 14/15 score on the alcohol test. I wanted to ask Mom about it, but I didn't want to tell on Susie.

"I am so sorry you had to see her like that," Mom soothed.

A tear splashed my bunny's back. It smudged more when I rubbed at it. I was glad that Mom wasn't saying Mrs. Smith was bad. But still, if it had been Mom, she would have stopped. "Wouldn't you have?" I asked her. "For me?"

Mom was quiet for a while before she spoke, "Drinking's not my challenge, Sweet Pea."

"Still…"

She cut me short. "We all have our challenges, even you."

I thought about volleyball, about history dates, about Jay being away.

Mom's eyes were as soft as a summer lake. "You haven't met your real challenges, yet," she said as if reading my thoughts. "But they'll come. They come for everyone. It is what makes life hard, but also wonderful."

I didn't know how sucking at volleyball made life wonderful. "Do you really think she'll get better?"

"I think she has a good shot. She's six weeks into the program now, and she's doing really well."

Her assurance settled on me like a blanket. If Mom thought Mrs. Smith would get well, then I could believe that, too.

"That's good," Mom said, indicating my bunny. Pleased, I looked at her admiring it. Then I coloured my paintbrush yellow to draw in daffodils. Mom also picked up her pencil. I half watched as she sketched new trees, flower-filled urns and green hedges. Shade dappled a table while two lounge chairs stretched in the sun.

"I like that one," I said.

Mom considered, twisting her lips to the side.

"It would be good to have a green oasis, particularly if you live in a city." Mom and I sometimes called our Garden Oasis. We had started that after reading Arabian Nights.

Mom angled her head first one way and then the other as she did when she thought in images. Her eyes returned to her other drawings. "Perhaps!" she said suddenly, taking another sheet. She sketched at high speed. Back were the trees, but the urns changed from pottery to metal and a trellised wall enclosed the space. The whole trellis was covered in vines of honey suckle, clematis and climbing ivy. She was erasing. I looked more carefully. Into the trellis she made unevenly-sized rectangular windows which gave views of the city like pictures framed in a living vibrant green.

"That's good."

"Mmm…" Mom answered, standing up with sketch pad and paper. She had her faraway look now. Absently, her fingers trailed the stone as she walked the Monastery's four small walls, her fingers tick-

ling the toes of each its cherubs as she circled by their nooks. Suddenly, she dropped to the sunny grass. Her hand flew. Her faraway look
had cleared; a smile played across her lips. I knew she had it then: a
Garden to be treasured; a place where all were made better just by
being within.

16

BABY

"You know how I feel about this," Jay said, his voice raised.

I froze in the hallway.

"It's like saying you didn't want Jill," Mom countered, her voice louder, sharper.

Never had I heard them be angry with each other. I slipped behind the grandfather clock outside the kitchen.

"I didn't," Jay said. "We had her for you, not me. I'm gone almost as much as I am here. What kind of father am I?"

"You're a good father, Jay."

"If we didn't have Jill you could come with me."

"I'm not going to spend my life following you around!" Mom's voice was cutting with anger.

"I'm just saying sometimes, like I come here. It would be nice if it wasn't always a one-way street."

Something clattered, a pan on a counter. "I don't believe what I'm hearing."

"What you're hearing is that I love you. I want to be with you."

"What you're hearing is that I'm having your son and I'm asking, just this once, that you cancel your god damn trip to be here when he's born," Mom responded furiously.

I slid down the hallway wall until I was balled behind the clock.

"I made a commitment." Jay sounded distant. "I won't back out. For Christ sake, I'm supposed to be on a plane in two days."

"What about your commitment here?" Mom demanded.

"I'm not doing it," Jay said with finality. I could hear his approaching footsteps.

"Jay!"

I pulled my knees in even tighter, trying to hide. The clock vibrated as it struck four. I shut my eyes. When the chiming stopped, Jay was standing there. Before he could speak, before he could tell me why he didn't want me, I pushed past him. I had to get out. I had to go somewhere. I raced toward the Olive Trees and then down the stone-strewn trail that led to Susie's. It was only as I saw Susie's house that I remembered. What had I been thinking? But I didn't want to go back, not now. I kept going. My eyes locked on the dusty trail growing quickly unfamiliar.

At the edge of the road across from the shopping mall, I stopped. The air smelled of tarmac and car exhaust. In both directions, the cars moved quickly. A big truck rumbled by, grinding its gears. A motorcycle swerved around it, buzzing like a gnat. My heart pounded as first one and then a second gap in the traffic went past. Finally, I sprinted, running clear into the mall parking area long after it was safe to walk.

Left over change from the Cake Sale **at school** clinked in the pocket of my red denim shorts. I thought to buy candy at the Penny Sweet Store. Inside the candy shop my heart raced. What if the cashier asked about Mom? I hovered in front of jelly bean jars. Silently I practiced saying that she was just next door buying paper. My hand trembled slightly as I held out the money. Silently, I cursed myself. The cashier hardly looked up.

The extra-sour lemon drop puckered my tongue as I walked slowly by the shops.

Jay didn't want the baby. Did that mean that Mom might not have it? I knew about abortion. Mom and I had talked about it when I had seen protesters once in front of Planned Parenthood. Mom wouldn't do that. I was sure of it.

At the bookstore, I climbed the familiar star-strewn stairs to the children's section. I hid in an empty bean bag half concealed by a book stack. I pulled out the first book I touched. I thought Mom was sure to be looking for me now, as I looked at a picture of the Mom and little boy feeding bread to the ducks. In the far end of the duck pond rested a flame-red flamingo. It stood quietly, its feathers dappled by a willow's shade. Seeing it made me yearn for home. Even if

I left now and went fast, it would take at least twenty minutes to get back. If Mom caught me off the property, I'd be in real trouble.

Footsteps. Someone was coming. Stuffing the last bite of liquorice rope into my mouth, I scampered to the far side of the stack, slipping around the corner just as people rounded the other side. I quickly hurried down the store's stairs. Outside was a phone booth. I patted my pocket. If Susie answered the first time, I might just have enough.

"Thank God," I said, at the sound of her voice.

"Jill?"

"I'm at a pay phone. Can you call me back?"

"Where are you?"

"Mom's having a baby."

"What?"

"Jay never wanted me."

"What?"

"It's true. I overheard them arguing."

"Where ARE you?" Susie asked again.

"At the mall."

"By yourself?"

"Can you come get me?" I asked, beginning to cry.

"Do you want me to ask my aunt?"

"Can't you take the bus?" Susie had ridden the bus two weekends before to our house. It had dropped her off at the far end of the mall.

"I don't have the money for it."

A tap on the phone booth made me cry out.

"Jill!" said Susie, alarmed.

"It's Jay," I whispered, turning my back to him. "What am I going to do?"

"You have to talk to him."

"I can't."

"It'll be ok."

"It's not ok."

The phone disconnected before she could answer. I hadn't given her my number. I had no more change. The disconnected sound began to scream in my ear. I hung up the receiver. Slowly, I slid back the phone booth door.

"Hey," said Jay.

"How did you find me?"

"I've been following you."

"Does Mom know?"

"I've called her and told her that I was with you."

Scared, I asked, "Did you tell her where I was?"

"She thinks we're together, which can be true if you walk home with me now. If we wait any longer, I think she'll want to come get you herself. She's pretty upset."

If Mom came, she would discover I had come alone. I was sure of it. I didn't want to deal with that, not now, so I headed back with Jay. I let Jay take my hand as we crossed the road, but broke free on the other side. At a rock outcropping below our Garden Jay asked me to sit with him. "There are things I need to say."

"What about Mom?"

"If she finds us here, we're all right."

From the top of the rocks, I could smell our Garden's wetness. Under my legs, the grey rock was still warm. Jay sat next to me. We both looked out over the valley.

"It's true that I didn't want children," Jay began.

I pressed my thumb hard in my palm.

"I wasn't even planning to get married until I met your mom. When she got out of school, we traveled everywhere together. My photography was going well, and we lived simply, so I easily support-ed us. Eventually, though, your mom wanted to do something for herself. We conceived the idea of starting a charity to help small Nep-alese villages increase their food production through more efficient water management techniques."

Mom had never told me that.

"But then she became pregnant. We had never talked about children. I had thought we would never have them. Your mom had always assumed we would. Her pregnancy changed everything. She wanted to move back home." Jay hesitated. In his eyes, I could see him collecting thoughts. "I felt angry. I felt that she had chosen a baby over us, as if she were trying to pin me down. That wasn't true or fair, but it took me a while to understand. When I finally met you..." Jay's eyes brimmed. "It was like your mom. Love at first sight."

"Then why won't you love my brother?"

He smiled in an odd way. "I will, sweetheart."

"Then why aren't you happy?"

"I am," he said softly.

"You didn't sound happy."

Jay hesitated again, his eyes searching the distance. "It took me by surprise," he said finally. "Already I am sad to be away so much. It's not fair on you. It would be even more unfair if there was another child."

"We're good when you're not with us," I told him.

He smiled. "I know you are."

"It's not always easy though," I admitted.

"It's certainly not perfect," Jay agreed.

"But then nobody's family is perfect, is it?" I asked, thinking about Susie.

Jay smiled all the way up into his eyes. "No sweetheart, nobody's."

17

BUSINESS

Charlie and his secretary Gina had been working on Paris from the moment I had agreed to go the month before. He had found hard-to-get tickets for the opening of the Gaugin exhibit and had upgraded our plane travel to first class, with miles.

"What do you mean you can't go?" Charlie said.

I spun in my office chair. Heavy fog obscured the city.

"I'm so sorry," I told him.

"It's all organized," Charlie insisted.

I knew all the effort that Charlie had gone to, but the secretary of the Window Boxes' CEO had just called, offering a breakfast slot. My long-prepared-for initial meeting with the Window Box buyer had gone exceptionally well. Window Boxes had agreed to take on both the statuary and the urn lines that I had pitched. What was best, however, was that the buyer had also become really excited about the idea of my developing an exclusive range of products for them. Now, the CEO, Chris Stanton, was asking for a meeting to discuss my concepts. I would have to work full-out to prepare. I had already contacted my Italian designer Giovanni to help me create drawings. If Window Boxes actually let me design an exclusive, it would be huge. My financials would go from red to black to *rapidly* growing. This was a once-in-a-business opportunity. I couldn't take any chances.

"We're leaving in less than thirty hours," Charlie protested. "You can't just back out now."

"You know how hard I've worked to get this business. Stanton has to think he's my biggest priority." What Charlie didn't totally understand was how close to the edge we had been running. Not even

Susie did. I wanted him to think we were as successful as he was. I wanted to be as successful as Susie, who was being considered for a Pulitzer.

"I should be your biggest priority." There was edge in Charlie's voice.

"You are, but let's just postpone it."

"We can't just postpone it. The Gaugin tickets, the plane tickets – all that's non-refundable."

"I'll pay you for the tickets."

"It's not about money," he said, his voice hardening.

"If you had a big client meeting I'd understand."

"I wouldn't want you to understand," Charlie argued. "I'd want you to tell me to go."

"That's not fair." I felt angry. He was being unreasonable. I didn't even believe it was true. Purposefully, I took a deep breath and let it out slowly. "We'll go another time," I said in the tone that calmed clients when they were upset.

"Oh I'm going," said Charlie coolly. His voice's edge had become steely.

I was taken aback. "By yourself?"

"I'll find someone."

"Now?"

"Sure." What he didn't say; what I was certain he was thinking was *Unlike you, there are lots of people who can be spontaneous.*

I heard voices in the background. "I've got to run," Charlie said, addressing me again.

"But…" I started. We weren't done. I needed to explain more. He needed to understand me better.

"I've got people waiting on me."

"Call me later?" I asked.

"Sure," he said, his voice now becoming neutral. It might have even been icy, he sounded so different.

****

I told Susie everything. Tim, Steve, even John couldn't make it, but it had turned out that Charlie's friend Jessica was game. "She's already got her ticket."

"You're the one who blew him off."

Her words stung.

"Don't you trust him?"

"Of course I do," I said, my anger turning on Susie. It wasn't that.

"You're just angry at yourself."

I looked down at the draft of the sales presentation I had been working on without stop. I saw the top page had a typo. I crushed it between my hands. "I had no choice," I said, my voice raising.

"There's always a choice," answered Susie calmly.

"I could design an entire exclusive line."

"So show it to him when you get back from Paris. He's already agreed to pick up your other lines. He's already committed to you."

"He might not give me another chance. He's CEO for God's sake."

"Did you even try?" Susie asked, reprovingly.

"You just don't *get* work," I accused.

"I work," she said, her voice growing cool.

"I mean business."

"You don't think I am in a business?" Susie's voice was steely.

"It's late," I told her. "I got to go."

"Jill," she began, the criticism in her voice easing, but I hung up. In the silence after, I made myself take up a clean sheet of paper. I rubbed my forehead, trying to refocus on explaining how exclusively designed products would be highly demanded by Stanton's customer base, as they would be developed for them purposefully. I tried writing it one way. I crossed it out. Another draft was equally unsatisfactory. *Damn you*, I admonished myself. *You focus.* After all this, *you better damn well concentrate.*

18

MOM

The noise of throwing up brought me running. Mom was on her knees, clutching the base of the commode.

"Mom?"

She retched, and again, and then again. Finally she flushed, closed the lid. She rested her head on top. Beads of sweat wet her pale face.

"What's wrong?"

She reached out her hand. "Pull me up."

I leaned back while she rocked to her feet. She went to the sink, splashed water on her face, and brushed her teeth. She seemed all better, but once in the hall, she groaned and sank again to the ground.

"Mom?"

"I feel sick."

"Should I call Maria?"

Mom lay on her side, curled in a ball. "No, I'm good."

She didn't look good. "Shouldn't you be in bed?"

"I think I'll stay here. The cold tiles feel nice." She closed her eyes. After a moment, her breathing deepened.

"Mom?"

"Mmmm?"

"Are you sleeping?"

She giggled without opening her eyes. The laugh made me feel better.

"Are you sure about bed?

"I'm pretty comfortable." That made us both laugh. I slid down on the floor to be next to her.

"Oh dear," she said after a while. "Thank goodness that's passed." She was pushing herself up, her back against the wall.

"You're not sick anymore?"

"A little queasy, but mostly better." I leaned against her shoulder; Lionel positioned himself on top of my pulled-in knees.

"What's wrong?

"It's just morning sickness," she assured me. "It happens sometimes when you are pregnant."

"Were you like this with me?"

"With you it was way worse. From the moment I was pregnant I threw up every day for four months. It became so bad that once I spent a week in the hospital so they could keep me hydrated."

"Is that going to happen now?"

"I don't think so. I have barely been sick this time. That's actually how come it took me so long to realize I was pregnant. With you, one day I woke up, and just like that, the nausea was gone."

"Really?" Lionel had shifted on my knees to look at her too.

"It terrified me," Mom said, touching Lionel's nose. "I thought something was wrong with you, but even before I got to the doctor's you gave me a big kick, so I knew it was all right after all."

This pleased me. "I did?"

"I thought you might be a circus star the way you somersaulted about the whole time."

I laughed, delighted, imagining my little self, tumbling and turning.

"In another week or so we will be able to feel this guy too," Mom said, resting her hand on her stomach.

I thought about the baby's little feet bumping against my hand. Jay would be missing it. He had been gone almost a month now, and I missed him more than I usually did. I think it was because Mom missed him more too. I could tell by the way she spent more time looking at his photos as she walked down the hall or the way she had taken to wearing his shirts when she went to bed every night.

Even though she was missing him, she was angry too. I had heard her talking about it on the telephone with Mrs. Smith, who was now out of the hospital and staying with Susie's aunt. I thought this meant that they would be moving back to the mountain soon, but Susie wasn't sure. Right now, Susie's aunt had said Susie wasn't to pester her mom about stuff. Right now, we were all still concentrating on helping Mrs. Smith get better.

19

CHARLIE

The ringing of the phone jolted me awake. I whipped my head up from my desk where it had been resting next to my completed Window Boxes presentation. I could feel dampness on the side of my mouth. The phone rang again. I wiped my mouth with my palm. My head felt hazy. I had been dreaming so deeply. Again, the phone buzzed.

"Hello?"

"Are you still there?"

"What time is it?

"4:00 in the morning," said Charlie.

I looked at my drafted presentation, waiting to be typed. I had been in the office without stop.

"I'm not going to Paris," he said.

"What?" I was awake now. "What are you talking about?" I looked at my watch. He should have already been on the flight.

"I gave the trip to Jessica and her sister."

"But Charlie, why?"

"I want to go with you. It was supposed to be about us going together."

"Oh, Charlie." I felt terrible. This was worse than ever. "Now I've ruined your trip too."

"It was our trip."

"I know," I said, nodding into the phone.

"We can't let this whole work thing swallow us up," he said, his voice quiet.

"I know. It's just that this meeting…"

"I get it," he said, cutting me off. "I do. But sometimes, we're going to say fuck it, all right?"

"Of course. It's just that..."

"I mean it," he said, interrupting. I could hear simmering dissatisfaction in his voice. "This is really important to me."

"It's important to me too," I said in a rush. But so was work. This company meant my doing something that was all mine, where I was totally in control, where all my efforts were an outlet to express a really important part of myself. Charlie needed to understand that too, but I wasn't going to say so. Not now anyway. I gripped the phone tighter, listening to Charlie's quiet. Right now I just wanted it to be all right with Charlie. I wanted us to be ok. I had felt sick every time I thought that my not going to Paris might have hurt us on the deepest level.

"What time are you going to be done?" he asked.

"I'm pretty done now."

"I'll come get you."

"Don't do that."

"I'm coming. Hurry and finish up."

20

PARENTS

Charlie's mom was turning fifty, and Charlie and I were flying to Maine for her birthday party. Susie had heightened the nervousness I had already been feeling by teasing me about what a big deal it was that Charlie was bringing me home for the first time. Also, I was up to my eyeballs in work now that Window Boxes had commissioned me to develop an exclusive line for them. Just the day before, my Italian designer Giovanni had sent over a whole new set of drawings that needed my comments. Yet after blowing off Paris two months earlier, there was no way I could even suggest that the timing might be inconvenient.

"My wallet!" Charlie exclaimed, patting his coat pockets.

I turned to look at him.

"It's got my license." He told the taxi driver, "We need to go back!"

The driver's eyes darted to the rear view mirror and then swept the road side to side. I looked at the dashboard clock, at the sign indicating the airport just a mile away.

"What time is your flight?" The driver's voice was deep and thickly accented. His posted license read Vladimir Slovak.

"In about two hours," Charlie said.

"Not much time," observed Vladimir.

"I know a fast way, but we'll have to sprint. I'll give you an extra $30 if we make it on time."

Vladimir Slovak's brown eyes lit up, game on.

* * * *

I gripped the door handle as we swerved back through the streets after getting Charlie's wallet. Time was running short. Charlie and Vladimir focused laser-like on the road as Vladimir gunned past slower cars. At red lights, together they held grim silence. The tension played on my already skittish nerves.

"We'll have to race for it," Charlie said to me when we finally skidded to a stop. Charlie talked us to the front of the check-in and security lines, but the gate was at the far end of the airport.

"Can you run?" Charlie asked, already sliding into a jog. My three-inch boots tap, tap, tapped the ground as my carry-on tugged at my arm. Soon, I was breathing hard. A stitch in my side stung. It felt like sand when my bouncing feet left the rubbery moving walkway.

"The gate's closing!" the ticketing agent called as we approached. Another was radioing down the walkway, telling them to hold the door. All eyes were on us as we went down the aisle. The stewardess followed, hovering while we stowed our bags, while we slipped into our seats, while our seatbelts snapped closed. Sweat trickled down my spine. Already, the plane was pulling back. Already, the safety demonstration was starting. I felt the pause of the engine building force. My stomach lurched as we left the ground.

I felt Charlie's hand. I opened my eyes. "You ok?"

The week before, Charlie had closed my apartment door while I was taking out trash with my purse and keys still inside. Susie had our extra set, which Charlie said was stupid since she was gone so much; then again, I never locked myself out. I tried not to be cross while we waited for the locksmith, while I missed first one and then the second of my morning meetings. At lunch, I got extra copies made, one of which I hid in the back garden. The other I kept just in case.

"It certainly made for quite the race," Charlie said, his eyes brightening.

I just looked at him.

"You got to admit Vladimir was brilliant."

I was coming to see that Charlie had this "all's well that ends well" attitude to life. Charlie did not focus on the fact that he had left his wallet, but that we had made the plane. Even more, there had been an aspect of trying to outsmart time and traffic that Charlie had found good fun. If it had been me, I would have been mortified.

"You ran great in your heels," he complimented.

I gave him a withering look.

"Honest. You've got real potential. I'd sign as your coach."

"My coach?"

"The quandary is whether to train you for the 100 meter heel sprint or to go for distance. To be fair, I saw talent in both."

"Heel running?" I said, starting to smile.

"Oh, I know what you're thinking. It's not an Olympic sport, but they add new ones all the time." He was speaking in earnest now. "Women would be all over it."

"To run in heels?"

"They're at it all the time, especially in the morning. There's nothing like the secretaries. Now Gina would be a challenger for you. When she has on her stilettos, nothing gets past her."

I laughed, remembering Charlie's call of earlier this week. When I had answered, his whispered voice had been strained.

"Where are you?" I asked.

"Under my desk."

"Your desk?"

"Gina's got on her red, four-inch stilettos. She's on the war path." In the background, I heard Gina tell Charlie to get out from under there. Charlie's whisper became more urgent. "She was making me clean up my paperwork. She says it is everywhere."

I had laughed, looking around my ordered piles and dusted surfaces. In his office, paperwork overflowed everywhere. I could never work like that.

"I might not make it out," Charlie said, his voice low, serious, urgent. "If I don't, know I love you."

I was totally taken back. "What?"

"You heard me," he whispered.

I could hear Gina's scolding grow louder. Then the line cut. I kept my ear pressed to the phone until the disconnect sound cried, a warm feeling spreading with my smile. The truth was that I think I had loved Charlie from our first night. Since then I had been working to play down my feelings, especially to myself. Statistics suggested that ours would be a passing affair. He had had so many girls, some he had even loved.

"Charlie!" a melodious voice called. A beautiful Asian stood close to Charlie, bringing me back to the present. Her smile was lively. He reached out to touch her arm. "What are you doing here, Mika?"

"I had work in Mexico; I'm connecting through." Her eyes cast around. "Where's Tim?"

"He's on the first flight tomorrow."

"Can you believe Milo and Oliver are coming to play?" she said breathlessly.

Milo and Oliver were two of Charlie's childhood friends. Their band Storm Chasers had just gotten a record contract. When Milo had called with the news, Charlie had been genuinely excited for them. Yet after, I could tell that he was also envious. That's one of the things I really liked about Charlie. He had more passions than there was time.

"Mom's way over the moon about it!"

"*Way Down Sally*," she said, cuffing his shoulder.

Charlie's smile broadened, as he caught her hand. "I wouldn't dance with anyone else."

"Tim too."

"You better believe it." They both laughed.

Mika's eyes moved curiously to me. Charlie shifted toward me to introduce us. Mika dropped Charlie's hand to shake mine.

"In fifth grade, Tim, Charlie and I entered the talent competition with a dance routine to *Way Down Sally*," Mika explained. "Tim insisted that we didn't need to practice."

Charlie rushed over her. "He said – and I quote – 'the sheer terror of not making idiots of ourselves would…'"

"'…lead us to some great spontaneity that would be better than anything we could do by practicing in advance.'" Mika joined in.

"And you believed him?" I asked.

"Tim can be very persuasive," Charlie defended.

"We were so awful," Mika giggled. "It was beyond embarrassing."

The drinks cart approached. "I better go," Mika said. "See you tomorrow night," she told Charlie, her hand touching his shoulder; Charlie's hand re-joined her arm. "Tell your mom that mine bought a new dress just for the occasion!"

"Seriously?"

"Can you believe it?"

I watched Charlie watch Mika's retreating figure, warmth lingering in his eyes. It hadn't occurred to me that there would be Charlie's childhood friends at the party too. "Are many of your friends going to be there?"

"Quite a few," Charlie said, swivelling towards me again. "Our house was the hang out, at least until we got the boat going. Everyone likes my Mom."

"Mika came on the boat?"

"Sure! She practically lived there our senior year."

It hit me. "You slept with her."

Charlie's expression changed, his smile growing awkward.

"You did!"

"Only once, as friends," Charlie said, rushing out the words.

"What does that mean?"

"Both of us wanted to try making love before we had to do it for real, so we decided to try it together."

"Wasn't that real?"

"You know what I mean."

I didn't know. I bit my lip, looking down at the seatbelt tail that I had been rolling and re-rolling between my hands.

"Don't look like that," Charlie said. "We were eighteen."

It occurred to me then, although I didn't want to know. "Will there be other girls there?"

"At Mom's party?" Charlie asked.

"That you've slept with?"

Charlie's expression grew more awkward.

Oh god, I thought. This guy is so going to break my heart.

* * * *

Charlie's parents were waiting at the airport gate. I recognized Charlie's father instantly. Charlie had his same dark hair and warm chocolate eyes. Charlie had told me that his dad crafted furniture in one of the barns on their property. Charlie's mother was elfin in size with silver hair that swung to the end of her back. She taught art and painted. Her water colours sold well in the tourist galleries up and down the coast.

"Charlie," she cried, closing the last of the distance in a rush. She hugged him tightly. When she let him go, Charlie's father wrapped him up.

"You must be Jill," his dad said, releasing his son. An Irish accent still sung in his voice. Its strength surprised me. His dad had come to America decades ago.

"I'm Mary," introduced his mom. Her hand felt tiny and soft. "We're so glad that you could come."

"Your mom's been cooking up a storm," Richard told Charlie as we walked. Richard had taken my bag.

"I thought you said that you'd let Dad cater it," Charlie protested.

"Their food was terrible, Charlie," she insisted.

Richard shrugged, smiling, "We tried out five different companies but none was good enough."

"You're just being impossible," Charlie scolded affectionately.

"I am not going to serve bad food at my party," she argued.

"You're not supposed to be serving at all because it is *your* party," Charlie countered.

Mary's eyes were green, just like Mom's, and they had a real fire in them now. I wondered what colour her hair had been. "It's my party so I can do what I want!" I could see in her satisfied face that she knew she held trump.

Charlie looked at his dad who was chuckling. "There's no arguing with her, son. I've tried."

"There's never any arguing with her," Charlie said, his arm around her now.

It was clear Charlie's mom took the complaint as a compliment. "I bet you're not stubborn like this old bull," Richard said to me.

"I don't know about that," said Charlie warmly.

"Good for you," Charlie's mom encouraged.

* * * *

Orange leaves drifted from the trees as we drove through the country roads past red barns and rambling houses. Charlie told them the story of his forgotten wallet, which his dad found hilarious. His

Mom just shook her head, catching my eye. I smiled brightly.

Eventually, we turned onto a long driveway. Their house sheltered amongst pines and maples. Out of the car, I caught the smell of sea; its scent mixed with chimney smoke, fresh fallen leaves and moist earth.

Inside the old house, I found that Richard had made most of their wooden furniture, which had a Quaker-like simplicity; richly coloured curtains, over-sized stuffed sofas and woven rugs added real hominess and warmth. Mary's water colours decorated many of the walls – fishing boats returning to port, fall trees blazing with colour, sea racing across rocky yellow sand, a brown-haired boy playing with a black and white dog.

"That was Rufus," Charlie said, indicating the animal. "He passed away a few months back."

"Richard and Charlie want me to get another dog," Mary said, stopping to look at the painting with us, her voice just catching, "but I still need a while."

The large kitchen smelled of cooking meat and the baked apple pie on the counter.

"Do you like lamb tagine?" Mary asked, tying on her apron. The round wooden table was already set for four. Richard's dad popped the cork out of a red wine bottle. His mom removed a large green pot from the oven. When she lifted the lid to stir, the rising aroma made my saliva pool.

"Can I help?"

"You just sit right down and relax," Mary insisted.

Charlie's dad held out my chair. So I watched as she fluffed couscous with a fork, whisked salad dressing in a bowl with mustard. Charlie's dad sliced bread as Charlie filled glasses with water. I was surprised when Charlie's Mom asked him to say a blessing. Charlie gave thanks naturally, in a way that was comfortable and familiar.

"Charlie tells me that you run your own garden furniture and accessory business," Mary said, setting off our conversation. It was easy to talk with them. They laughed often, especially his dad, who had this way of making things funny. They told me stories of when Charlie was little; his whole sixth year, for instance, he wouldn't take off his Superman costume. Charlie's mom eventually ended up buying several just so she could make sure his clothes were regularly washed.

"Even to school?" I asked, looking at Charlie.

"No one was coming between me and my Superman," he said, not the least embarrassed.

"He's like that," said his mom proudly. "Charlie never follows the crowd."

Indeed, from my experience, the crowd followed Charlie.

"Has he taken you on his boat?" Charlie's dad asked, passing me more salad.

"He has," I said. Charlie caught my eyes, raising his eyebrows. Under the table, his feet found mine.

"I'm not much of a sailor myself," his father continued. "I go green as the sea even if I so much as set eyes on a boat."

"I like to sail," said Charlie's mom enthusiastically. "Don't I Charlie?"

"Like a seadog," he assured her.

After lunch, I helped Charlie's mom clear up while Charlie went to see the new furniture his dad was making.

"I'm so glad you're here," she told me as I wiped down the table with a cloth while she emptied the remains of the tagine into a plastic container. "You are all we hear about when Charlie calls."

I was completely taken aback, but also touched. I hadn't yet told Jay about Charlie. That made me feel bad.

* * * *

Curiously I looked around Charlie's childhood room when he showed it to me after lunch. Watercolours of the sea, of his sailboat, and of a younger Charlie were interspersed with teenage posters of Charlie's favourite piano players who ranged from a young Elton John to Keith Jarrett, whom I wouldn't have known before Charlie had introduced him to me. A quilt covered his navy blue single bed, to the side of which was a very large pin board covered with photos.

I moved in to look more closely. There were images of Charlie on bikes, at Christmas, disguised for Halloween, on his boat and more. A Superman-attired boy Charlie raced down a long grassy hill with his arms out, as if flying. In almost every photo, friends flanked

Charlie. Many of the faces morphed older over time. Even as children, I could easily identify Mika and Tim.

"That's Milo and Oliver," said Charlie, moving close, his hand resting on my back. "John hates that picture," Charlie said, pointing out an acne-speckled, red-headed boy with braces. I keep it up there just to piss him off. And that's Stevie." Several photos showed Charlie with his arm around a very pretty girl with long brown hair. "That's Lyndsey," he said. "We dated freshman year." So he'd slept with her too. "And those are Janet and Allie and Jessica. You'll meet all of them at the party." There were a couple of pictures of Allie and Charlie holding hands when Charlie looked to be about fourteen or fifteen.

It struck me how different our childhoods had been. His house, close to the school, was in a small town where he could ride to everything on his bike. I had seen how close we were when we drove in from the airport. He had clearly been popular. Pictures showed him holding winning baseball trophies, shooting basketballs or hugging team members after what had clearly been a just-scored soccer goal. All the pictures gave this feel of Charlie always being at the center of everything. Instead, I had grown up isolated in a Garden on a mountain where most of my play was with Susie or alone in my own imagination.

What struck me too was how carefree and happy everyone looked. I would have stared back from similar pictures hurt and hollow. Maybe growing up like this explained Charlie's almost cavalier quality. He could lock himself out, forget his wallet, change plans on a whim because he had never had any reason to be more careful; everything for him had always been fixable. He could love and love again because his deepest pillars of love remained firmly on their foundations. I guarded love more carefully. Mine didn't flit or cavort. Once embedded, my love grew deep and tenacious and could only be ripped up; thick clumps of me like earth would cling to its torn roots, roots now exposed and already dying. A whispering voice like an intractable habit warned me again not to become too entangled. I shook my head clear of it as if scaring away a buzzing mosquito.

* * * *

After exploring his room, Charlie took me for a walk along the coast. My hand that wasn't holding his was pushed deep in my jacket, which was zipped up to the top against the air's frosty bite. The autumn waves hit the beach with force, raking fiercely back across the pebbly shore. Charlie hummed.

"What song is that?"

"An Irish folk song that Dad used to sing to me when I was little."

"Sing it to me," I asked.

I leaned into him as he sang, made happy by his soft, deep voice. Eventually, we went down a cliff into a small cove protected from the wind. Below the cliffs, it was warmer. From his backpack Charlie removed several blankets. He shook one out, and we sat on top of it way back from the restless water.

"Mom's not going to let us share a room," Charlie said.

I had wondered about that.

His fingers began stroking my thigh. My eyes opened wide. "Someone will see."

Already, he was shaking another blanket over us. "Not here," he assured, slipping a hand inside my jacket. "Cold," I protested, squirming away from his touch.

"Not for long," he promised.

* * * *

Well into the night, Mary's party rocked. When we weren't dancing, Charlie joined the Storm Chasers on a second keyboard; the barn thrummed with their sound. Mary and Richard were great dancers. Mary hadn't sat down all night; if she wasn't dancing with Richard, someone else whisked her off to clapping hands and appreciative whoops. Now Tim twirled her round in floor-length, emerald dress. Mary laughed in delight as Tim dipped her down.

Suddenly, the lights cut. The music stopped. Richard came carrying an enormous cake, covered with the full fifty candles. The Storm Chasers struck up Happy Birthday, and Charlie was by his mom now, his deep voice rising above the rest. It took her two tries to extinguish all the candles. The barn became black when the last candles went out, and people cheered and made spooky noises until someone found the light. Mary, Charlie, and Richard hugged. She had tears in her eyes, as everyone shouted *hip-hip hurrah*.

21

FIRE

Fading daylight had drained the Garden colours black, and Mom and I were already in front of the fire. Our fireplace was huge and had once been in a medieval castle. I often imagined that our Fire was an injured sun, resting in our hearth as if in a hospital bed. We fed her sticks and logs which were both her food and her medicine. Without them, Fire would die, and the world would be forever plunged into eternal blackness.

"We'll have to get a fire grill before the baby comes," Mom remarked as she beaded my tree costume for our Ecology Day play. Next to her, I searched for greens in the jumbled-up bead box. I liked the glossy slippery feel when I plunged my fingers deep into its pool.

"Did you have one when I was little?"

"We didn't have a fireplace."

"None at all?"

"We put this one in when you were about four."

"I remember that!" Although I hadn't thought of it before, now I could see dusty men hammering a hole with big, black-headed mallets. Their loud crashes had hurt my ears. "Do you think the baby will come early like I did?" Already, Mom's belly was huge. She looked as if she had swallowed a basketball.

"The doctor says he's certainly big enough."

Holding up my shirt bottom to form a vessel, I poured the collected beads in Mom's wicker basket.

"Jay was stupid to have gone."

Mom looked up from my costume. On a green shirt, she was stringing beads on wire circles to make leaves.

"I mean, would you have gone if you were him?"

Thoughts flitted across her eyes. I couldn't tell if she was working out what she actually thought, or what she thought she should tell me. Mom kept trying to act as if this was just another of Jay's trips, but I knew his absence hurt her. Once, I had seen her hacking apart a cactus that she had been replanting. By the last shovel blow, she was crying. Not sure what else to do, I had run to get Maria. She said we should surprise Mom with her favourite dinner. That night Fernando was so funny that he had Mom crying with laughter. Mom cried easily these days. She said it was because of the hormones.

"No," she answered.

"Me neither," I agreed. After a moment I asked, "Will you always be angry with him?"

Her eyes skipped back. My question had surprised her. "No," she said finally. "Staying mad takes work. Eventually it'll wear. Besides, Jay is really regretting his decision."

"How do you know?"

"It's what I hear when he reaches me. He only wants to talk about us and the baby."

I thought about Jay trapped in the cold with no way to come home.

"If there had been more time," Mom said, "Jay might have been able to find someone else."

"So it was time's fault that he went?"

Mom's smile was sad. "Not completely."

I reached to rest a hand on her tummy. I felt a ripple and then a strong jab to the inside of my palm. We both smiled. "He's so strong."

"All that good healthy food we have been eating."

I rolled my eyes, but then I thought about Susie being smaller. "Do you think Mrs. Smith drank when she was pregnant?"

"Probably some."

"You didn't drink with me did you?"

"I had a little wine a couple of times." Mom's eyes crinkled at my expression. "A little wine is ok, you know."

"You won't drink now though, will you?"

"Haven't yet."

"Don't," I insisted.

Mom stroked hair away from my face, tucking it behind my ear. My scalp tingled pleasantly. "Mrs. Smith's drinking has been scary hasn't it?"

I nodded.

"You have been a very good friend to both of them," she told me. "I'm proud of how good you've been."

* * * *

A bad dream woke me with a start, but it faded like a ghost before I could remember what it was about. Outside, branches scratched against my window like witch's nails. I pulled all my animals close. The night before, Daisy Deer had been up with a cold and had awoken all the others. It had been a real job resetting them all, so that Lionel and I could finally sleep ourselves.

"Hey," Mom said, as I appeared at her door. She was sitting up in bed, her face lit by the television's glow. Lions lay sleepily under a tree while two cubs frolicked close by. Lionel instantly perked up at their sight, watching intently from the door. "What are you doing awake?"

"I had a bad dream," I said, looking at the lions.

"What about?"

"I can't remember."

"You should go back to sleep."

"I can't."

"You are going to be tired for school."

"Branches are scraping."

"Come here," she said, pulling back the covers.

I leapt into bed, not needing to be asked twice. I snuggled close.

"Can I sleep with you?"

"If you promise to sleep right away."

"Can we watch the lions for just a little while? Lionel's very interested."

"For a little while then."

"I think Lionel's missing Africa," I said, as he watched the lions stalk antelopes.

"If he were in Africa, he would miss you more."

I kissed his well-worn nose. "All those thousands of years of instincts," I countered. "The draw would be too great."

"Love is greater," Mom said. "Nothing is greater than love."

I was almost asleep when Mom softly moaned. I turned to look. Her eyes were closed, her face pinched tight.

"Mom?"

She found my hand.

I scooted up. "Mom?"

"I'm all right, Sweet Pea," Mom said, her ragged breath easing, her eyes now open. Little beads of sweat dotted across her lip.

"What's wrong?"

"I seem to be practicing my contractions."

"The baby's not supposed to come yet."

"I think I'm just practicing."

"Shouldn't we go to the hospital?"

Mom laughed. "We're a long way from that. My guess is that this will settle in a bit."

"How do you know?"

"Well, for one, we can time them."

"Shall I get my stop watch?"

Mom laughed. "Why not?"

I leapt out of bed. "I'll get a pencil and paper too."

"Now's the time to be really brave, right?" she said when I got back.

I nodded solemnly.

"It's natural for even the practice contractions to hurt, right?"

I nodded again.

"So, you'll try not to be scared?"

"I'll try."

"Good girl, 'cause here we go again." Mom said, her voice going tight. I raced down the hall.

An hour and a half later, Mom said, "I think we better call Mrs. Smith."

"Should we go to the hospital?"

"Not quite yet. But we can call the doctor too."

Mrs. Smith's voice was heavy with sleep when she answered the phone.

"You have to come," I pleaded, giving way to the panic that I had held back. "Mom's having contractions every seven minutes. I'm timing her. She won't go to the hospital."

"Where's your Mom now?"

"In bed."

"All right honey," she said. "I'll be there record fast."

By the time I returned to Mom, she was leaning head against the wall, groaning horribly. I wished that Maria and Fernando weren't away in Mexico.

"Are you ok?" I whispered.

"Just great, Sweet Pea," she said through uneven breaths.

"We're not practicing are we?"

She tried to smile. "I don't think so."

Twenty two minutes later, the doorbell sounded. I flew down the hall.

"Now every five minutes," I told Mrs. Smith.

"Jesus, that's fast." She was already striding toward the bedroom.

Susie snatched my hand as we quickly followed.

"Jesus Fucking A-Hole Christ!" Mom roared.

Susie and I froze. Never ever had I heard Mom swear.

"Fuck, fuck, fuck!" I heard her shriek again. I dropped Susie's hand and ran to the door. Mom was on hands and knees with her head leaning on the floor.

"Mom?"

She looked at me with wild eyes. "It's all right, Sweet Pea," Mom said through clenched teeth. "It's not as bad as it looks."

Mrs. Smith snorted.

"Oh, God," Mom said. "God, please no."

"Breathe with me now, Becky," Mrs Smith said, kneeling by her. "You squeeze my hand and breathe."

When the contraction passed, Mrs Smith said, "Come on Becky, we're getting you to the hospital."

"But it's too soon," Mom protested.

"The rate you're going, you're going to have this baby within the hour."

"Please Mom," I added, in tears now. "We have to go."

"Give me a minute," Mom implored.

"I want you in the car before your next contraction," Mrs. Smith insisted, pulling Mom to her feet. Mom stood shakily. As she rose, liquid gushed from between her legs.

"Oh, God," Mom said, falling to the floor again, as the next contraction took her.

"Christ," Mrs. Smith said. "You're doing great honey. Just breathe." She looked up at us. "Girls we have to get her to the hospital because the baby's going to come quick now. As soon as this contraction's done, we are going to get her in my car no matter what. OK?"

We both nodded. I was terrified.

"Jill, you get under her arm, and Susie you stand next to help."

We barely got Mom to the car. Mom shrieked at the next contraction, and then her voice subsided to a low moan.

"This is too horrible," I said, tears running down my cheeks.

"It's ok, honey," Mrs. Smith said as she roared down our bumpy dirt drive. "You'll forget all about this when the baby comes."

I won't, I thought. I won't ever forget about this.

"I need to push," Mom cried.

"Shit," said Mrs Smith. "Becky hold on." She sped through the empty pre-dawn streets. She didn't stop at the red lights, just slowed down to look before hurrying right through. I gripped the door handle as we skidded to the hospital entrance, throwing us against our seatbelts. Mrs. Smith ran into the hospital. Two men with a gurney raced out behind her. The doctor hurried with them.

"It's coming," Mom cried, before she was eclipsed again by pain.

"I can see the head," the doctor said, looking between Mom's legs. "Get her on the gurney!"

They heaved her on the stretcher and sped her through the hospital doors.

"Mom," I screamed.

"Susie, you hold on to her," Mrs. Smith said, racing after them. "Find the waiting room."

I tried to go after her, but Susie was strong.

About twenty minutes later, Mrs. Smith came back wearing a big smile. "Let's go meet your brother!"

Mom's copper hair was matted to her face. She shook, although she was under a pile of blankets. She smiled when she saw us, looking up from a bundle wrapped in a white blanket with teal trim. A little blue hat covered my new baby brother's tiny head. His blue eyes were open wide.

"This is your big sister, Jill," Mom told him as we all looked down.

"He looks just like Jay," said Susie.

"Like a little Jay," I agreed.

Mom looked at me, her eyebrows raised. We had been debating names for months. I liked Luke, Scott and Dylan. Mom was keen on Matthew or Mark. "Little Jay?" I suggested.

"What about John Jay Tuttle," Mom answered. "That way he'd never be a junior."

"That's good!" said Susie excitedly.

"It's perfect," I agreed.

"Do you want to hold him?" Mom asked, making room on the bent bed. I cuddled close and she slipped John Jay into my arms. He was so tiny, just like a doll, except for his blue eyes, alive and real. "He's beautiful," I whispered.

"Exquisite," Mom agreed. We laughed, unable to believe our good luck.

"Smile," Mrs. Smith called. We looked up, and the camera snapped. She came near and clicked John Jay's face. The flash made him startle. He furrowed his little brow and began to whimper. His cry sounded more cat than human.

"Hey, hey," Mom cooed, taking him from my arms. "Look, look," she comforted in a sing-song voice. She offered him her nipple. He latched on and began to suckle; his blue eyes still open. I watched, fascinated.

"What a good boy," said Mrs. Smith approvingly.

"He is a good boy," Mom echoed. "My beautiful, good, amazing boy."

My wonderful, brand-new brother.

22

FIGHT

My mood was as black as the dregs of the coffee that I had accidentally tipped over my papers. A month ago, just after we had gotten back from Maine, I had wrongly commissioned an order with my Italian manufacturer Giovanni after an unexpectedly late night with Charlie. It was an expensive mistake. I had wrongly doubled the indoor/outdoor benches and red vases that my new customer Stanton had wanted, and I hadn't ordered enough of the elf statues by misreading the notes that he had faxed through. I could cover the elves from inventory, but the additional benches and vases I would have to absorb as a loss, unless the first order sold unusually well. They were exclusive to Window Boxes, etc. commissioned especially for Christmas; I couldn't sell them to anyone else. Anxious to secure the business, I had already slimmed my margins. Absorbing the extra inventory would cut deeply into my profit.

The smell of – I sniffed again – enchiladas greeted me as I entered Charlie's apartment.

"I hope you're hungry," said Charlie as he scurried back to the kitchen.

I felt fat. I hadn't exercised all week, and I felt all bloated. I knew this was because I was getting my period, which always made me swell like a zit, but I had also been eating chocolate chip cookies all afternoon, trying to combat fatigue. Charlie cracked open a beer and sent it my way across the counter. I didn't want beer, actually.

"Good news," said Charlie as he removed the enchiladas from the oven. The abundant golden cheese melted into the bubbling red sauce underneath. "Maine's coming."

I could feel my own forehead crease. "What?"

A whole group of his and Tim's friends were coming for a three day visit. The four staying with Charlie were all girls, two of whom he had slept with. There was Mika, but also Lyndsey.

"They're staying here?" I said to Charlie, incredulous.

"Why's that a problem?" he asked, setting plates on the counter for us.

I opened my eyes wide, raising my eyebrows.

"Oh come on Jill, really?"

"Why can't the girls stay with Tim and you take Stevie, John, Milo and Oliver?

Charlie served enchiladas onto each of our plates. "Are you jealous?" he teased.

I wasn't in the mood. Susie hadn't been in touch in over ten days. She was covering a story on the resurgence of honour killings in rural Turkey. I was worried about her. "It's just weird."

"What do you think I am going to do, have a *manage-à-cinq*?" He said *manage-à-cinq* while wiggling his eyebrows playfully.

I set down my untouched beer. I had had enough. Charlie never asked. He was always springing things on me. "You do whatever you want. Susie should be in town anyway."

"I thought she was joining us."

"Not now."

Charlie leaned back against the counter, his arms crossed. "You're being ridiculous."

I stood up from my stool, taking my purse and jacket. I didn't need this stress. I would never have invited four guys to stay at my apartment without asking Charlie first.

"Jill," said Charlie.

The day before, we were supposed to go out for sushi, but when Charlie picked me up on his motorcycle, instead of the car, I found out that he had agreed instead to meet Tim and friends for pizza and a movie. I had been looking forward to sushi and an early evening all day. We had a great time, but it wasn't the point. Riding his motorcycle scared me.

"Come on, sit down!"

I could feel tears threatening, which made me even more cross.

I had to get out. I had never cried in front of Charlie, and I wasn't about to start.

"Jill!" Charlie called, as I went for the door. By luck, an empty taxi was passing just as I reached the street.

* * * *

I found Susie's bag waiting under my Nepalese photos when I entered the apartment.

"There you are," she greeted happily. She was wearing my sweat pants.

"What are you doing here?" I asked – more accusation than question.

"The university is holding an international conference on Women's Rights. I read about it when I was researching my honour killings article which…" A big smile broke on her face, "my editor loved!"

"Why didn't you call me?"

For a moment Susie looked confused, and then her expression cleared. "We were way out in the mountains. No cell reception at all."

"You could have at least called to say you were coming now."

"I barely made my plane as it was; this was very last minute," Susie said, a tinge annoyed. Susie didn't like feeling cross-examined.

The doorbell rang and then rang again. My stomach dropped. "I'm not here."

Susie looked at the door. "What are you talking about?"

"It's Charlie."

"What happened?"

Knocking sounded. "I'm not here," I insisted, moving down the hall.

"I can't tell him that."

But already I was making my way to the bedroom. "Please," I said, tears pooling. "I can't see him right now."

I hugged Lionel while I waited, trying to make out their muffled sounds. About ten minutes later, Susie rattled the locked door handle. "He told Tim to take the girls," she said, coming to sit across from me on the bed.

That made me feel even worse. "Can you believe him?"

"I don't believe you," said Susie.

"Me?"

"He's a guy that has friends as girls. You've got to get over it."

Her words stung, and not just because of the rebuke. She had sided with him again. I needed air. I needed to think. I started to get up.

"Don't you even think of bolting," she warned.

"You've said what you think."

"Jill," she said, taking my hands. She dipped her head low, so she could catch my eye. "What's the matter with you?"

I didn't even know how to describe it. I just felt wrong. Charlie had this erratic quality that made me feel totally exposed. Friday afternoon he had shown up at my office unannounced and then had proceeded to rib me about how ordered everything was. Having things well sorted made me feel in control, protected, like a defensive shield against a world that could be cruelly unpredictable. I knew my tidiness was a bit over the top; I didn't need it pointed out.

"He's spontaneous. That's a good thing."

"It's not just that." We were always in a rush because he was always running late. He kept losing my apartment keys. "I've had to change our lock twice."

Susie smiled, which just irritated me further. "Those keys didn't have any identification on them."

"Changing the locks was the right thing to do," I argued. "And that's not the point."

"What is the point?"

I ripped at the balled tissue I held in my hand. "It was all going so well before him."

"I'd say it's all going better now."

"I just need some time."

Susie's brow creased. "You're blowing this out of proportion."

"I've been with him almost every night for the last six weeks."

"That's because you like him," Susie said gently.

"I like him too much," I whispered.

"But that's a good thing."

"No," I said, covering my face with my hands. We were just too different. I felt like a fool.

"He wants you to call him."

"I can't."

Susie pried my hands from my face, her mouth set. "You're going to have to talk sometime. He deserves better than this. After all, he's done what you wanted."

* * * *

I didn't call. By chance, I had been scheduled to travel to a garden convention for the rest of the week. Away, I went from early break-fasts to serial meetings to late dinners. The non-stop schedule meant that by the time I hit my bed, I was asleep instantly. Each morning the alarm clock shattered uneasy dreams, and I awoke exhausted, my eyes black-ringed.

Charlie kept calling. Each ring felt like a scalding, but his silenc-es were worse. Susie was becoming increasingly mean each time we spoke. During our last call, she had made me angry enough that I had decided not to come home for the weekend despite it being her last days in town. Instead, I checked into a small hotel at the edge of the desert about a hundred miles from the convention hall. Early, before the sun burned, I took long hikes. In the day's heat, I hid under the umbrella by the pool.

I knew that Charlie wouldn't cheat on me. Susie was right that the girls shouldn't have set me off so much. I had liked them all. I could have stayed with him at his apartment. He could have left his apartment to the girls, and slept at mine.

I wanted to be with Susie, not here alone, but she kept implying that I was creating problems with Charlie so I could avoid the risk of being in a relationship. I wasn't afraid of risk. I swirled my turquoise bracelet around my wrist. That just made me plain furious. Hadn't I started my own business? I could have lost all my savings. How risky was all the mountaineering I had done? Yet, the truth was, my feel-ings for Charlie scared me more than any mountain. He felt too good to be true; instinct warned me to pull back before I was completely lost. That was the point. Charlie had had so many girls. Maybe it was time for me to get out while I still could, before the inevitable. After all, it was Susie who had said that it would be good if I had more experience. Maybe what I really needed was a break, just for a while. I just need time to get a grip on myself.

Susie had said that Charlie was really hurt, that it would serve me right if Charlie dumped me. I had proven that I wasn't mature enough to be in a relationship in the first place. Tears slid down my cheeks.

* * * *

By the time I came home Sunday evening, Susie was already gone. I had tried calling, but her phone just rang to voice mail. I didn't even know what time her flight had departed. Always she left her itinerary, but the table was empty.

In the living room, there was Charlie's sweater thrown over a chair; in the bathroom, specks of his brown beard still dirtied the sink; in my bedroom, a pair of his discarded underwear rested at the top of the hamper. I imagined collecting his things into a brown paper bag. I imagined sending them to his office or worse handing the bag to him as he waited in the hall. It all felt just too horrible to think about.

23

JOHN JAY

Since John Jay had been born, I had started riding the bus home. I was always the last stop. After all the other kids had gone, I would move across from Sam, the bus driver. Sometimes we talked about his wife and grown-up son. Sam liked to talk about the traffic. I always gave him what Sam called the John Jay report – how much he had slept, how he had started to smile, how he kicked his legs and waggled his arms when I talked to him. The more I told Sam, the more I missed my brother, until I was so excited to see him that I would burst from the bus as soon as it arrived.

"Mom?"

"In the Lavender Room," Mom called. On the patio table, milk, red apple slices and graham crackers waited on a tray. I scooped up slices and crackers, skipped past Elf on his moss-covered mushroom, through a brick arch into a sun-baked room filled with lavender, rosemary and sage. A cold water brook burbled in one side of the room and out the other. I hopped across its stepping stones, scattering two small sparrows.

"How was school?" Mom whispered. She stood under the branches of a large olive tree. John Jay fussed in her arms. Mom's expression creased. "This baby!" she muttered loud enough that she might as well have been talking, frustration clear in her voice. "I've been trying for forty-five minutes to get him to sleep."

"I'll take him," I offered. Mom didn't hesitate. I nestled him close, bringing my cheek in to touch his so I could inhale his milky smell. He gave me a lopsided smile. Bewitched, Mom and I returned big, exaggerated grins. He beamed again, bicycling his feet. I laughed.

"He doesn't seem very sleepy."

"Mmm," Mom said, in her I'm-not-so-sure-of-that way.

John Jay cooed.

"You tell mean Mommy not to make you sleep when you want to play," I told him back in a sing-song voice.

John Jay kicked his legs vigorously.

I laughed, encouraging him, "That's right, you sweet thing!"

"There's someone who adores his big sister," Mom observed.

"This big sister adores her baby brother," I said, kissing his nose.

"Sit down," Mom said, already stretching out on a lounge. "What news of the day?"

"I got my history test back," I said, extending myself beside her. I rested John Jay's back on my bent knees so his bottom tucked in my lap. I swung my knees to rock him while I gently massaged his feet. He gazed up at the quivering olive leaves.

"And?" Mom asked.

"Eight-nine."

"What was the high score?"

"Ninety-four. James got it."

"Mmm," said Mom, her lips pursed.

"I was third in the class!" I protested.

"Only third?" she said, both as a joke and because she meant it. I ignored her. She didn't press it, which meant she wasn't really displeased. Instead, she stripped lavender from its stalk, crushing its purple flowers in her hands so that its scent released. Lavender made you sleepy.

"Lunch was chicken pot pie," I told her.

"Ugh."

"I don't know why they make it, everyone just bins it."

"He's falling asleep," Mom whispered.

We both watched as John Jay's eyes shut, his little arms dangling downward.

"It's amazing how he'll sleep for you," Mom admired. "Even Maria couldn't settle him today, and she's better at it than I am."

Pride coursed; everyone said I was a natural with babies; that I'd make a great Mom one day. I thought it was because of all my practice with my animals.

"Do we dare move him?"

I stopped the back and forth rocking of my legs. John Jay didn't stir.

"I think he's out."

"Thank goodness," Mom breathed.

* * * *

"What's that?" I asked, after I had settled John Jay in his kitchen bassinet. A blue rectangular machine rested on the table, clear plastic tubes coming from its center.

"A pump," Mom said, turning on the stove to boil water.

"For what?"

"For pumping milk."

"Whose milk?"

"Mooooo."

"You're kidding!"

"I'm planning to pump extra milk to freeze," Mom explained. "This way, he can have a bottle if I'm busy."

I tried to imagine it, remembering a TV show about dairy cows.

"I'll show you," Mom offered. "I need to pump anyway."

I watched, fascinated as her now huge breasts spilled from her unsnapped bra. She placed plastic cups over each of her nipples. The machine whirred, and little streams of milk squirted out.

"Does it hurt?"

"Not really," Mom said.

"There's not much milk."

"That's because I've just started pumping. Over the next few days, my body will ramp up."

"Can you keep making more milk forever?"

"Up to a point," she said. "But as long as you eat and drink enough, the body has amazing capacity."

When she had finished, I detached one of the milk-capturing bottles and sniffed. I stuck my finger in.

"Hey, don't do that!" Mom said.

I kept pushing my finger in until it was wet. It tasted light, but not at all like milk.

Mom's expression softened. "And?"

"Not as bad as I thought."

"Thanks a lot."

I set the bottle back on the table. "It's amazing that John Jay can live off of this stuff."

"Isn't it?"

"And that you're making it."

"It's a miracle," Mom agreed.

* * * *

Still more asleep than awake, I heard Mom cry out. I went toward her, padding across cold tiles in the still dark. Her night light glowed like an inside moon. With John Jay in one arm, she sat on the bed, rubbing her toe.

"Are you ok?"

On hearing my voice, John Jay swiveled his head.

Mom grumbled. She looked cross and fed up. "He's been up every hour all night," she said, her voice catching. The bedside clock gleamed 5:06 a.m.

"Give him to me," I said. John Jay beamed as I came near.

"Are you sure?" she asked, looking from John Jay to me. There was longing, but also concern in her voice. Her eyes were raccoon black. "If you have any problems, you must wake me."

"I will."

"Even if it's only after fifteen minutes."

"I will," I promised, holding out my hands.

Back in my room, I laid him in the center of the bed while I collected things for us to play. All the time that I gathered, I chatted, "You must be nicer to Mom, monkey. She works very hard to take good care of us."

Unloading my armful of toys next to him on the bed, I caught his legs, bicycling them fast, slow and then faster again. He smiled, delighted. After, I showed him a jingling bell that I swung from one side of his head to the other. His eyes followed it like a stalking cat. I tickled his face with my Barbie's hair. I tried to get him to hold a squishy ball. After we had finished the toys, I lay next to him and read. Early on I had discovered that John Jay loved reading, and now Mom and I combed book stores to find pop-up books.

"Well, little boy," I said, dropping the last of the books to the ground, and sweeping him up above me. "Shall we go to out to the Garden?"

Outside, the dawn air was cold. I had John Jay in the snuggly with his back to my stomach so he could face out to see. All his squirming had stopped. The cold, the scent, the breaking light, the waking birds – all of it had caught his attention. His little hands gripped my fingers tightly.

Each time I took him to the Garden, I shared another secret. Last time, I took him to meet the Flamingos. Without my guiding his hand, John Jay reached out to touch each in turn, and they tinkled and sang in their whispery way, and John Jay heard, kicking his legs excitedly. The time before, I had let him suck mountain-cold stream water from my dripping fingers. After, we had gone into the Green House and I had mashed the tiniest amount of strawberry between my fingers and then slipped the pulp into his mouth. His eyes had lit up at its flavour.

This morning, it was time to catch lizards. He was my brother after all, and catching lizards was going to be a key skill. Keeping him steady with one hand, I moved among the rocks by the edge of the Garden. The Landslide still looked like a gash, despite all of Fernando's landscaping. Yet, lizard hunting was better here now. The newly exposed rock and the new foundation walls acted like a heat trap. Always now, languid lizards could be seen baking on the rocks in the hot afternoon sun.

"Watch how it's done," I whispered to him, spotting a six incher which had crawled out to soak up the morning's first warm rays. Quick as a frog's tongue, I caught the lizard's tail, lifting him off the ground. The lizard whipped back and forth trying to bite. I held him so John Jay could see.

"You've got to grab him behind the neck now," I instructed. "Get a good hold so he doesn't snap at you." I plucked him from the air and pinned him on a rock by his neck. Guiding him gently, I took John Jay's hand to touch the lizard's back. "Softly, softly," I coached. "The most important thing is not to hurt him."

After we released the captive lizard, I pointed out to John Jay the two rock outcroppings in the parkland close to our house. One cluster of rocks Susie and I called Vulture, because the largest rock was shaped like a sharp-beaked bird. The two smaller rock mounds in front of the Vulture were the Rabbits. Both were dying, and the Vulture was moving in to feast on their flesh.

Slightly behind Vulture and to the left, Genie's Bottle was a taller rock formation that looked like a squat chemist's bottle. Half way up the bottle was the Genie's face. Susie and I believed that Genie had been trapped long before by Ice Man, who lived in the peaks above the Garden. While Genie could not escape, he still had powers. His parched breath could agitate for days, covering the surfaces inside our house with a fine red dust.

"That's where your daddy, Jay, will first teach you to climb rocks," I told John Jay. "That's where he taught Susie and me. I'm quite good at it now. In fact, maybe I can even teach you."

Back in the kitchen, the frozen plastic baggy half filled with breast milk melted fast as I ran it under hot water. On his blue-checked changing table, I dressed John Jay in a dry diaper. I brought him back to my room for his bottle. At first he rolled the bottle's nipple in his mouth because it wasn't Mom, but he had gotten hungry, and before long he settled to sucking. He was asleep before the bottle was finished. I laid him on the bed and curled around him.

I opened my eyes to find Mom staring down at us. John Jay was still asleep, his whole body pressed against mine, his hand thrown over my tummy.

"What time is it?" I whispered.

"Past nine!" Mom whispered back. "When I saw the time, I couldn't believe it. Are you all right?"

"We had lots of fun," I told her. "I gave him a bottle."

"I see."

"Shall we let him keep sleeping?"

"Definitely," Mom said. "Do you want me to lie with him?"

I stretched a little, yawning. "I'll stay," I said. "He's very cosy."

24

GIOVANNI

Even though I had been working with Giovanni closely over the last two and a half years, I had yet to meet him. Now he was spending a day with me before going off to meet friends on vacation.

"So you'll be picking me up from the airport?" Giovanni asked.

"How will I know you?"

"I'll know you. I have seen your picture. You are very beautiful," he said, his voice warming.

I laughed. Giovanni's professionalism was impeccable; when necessary, he had even run his family's factory all hours to meet unforeseen demand. Still, every now and then he would throw out the unexpected flirty compliment.

"But how will I know you?" I insisted.

"I'll be the drop-dead Italian."

"You mean drop-dead good-looking Italian?"

He lowered and lengthened his voice. "Can't you hear it in my voice?"

The next day, when I found Giovanni at Arrivals, I discovered he was not handsome in a typical way, but he possessed a merry, mischievous face as well as an athletic build.

"Well?" he teased, his eyes gleaming over his proffered hand, which I took to shake.

I cocked my head first one way, then the other. "Not half bad," I said. "But I still only like you for your pots."

"We'll see about this," he said, his eyes amused. "But first, we go to dinner?"

"I made reservations at a great Italian," I told him. I knew

Giovanni and his family loved food. That I ate lunch at my desk had been a topic of constant horror for them. Several converted barns on their land housed their factory. On nice days – most days in Southern Italy – they all sat outside together for his mama's three course lunches. I had seen pictures of their shade-dappled dining patio, as my planters now stood grouped in its corners.

Giovanni's face dropped.

I pushed his shoulder with mine. "I'm joking. We're doing Chinese fusion."

His face lit up again, like Mediterranean sunshine.

At the restaurant, Giovanni ordered enough food for a small army, and then sent back the first wine, before heartily approving the second. He did it in a way that complimented the wine master. Now, as he sat back, his eyes seemed to vacuum up the restaurant's every detail.

"All good?" I asked.

"Perfect," he said happily. His smile broadened. "I have something for you."

"For me?"

From his briefcase he removed a small portfolio. Curiously, I opened it. Inside were highly accurate watercolours of my pots, each blooming with plants typical of the climates in our primary markets. In each drawing, the planters had been integrated into gardens in ways I hadn't before considered. They were exquisite. Already I imagined them framed on my office wall.

"Oh Giovanni," I breathed.

Giovanni smiled. "My idea is that we can be attaching variations of these drawings as tags to each of the pots," he said, withdrawing mock-ups from a vanilla envelope. Tasteful brown card stock framed the coloured ink drawings. Beneath each was listed a tag with an accompanying retail price. Immediately, I could see how the tags would encourage buyers. "They are also a present," he said, pushing them toward me. "For your business."

I struggled to find the right words to thank him. The drawings were so unexpected, yet so perfect. I would instantly put the tags in mass production.

* * * *

Giovanni and I spent the next morning at my office. He was curious about all my lines, not just those he manufactured. In the afternoon, I took him on the Tide Pool Trail. He kept up with my fast pace easily; he told me he raced bikes on the weekends.

"The local bank sponsors our team," he explained. "My oldest sister, she manages the bank. She is ruthless. If we don't win, it is all I hear about." The more emotional Giovanni became, the more his hands gesticulated. When he spoke of his oldest sister, his hands flew everywhere. "I am the only son," he said. "I have five sisters." It was clear that he was doted on, not just by his mother and father – with whom he still lived – but also by his sisters. "I tell you it has been a curse to be raised among all these women." An unexpected jealousy pricked as he spoke; I had always wondered what it would be like to be part of a big family.

Later over clams and crab cakes at Peet's, Giovanni removed a sketch book from his pocket. "As we walked, I've been thinking about your business." Spreading his book flat, and sliding it between us so that I could see, he began sketching. I had thought someone else had drawn the pictures he had given me yesterday; now I saw that he was the artist. His ideas flowed across his pages as fluid as water, and not without its sparkle. "We have bought new plastic extrusion and stamping machinery," he told me, his voice and his demeanour turning seriousness now. "I might not be able to make your lines much cheaper, but I am sure I am making them better."

Giovanni ordered celebratory beers after I agreed to try his window box prototypes. Several beers later, he began drawing caricatures of the people in the restaurant, inventing funny stories about them as he inked. I rippled with laughter.

"But that's me," interrupted a middle-aged blonde. I looked up from the drawings littering our table. Giovanni had said she was secretly a witch because of her red fingernails; in his drawings, they had become talons and he had elongated her nose to an evil point.

"I am a street artist," Giovanni explained without missing a beat. "She has quintuplets," he said, indicating me. "She invited me to dinner to convince me to do portraits of her children."

The women's head swivelled between us.

"But two, he said, leaning in confidentially and tapping his head, "aren't right here, so I am saying no despite this dinner."

He turned to me. "I am sorry, but I must be honest."

"You have quintuplets?" the woman exclaimed.

"Actually, she is telling me she has seven children from three fathers," Giovanni jumped in. Despite the ridiculousness of his reply, I felt the hot flood of embarrassment.

"To me, these nails here are like extensions of your soul," he was telling her, "warm, passionate, on fire." Unbelievably, by the time he was done talking, Giovanni had convinced her to buy his drawing for a tenner.

I wiped the silent laughter from my eyes as I watched the woman retreat, a big smile on her face. Giovanni grinned back at me as if he were a boy at an ice cream counter sitting before an enormous sundae.

"You are bad," I scolded.

"You're not married," he said, his eyes flicking to my fingers.

I was caught aback at his change of subject.

"Boyfriend?"

My stomach tightened. It had taken three weeks for Charlie's calls to stop completely. Now, almost two months later, I still missed him terribly. Unexpectedly, it was often worse at work. By mid-morning, unless I was busy with clients, I still felt the absence of his calls like physical pain. Without ever talking, I had messengered all his things to his office. He hadn't done the same for me; he hadn't even sent a message through Gina about my box having arrived.

At night, I often found my thoughts interrupted by our memories. The previous night, we had lain together on his couch, his head in my lap as we listened to his vinyl collection. A South African group played; their tribal singing had in it the sound of a lone train passing; it had been so evocative in the candle-lit room that the train had passed through me like a shiver. Charlie had seen me connect with the music; he had tightened his grip on my hand, urged me deeper.

Susie had long since stopped her admonishments. She still said that Charlie deserved the respect of an explanation. Yet she understood me. Over and again, she promised it would get better, that given time, I would grow through this. Given time – how these oft repeated words were bitter to me, like medicine without water.

I shook my head.

"No boyfriend at all?" Giovanni persisted. "But how is this possible?"

"What about you?" I deflected.

His smile broadened widely. "I am not dating seriously, either. Although my mama, she's telling me all the time that I must find a nice girl now. My mama likes her children married. All my sisters are married but one, and she has a serious boyfriend."

"Maybe she just wants you out of her house?"

"You don't know my mama," Giovanni said confidently. "I think she wants me to marry so my wife will move in. She gets lonely with just the four of us, now that my other sisters have left us."

* * * *

"Where do you live?" Giovanni asked as we left the restaurant.

"Not far from your hotel." I raised my arm to flag an empty taxi. "I can drop you off."

"This is not possible," he said, reaching to open the taxi door for me.

"What do you mean?" I asked, turning.

"I am Italian," he said, his voice playful, but his eyes serious. "It is I who drop you off."

There was no telling him otherwise. On our way, I pointed out sights as we weaved through dark streets. He shifted near to see our Catholic cathedral; when the church was gone, he remained close, and I became very aware of our touching ankles. I was sure Giovanni felt us too, but he gave no indication. Instead, he told me how, as a choir boy, he had once convinced the others to smuggle in frogs under their robes.

"During Mass, they began croaking. This boy, he sets his free, and then we all do, and then it is everywhere – these frogs. The priest, he gets very angry, but I pretend innocence. I ask him, 'Doesn't God also want the frogs to be Christian?'"

I laughed.

"What could he do?" he asked me.

The taxi slowed to stop at my building. "You're going on to 335 Baker," I told him.

"Actually, I am thinking of walking," Giovanni told the driver. "I am liking walking in new cities."

* * * *

"Well…," I said, after I had given him directions back to his hotel. Tomorrow, Giovanni was going to meet two friends from home in Las Vegas. "Thanks again," I said, indicating the sketches that Giovanni had torn for me from his notebook.

"I will have the prototypes ready by the end of next week," he promised again.

"Well…," I repeated, feeling palpably the presence of my apartment. I offered my hand.

Giovanni took it, moved in. "I like you Jill."

"Giovanni…"

He cupped my chin, brushed his thumb over my lip. I thought to step back, but he kissed me and when his tongue probed, I opened willingly.

"Wrap your legs around me," he breathed in my ear. Already he was lifting me, tilting me, kissing me again. With my legs around his waist, my back against the wall, he began moving against me. As his movements gathered pace, as our breathing increased, I strained to feel him deeper while he squeezed my nipples under my shirt. When I cried out, and threw back my head, he pushed harder still until he collapsed in my hair.

"Giovanni… Already doubts were rushing in like flood water.

"Hey, Hey…," he said, brushing hair from my face. "This can be nothing," he whispered. "If you want, this can be nothing at all."

* * * *

"And then he faxed over a drawing."

"A drawing?" asked Susie.

"It was of me right after – you know. It could be a picture it is so alike," I told her, looking again at my thrown back head. Its intimacy unsettled me, but even I thought I looked beautiful.

"With a note?"

"Only his name at the bottom," I told her.

"That's too cool," Susie approved.

"What am I going to do?" I breathed.

"The hypocrisy is rich," said Susie, laughing.

"Don't you think I know it?" I asked, my voice rising, devoid of humour.

"Calm down," Susie soothed. "He's Italian for goodness sake. You live 6,000 miles away. From his perspective, I am sure this won't affect your work relationship."

"So you are saying it was just physical sex," I said, hurt despite myself.

"You know that's not what his drawing means."

"What does it mean?" I asked, looking back at the image of myself, my eyes half closed, my cheeks tinged.

"I think he's saying it can mean whatever you want it to mean."

"That's exactly what I am afraid of."

25

SHADOW

"John Jay looks more like Jay every time I see him," Susie said. Together we lay on the Great Lawn. At just four months, John Jay had mastered rolling from back to belly. Now on his tummy, he lifted his head and smiled his inimitable clown grin, trilling.

"Good boy!" I exclaimed. After the initial joy, he began to fuss. He disliked being belly down. Gently I flipped him to his back, tickling his tummy. He laughed, then immediately set back to rolling.

"Jay had to be just like this when he was a baby," Susie said.

Tummy down, John Jay pushed up on his arms, but they buckled and his face crashed into the blanket. He shrieked. I scooped him up, rocking. John Jay's crying stopped.

"What do you mean?"

"John Jay is constantly trying to master movement. Jay does that even now."

I had never thought of it like that.

"When's Jay coming back anyway?"

"In a few weeks."

"He's missed so much."

"I can't even remember what it was like without John Jay."

John Jay sat on my lap chewing his fist. Susie nibbled his toes. John Jay clown-grinned at her, and we both laughed.

"Hey girls," Mom called. "I'll trade you a baby for a snack."

"Thanks Mrs. T," Susie said, as Mom set down a tray of milk, melon and lemon bread.

"It's you that I need to thank," Mom said, lifting John Jay from my lap. "I finished all the invoices!"

* * * *

"So what do you want to do?" Susie asked as Mom and John Jay moved away.

"I don't know," I said, biting into lemon bread. Tangy lemon syrup saturated its sweet crust.

"Want to play Shadow?"

I hesitated, but only briefly. "Sure."

Quietly, we finished our snack. We drained our milk. In silence, we went to the Mirror Room where honeysuckle covered stone walls. Inside, the Heaven Mirror gleamed like melted mercury, reflecting sky and bits of feathery Willow whose whispering leaves rippled like green liquid in Mirror's silvery, shimmering interior.

Slowly, we circled, chanting. "Forgive us, Mirror, for we have sinned. Help us, Mirror, for we have fears. Bless us, Mirror, for we have wishes." Ten times we went round Heaven Mirror, each collecting our thoughts. Shadow made us expose our deepest secrets, yet we could not comment on these revelations until we had asked for forgiveness, until Angel's water redeemed us.

We began by falling to our knees before the plaque of Medieval Knight, set in the wall by Willow.

"I stole money from my mom's purse," Susie confessed.

I peeked at Susie, surprised. When her mother had been drinking, Susie often took money to buy food, but why now?

"I snuck sweets from the cupboard." I admitted.

We touched Knight's sword.

In silence, we slipped to the Nasty Frogs. In Shadow, there was no seeking security by stroking Griffin.

Susie said, "I stole a calculator from a girl at school."

"What?" I thought, but said instead, "I fought with my mother when she asked me to set the table."

From the Frogs we went to the Lily Pad Room, where Bronze Deer stretched her dainty metal neck to reach the clear green water. "I stole nail polish from a store."

This time I looked at her frankly. Defiance blanketed her hurt. "I fear...," I began.

"Have you no more sins?"

"I picked my nose and ate it," I owned up, my cheeks flushing. We stroked the Deer's pointed ears.

Next to the Blue Marble Rabbit, Susie revealed, "I lied to my mother about the calculator."

That reminded me. "I lied to Mom about brushing my teeth." The rabbit's nose felt smooth, its brown glass eyes penetrated.

In amongst the Cutting Beds, nine glass blossoms on tall green glass stems sparkled in the afternoon light. They cast coloured shadow on the sun-baked stone hot against our knees.

"I lied to my Mom about going to a friend's when I really went to buy books with the money that I stole."

"I stayed up late twice last week, and then was grumpy because I was tired." We tapped each flower before continuing.

In the Green House, Wooden Monkey scampered up the Orchid Tree. "I lied to my Mom about having friends, because I wanted her to think I am happy," Susie said.

What about Donna and Diane that Susie always talked about?

"I was jealous of Donna and Diane," I confessed.

In front of Gentle Bear that wandered deep in the Pines where our Garden became the Wild, Susie said, "I called Donna and Diane bitches yesterday." I could just catch Susie's face in my periphery. She must have been really upset to have called them such bad names.

"I fear that you will get caught stealing," I said. This time, Susie did not challenge my change to fears.

By the Peat Porcupine, Susie said, "I cut myself with a razor yesterday." She pushed up her shorts. Three small scabbed slits streaked across her inner thigh.

"Why Susie?"

She just shook her head, her eyes moist.

"Susie, I'm afraid of all the things you're doing." We dipped our fingers in the snow-cold water of Porcupine's Pool.

"I'm afraid I'll get caught stealing," Susie said at Lion's Table.

"I was afraid that if you were really happy in your new school, you wouldn't like me as much. I am so sorry. I wish you were happy."

"I wish I had just one friend there that was just a quarter as good as you."

"I wish you would never cut yourself again. You mustn't Susie!"

We stroked the Table's stern lion, and then, without warning, Susie tore across the Garden. I raced too until we collapsed on the Olive Gazebo's shadow-checked floor. A little metal heart shone from its center.

"I wish I could move back," Susie said.

"I wish you could move back, too." We stroked the heart together, and then quick as lightning, Susie lit out again. I went after her. At Angel, we circled, chanting, "Good Angel, Good Angel, forgive our sins. Good Angel, Good Angel, conquer our fears. Good Angel, Good Angel, grant our wishes." We sprinkled her cleansing bird bath water on our shoulders and face.

After, I searched Susie's eyes – embarrassed, defiant, scared.

"What's happening Susie?" I whispered.

"I don't know."

"Why are you stealing?

"I just can't stop somehow."

"Does anyone else know?"

"No!"

"You haven't told anyone at school?"

Anger hardened her voice. "Like who?" She was trying not to cry.

"Donna? Jane? What about that girl Megan you told me about?"

"They haven't been nice at all."

"What do you mean?"

"Sometimes, they'll sit with me at lunch, and sometimes, they sit purposefully where there aren't enough chairs for me to join. Sometimes, they'll talk to me; other times, they stop talking when I come up. I never know what they'll be like." Her tears fell.

"They are bitches," I said, trying out the word for the first time.

"I don't know what I am doing wrong," Susie said, wiping her eyes on her shirt.

"They're wrong, not you."

"Stealing feels like getting them back."

"But that's just hurting yourself."

"I know. That's why I cut myself, for punishment."

"But Susie, that's even worse!"

"I know," she said miserably. We sat now, cross-legged at the feet of Angel. I took her hand. "Have you talked with your Mom?"

"About stealing?"

"About everyone being mean?"

Susie shook her head. "I'm afraid to upset her."

"She's going to be more upset if you get caught stealing. You'll get caught eventually. You know that, right?"

Susie suddenly seemed small, like a balloon losing air. "Yes."

I squeezed her hands. "Don't worry. We'll figure out something."

Susie looked away. She looked so sad. I shifted my head so that she would have to see me. "OK?"

"OK," she said finally.

26

GIOVANNI

"The prototypes were fantastic," I told Giovanni.

"Yes?"

"Even better than I expected. Let's put them in production."

"Excellent!" cried Giovanni. His distant voice seemed to soar. I smiled; his enthusiasm was irresistible.

Giovanni's voice changed, softened. "How are you, Jill?" In our brief conversations since that night, we had kept it all business, which I had quickly rationalized as positive.

"Good," I said, keeping it light. "How was Las Vegas?"

"Like a whore." His said it like a compliment.

"How would you know what a whore's like?" I teased

"It's as you hear. You pay money to have a good time with something garish."

I laughed.

"Actually, I wasn't paying," he said, cockiness seeping into his voice. "I won five thousand at the black jack table!"

"Seriously!" I had never known anyone to win, not that I knew many who bet. Still, at the Annual Garden Convention Show, people talked about their gambling escapades. For me, life was already too much of a wager to add chance in the form of monetary entertainment.

"I quit while I was ahead, but my friends, they lost, so I was buying drinks and meals for the whole weekend." He chuckled. "Which I guess means that I lost too, as my friends, they were choosing only the best restaurants."

It was clear that Giovanni approved.

"But I am really asking how you are about the night." Giovanni's voice was more serious now, and insistent.

I didn't know what to say.

"It is my rule not to mix my business and my pleasure."

Unexpectedly that hurt. "Me too," I rushed in.

"My father was not impressed."

"He knows?" I was aghast.

"He guessed. Actually, it was my mama who was guessing and telling my father. My sister, she said..."

"Your sister?"

His voice was apologetic, "We are a close family."

"Let's just forget it," I cut in. "Make it like you said." My embarrassment was acute.

"But this is the thing, Jill – I am not wanting it to be nothing."

"But Giovanni..."

"I know all you will be saying," he said, "because I have been saying it to myself as well. This is why I haven't been talking to you before. But this is the thing – I don't want nothing."

I swivelled in my office chair, both uncertain and pleased. Despite the fog, a scattering of people sat in the square cupping takeaway drinks. Tall yellow tulips sprouted from the planters like little suns.

"Can I see you again?"

"Your family..."

Giovanni cut in. "They agree, my family. They feel about you like I do." His laugh was low, this time, guttural. "Well, maybe not exactly like I do," he teased. The playfulness in his voice made me smile.

"Maybe I could come see you when our shipment arrives? Besides, I have a surprise for you."

"Surprise?"

"Two additional boxes."

I wanted to know what was inside, but Giovanni wasn't telling.

"I'll get a hotel room, of course."

In my head, everything replayed that I had ever told Susie about getting together with people from work.

"The truth is, Jill, your business is very important for my family," Giovanni said, as if reading my mind. "I promised my father that I wouldn't let my dick mess this up."

I shook my head, simply incredulous. You had to love Giovanni's family.

"So maybe we can just be friends for a while."

I thought again about my legs around his waist.

"Take it slow like an Italian snail."

"Italian snail?"

"They're the ones with the Fiats."

I laughed with Giovanni. I wasn't quite sure why Fiat snails were funny, but Giovanni was very amused, which was funny in itself.

"What are you saying?" he urged.

"OK."

"Bravo!" he cried.

"OK," I said again, louder this time, so that I would make sure that I heard it, that I would not forget my acquiescence sometime later.

27

NEW DAY

The first grey light penetrated the darkness. I closed my eyes hoping sleep would return, but the sky was blanching quickly. Beside me, Susie murmured, rolled over. Through the half opened window a bird sounded, then another answered, back and forth. Slipping from the covers, I padded to my wide glass bay. There, the animals had already gathered. Lionel stood on my knees, king, friend, and guardian.

I could hear a third bird now. His note excited the other two. As the light whitened, shapes emerged from night – trees like black ghosts, fat bushes like squatting trolls. I pushed the window open wider. Cool air came in like a streamer, carrying drifting Garden smells. I shivered, once.

"Mom, I didn't do it!" Susie cried.

Susie could sleep talk whole paragraphs, which usually made me smile. This morning, though, I thought again of yesterday's Shadow. I imagined Susie's angry teacher pacing the desk rows looking for the calculator thief. We had to stop all the bad things she was doing. She was sure to get caught if we didn't.

A fourth bird joined the morning chorale, then another and a sixth. I paid careful attention now. Sun's first rays would soon shoot into the Garden like arrow quivers. As they struck, black trees and plants would regain colour. Susie and I believed that seeing the first yellow light was seeing God, but just for that millisecond. God came as a blessing, captured like a secret.

Another bird sang, and I wished John Jay were with me. John Jay loved birds. Often he rose early, and frequently I took him now if Mom was tired. In the Garden, our new favourite game was to bird hunt. When John Jay saw one, he kicked his legs excitedly. On the days I woke before him, I liked to climb into his crib, curling around him so his milky breath blew warm across my neck.

There! A yellow streak! Lighting the peach roses! Then more light crossed the mountains, and as quick as breath, God was gone. The birds reached their raucous, melodious crescendo, singing morning's coming, the sheer joy of breaking dawn.

Once the Garden was fully lit, I spent time dressing and settling my animals. Michael Marmot and Harry Hedgehog played at running races while Red, Daisy, Squirrel and Rascal were all tumbling around. I left them playing happily, stealing past sleeping Susie down the chilly morning hallway. I paused in a warm early sun patch at John Jay's door. Even from the threshold, his baby smell was strong. My eyes lingered on the pop-up books spilled across the carpet. Ready diapers were piled on the changing table next to a furry ball and a plastic rattle. John Jay now resisted diaper changes, which was hard when his diaper was poopy. Toys were needed to distract him, so his bottom mess wouldn't go everywhere.

I yawned. I was glad he was still asleep. It would be delicious to curl up again for a while. I tiptoed as quietly as I could. As I reached his cot, I smiled. If John Jay was going to wake, it was usually when I got this close. Instead, he was very still, a strange blue-white. I reached to touch his cheek. It was unnaturally cold. I rustled him gently, tickling chilled feet, and then shaking his tummy, harder, then harder still. I screamed.

"Jill?" Mom rushed to us. "Oh God," she cried, as she took John Jay in her arms. "Oh, my baby." She rocked him against her chest as milk wet her shirt. "My little baby boy."

"What's wrong?" I cried. "Is he all right?"

Mom was rocking, rocking, "No, no, no!"

I backed away.

"Jill? What's happening?" Sleep still confused Susie's face.

In the hallway I could hear Susie giving Emergency our address. I could hear her imploring them to hurry. He didn't even have a cold. What had God done? Realization made one pin-hole prick into the unfathomable. That prick brought red-blind feelings. The rose bush! I rushed into my room, knocking my animals off the bench, as I went out the window. Taking clippers resting nearby, I hacked. I pulled at stuck branches with raw hands. The thorns cut and scratched.

"Jill!" Susie called from the bedroom window. "Stop!"

Before Susie could get to me, I ran. I had this sense that whatever had just happened wouldn't be real if it couldn't catch me up. Garden rooms blurred. I careened by the Landslide, down the steep path toward Vulture. A stitch burned. Once there, I climbed, hearing everything Jay had ever told me about the importance of safety ropes. But I didn't care just as Jay didn't care. I hated Jay.

From the rocks' height, I could see a dusty trail on our driveway, meaning cars were coming. It occurred to me that they would take John Jay. It occurred to me that I had to stop them. Quickly, I began scrambling down. Some distance from the bottom, I slipped. My fingers tried to grip, but my momentum was too much. When I hit bottom, my legs crumpled underneath me, but I forced myself up. My side seared; already blood seeped through my pyjamas. But still I ran, and kept on running.

"Wait," I screamed as the ambulance began to back up.

"Jill," Mom cried.

The ambulance stopped. Men jumped out.

"I want my brother!"

"Jill," Susie started, but I knew what she was going to say. I spun on her. My ankle seared. I reached to grasp it, but I fell, shrieking out.

28

HOSPITAL

I hurt all over. The dim room was unfamiliar. In the chair, Mom slumped. I went to push myself up, trying to figure out what was going on. I found my leg in a cast. White bandages wrapped around my palms. My stomach stung.

"Mom?" My voice croaked.

Mom jolted. She leaned over, stroked my forehead. "How do you feel?"

"What's happened?"

"You've fractured your ankle," Mom soothed, "but you'll be right as rain in a few weeks' time."

I remembered now. "My stomach hurts."

"You had a bad cut that took quite a few stitches."

I looked at my hands.

"They're quite scratched up," Mom said, following my eyes. "In a couple of days they'll be fine."

"John Jay?" I whispered.

Mom shook her head, tears in her eyes.

Hurt scorched. "Why?"

"He just stopped breathing." Mom's voice choked. "No one knows why."

* * * *

Mom's sweatshirt lay over her empty chair. The room was brighter now, even with the drapes partially closed. My skin felt on fire. Painfully, I scooted myself up. A doctor came in as I struggled with the water pitcher, the bandages making my grip awkward. "Let me help you with that," he offered.

I gulped, coughed, sputtered.

"Easy does it," he said.

I panted a few times, and then drank until the water was gone. I rested back against the pillows, exhausted when I was done.

"How do you feel?" he asked. He placed a hand on my forehead. His skin smelled like soap.

I looked at my blankets.

"I'm sorry about your brother," he said, as he brought his stethoscope to my chest.

I didn't know what to answer. When he finished, he wrapped the stethoscope around his neck, sitting in Mom's unoccupied chair. He took my wrist between his fingers.

"I was telling your Mom last night that I also lost my brother when I was nine."

He had brown hair and dark eyes.

"He was my best friend."

With my free hand, I pressed my sheet against my eyes.

"It takes a long time to feel better when you love someone as much as your mom told me that you loved your brother," he said, handing me a tissue.

Just yesterday, John Jay was rolling over, laughing.

"For a long time after my brother died, I just stopped caring about things," he said, sitting in a chair next to me. "I thought that if I were happy, that meant that I didn't love my brother any more, and that I was beginning to forget him, but I was wrong. I squandered a lot of years of my life before I understood that my brother would have never wanted me to stay sad forever."

"How could he just stop breathing?" I whispered. Hurt made it hard to speak.

"No one knows why it happens exactly," he explained gently.

"But he barely got a chance."

"No, he didn't."

A slat of sun fell across my bed from the cracked curtains. I saw again God lighting the peach roses. "I hate God."

"I felt that way too, and I am a deeply religious man," the doctor told me.

The doctor stood, went to the window. He pulled open the drapes. The sun's full light spilled across the room. The doctor turned back to me. "What makes your mom feel better might not make you feel better. Everyone has to get better in their own way and in their own time." He came and sat by my bed again. "Life is like the tide," he said. "No matter how far out it recedes, life always comes back. Sometimes it rushes in, and sometimes it just laps in gradually, but life will come back, and you will feel better as long as you let yourself. You mustn't feel bad about it. I also told this to your Mom."

The sun at his back darkened his face. "You go home today."

Mom came then. Seeing me awake, she hurried forward. "How are you?" she asked, looking between the doctor and me.

"I was just saying that she's going home," the doctor said, standing. He removed a prescription pad from his pocket. We watched as he wrote.

"Antibiotics for Jill," he said, handing Mom a prescription, "and a sleeping aid for you. Sleep's important, for both of you," he emphasised.

"Thanks," Mom said, taking the white paper squares. "Thanks for everything."

"You're most welcome," he said, touching her shoulder. He looked down again at me. He gently squeezed my arm. His voice echoed. "I'll be thinking of you Jill."

29

SAD

The bright daylight made me blink. Although I had a walking cast, the nurse had also given me crutches. The crutches pulled at my hurt skin as I swung forward step by awkward step. It was a relief when we finally reached the car. Mom helped ease me in. Once buckled, I sank against the already hot seat. Cars, trees, houses, people passed as we drove, but they felt unreal. Familiar things now felt wrong. It made me feel as if I were inside an empty jar, sealed off. "What a joke," I heard Susie's say in my head. "What a very bad joke."

On the slow drive up our long dirt road, the hurt caused by our Garden's nearness started to cause cracks in the jar that I had become. Impossible took on the first hint of real. Home was John Jay. A strangled noise escaped Mom. Tears streamed down her face as she clutched the wheel with both hands, her body angled forward as if she was trying to see through a storm. At our house, she rested her head on the wheel while tears made water marks on her pants. Then she began hitting her head hard on the wheel's plastic.

"Mom!" She was scaring me.

My cry stopped her. Her hollow eyes struggled. Familiar concern finally returned, and she looked more like Mom. She tried to smile. "What if we sit you on a lounge chair in the Garden?" Her voice sounded too high, off somehow.

I just looked at her.

"Are you hungry?" she asked in the same strangled voice. "I'll get you something to eat."

I shook my head.

"You must eat," she insisted.

I didn't answer, because what was the point? She'd make food regardless. I struggled to get out of the car before she could help. It was hard manoeuvering crutches on the irregular path. A thyme scent arose when my sticks crushed against its over-hanging leaves. Our blanket was still spread on the Great Lawn. My stomach clutched. Two bluebirds pecked at leftover lemon bread crumbs. Was that really just yesterday?

I saw John Jay flip onto his stomach. Wasn't it *now* that was impossible? Wasn't this all some bad *mistake*? My crutches caught. Before I could catch myself, I catapulted hard onto the stone walkway.

"Jill!" Mom cried.

Pain exploded. This wasn't a mistake. With a grunt, Mom lifted me up. She carried me quickly, my crutches left behind. I felt new blood trickle down my stinging cuts.

* * * *

Mom set down fruit, lemon bread. "You need to eat."

"Oh God," I thought, "Not the lemon bread…" Lecturing came and then drifted from her eyes when I made no move toward the plate. "Why don't you rest," she said instead. "I'll just garden for a while." I kept back tears as she went to the beds. On her knees, at nearby beds, I imagined her ripping out still fresh flowering plants. Their pried roots tore audibly, like a cry. Afterwards, she emptied bag after bag of dark soil into the bare earth, digging it in deep. When I awoke, red flowers rioted, where before soft pink flowers had gently waved. Mom sat by me, cupping tea. She looked exhausted.

"Mom?" I was so parched. It was hard even to whisper.

"Hey," she said, quick to kneel beside me. She held her tea to my lips. Honey made it sweet. I drank three cups. All the while, Mom soothed my hair.

"Better?" she asked when I had finally finished.

I nodded.

"Can you eat something?" Her voice was hers now, but tired.

I shook my head.

"You have to eat something."

"Have you?"

A trace, what normally would have been a smile, touched and left her lips. I could see her considering a lie.

"You haven't," I answered for her.

Ruefulness left just as it had formed. She took an apple slice and bit. "Your turn," she said when it was gone.

I took the thinnest piece of apple, and from its corner took a small bite. It was juicy and delicious, making my mouth water. The apple was gone almost before I had started. I ate another slice and then a third.

"Good girl," Mom encouraged.

I had grapes, but then I was done.

"Have you told Jay?" I asked.

"Yes," Mom said.

"What did he say?"

The lines on Mom's face seemed to have been etched deeper almost overnight. "He's trying to come home."

"He's missed him completely."

"I know."

"That's so sad," I said, tears starting.

Mom was crying too. "I'm sorry," she kept saying, coming beside me on the lounge, pulling me close. "I'm so, so sorry." My whole body pushed into hers. Under my ear, her heart knocked as her chest shook. After a while, our crying subsided. A flitting caught my eye, and I saw a little bird dash from one branch to another, and then I saw a second bird and a third. One trilled: *tree, tree, tridil; tree, tree, tridil*; another answered, *tridil tree, tridil tree*. Oh, John Jay.

"Susie called," Mom said.

I looked at her.

"They're down the mountain. She'd like to see you."

"Do I have to?"

Mom's eyes stood back. "No," she said gently.

"I just want to be with you for a while."

Mom hugged me again. "I feel the exact same way."

* * * *

I awoke with a terrible sense of something wrong. Uncomfortable, I shifted in bed. My stitches throbbed, and I remembered, and pain struck like a slap. I coiled my chest to my knees, curling against any further attack, as sobs wrenched. Afterwards, I felt empty, hollowed out.

Again, I awoke. Was it just the same night? I tried to make sense. Painfully, I pushed myself up until my back was wedged against the pillows. I pulled in my casted leg with my hands, wrapping my arms around tucked in knees, rocking, rocking, trying to think, to not think.

Maybe there wasn't a God! I mean, what had John Jay ever done that had ever been bad? He had been too young to be bad! Faster, I swayed, but not fast enough. Pain seared like hot iron, and I broke under its blistering. I wanted to call Mom, but pain swallowed my voice. Tears fell like draining blood. When I finally stopped, I felt cold – so cold. I thought about covers, but then, why should I be comfortable, when John Jay was – where? Heaven? If there were no God, there was no heaven. Maybe there was just…nothing. No! There had to be God! Thinking of John Jay anywhere but Heaven was unbearable. John Jay couldn't just be erased.

I roused, slumped over on the pillows. Had I even slept? Yet the night's light was different. I felt icy, thirsty. If I could just get some tea. I eased my legs to the floor. My legs were stiff and hurting when I stood. I made my way painfully to the window past animals still thrown on the floor. Stars glowed brightly in pale darkness. When I was little, I had once asked Mom, "When I get to Heaven, will you put up your hand so I can find you?" Who would raise their hand for John Jay if there was no Mom and there was no me?

****

John Jay's door was closed. I hesitated, and then crutched quickly until I was clear. In the living room, I found Mom, motionless, her beading untouched. She did not see me as I came in.

"Mom?"

She startled. "What are you doing here?"

"I woke up."

Mom nodded absently.

"Are you beading?"

It was as if she didn't understand.

"Beading," I repeated, indicating the box of beads in her lap with my head. She looked down. She shook her head.

"Mom?"

Sobs shook her shoulders.

"Mom?"

She cried without answering.

I crutched to the couch. Not knowing what else to do, I put my hands on her leg. I rested my head on her shoulder. "It's all right," I said over and over. "It's going to be all right."

After a while, Mom's crying eased. Finally, she really saw me. Worry focused her eyes. "Can't you sleep?"

I shook my head. Her concern brought my tears, and Mom wrapped me in her arms.

"Will it ever be ok?"

"Yes," she whispered.

"It doesn't feel like it's going to be ok."

"I know," she said. "I feel that way too."

* * * *

Grey began to colour the night's moonlight as Mom settled me at the table, waiting for me to manoeuvre my legs underneath before sliding my chair forward. I watched as she took the kettle from the stove, swiveled to fill it. The kettle clattered. She swayed. I pushed myself up. She gripped the basin, catching herself. Then I saw it too: John Jay's bottle. I sunk to my chair. Mom's body tightened, as if she was pulling into herself. Her face changed – determined, angry, she took out a plastic storage container and quickly, she swiped all his bottles from his shelf, and then put in the one from the sink, sealing the top shut. Milk leaked through her cotton shirt as carried the container to the pantry. She climbed the always-waiting step ladder, sliding the container to the very back of the highest shelf. When she came back, she cleared all the frozen breast milk from the fridge, throwing it and the pumping machine into the trash.

"Mom?" I whispered.

She turned to me, her eyes wet. Back at the stove, she held the kettle to her chest. She looked so sad, nothing but broken pieces.

* * * *

"How do you know?"

Mom looked up at me from where she was kneeling by the hearth, turning a log. We had skipped our tea; instead I had water. Now I was so tired, yet each time I closed my eyes, panic struck like sudden falling.

"How do you know it will ever get better?"

Black ringed Mom's green eyes. She set down the iron poker. "Grandpa died, remember?"

I was six when Grandpa died. I hadn't known him well, but I had a vivid memory of Mom crying.

"Remember how sad I was? But remember how I got better?"

"How much time?"

"I don't know," she said. "For now, we are both sad. That's all I know, and that's all right. It's good in fact."

"Why is that good?" Sudden anger coursed. Was it good that John Jay was dead? I pushed myself up on the couch.

"Hey," Mom said, near me now. Her hand eased apart my fingers where my nails had been cutting into my wrist. Red marks dotted where my nails had dug. She took my hand in hers.

"How could that be good?" I repeated, anger deflating as quickly as it had come. I felt that wretchedness was all there had ever been.

"We have to feel the sadness now or it will bury inside us, and make us sick. We have to be sad now so we can be better later."

"But it hurts so much," I said, my voice barely a whisper.

With her thumb, she stroked the top of my palm. "I know."

"It feels like I will cry until there will be nothing left." Again, my eyes welled.

Mom smiled, tears spilling down her cheeks. "Your soul's so big an ocean of tears wouldn't dent it a bit. You cry Sweet Pea. That's the right thing to do."

"It scares me," I whispered again.

"I know."

"To see you so sad."

"Oh, Sweet Pea," she said, taking me in her arms. "I've got to get my pain out too. Can't you see?"

I nodded, wiping my eyes with my palms. It was so hard to see. "We'll be ok."

I nodded again.

"With enough time, we will get through this."

* * * *

The sky's colours burned bright. The birds were most fraught in their song. When the day's blue sky finally came, we watched it deepen, darken, until it was limitless. I was resting against Mom's tummy on a lounge, warm under our blanket.

Eventually Mom said, "The doctor insists no school for the rest of the week."

"I don't want to go back this year." I had been thinking this as we watched the sunrise.

"You can't just miss five weeks of school."

"I'll do my work here. School can send it. Fernando can help me if I get stuck." Fernando was a great teacher. When he was young, he had skipped ahead two classes.

Mom shifted me to the side so she could see my face. "Don't you want to see your friends?"

"I want to build John Jay a Garden room. I want to put in it all the things that John Jay loved. It'll be his special place where I can go when I am missing him."

Already I felt Mom liking the idea. I felt her imagining where to build it, what it would look like.

"I want to build it by the rocks there," I said, pointing to a place near where the land dropped off more sharply now because of the old Landslide.

She nodded as she began to see it. "It could have a bird bath."

"He'd love that," I said.

"What about climbing honey suckle?"

"I'll think about it."

"We'll definitely need a few trees to dapple the sun."

"But outside the walls."

"One inside could be nice."

"Maybe."

"But…"

"Mom," I cut her off. "You make your own room for John Jay if you want, but this one's mine."

Mom went quiet. She was turning it over.

"Can I?"

She was quiet for a long time.

"Can I?" I repeated, thinking she hadn't heard.

"Yes," she said finally. "I think it's a good idea."

* * * *

Alone, I crutched slowly through the Garden, having convinced Mom I was healthy enough to walk a bit. Under the Pines, by our Stream, I eased down. The shadowy air felt good. I watched Stream burble needles around rocks as they floated steadily by.

"Hi." Susie stood slightly away, tentative. "I know you don't want to see me." Hurt cut her face. She was crying.

I hadn't thought of Susie being sad too. I reached out my hand, and in a rush, she caught it and came to sit so close that her whole body pressed against me. I leaned back, and her firmness sustained me.

"What gets me most," said Susie, "is there is nothing we can do. Even with Mom, there was always a chance to fix it."

I nodded through tears. Talking about John Jay with Susie made his death feel that much more real. Sharp pain became that much more cutting.

"I'm moving back."

"What?" I said, pulling back to look at her.

"We're moving back," she said, her voice rising.

"When?"

"Now, today. I'm finishing the school year with you!"

"I'm not going back to school."

"What?"

I told her about the room.

"Your mom's letting you off school?"

"I just need to be alone for a while."

Susie's expression reeled back.

"And with you," I said quickly. "It's already better seeing you."

Susie's Mom's voice carried across the Garden.

"We have to get to school early to re-register."

Suddenly, I didn't want Susie to go. "Will you come after school?"

"I promise."

Mrs Smith's voice was closer, more insistent.

I looked over my shoulder. As much as I loved Mrs. Smith, I couldn't bear seeing John Jay gone in her eyes too, not right now. "Go before she finds us."

Susie nodded. She chased down Creek Path and up the other side. When she had made some distance, I heard her call.

In the silence afterwards, the sounds of the breeze, the dragonflies, the water all became louder. The Garden sounds created an emptiness inside me that was so great that I felt suddenly unstable. I was so relieved when Mom's footsteps came, and then her arms. She searched my face, her cool hand touching my damp forehead. "You need bed," she said, lifting me. Suddenly, I felt so tired. When we got to my room, my sheets felt cool and good. A pillow between my legs eased the pressure of the cast. Mom stroked back my hair.

"I'm so glad about Susie," I said.

"So am I," Mom agreed.

Fatigue was blurring my thoughts.

"Shhh," Mom cut me off.

Mom's weight shifted. "Don't go. Please."

She took my hand. "I won't go anywhere," she promised.

* * * * *

"Mom?"

"How are you feeling?" she asked, stroking my face.

"What time is it?"

"Almost four."

I've slept all day?

"How do you feel?"

I stretched gingerly, careful not to pull at the torn skin. Afternoon light streaked in at a slant, the way it did after school. "I'm a little thirsty."

"Are you? Tea?" Mom asked, perking up. "Or maybe milk's best."

"Tea please."

Carefully, Mom lifted me up to a sitting position, helped me slip on a t-shirt and gym shorts. "Your chariot," she said, kneeling.

After I had finished tea and a sandwich she said, "I have a surprise for you."

"A surprise?"

Mom handed me my crutches. "I'll show you."

The sun's heat felt good as I swung my crutches cautiously so as not to snag them on the changing path.

"Careful here," Mom said as we neared the far end of the Garden. The ground had been freshly torn; Fernando and two of his men were working there. Already, they had dug irrigation ditches toward the place I had chosen for John Jay's room, and now they were reinforcing the retaining wall that supported the hill.

"What do you think?"

I returned Fernando's wave.

"It should be ready for you to take over day after tomorrow."

"What's going on?" Susie asked.

I hadn't heard her come up. "It's going to be John Jay's room," I said, sweeping my arm in the room's direction.

"Are you burying him here?"

The question took me aback. Mom's face had gone white.

"I'm sorry, Mrs. T," Susie stammered. Her eyes began to tear.

"It's all right sweetheart," Mom said, wiping her eyes. "We're cremating him actually."

"Cremating?" I hadn't thought about what we would do with John Jay.

"I thought we would spread his ashes by the rocks," she said, pointing at Vulture and Genie.

"Why not in the Garden?" I said, my voice rising.

"I was thinking that the park land is protected. If we ever sell this place..."

"We won't sell our Garden ever. It will be my Garden and my daughter's."

"It won't matter," Susie said, breaking in. "We'll all be together in Heaven then anyway."

Mom choked on a sob; tears streamed down my cheeks. Mom pulled us close. Over my shoulder I could see Fernando watching us.

"Won't he even have a gravestone?" I whispered.

"I was going to put a gravestone in the cemetery," Mom said. "I thought we could bury some of his ashes in a little urn underneath."

I liked that idea. "When?"

"I was waiting until I thought you were well enough and for Jay."

"Jay's coming?" Susie asked.

"He's trying. It's not easy to get out of Antarctica."

"Why does he have to come?" Suddenly I felt lit up.

"Of course he'll come if he can," Mom said.

"He's John Jay's dad," Susie reasoned.

"He's hasn't even met him. You can't be a Dad if you don't show up."

"Jay's hurting too," Mom said.

Furious, I swung my crutch down hard on a nearby lilac, breaking a branch.

"Jill," Mom said in a voice meant to stop me.

I didn't care, but Mom was quick. Before I could build momentum again, she grabbed the raised crutch, twisting it from my hands. She threw it out of reach. I went to hit her, but she had me wrapped in a tight hug, my arms pinned at my side. Already, my whole side burned. "He doesn't care."

"He does, Sweet Pea."

"If he did, he would have been here. If he had been here, John Jay might still be alive."

"That's just not true," Mom said, but there was something in her voice that made me realize that a part of her believed it too.

That made me stop; I couldn't go there, not if Mom went too.

****

Jay didn't make it for the memorial service. Bad weather didn't let the plane in. Without him, with friends, we buried a little of John

Jay in a Moroccan pot that Mom had bought the day she had met Jay. The next day at first light, just Mom and I sprinkled the rest of him in the Garden and out by the rocks. The dawn breeze lifted him up, skyward. The flamingos keened when his ashes whispered past their faces. Feeling their cries was like hearing my own anguish, but it was also more. I felt encircled, as if they were draining some of my hurt into their hearts, their kindness lessening a sadness so unbearable that I was being crushed by its force.

After that, I went to work on his room. I pushed myself hard and found a rhythm – for the walls: cement, brick, scrape; cement, brick, scrape; for making the earth inside fertile: dig and dig and new soil and turn and dig until my hands blistered and then calloused, until my muscles throbbed, until I dropped into ragged instant sleep each night. Still, I awoke at all hours, panicked. It was always a variation of the same dream – John Jay falling before I could catch him. Each time, jolted awake, for one split second I would think – it was only a dream! But then again what was real hit me like a wall at full speed.

Sometimes even at night I would go back to work. Mom watched or worked herself. Like me, she gardened long hours now, searching out the hardest jobs: pick-axing irrigation trenches, sawing off big branches, repairing fences, digging posts, clearing bramble, hauling stone. Sometimes, a new tiredness came again quickly, and without even realizing, Mom was carrying me inside. No matter how little I slept, I always woke at first light. I always watched for the sun's yellow rays, but I no longer believed these rays were God. Sometimes when I worked, I thought of Jay. Just thinking of him made me mad. I felt he was somehow to blame, although I couldn't explain why. Sometimes all I saw was John Jay's lifted little hand. "I'll know you," I'd call to him in my head, my tears falling. "I'll know you even without your hand."

I had finally collected my animals from the floor, and set them back in their home on the seat of the Bay Window. Michael, Harry, Daisy, and Rascal were always crying. Squirrel sat off by himself hardly moving anymore, while Red Rabbit just thumped from one side of the seat to the other whenever I sat with them. Lionel was with me, always standing guard. He came to the Garden when I worked;

he came to the bathroom when I toileted; he stood on my pillow at night keeping careful watch.

In the afternoon, Susie came. She brought my school work, and we studied together. Susie had tried several times to convince her Mom to let her stay home too, but Mrs. Smith would not agree. I was secretly glad. I liked my time alone.

Today, as I leaned against my shovel to wipe away sweat, I felt as if my eyeballs were dragged down by lead balls. Last night, I had been up working for hours, and I was exhausted, but daytime naps invariably ended in nightmares that were worse than being tired. So instead of stopping, I forced myself to turn soil. If I kept moving, sometimes the tiredness would burn away like morning mist.

In the house, on route to the kitchen, I stopped before John Jay's door. Usually, I went by quickly. This time I turned the handle. The smell of diaper, of lotion, of John Jay was strong even from the hallway. I sank to his floor. How could his room be exactly as it had been when he was gone? Blankie's blue corner poked from between the crib railings. Elephant rested on top. I heard again his cooing voice; I saw his face tinge red as he pooed; I could even smell its odour.

"Hey."

Mom's voice startled me. I looked to see if she was angry, but instead her eyes were lost in their own John Jay memories. She came inside too, and I watched as she touched each thing in the room, lingering. She picked up Elephant from his crib, brought it to her face, inhaled deeply. I saw John Jay chew on its rubbery tail. She pulled Blankie through the bars. Cradling it, she sat by me. Her tears fell. Her crying no longer frightened me. Together, we had learned how to cry.

"It's so hard," she whispered, after a while.

I rested my head on her shoulder. "But he was worth all the hard. I wouldn't have missed him for anything," I told her. "No matter how hard it is now."

Through tears, Mom smiled. "Me neither."

"Are we always going to keep his room like this?"

Her eyes shifted up, out. "No," she said finally.

"Maybe you'll have another baby," I said, looking up into her face. "I'd like another baby."

Mom winced. "Maybe," she said after a bit. "But then that baby should have its own room, don't you think? Living in here would be like living with a ghost."

That seemed right.

"I was thinking of giving his things to Patricia." Patricia was Mom's friend who was pregnant.

"Wouldn't she have his ghost then?"

"No," Mom said quietly. "If his things are all rearranged in a new place, it would be more like his blessing."

"I think he would want that," I said, my voice rough.

"Me too."

"Can we keep his animals?"

"You can keep anything you want."

"Are you going to keep anything?"

Mom's red wet eyes scanned the room. "I think I'll collect a little bit of everything."

"I want to keep his books. I love his books."

"We can put those in a box too," Mom agreed.

We sat quietly for a while, each absorbing what we had decided.

"But we don't have to do it now, do we?"

"No," said Mom. "I think we should wait a bit."

"Me too."

"We'll know when it's time."

I accepted that. Before, I would have wanted to know how we would know, but now I knew feelings were like rapids of a fast flowing river. They spun, dunked, smashed against rocks, threw us up, gasping for breath. Every now and then was a pool of calm, but just as I'd be about to claw my way out, feelings would drag me back down, and all I could do was hold my breath.

From the cracked window, we heard a car. It was sure to be one of Mom's project managers who always came Mondays to gather stock. The driver killed the engine, a door shut. I could feel Mom's body anticipate movement. She wiped her eyes.

"Do I look a wreck?"

"You look beautiful."

Mom smiled. "Somehow that's hard to believe."

"I think you are the most beautiful Mom in the whole wide world," I told her.

Mom looked down at me, the smile reaching her eyes. "And you're the best daughter ever."

30

GIOVANNI

"This box is my surprise for you," Giovanni said, the excitement clear in his voice.

I sliced open the large brown box with the pen knife I kept on my key ring. Reaching inside, I pulled out a large ceramic pot. It stood on three legs. An owl's face peered from its center. Painted feathers spread prettily across its surface.

"There are more," Giovanni said, now helping me to unpack the earthenware, as I admired the first piece held in my hands. The second was the lopsided face of a man; a rabbit poked out of a third, the pot's big looped handles being its floppy cream and brown ears. The curving shape of the fourth made its gentle, beguiling face seem more siren than woman.

"Oh, Giovanni," I breathed. "They're amazing!"

"The inspiration is coming from Picasso."

"You made them?"

A timidity replaced the usual cocky joviality that was his smile. "I thought they might be good for your business."

"They're incredible," I breathed, turning Owl round in my arms. "Do you think they will sell?"

"Like hot cakes!"

Giovanni lit up like a carnival. "I have many drawings! These are only the first of my ideas," he said excitedly, pulling out his sketchbook. Deer, raccoons, squirrels, children, a pottery elf and more, filled his pages, each as fanciful and striking as the next.

"Can you really make these in large numbers?"

"Yes," he assured me. "I have ideas."

****

The windless, sunny afternoon calmed the cold sea which spilled up the wide beach in lazy foam. It rushed around our ankles, pulling sand between our toes. One hand swung my shoes while the other Giovanni held.

"After art school, I was starting to work with my father," Giovanni told me. "Our factory supports our land that has been in my family for generations."

"Couldn't one of your sisters have taken over the factory instead?"

"Three of my sisters are helping with back office, but only I am the one good at making things."

"But do you still paint, I mean, when you're not working?"

Giovanni's smile was sad. "Not so much," he said. "After work, there is not so much time." He laughed a little. "We Italians are not all cappuccinos like you Americans think. At our factory, we are working a twelve hour day. My father, he is not like he used to be. I must be working twice as hard, and as fast, so that he works less without us saying so. He would not slow down even if we asked him too."

Washed up on the beach, a large drift wood log rested. Giovanni led me to sit against it. It was warm from the sun, and the hot sand warmed my chilled toes as my feet buried into it.

"I am seeing in light," Giovanni told me unexpectedly, like a confession.

I looked at him, confused.

"I always have, from when I am small." The back of his hand rhythmically rubbed against my palm, then re-traced its path with light, tickling fingers. "Where you are seeing the sea," he said, waving his hand to take in the expanse, "I am seeing the light on and around the sea, and its absence in its shadows."

I tilted my head, trying to imagine.

"Light-seeing has made me always on the outside, because I am not seeing the world like other people. Light, she is always glinting at me, and some days I am having lots of trouble thinking because of her movements."

"What about cloudy days?" I asked, trying to understand more.

"There is always light, even without sun, but too many cloudy days, and I am getting sad after a while."

"What about night?"

"I am reading shadows like I am reading sun. People too," he said, glancing at me sideways with a little smile. "They are all dark and light too, and it is not just their surface. Before they're even talking, it is like I am seeing their good and bad. I am very good at judging people."

"I see in smells," I admitted. "I mean, not really see, but sometimes I feel like I am aware of smells in the same way you are of light."

Giovanni's wide smile broke. "What am I smelling like?"

"Good, peppery, like a spice shop," I said without hesitation and then blushed.

Merriment danced in his eyes. "And if I get closer? Is my smell changing?" His lips feathered across mine. I leaned in, wanting him. His kiss deepened and I parted my lips as he pulled me down to the soft graininess of the warm sand.

"I am promising my father," he said with a groan as our breath quickened. "That I am keeping on your clothes."

I laughed and was embarrassed simultaneously.

"But I am Catholic," he said, brushing my nipple through my shirt. "We are very good at this."

* * * *

We made our way across the sand to Peet's. Giovanni wanted the clams again. He had told his mother that Peet's clams were better than hers, which Giovanni said would have offended her greatly if she had not outright dismissed the idea. Still, she had made him promise to go back to see exactly how they were made. If it was the wine, as she expected, he was to bring back several bottles.

"Isn't it strange," I asked as we walked, "not to have any privacy?"

"What are you meaning?" he asked, swinging my held hand.

"Your family, they know everything."

Giovanni laughed. "Not everything."

I looked at him sceptically. He was promising his father how he would not make love, for goodness sake.

He shrugged, unconcerned. "It is what I am used to. We have always lived with honesty."

I hadn't thought of honesty like this before. The idea took me aback, but as I considered, it was in fact how I was with Susie. At the parking lot, we paused to replace our shoes. Giovanni retook my hand as we crossed to Peet's entrance.

At the door, I froze. My stomach dropped. "Charlie." Tim followed him out the restaurant door with two men who seemed like clients. Charlie saw our clasped hands. Hurt fragmented his face.

"Hi, Jill," Tim said, stepping in. I shook awkwardly a hand I had never before shaken. After, I crossed my arms across my chest.

"Let me introduce you," Tim said breezily, exchanging my name with his clients. I avoided Charlie's eyes that I felt bearing into my face. Tim paused at Giovanni expectantly. Giovanni put forth his name before I could even gather my wits. Charlie and he locked eyes as Giovanni took his grip.

"We are from Denmark!" one of the clients told Giovanni, the way that Europeans do when they meet up in another place. Tim made their excuses quickly. Charlie said nothing. Our eyes met once before he left. I felt tears sting; he shook his head as if admonishing himself.

* * * *

Giovanni was thoughtful, quiet, as we sat in our booth by the window. It was taking all my energy to pretend nothing had happened. We busied ourselves ordering, and then spreading butter on the bread.

"You have feelings for him," Giovanni said finally.

"No," I said, not even pretending to wonder about what he was saying.

Giovanni raised his eyebrows.

I didn't know what to say.

"Did he end it with you?"

"No, it was me," I admitted, setting down the bread for which I had no appetite.

"Was he kissing another girl?"

"No," I said quickly. In my lap, I twisted tight my paper napkin.

Giovanni sat back in his chair; he considered me carefully. "You are scared of these feelings then."

"No." It was just too hard to explain. No matter how hard it felt, it was just better this way.

He cocked his head. "He loves you," said Giovanni. "That is very clear."

"No." Not after my leaving as I had; he couldn't. As Susie had kept pointing out, Charlie deserved way better than how I had behaved.

Giovanni nodded thoughtfully. "He has a good light. So does this Tim." He smiled as if amused at his own paradox. "In another world, I am liking both of them."

* * * *

Seeing Charlie had changed the tenor of our evening. Giovanni carried the conversation, chatting about life in his small village, about going to Rome to study art, about his clever dog Rico. We did not linger.

"Let's walk," Giovanni proposed.

"Home?" It was a long way to his hotel.

"Why not? It is a young night."

He took my hand as we began the long hill that led away from the beach. His hand felt good, enveloping, and I felt I could lose myself in its feeling completely, like nakedness under a duvet. As we climbed, I began to feel less out of sorts. I quickened my pace, grateful for the hill's steep ascent. Giovanni matched my steps easily.

"Have you ever been in love?" I asked Giovanni as we started down the hill's flank.

He smiled. "A few times."

"When was the last?"

"Elizabeth. I met her in art school. She was from London. It is from her mainly that I am learning my English."

"What happened?"

"She fell in love with another man."

"Oh, Giovanni," I sympathised.

He smiled. "You see, I am knowing how this Charlie feels."

I wanted to protest against Charlie's feelings, but Giovanni's gentle look kept me honest. It was a small trough before the hill's next rise.

"What is it about Charlie?"

"About Charlie?"

"That you love?"

"Loved," I insisted quickly.

"What?" he persisted.

A million thoughts flashed – his humour, his spontaneity, the way he was at ease with people, how he was with his friends, his love of music – but really, it was much more, it all blended into something indescribable, more overall feeling than a single idea. "Being with him was like finding the best of me." Without thinking, I added, "Maybe that's what it means to be a soul mate." I regretted the words as soon as I had said them. Giovanni's eyes flinched. "But that is how all good relationships are, don't you think?" I rushed on. "You bring out the best of each other?"

"Have you had many good relationships?" Giovanni asked.

I shook my head. I felt embarrassed. "He's the only one."

"Ahhh…" His expression changed. "The only, only one?"

I blushed. I knew what he was asking.

"Ahhh…" He nodded, as if it were all making sense. After a bit, a slight smile played across his lips.

"What?" I asked.

"What does he smell like?"

"What?"

"This Charlie?"

How could I express it? Blue seeped into dawn. "Clean sky," I told him finally.

Giovanni laughed a little. "It's like his light," he said. "That's funny, isn't it?"

* * * *

At my door, Giovanni turned and took my face in his hands. "I am not asking to come up," he told me. "I like you too much."

I smiled.

"To be second to anyone."

He cupped his fingers under my chin so I would look at him again. "You need to talk to him."

"There's nothing to say."

"The conversation isn't even starting," he said. "Until you start, it can't end."

I felt like I was breaking.

"It's ok," he hushed. He brushed his finger across my lips, kissed my eyes, my mouth, but only for an instant. "I am waiting," he promised.

"But Giovanni…"

He crushed my lips with his, and then broke away. "I am waiting," he said again. He turned my shoulders to the door, his touch playful, but also insistent. "Now off, before my man parts do something that both of us are not yet wanting."

I rooted my key into the lock. When I turned to close the door behind me, he had moved back almost to the pavement's edge. He raised one hand up in farewell. I mimicked his gesture, wanting to press my fingertips to his through the distance of our space. Then he turned down the hill; I stood to see him go before I shut the door.

I was wide awake in bed when the fax machine beeped. Giovanni's picture was me resting against the tree, my feet covered with sand. My eyes had a faraway look as if I were seeing out across all the sea. Off all of the surfaces, light bounced chaotically.

31

DREAM

I sputtered trying to clear water from my lungs. The boat plummeted. The hull shuttered ominously as it hit the trough hard.

"Just singing in the rain. . ." What was that? I swivelled my head, trying to see in the black watery chaos. Salt water stung my eyes. It worked under my palms, making them slip on the rail to which I clung.

"What a glorious feelin', I'm happy again." I could see nothing through water and night.

"I'm laughing at the clouds, so dark from above."

The singing was getting louder. I wanted to wipe the sea from my eyes, but the next dangerous wave crest loomed.

"The sun's in my heart. I'm ready for love."

Charlie! He was there now, by the rudder, in his yellow storm gear. His feet tapped across the steep deck as if it were at dock.

"What do you call it when it rains geese and ducks?" Tim was pulling on a rope.

"Fowl weather!" Charlie shouted out, his shoes beating out a *ba, ba, bing.*

Tim secured the sail now full to the wind. "What is the king's favourite type of weather?"

Charlie did an air-born caper. "Hail!" he yelled, feet landing.

Were they insane? Even Tim was now doing a jig. But already the boat climbed less steeply.

Laughing Tim roared, "How does one lightning bolt flirt with another?"

Charlie twirled, and cried, "They electrocute each other."

"Come on, Jill," Tim encouraged. He was motioning for me to get up, join them. He was working another rope now. "What does one raindrop say to another?"

I shook my head disbelievingly.

"My plop is bigger than your plop," both boys bellowed together.

That wasn't even funny. They were in hysterics. I couldn't help but laugh at their complete ridiculousness. My laughter woke me. Already the dream was fading. I shook my head. *My plop is bigger than your plop?* I saw again the pages of a Dr. Seuss riddle book that I had loved as a child. I lay in the dark thinking of its other jokes, waiting for sleep to return. 'What is black and white and read all over? A newspaper! What is brown and sticky? A stick!' Maria, Fernando and I had thought the jokes were so funny when I was little.

Finally, sleep still elusive, I padded to the kitchen for tea. Staring out into the city, I realized that Giovanni was right. Ending it with Charlie in the way I did had left me feeling unresolved, even conflicted. Yet, I couldn't imagine calling Charlie. What I could possible say? "I'm feeling bad because I left you like a jerk? Can we talk so I can move on with my life?" I remembered all the blue airmail letters that always came from Jay. Maybe I should write – that I am sorry, that he is an amazing guy, that it was all my fault, that we just weren't right. Suddenly, I felt tired, heavy.

On my bedside table was Giovanni's first picture of me. The penned drawing was so much my likeness, and not just because it resembled my features. I thought again about his seeing in light. I wondered what it would be like to read the world as he did – sunlight's luminous reflection, bouncing, bounding everywhere.

32

CHARLIE

Overnight the fog had spilled in, its mist dampening surfaces, darkening the ground. The idea of writing Charlie felt quite impossible now that morning had come. I couldn't think how to put into words what had made me leave, without it feeling like an attack. I didn't want to attack Charlie. His spontaneity and chaos were at the heart of who he was. It didn't unbalance him, only me. Love was supposed to make you feel solid, but my feelings for Charlie made me feel wide-open, exposed. Since John Jay had died, I had re-built myself like a Jenga tower, stacking criss-crossed blocks layer by layer. Being with Charlie felt like removing one brick at a time, then replacing them back on top. Yes I was taller; yes openings appeared where once I had been sealed off, but I was more wobbly now. I felt as if I could suddenly collapse at any point, like a snow ledge threatening to cascade precipitously.

A little brown and white dog trotted by gaily. I smiled. This morning Giovanni had faxed me a series of funny sketches of me and his motley Rico. The first was Rico looking at my image: "Wow, she is beautiful!" Another was Rico turning his head as if looking at Giovanni: "You told her what?" Yet another was Rico with his paw covering his face: "You idiot!" Then there was Rico sitting, hang-dogged: "If only he is letting me handle it." The last image was a drawing of the backs of Rico and Giovanni sitting in front of the sea: "Thinking of you," it said.

I wished Giovanni could write my letter, or at least talk it through with me, although really, I didn't want that either. This was between just me and Charlie.

I started up the last crest before the steep descent that led to my office. Coffee shops, baking bagels and diesel fuel replaced the sea scent that wafted by my house. At the summit, a lone flamingo stood by a water pool. It lingered in the back of the diminutive garden of an old Victorian, painted entirely in shades of purple. Seeing it always made me inexplicably happy, no matter how grumpy I was before I reached it. The flamingo made me think of Susie; she had spotted it first, back when we were still new to the city.

I calculated her time in Africa. I tried to think what she would tell me about writing. For the first months, Susie had pushed hard for me to talk to Charlie. Now, though, I think she might say to let sleeping dogs lie.

Work thoughts had infiltrated my ruminations by the time I reached my office. My pace quickened as I started up the two flights of stairs. Giovanni's product cards were such a success that I was doing them for all my lines. First up this morning was to think of ideas for these. At 10:30, I would discuss the ideas with my local graphic artist. Before all this, however, I had a 9:00 call. I needed to hurry to be ready.

'*What dog keeps the best time?* A Watchdog!' I smiled as I started floor two.

'*What time is it when an elephant sits on a fence?* Time to get a new fence!'

I shook my head, chuckling, as I saw again the image of a huge elephant shatter a thin picket fence. Wait until I reminded Susie; she loved that book as much as I did. Even better, I'd joke talk to her. Susie, "God I'm exhausted." Me, "*Why do bicycles fall over?* Because they are two-tired!"

Susie: "The tribal fighting in the Congo has been terrible." Me: "*Why don't skeletons fight each other?* Because they don't have the guts!" Susie: growing irritated now: "Jill stop! You're not funny." Me: "*Why did the baker stop making donuts?* He got sick of the whole business!" I laughed out loud. It was going to be classic; I was going to really make her mad, which would be as good fun as the jokes.

****

Photographs of various garden settings covered my desk in a colourful mosaic. I had taped pictures of our products to each of the images in ways that I thought were alluring. I sat back in my chair, surveying. It was good. Pleased, I swiveled, and then froze. In the square across the street stood Charlie; he held a kaleidoscopic clutch of coloured balloons. Seeing me, he raised his hand. As I waved back, he let the balloons go. He, I, and the people in the square all looked up as they floated away. When my eyes returned to Charlie, his mobile was pressed to his ear. My office phone trilled.

My voice shook as I answered.

His voice sounded not altogether his own. "Thanks for picking up," he said, "although, since when have you said no to balloons?"

I laughed. Once we had spent a Sunday afternoon lazing around Fisherman's Pier with its rides and amusements. I had cooed over foil baby-seal balloons that I had spotted at a balloon stand. Charlie had bought two, and tied them to my belt loops at the back of my pants. They had followed us all day, even to a not-so-casual restaurant. Charlie had earnestly explained to the hesitant maître d' that they were seeing-eye seals; I was constantly getting lost, he explained, and with the seals floating above me, Charlie could use his "seeing eye" to find me. The maître d' had laughed, and let our seals in. Once home, my seals had floated at the top of my ceiling for weeks, only slowly deflating. Many times Charlie had threatened to harpoon them; each time, I had whacked warningly. Their deflated shells were now hidden in my memento box.

"I need to talk to you," Charlie said, his voice all seriousness now. "In person, today."

"I have a meeting," I said, my voice catching. The designer was to arrive in twenty minutes.

"I'll wait," he said, all the time looking up at my window. "If it takes all day, I'll wait."

"Charlie," I started to say, but he clicked off. Tears swam; I dabbed with my sleeve. I knew what Susie would say. "Cancel the designer," I told my secretary as I grabbed my jacket.

Charlie was still looking up at my window as I came out of the building. I was almost across the street before he saw me. He stood. I was trying very hard not to cry. It had been so long. I had tried so hard to move on.

"How are you?" His brown eyes were dark, serious.

It was hard to talk. I nodded.

"I've been better," he offered. I could hear hurt in his voice.

It was hard to look at him.

"What happened?"

"Happened?" Even though, I knew what he was trying to say.

"Why did you just shut us out?"

I shook my head.

"Tim and the girls were completely with you, you know."

I looked at him in surprise.

"Mika said if it were her, she would be chewing nails and spitting rivets."

I smiled. Affectionately, Charlie had told me once that I shouldn't let Mika's sweet demeanour fool me; she was strong-willed, stubborn, and intensely jealous.

"Tim said he would have been pissed, especially if he hadn't been consulted. He asked how I would have felt if you were shacking up with a whole bunch of guys for the weekend, especially if they were ex-lovers."

"Susie sided with you," I admitted.

Charlie smiled. "Did she now?"

"She said it was a good thing that you could be friends with your exes."

For a moment, his eyes were pleased, but right away they again grew sad. "But none of them would have just cut out, without even trying to talk about it."

I could feel my cheeks grow red.

"We're not always going to get it right. *I'm* not going to get it right. There has to be some room to make mistakes, without you leaving at the slightest trouble."

I tried to explain with my tear-pooling eyes.

"Don't you think I'm scared too?"

I bit my lip hard. I didn't want to cry.

"Don't you get how much I love you?" Charlie asked.

How could I explain?

"I think I knew I loved you from our first night, but I didn't understand how much until these last few months."

His hand reached to brush away tears. "Don't cry." I felt the warmth of his touch, not just on my face. When he bent to kiss me, I leaned in wanting more.

Afterwards, I felt so confused. "I just need to think."

"About him?" he asked.

For a second, I didn't even know what he was saying. But it wasn't Giovanni; it wasn't that at all. "No."

"No?"

I shook my head.

He took my face between his hands. "Do you love me?"

"Yes," I whispered.

"What else do you need to know?" His lips brushed mine again. "Everything else we can figure out. If you'll just stick with me, we can do this. I promise you, Jill."

* * * *

"Hi." I was so nervous it was hard to speak.

"You are choosing him."

"Giovanni...," I began as a way of explaining.

"It's ok," he said, his voice gentle. "I already knew. Rico was telling me," he tried to joke.

I laughed a little. I saw Rico's paw over his eyes.

"I am really liking you, Jill. You are a good person. We will be good friends."

"Really?"

"How are you asking, really?"

"We can be friends?"

Giovanni laughed a little. "What else would you think?"

33

JOHN JAY'S ROOM

Three brick rows were off-center. When I showed them to Fernando, without saying so exactly, he made me aware of what I already sensed: they would have to come down. He, of course, wanted to do it, but I refused. However, loosening brick from mortar proved impossible. I would have to get help, but right now, getting help felt like failure. Instead, I whacked, whacked, whacked wildly with my shovel, each stroke making nothing but divots. The heat beat through the shading fabric. The sweat inside my cast made it itch madly. I was exhausted. The night before, I had hardly slept at all.

"Hi."

I jumped. Jay must have been watching. There were questions in his eyes.

My chest tightened. "What are you doing here?" My voice was hard.

Jay looked taken aback. That felt good, but then I recognized his understanding. Turning away, I raked my arm across my face. I didn't want to see him, not this way. Why didn't he call? Why did he always just show up? What was Mom going to do when she saw him here? She was angry at him too. She didn't need this right now. I turned to walk away.

"Please don't go."

Something in his voice made me pause, but I was still furious. "Why should I when you never do anything we want? Mom asked you not to go, but you didn't care. He might still be alive if you had been here." I think I believed that. Maybe somewhere in her heart, Mom believed it too. If Jay hadn't gone, he would have changed things. He might have been up with John Jay that night, so at the moment John Jay stopped breathing he would have seen him. John Jay might have been outside more, inside more; we might have bathed him earlier or later. It would have been different. That difference would have saved him. His death had been random; something random could have changed it.

Jay's eyes recoiled.

"I hate you," I said, turning.

He grabbed my left arm to stop me. My right arm swung at him as hard as I could. I caught him in the side. The impact caused him to loosen his grip for just a second and I wrenched myself free.

"Jill, stop!" Worry gave command to his voice.

I tried to go, but he caught me easily. My hands pummeled him, but he pinned me close.

"I'm so sorry," he said over and over as I struggled, his voice hoarse. I felt him start shaking. I looked up. Jay was crying. He had never even met John Jay and yet he was crying.

* * * *

"What happened?" Mom asked.

"She became upset," Jay answered.

"Of course, she's upset," Mom said, provoked, her voice carrying easily to my bedroom. "Did you ever think to call and let me know that you were close?"

It was her rage that had woken me. I looked at my clock. Mom must have just come in. After seeing Jay, I had been too tired to work. Even though I hated sleeping during the day, I had been too tired for anything else. Mom sounded even angrier than she had when she told him she was pregnant.

"Have you ever once thought what it was like for us to have you breeze in and out at your own whim?"

Jay didn't say anything.

The coldness of Mom's voice scared me. I twisted my silver turquoise bracelet. Susie's mom had driven her dad away. Despite everything, I wouldn't want Jay gone forever – not after John Jay.

With effort, I stood. I felt woozy. Carefully, I made my way down the hall. A drawer banged loudly.

At the kitchen door, I peeked in. Jay stared into his favourite tea cup, hurt etched on his face. Mom hunched over the stove. I ducked back when she turned, but she had seen me.

"Jill?"

I stepped into the door frame. She came over to me, worry clear on her face. Her eyes were glassy, bright. She looked all washed out.

"I just woke up," I said.

"Are you all right?"

"I'm fine."

"Are you sure?"

"I'm fine Mom," I said, breaking past her. At the kitchen table, I sat right next to Jay.

"Hi," I said very quietly.

"Hi," he whispered back.

"You ready to lose at chess to me later?" I could feel Mom looking at us.

"I'd like that," he said.

"What's for dinner anyway?" I asked, looking up.

"Lentil soup," she said.

"With dipping bread?"

"I stopped at Mario's on the way home."

Mom returned to the sound of the bubbling soup which needed stirring. At the stove, she braced herself with her hand. She rubbed her head. She didn't seem right. I went over to the stove. "Can I stir?" I asked, putting my hand on her back. She felt wrong through her shirt. "You're hot."

"I'm fine."

Jay came to us, too. He put his weathered hand on her neck, laid the back of his fingers across her cheek. "You're burning up," he told her.

"I'm OK," she insisted.

"You're not, and you're going to bed." His voice was in charge again. Mom tried to protest, but Jay just scoped her up. "I'm not arguing about this Becky," he said carrying her off. I followed, panic closing in on me like a vice. The bad feeling got worse as he slipped off her shoes and shorts, and then put her under the covers. He got her water and aspirin, and insisted she take it. What scared me most was that Mom had stopped protesting.

What's wrong?" Mom was never sick. "What's wrong?" I insisted.

"It's just a virus," Jay said, looking up from where he sat on the side of the bed, his voice quiet. He was stroking her hair. Already Mom's eyes were closing. She too had been up most of last night. Her shifting legs moved the lumps made by the covers.

"How do you know?"

"She just needs rest sweetheart," he told me. "A little rest and she will be right as rain."

* * * *

I awoke, heart pounding. Something was bad. Mom – what if something was really wrong? Taking up Lionel, I went down the hall. From her room, a snug glow seeped. Jay was in a chair by Mom's side. His gaze shifted toward me as I approached.

"How is she?"

"Sleeping well," he reassured.

"Is she better?"

"Getting better," Jay said.

"How do you know?"

"Her fever's already down."

I nodded. I still felt scared.

"Come here," he said, holding out his arms. I walked toward him and he slid me on his lap. I leaned against him. He was broad and strong and comfortable. "It's all right," Jay reassured again, kissing the top of my head.

"I couldn't live if she died."

"She's not going to die," Jay said firmly. "She's just tired herself out."

I nodded, wiping at my eyes. Watching her, I pulled Lionel close so that his soft ears brushed against my cheek. The grandfather clock chimed twice. In our quiet, Jay's chest rose and retreated, rose and retreated. I began to feel sleepy. My cast leg itched.

"When do you get this off anyway?" Jay asked, as I scratched at the skin at the cast's top.

"Tomorrow. They're cutting it off with a saw."

"I'll take you," Jay said. "Maria can be with Mom just in case."

"All the information is under the frog magnet," I explained.

I could feel him nodding into my head.

"I want to keep it. It has signatures," I told him, holding it up so that he could see.

"That's quite a collection."

"You can sign it, too, if you want."

"I'd like that," he told me.

* * * *

Jay was in John Jay's room, holding the picture of him that sat on the changing table. Jay's shoulders hunched forward. When Jay looked up, his wet eyes were sadness.

"How's Mom?"

"Much better," he said, attempting to smile.

"Where is she?"

"Still sleeping."

"Still?"

"It's going to taking a little more sleeping still," Jay said. "She was very, very tired."

I nodded. I knew that was right. She never slept anymore.

Jay looked again at the photograph. I could see the photo without even looking; John Jay smiled, kicking his feet.

"He was so much fun," I said.

"You can see it from the photo," Jay said, his voice choking. He replaced the photograph on the changing table. In the photograph, he had his light-blue elephant.

"That's Felix," I said. "John Jay liked to bite his tail."

Jay smiled, but his tears brimmed.

I stepped toward him, into John Jay's baby smell. "He could be a real monkey when you tried to change him. To clean his diaper, you had to distract him with a toy. Felix was one of his favourites. It might have been his Lionel."

"Mom told me all the time about how good you were with him."

I blushed with pride. "We were such good friends," I told him, "which must sound funny, since he was so small."

"That doesn't sound funny at all."

"He liked this picture," I said, coming close to pick it up. "We put it into that rubber frame so he could mouth it while looking at himself."

Jay smiled.

"He liked when you dangled keys above his head too," I said. "He liked it even better if he got hold of them himself, although sometimes he hurt himself with their metal. You had to watch him like a hawk."

Jay nodded, as if he could see it.

"We named him after you, the instant we saw him." I asked then, because I had wanted to know, "Isn't it strange that you had a son that you never saw?"

"It's terrible," Jay said, and he looked so devastated that I was immediately sorry for the question. "I'll never take another assignment where I can't get back, quickly." His expression had changed, his eyes hard. Even Jay was angry with Jay.

"What about the penguins?"

"They'll have to be for someone else now."

"Won't that make you unhappy?"

"Not compared to this," he said, sagging suddenly. Like us, grief rendered him powerless. I realized then that, while Jay did not know Mom's and my sadness because he did not know John Jay, he had his own sadness, which we didn't know. I would rather have mine any day.

"I'm building John Jay a Garden room," I said. "You can help if you want, and I'll tell you everything I can remember about John Jay while we work. I'll tell you all of it."

"I'd like that," he said, his voice raspy. "I'd like that more than anything."

34

THE MOUNTAIN SURPRISE

Since we had gotten back together three months earlier, Charlie and I had spent just about every non-working minute together. In real ways, our relationship had changed. A certain tacit intensity replaced our previous insouciance. Charlie was quick to clarify plans, to listen more carefully, to spend more time making us both aware of our feelings. The change was subtle. Charlie was still Charlie – playful, spontaneous, up for fun however it presented itself, but he was less apt to assume that how he felt was how I felt; that what was good for the gander was good for the goose. He hadn't once shown up on his motorcycle. Often now, he chose for just the two of us to hang out. We took long walks or sailed entire days by ourselves. He asked me about the Garden, about John Jay, about Jay and Mom; and he told me lots of stories of when he was young.

Recently, he had surprised me with plans for a long weekend of camping and hiking. He had been vague about where we were going even when we arrived at the mountains. He wanted to surprise me, and that required us to be up the trail by sunrise. To do this, we now hiked through black night, our miner torches tossing disseminated light on the rocky trail that steadily climbed. I tried to identify the blossoms briefly illuminated by our passing beams: purple vetch, blanket flower, balsamroot, bear grass. Above us aspens rustled like foliage chimes. Somewhere, water poured.

After a while, we came out into to a wide valley. Out from under the trees, thick stars cast good light, and I could make out steep mountains rising up on all sides. Water wound like a black snake across the valley floor. In the soft breeze, I caught the scent of wild spearmint, and another scent that smelled of sage.

"You hungry?" Charlie asked, slowing so we could talk more easily.

"Starving."

"We're almost there. There's a rock shelf close by where we can stop for breakfast and watch the sunrise."

Taking my hand, Charlie led me across a field of boulders. We hopped from one to the next as we ascended. Charlie stepped effortlessly. Like Jay, he moved in accord with whatever he did. Once, when I stumbled, he steadied me. At a stone plateau a bit up the valley wall, we stopped. I shrugged off my pack, sank down gratefully. Charlie unloaded a thick foam mat and food. I shifted to the mat as the aroma of chocolate rose from the unscrewed thermos. Piping hot, delicious. I sipped while whiffs of cinnamon and apples rose as Charlie stirred steaming milk into oatmeal.

Charlie sat so that our shoulders and thighs touched. I ate hungrily. When I finished the double serving of oatmeal, I started on fruit and then an energy bar. The light was changing quickly now, bleaching the sky white. Soon, I saw that wild flowers blanketed every part of the valley.

"Charlie?"

"Surprise."

"It is so beautiful," I whispered, taking in the flowery kaleidoscope.

"I've wanted to bring you here from the moment you told me about your Garden," he said, kissing me. Immediately, I was aroused. Sensing it, Charlie kissed me deeper, shifting me down on the foam mat. It occurred to me that someone might come, but already he was taking me.

"What?" he asked after.

I shook my head, blushed.

"What?" he pressed.

"I'm like a rabbit."

"Rabbit?"

"At this point, I'd probably rut with you in a restaurant in front of the waiter."

"Rut with me?"

"This can't be normal."

"We are collecting our places," he laughed. Then playfulness disappeared from Charlie's eyes. He shifted to his knees. "I have something for you," he said pulling me up. From the pocket of his discarded jacket, he withdrew a box. He eased open its black velvet lid. The diamond glinted in the early sun.

I was dumbfounded.

"I love you with all my heart."

"You want to marry me?"

Charlie laughed. "I am proposing."

"But Charlie..." I didn't know what to say. I was utterly surprised. Had we even known each other long enough? Was this the right choice? Yet who was I kidding? I loved him more than anything. I loved him enough to *trust*. "But... " The thought dropped on me like ice water. I didn't want children. Of all the things we had talked about, somehow the subject of children had never come up.

I could see his surprise when I told him. How could I not say how I felt? Not when he was asking me to be his wife. I heard him swallow. He licked his lips. He missed only a beat. "It doesn't change how I feel, Jill. I want to marry you, with all my heart."

Tears slid down my cheeks.

He brushed them away with his thumbs, framing my face with his hands. "Marry me."

I had assumed that without children we would have no reason to get married. "Really?"

Charlie laughed. "Of course really."

"Yes," I whispered.

"Yes?" he repeated, his eyes shining.

I nodded through tears. "Yes."

He slipped the ring on my finger, pulling me toward him. I felt him harden. I moved on to his lap and he plunged inside. Clinging, my eyes closed, my head on his shoulder, I wrapped my legs tight around his waist. He caught my ear lobe in his mouth. Charlie chuckled so quietly it was more vibration than sound. There was something about his laugh. I pulled back, felt bare in his gaze. "It's all right," he promised, sensing my fear. "It's going to be so good." His mouth was back at my ear. His movements brought sensations so intense I thought I couldn't bear them, but I wanted them more. My fingers dug into his back as I cried out in total abandon.

35

MARRIED

"Married!" Susie exclaimed. We were in our back Garden. Susie was jet-lagged. I had finally coaxed her from bed by baking oatmeal chocolate chip cookies which she loved best hot. Figs and steaming mugs of Indian Chai tea flanked the cookies on our tray.

"Married!" she repeated. I could see arguments marshalling in her eyes. "You barely know this guy!"

"Since when is he '*this guy*'?"

"Don't you think this is all a bit rushed?" She still held a fig half-way to her mouth.

"Of all people, how can you say that to me?" I asked, setting down my tea.

"What do you mean me of all people?"

My eyes were beginning to sting. "Don't you like Charlie?"

"You know I adore Charlie."

"What is it then?"

"How do you know this is right?"

I realized then that it was the idea of marriage that was difficult for Susie, for both of us. It wasn't Charlie.

"He gets me, Susie, at times better than I get myself," I told her, trying to explain why marriage, why now. "Sometimes when we're talking, he'll say things, and I realize it is exactly what I have always thought without even realizing. He's fun and funny, and I feel safe with him. I haven't felt this safe in a really long time."

Susie didn't say anything, but the creases between her eyes softened.

"And the sex is so good."

Susie laughed.

"Coming home, we did it on the airplane. The stewardess caught us coming out of the bathroom. I could tell that she knew exactly what we were doing," I said, reddening with remembered embarrassment. "He is everything to me."

Susie studied me. Her eyes were changing.

"I just know."

"Oh Jill," Susie said, eyes tearing.

I squealed. We both squealed. I fell into her arms for a hug.

"You'll be my maid of honour?"

"Do you even need to ask?"

"I found the perfect dress!" I said, pulling back. From my back pocket I removed a glossy magazine page. A heavily made-up blonde girl modeled a ruffled, floor-length, lavender dress. "Isn't it perfect?"

Susie stared at the picture silently.

"It's your favourite colour! I chose it, especially."

A look of forced enthusiasm masked what I knew to be utter horror.

"What?" I said, feigning hurt.

She wouldn't even look at me.

"You don't like it."

"It's great." It was obvious she was lying.

I burst out laughing.

She looked up.

"Got you!"

"You ass!"

"Frilly lavender taffeta?"

"It's bad enough you're getting married. But purple taffeta! It was like I had lost you already."

"You'll never lose me. How could you even say that?"

She pressed her covered sleeve against her eyes.

"Do you really think that I could function without you?"

"No," she said in all sincerity.

"See," I said, bumping her shoulder with mine.

Susie rubbed at her eyes again, pressing so that her whole side was against mine. She took a sip of tea, shifted so that even our legs were touching. "So what do you want me to wear to this wedding then?"

"Anything you want. It's going to be really small. We're thinking of getting married in the valley where we got engaged."

"When?"

"As soon as we can."

"Have you told Jay?"

The sun disappeared behind a single cloud. The sudden withdrawal of heat made goose bumps rise across my arms.

"Not yet."

"They want me to stay in Africa six months this time round."

"But Jay should be home in three."

"I'll be back whenever you tell me," she promised.

"What do you think Jay will say?"

"He'll think it's great."

"How do you know?"

She smiled. "Cause he fell in love with your mom in the exact same way."

36

ENGAGED

Naked before the mirror, I acknowledged my newly acquired muscle tone, still critical of fat. After a moment of admonishment, I slipped into the bath. The scalding water was rapture to muscles already tightening after the morning's training session. A couple times a week, Charlie had taken to feeding me tennis balls two hours at a time.

Now dry, after the bath, I stroked on vanilla ginger lotion. A white t-shirt went over a pink lace bra and matching undies. My unclipped blond hair fell long and a bit damp down my back. I pulled on my jeans, brown boots, my crystal necklace that hung sparkly between my breasts on its long brown cord. Mascara, blush, lip gloss, a little hair spray to keep brushed hair back, and the doorbell rang. Charlie must have forgotten his keys again.

"You look beautiful."

I blushed. "Don't."

"You're going to be my wife. Can't I tell you you're pretty?"

"It makes me uncomfortable."

"How could I make you uncomfortable?"

Suddenly, doubts – the ones I told Susie did not exist – came from nowhere, flooding me. What if we were making a mistake? What if we were moving too fast? What if...

"Are you ok?"

I looked down at the floor.

Charlie lifted my chin. "Tell me."

"We're getting married." I stopped. "It's just that..." I wasn't even sure what I was trying to say.

Charlie pulled me into his arms, his heart thumping in my ear. "I'm scared too," he said softly.

I looked up at him. "Are you scared because you have doubts?" That he could be uncertain made my doubts morph into something bigger.

"Not about us, but about me. What if I don't make you happy?"

"What if you stop loving me?" It was out now – the fear that had been niggling without my even realizing. What if he decided one day that enough was enough?

His eyes softened. "I'll never stop loving you."

"How do you know?" After all, fifty per cent of marriages ended in divorce. How did he know that it wouldn't be us? "I'd rather not get married in the first place than see us die a horrible, divorced death."

"I've also thought about that."

"You have?" I was surprised.

"Asking you to marry me wasn't some spur of the moment decision," he said, smiling down at me.

"But how do you know it's the right decision?"

"I keep coming back to our values," Charlie said without hesitation. "That's what Dad and I talked about – how our values will keep leading us to the same places no matter where life takes us."

"What do you mean?"

"You're generous; so I am. We are both apt to help friends and family in need. We're both adventurous. We both like hard work. We both like to be fit. I could keep going and going. Your tendencies are like my tendencies; your instincts are like mine."

I had never thought about it in quite this way before, but Charlie was right. It was why I felt so comfortable around him. It was like being comfortable around myself.

"And we love each other."

I loved him more than anything.

"And we have lots of fun."

So much fun.

His eyes twinkled. "And the sex!"

I hit him in the arm with my hand.

"What more could we want?"

"Luck," I said, admitting what probably scared me most about loving Charlie. Life could carry it all away in an instant, even if we did nothing to mess it up.

"And faith that it'll be all right."

"You mean that nothing bad will happen?" I couldn't have faith in that. Bad things happened all the time.

"I have no doubt we'll face hard things," Charlie said. "I'm talking about the faith that no matter what comes our way, we can get through it together: faith that together, we'll be all right."

"Do you really think that?"

"There isn't anything I wouldn't be able to face if you were by my side," he said, his voice pure conviction. "It's been quick, though, hasn't it?"

Like a whirlwind.

"We don't have to get married, you know."

Was he backing out?

He smiled. "Don't get me wrong. I'm ready to marry today if you want, but I am also ready to wait as long as it takes for you to feel comfortable. I don't want you to feel rushed."

"You're really that sure?"

"I knew it from the moment you spilled coffee on me."

"That's so not true."

"It is." His twinkle was back. "When you stained my shirt, you branded my heart."

37

WATERFRONT

Charlie and I were at the wharf. Lost amongst the port's old warehouses were hidden art studios, unmarked restaurants, and a few galleries featuring cutting-edge art. The artists squatted in dilapidated buildings, unused, by the docks. If ship traffic was high, these marginal warehouses might be temporarily reinstated, and the artists would then need to move on. Artist-run galleries and restaurants followed the artists, the cafés operating on portable stoves with simple menus. The cafés serviced both the artists and those working at the docks.

I had not known about the warehouse art scene before Charlie. Charlie was always showing me something new about the city. When I had first trailed Susie here, we'd spent all our weekends walking its neighbourhoods. Charlie, however, had this way of finding things others often did not notice. Even on blocks with which I was familiar, Charlie knew not only that the Indian 99 cent store sold the cheapest batteries, but that it was run by an Indian Muslim recycling expert who had abandoned his work in India when Hindu-Muslim unrest had driven him from his village. It was always like that for Charlie. If he gave someone his business, eventually they gave back their stories.

"I finally talked to Susie," I told Charlie over lunch.

"What did she say?" Charlie asked, buttering bread.

"Only that she's on deadline."

"What's she working on?"

"She didn't say."

"When's she coming?"

"She wasn't sure exactly, only that she would for sure be with us day after tomorrow."

"Is Bob coming?"

"She didn't say. I don't even know if they're working together right now."

"Not much of a conversation," Charlie said, smiling.

The waitress came to take our order – clam chowder for me, stew for Charlie; we each ordered wine.

"She did say she finished her first Five Year Plan. She's all pumped up about it," I said, ripping off a slice of bread from the loaf.

"Five Year Plan?"

"She got the idea from China."

"You mean a business plan?" Charlie asked.

"More like her five-year goals," I said, amply buttering.

"What's on it?" he asked curiously.

"Write two books, one non-fiction, one fiction."

"Susie writes fiction?"

"No but she wants to try. She has an idea about a native Indian character who only finds success in the white world by drawing on what's most Indian inside her."

The dreadlocked, multiply pierced waitress returned with our food. The soup steamed. Charlie doused his stew with pepper. As I took my first bites, dock workers sat at the table by the open door, and immediately lit cigarettes. Dark wool caps were pulled low over lined, ruddy faces. They ordered coffee and selected donuts from the white china dish that sat under a glass cover on the counter.

"So what else was on the list?" Charlie asked, between stew bites.

"Win a Pulitzer, learn to surf and to play the electric guitar. . ." Unlike me, Susie was quite musical. That said, I had laughed when she had told me, as I could just imagine her wailing away, her strings screaming.

"Nothing about relationships?"

"What do you mean?"

"You know, find a boyfriend."

"A relationship's not a goal."

"Why not?"

"It doesn't work that way," I said, dipping bread in my soup.

"What's Susie's number one problem meeting someone?" Charlie challenged me.

"She's always traveling."

"Exactly, so if a relationship was her goal, step one would be to work locally."

"Just because she isn't traveling doesn't mean she'll find love." Besides, Susie would never give up her international travel.

"True, but staying in one place for a while would at least give her a fighting chance. Then she could ask friends to set her up, try dating services. . ."

"There is no way Susie would use a dating service!"

"Get a dog."

I rolled my eyes.

"You laugh, but dogs are a great way to meet people."

"None of that is guaranteed to work."

"It's not guaranteed she'll write a novel either."

I considered this, licking a trickle of melted, soupy butter from my pinkie.

"Do you have long-term goals?" Charlie asked, his eyes thoughtful.

"Do you?" I countered.

"Be the best husband ever."

"Besides that."

"The most imaginative lover."

"I'm serious."

"So am I."

"Need anything?" the waitress asked. From underneath her spaghetti-string top, brown arm hair fluffed.

"We're good," Charlie answered.

The waitress' long peasant skirt clung to her round, firm bottom. I watched the dock workers watch it as she returned to the counter. They were pushing back their chairs. The waitress waved from behind the counter. She hadn't charged them.

"Charlie," I said, leaning in and lowering my voice. "Those guys haven't paid."

Charlie glanced at the departing figures. "I think it is part of the informal rent agreement."

The waitress went over to the abandoned table. Under a plate, money had been tucked.

"She's pocketed the money the workers left," I whispered to Charlie.

"It was her tip," he returned in a bemused, false-whisper.

"Three dollars for coffee and donuts?" I whispered back.

"Three dollars for good service," Charlie answered, playing at being conspiratorial.

"What good service?"

"The not-charging-them service."

I was fascinated. "Do you think they are part of the mob?"

Charlie shrugged. "Might be."

"Do you think they've killed people?"

Charlie laughed. "Highly unlikely."

I wasn't so sure. There was another group of workers by the wall, but they had a check.

Charlie pushed forward his emptied stew bowl. "One thing I would like," said Charlie, continuing our conversation, "is two hundred acres on a hill."

"Where?"

"I'm flexible. I'd just like the idea of having a little piece of the world where we could get away from it all."

I pictured a log cabin on top of a sunny mountain.

"I've always wanted a tractor."

I laughed.

"What?"

"I'm imaging you in overalls."

"How did I look?"

"Cute," I said. "Very, very cute."

"It'd also be great to play in a band again."

I thought about Charlie's friends with their recording contract.

"What about you?" Charlie asked me.

"I'd sail with you across the Atlantic."

Charlie was surprised.

"The idea has been growing on me since I have been reading all the Patrick O'Brien novels. I like the idea of seeing nothing but sea for days without end."

"I'm game," said Charlie.

"Someday I'd also like to build a new school in Maria and Fernando's village."

"That's a great goal."

"And be a big sister mentor."

"That's unexpected."

"Why?"

"I just wouldn't have guessed it."

The waitress came to take away plates. "Anything else?" Her voice was soft, melodic; it sounded incongruent with her grungy appearance. Charlie looked at me; I shook my head.

"Just the check please," he told her.

She produced a pad from her pocket, calculating quickly. She placed the bill pointedly in front of me. I felt the challenge. Charlie reached for the check, but I took it first. I felt oddly foolish. A trace of a smile flickered across the waitress' lips.

* * * *

Sea water sloshed chaotically underneath the dock slips as Charlie led me deep into the wharves. We followed old trolley tracks once used to shift stowage from ship to store. This oldest section of the wharf was historic. The warehouses were smaller here, close together. Paint peeled from their huge sliding doors. Into these doors, smaller ones were cut, secured by big, old-fashioned padlocks.

"Here," Charlie said, leading me in an open door. Inside, silent movies projected screaming people on the walls: in terror, in frustration, in insanity. Large cages filled with rabbits rested before each projected scream, white bunny coats constantly changing colour in the casted light, their moving shadows blacking out pieces of the projected images. Repeating in unlike voices, in varying volumes, at different speeds, people chanted: "Hop. Hop hop. Hop." In the room's center, in a cage sheared open by wire cutters, a large brown hare lay impaled by a knife in a pool of blood. I recoiled. Only when we edged closer, did I see the dead bunny wasn't real. It was still horrible. I was glad to get out.

In another warehouse studio, cloudy light streamed through the large skylights. A red carpet was flanked by a velvety red rope supported by shiny gold posts in the otherwise empty room. This red carpet rope collapsed in parts, sometimes folding over itself. I thought the exhibit clever. The wilting rope was exactly how I felt at the end of a party – still dressed up, still glimmering from the evening's fun, but with high heels off, slumped, tired. In the corner, two black-clothed guys huddled deep in quiet conversation around a coffee-cup-strewn table.

The next gallery showcased nails – hedgehogs and porcupines bristled with nail-quills; women's privates were spikey metal; chains of welded nails fell like long hair down their backs. It was their expressions that struck me – people and animals alike. Each seemed to be captured at an exact moment of thought. One animal, for instance, looked to be contentedly eating; another was startled by imminent danger.

Yet, of all the art we saw, it was the photographs of the children that touched me most. Pictures showed children skeletal from malnutrition, limbless from war injuries, bruised and hollow-eyed from abuse. Each was making art – drawing in the dust if they were too poor for paper, colouring with crayons, one girl painting with the blood seeping from a wound. Each of their creations was unexpectedly beautiful, the beauty of their art contrasting starkly with their desperate situations.

Charlie clasped my hand tightly as I whispered, "This is too hard."

"Yet humanising."

How could this abuse be humanising?

"Art is what makes us human. Seeing children create art despite their hardship talks to the best of human tendencies even as the exhibit exposes our worst."

"It just makes me want to sweep them up to make them safe."

"I know," said Charlie, clearly moved. He put his arm around my shoulder to hold me close, and we walked a long time without talking. It felt good to be outside. The biting sea breeze cleansed.

"Penny for your thoughts?" I finally asked.

Charlie smiled. His distant eyes refocused. He looked at me sideways. "I was just thinking about how upset you were seeing the last exhibit."

"Anyone would be."

"Do you think you don't want kids because of your brother?"

Even after all this time, my heart constricted, as if it was closing up. "It's not because of anything. It's just how I feel." My voice had an edge. I took a deep breath and let it out slowly.

Charlie nodded, but I could tell he wasn't convinced or satisfied. I realized I had never asked Charlie if he wanted kids. Now I was afraid of the question. I waited for him to say, but he didn't. Instead, he was quiet, swinging my hand in pace to our steps. If he really wanted children, he would say, wouldn't he? Besides, if he really wanted children, he wouldn't be marrying me. If he wanted to talk about it more, he would. What else could I really say?

38

NOT THERE

Mom stood, resting her back on the stove. She stared past me; a glance over my shoulder showed nothing but pantry and shelves.

"Can I? Mom?" I asked again.

She blinked, her brow furrowing. "Can you what?"

My anger flared.

"Order the plants," Jay cut in. Concern tinged his expression. "She gave you her garden plan yesterday," Jay reminded Mom gently. "Jill wants to start planting by Friday."

"Have you even looked at it?" I demanded. I had spent hours on it. Against my objections, Mom had insisted that I make a plan before she would start purchasing any materials.

"Why don't you go get it now?" Jay suggested, looking at me meaningfully. "It'll be good," he continued, addressing Mom again. "This way we can all talk about it."

* * * *

"Why does she blank like that?" I asked Jay after, as we swung. It had been his idea to build a porch and swinging bench in front of John Jay's room. The rocking gently sloshed my lemonade. It tasted tangy-sweet, cold all the way down.

"She's not sleeping much," Jay offered.

"Neither am I," I argued.

Jay didn't say anything for a time. Especially since building this room together, I knew that it sometimes took Jay a while before he had his thoughts just right.

"Losing John Jay left a big hole," he said finally. "Right now, your mom keeps falling in. But every day she throws a bit more dirt on top. But like you with this room, she doesn't just want to bury him. She is trying to find a way to keep him close, where his nearness doesn't constantly slice her up. She's struggling with the balance right now. It takes time."

Anger surged. "If I hear one more person tell me it takes time, I swear to God. . ." I wasn't even sure what to threaten. I threw my glass. The lemonade scarred the dust. "What about now?" I demanded. "Time doesn't help now."

"This room is your *now*," Jay said firmly.

"This room isn't helping Mom." I wanted to strike out. I was angry that Mom was sad, that I was sad, that John Jay was not alive. I felt angry that I was angry, that I was helpless before my feelings that could lash out like a storm.

Jay leaned his body against mine. "She's getting better, sweetheart. She's getting better all the time."

"How do you know?" I asked, a rogue tear spilling from my eyes.

"Because life is irrepressible, particularly for someone like your mom. Life wouldn't let her sit it out, even if she tried. The fact that she is struggling so much is a good sign, as it means she's really grieving. Proper grieving is what makes you better. It's what stops you from getting bitter and closed off inside."

I felt so uncertain.

Jay squeezed my hand. "Remember the elk?"

The one Jay had seen on the trail when he was young.

"He was like the red poppies that bloomed on the World War One battlefields that we talked about the other night. After all that destruction, wasn't it wondrous that something so beautiful could grow? That despite all the slaughter, life was resilient enough to create something so good?"

"But the dead soldiers didn't see the red poppies."

"No they didn't."

"So for them, life wasn't resilient."

Jay's eyes searched the horizon, and then came back to mine. "For them, life was unfair, but not pointless. I believe their sacrifice became the example that asked our generation to be better than the one that came before."

Trying to understand, I walked the swing back until I was just on my toes. We picked up our legs, and the swing swooped.

"We are all interconnected," Jay continued. "Without even knowing it, we can set off a chain of events which can have immense repercussions. Like if I drop $20. All I'd know is that I lost money, but for the person who found the twenty, it might be the twenty that changed his life, as with it maybe he bought the pie that made him finally realize that he wanted to be a chef. My loss becomes his resilience."

"Or he could just have an extra $20."

Jay smiled. "That too."

A warm, soft wind caught my hair. I looked across at Genie. High clouds cast streaky light, deepening the contours of his rocky face, and making his eyes seem like Mom's, dark-rimmed and sad. Recently Mom had taken to gardening in the dead of night, long after I should be sleeping. I watched the glow of her miner's light as it moved from bed to bed. She liked to be out there alone, not even with Jay.

"The Garden's Mom's now?"

Jay nodded. "It's definitely hers now. It's helping her, like building this room is helping you."

"So she won't be cut off?"

"Not your Mom. She has more capacity to see and create beauty than anyone I know. It is one of the many things that I love best about her."

A bluebird twittered on the grass right at the edge of the old Landslide's precipice. In order to give the soil better grip after the hill's collapse, Fernando constantly blanketed the area with wild grass seed. Maria complained that he had become obsessive, sprinkling seed like holy water. The upshot was that birds now flocked along the drop-off. It made me glad to watch them flit and peck. Maybe that was what Jay meant about resilience. Despite everything, the darting birds made me smile.

"We just need to be patient. Can you? For a little while yet?"

It wasn't the first time Jay had asked me to be patient. But I had felt out of patience for a long time. Mom might go absent, but I

raged. Little things set me off. Most recently, when I had accidentally dropped a plate, I became so mad that I tried to break another
before Fernando came and pinned my arms until I calmed.

"I'll try," I told Jay softly. Because really, I had no choice.

39

WEDDING SHOPPING

Two sea gulls perched on the front fence, disappearing and re-emerging, like feathered spectres in the wafting mist. I watched them from the kitchen as I cupped my coffee.

"Where's the bread knife?"

"Dishwasher," I called to Susie as I moved to the ringing phone.

"Hello bride-to-be."

"Hello groom."

"You're going to shop for a wedding dress today," Charlie sing-songed.

"Mmmm."

"Come on," he persisted, "you've got to be a little excited."

"Mmmm." I was certain shopping for wedding dresses would be like trying on bathing suits in front of an audience.

"You know you can wear anything you want," Charlie said. "You know I don't mind if you come in jeans."

"I know." I didn't want to wear jeans.

"You'd look beautiful in a sack," he encouraged.

"Mmm," I said doubtfully.

* * * *

Susie and I were just leaving when the phone rang again. It was Pascal from Plant Design. Our latest shipment had a lot of broken inventory; he had built a promotion campaign in which our pots were featured. He was not happy.

Susie caught my attention, pointed to her watch. I held up my finger to her, indicating one minute. Ten minutes later, I determined that almost 40% of what we had sent had been cracked or chipped. I checked my watch. It was three o'clock Italian time. I could still reach Giovanni.

"Oh, no you don't," Susie said firmly, putting her finger on the disconnect button as I started to dial Italy.

"Are you crazy?" I said to her, my voice rising. "You heard that call. I've got to call Italy."

"No," she said firmly. "You've got to choose a wedding dress, wedding cake and flowers."

"Just give me five," I insisted.

"Jill," she said, squaring off in front of me, "I have flown from Africa, dragging my poor photographer on the flimsy scam of writing a piece on oil tanker traffic in Alaska that must be done in three days' time. You are getting married in a little over two months. We need to get this done."

I tried to protest, but she cut me off. "As Maid of Honour, I have the right to make you do what I say."

I rolled my eyes.

"I mean it," she said, her anger growing. "I worked hard to get these appointments."

"I'll call in the car."

"Fine," Susie said. "But we leave now."

"I'm just so not in the mood for this," I grumbled.

"Well then you should have turned Charlie down."

* * * *

"Yes," I explained to Giovanni, as Susie and I climbed the winding wooden stairs of the old Victorian house in which the wedding shop was located. "The replacement goods must ship today. We can't lose this account."

"Off," Susie mouthed to me as we reached the shop's entrance.

I held up my finger.

"Off," Susie said more loudly.

"Wait," I mouthed back to her. "It would be better, Giovanni, to say we are going to deliver on Tuesday and have it there on Tuesday, than say Friday and not have it there until Monday."

"Off!" Susie insisted, this time loudly enough for Giovanni to hear.

I covered the mouthpiece. "Would you just wait!" I said exacerbated.

Susie snatched my phone. "Giovanni, this is Jill's Maid of Honour," she said, turning her back on me so I couldn't get the phone back.

"Susie, no!"

"We need to shop for her wedding dress right now."

"No!" I said again, my voice rising.

"Hold on a sec." Susie handed the phone back to me. "He wants another word. He promises to make it quick."

I was fuming.

"Why aren't you telling me you are getting married?" he asked.

I didn't know what to say.

"You were feeling awkward," he volunteered. "I am understanding that. I am very happy for you, Jill."

"Thanks."

"Truly," he promised.

"Off!" Susie said again, moving her face closer to the receiver to be sure that Giovanni could hear her.

Giovanni laughed, "Go choose your wedding dress," he told me. "I am taking care of everything. New pots will be going out this afternoon."

Susie again grabbed my phone. I tried to kick her hard in the shin, but she dodged. She was saying goodbye while already moving into the wedding shop. The scent of fresh coffee greeted us as we went in. Classical music soothed.

"Morning Susie," an immaculately coiffed, blond-haired woman called. "And you must be Jill, she said, stretching out her hand. "Many congratulations," she said warmly. "Can I get you a cappuccino? Latte?"

"Cappuccino double shot for me please," said Susie eagerly.

"All the dresses are ready," the assistant said. "I arranged them as we discussed."

"You've been here before?" I whispered, as she went to get our coffee.

"Yesterday," Susie said lightly.

"I thought you were working yesterday."

"Trust me," Susie said. "I was."

"Would you like to come see the dresses?" she asked after we'd had a minute to sip our drinks. "Seeing you, I think Susie got them just right. There isn't anything I would have added to what she has already selected."

"You've chosen my dresses?" I whispered to Susie.

"Wait until you see," the woman said, smiling over her shoulder at me.

Five full-length, white and ivory dresses flowed from display hooks, each different, yet each quite exquisite. My eyes stopped on the third in line. Ivory, sleeveless, fitted at the bodice, neckline scooped with pearls, it opened to a long full skirt. I spread out its skirt in my hands, admiring its silky, translucent simplicity.

Susie came up to me from behind, resting her chin on top of my shoulder. "I knew you'd like this one best."

"It's perfect," I murmured.

"But try on the others first. Like this one," she said, holding up what Scarlet O'Hara might have worn, white, wide-skirted, and amply ribboned.

"It's going to look horrible."

"You'll be quite surprised," the woman encouraged.

I looked at Susie dubiously.

"Just try," she coaxed.

"Don't say I didn't warn you."

The woman swept forward. "A strapless bra and shoes are waiting in the dressing room."

I was moving to follow her when my phone rang. Before I could get it from her, Susie answered. "Jill Tuttle's line. Giovanni, Ciao! Yes, she's trying on her first wedding dresses right now."

I lunged at her, bristling. Susie evaded me.

"The trucks are picking up the damaged order in the next two hours. Excellent! She'll be very pleased. Yes, she would love flowers," Susie said, looking at me for emphasis. "Yes, just send them to the office. Perfect! Grazi Giovanni! Ciao!"

"Do you realize how unprofessional that was?" I demanded.

"On the contrary, Giovanni seemed doubly motivated to make things right so as not to mar your wedding preparations."

"Give me my phone."

"First get into a dress."

I didn't move.

"Quicker you start, the quicker it's yours," Susie said, stepping back and waving the phone above her head and out of reach. I thought about springing for it, but Susie would only run. Susie wouldn't hesitate to race around a wedding shop. Her eyes gleamed.

Scandalized by the scene I conjured, I took up the first dress... When I finally turned to the mirror, I couldn't believe my reflection. The dress was antebellum yes, but in a fresh, modern way. I swirled. It was beautiful. I looked beautiful. I couldn't believe it.

"See?" Susie said.

Again, I twirled, the dress ballooning like an umbrella.

"Come to the main room so you can see the dress in the natural light," the woman encouraged.

I rustled after her.

"Here," she said, taking my hand as I stepped up on an elevated platform in front of a three-way mirror.

I swished side to side for the pure fun of it. Standing on a step stool, Jennifer fitted a white lace veil which fell to my waist.

"You look amazing," Susie breathed.

"Never in a million years would I have thought," I told them both. "I really love it."

"You can't decide yet. Try another first," Susie insisted.

I was eager now.

The second dress was whiter, imprinted with little daisies so subtle that at a distance they seemed part of the texture. Empire style, it came in below the breast and then fell unimpeded. Its silk glistened. Sweet, tiny daisies wove into its matching veil.

"Gorgeous," Susie cried, as we stood admiring before the mirror.

"I just love it."

"More than the first?" the woman asked.

"Gosh, it's hard to say."

Susie said, "This one is great, but I can imagine you having a dress like this as an evening gown. I can't ever imagine you wearing something quite as elaborate as the puffy again. It makes it seem more once-in-a-lifetime."

"Try another," the woman said.

Once in the third and before the mirror, I knew it was the one. Its simplicity highlighted me instead of the dress, from the exact way it hugged my figure, to how its hue of ivory brought out the colour in my cheeks. It wasn't quite as full as the first one, but ample enough so that I could never imagine wearing it for anything other than my wedding. The floor-length veil was fitted. If I'd ever had a dress of my dreams, this would have been it.

Susie came behind me, tears glistening. "Perfect," she breathed.

"It is," I said, elated. "It really is."

* * * *

It had been a full but, productive, day of flowers, cakes and wedding registration. Susie had been to each purveyor before, making sure they had exactly what she knew I would want. After, Susie took me to a new age spa, where she treated us to massages, manicures, pedicures, and a hot tub.

Bob was already at Jimmy's, where we were meeting the guys. "You got your hair cut," Susie said to Bob by way of greeting when she saw him, running her hand through his blond, short curls.

"This morning."

Susie flopped down in the booth next to him. She helped herself to a long sip of Bob's drink. "Good mojito!" she said. "Let's order all around."

"To the bride," Bob toasted when our drinks arrived.

I blushed.

"Did you choose the dress with the pearls?"

Flummoxed, I looked from Bob to Susie. "Did she really drag you around with her?"

"All day yesterday."

"Oh no."

"I told him it would come in handy for his wedding," Susie told me serenely.

"Are you getting married?" I asked, surprised.

Bob laughed. "Not any time soon."

"Aahh," I said.

"And what about that fig and ginger cake?"

"Fig and ginger?" I asked.

Bob turned to Susie. "They weren't . . ."

"All chocolate," Susie confirmed.

"Do you even like chocolate?" Bob asked.

"I do actually."

From across the room, I spotted Charlie. "Please don't say anything about the wedding dress," I said, nodding my head in his direction.

"Mum's the word," Bob promised.

Charlie eased into the booth next to me. I leaned into him. He smelt like fresh clean shower. He slipped his arm around my shoulder.

"Mojito?" Susie asked as the waitress appeared.

"Sure," Charlie agreed.

"Another round," Susie told the waitress. My drink was half finished, but both Bob's and Susie's were empty.

"Did you find a dress?" Charlie asked me.

"I did," I said. "But that's all I'm saying."

We talked and ate and danced to rock and roll. Charlie told a story of how, in order to win a contract for his wind turbines in Scandinavia, he had spent one night alternating between hot sauna and cold snow *au natural* while drinking vodka shots. He had become so drunk that after ten shots the clients had to dress him, take him back to the hotel, and dump him in his bed. When he woke the next morning, he was convinced that he must have lost the business. Instead, when he arrived at their offices the next day, he found pleased Swedes who were slapping his back congenially.

"You got that drunk on ten shots?"

"Are you telling me you wouldn't have?"

"Nope."

Charlie considered Susie. In the friendliest of ways, Susie had been ribbing him all evening. "I don't believe you."

"Is that a challenge?"

Charlie broke into a slow, amused smile. "I think that is."

"I don't think that's such a good idea, mate," Bob told Charlie.

"Bob's right," I said. "Susie can drink more than anyone."

Susie leaned back in the booth, delighted.

I could see Charlie sizing her up. He probably had eighty pounds on her, and she was two drinks ahead.

"It is."

"Name your poison."

"Tequila shots."

Susie looked as if she had hit the jack pot. "You're on!"

Charlie flagged the waitress. "Eight tequila shots please," he ordered.

"Eight?" I asked, taken a back.

"A shot each for you guys, and three each for Susie and me."

"Could you make that twelve?" Susie asked.

Charlie looked at her.

"Or does that sound like too much?" she asked.

Sometime later, we were all rocking. The band played the Rolling Stones.

"Come on Charlie, dance with me," Susie said, pulling at his hand. Charlie stood, wavered, and sat back down. "Think I'll sit this one out." Susie bent down to look at him directly. "Are you conceding?"

Charlie smiled, and then nodded. "Yes mam, I am."

"*Whoo hoo*," Susie said, punching the air with her fist. She grabbed my hand. "Come dance with me." I stood up to follow, but Bob cut in. "Do you mind?"

"I thought you didn't dance," Susie said, swaying slightly.

"I am tonight," he said, grabbing her hand.

I watched as they went to the dance floor. He spun her deftly, and then took her in his arms.

In fact, he danced well, sexy, easy with the rhythm. I watched Susie's face change with surprise. He pulled her in close until their whole bodies connected. She rested her head against his chest. "She likes him," I thought as I watched her close her eyes. "I wonder if she even realizes."

40

PERIODS

The fecund, moist air of Green House washed over me like a bath, warming after the cold chill of the early morning. Cockatoo Pug squawked alarm at my intrusion. Cockatoo Pat watched, one eye cocked, from an upper branch. One of Mom's clients had given her the pair as a thank-you present. Now they held dominion over Green House and complained loudly when anyone entered.

I stopped, surprised; Mom was singing. Her voice carried from the far end of Green House's Extension. Over the last year, she had filled Extension with vegetables and fruit trees. We now provided all the produce for two homeless shelters. I walked toward Mom as quietly as I could with a squawking cockatoo overhead, listening. I had a bad voice, but both Mom and Jay sang in a way that made you feel right when you listened. She looked happy when I found her.

"You're up early," she said as I came close.

"You're up even earlier," I said, hoisting myself up on the planting table next to a strawberry plant heavy with berries. I plucked the ripe berries, mashing them on my roof with my tongue to suck out their sweet juiciness. Mom placed tiny blue labels on diminutive bottles.

"What's inside?" I asked, twisting off a cap before she could answer. A honey suckle fragrance rose. Mom had taken to capturing scents in oils that she dropped in our baths or dabbed on her skin. Since John Jay's death, she scented liberally.

"I woke from the funniest dream about John Jay," Mom said. "He was in Heaven, but somehow he was also back with us. Since getting up, I have been remembering all kinds of things about him."

"Like what?"

"His smile; the way he looked when he slept; that time in the lavender room when I couldn't get him to go to sleep no matter what, remember?"

I nodded.

Mom wiped at her eyes with her sleeve. "It makes me miss him so much, but right now I feel happy. I am so grateful we had him for the time that we did."

"Do you think he is living in Heaven?"

"Yes."

"Do you think we will see him again?"

"Yes, I do."

"In Heaven?"

"Heaven is as good as a word as any to describe the indescribable."

"If it is indescribable, how do you know?"

"I just feel it," she said.

Pug landed on the edge of the lettuce box on the shelf above us.

"Oh, no you don't," Mom called up to him.

I looked at him as he turned first one eye and then the other in our direction.

"What's he after?" I asked.

"The strawberries. He's mad about them. I wouldn't mind so much, but they give him terrible runs. The cherries are even worse. He has been pooping pits everywhere."

I laughed.

"They're nightmare birds."

"You love them."

Mom screwed up her face in protest, but it did no good.

Pug made his move. Swooping down with a caw, he plucked a strawberry before we could chase him off. He then landed on the cherry tree behind us. He gulped the strawberry down in two bites. Mom jumped to pursue. Pug flew off in a commotion of wings and feathers, a big cherry dangling from his beak.

"Honestly!" Mom shut the doors between Green House and Extension. She opened the glass doors to the outside and wheeled the cherry tree out, then shut the door again. Having safely removed the cherry tree, she reopened the connecting doors.

"Mom?"

"Mmmm?" she said, returning to her bottles.

"Something is happening with my breast."

She looked up at me.

"The nipple has gotten puffy and hurts when I rub against it.

Mom looked at my breasts hidden under my sweatshirt. "Want to show me?"

I pulled up my shirt.

Mom smiled. "They're starting to grow."

"Does that mean I am going to get my period?"

Mom's smile broadened. "Probably not anytime soon. It will take a while still."

My relief was real. "How old were you?"

"About thirteen and a half."

"How old do you think I will be?"

"Probably about the same."

"Where were you when it happened?"

Mom put the last of the labeled bottles in a wooden box and fastened the hook, sliding it on the shelf. "At school."

"Wasn't that horrible?"

"It wasn't ideal," Mom said, easing up onto the bench next to me.

"What did you do?"

I put toilet paper in my pants. When I got home, I took some of my mom's napkins."

"Didn't you tell her?"

"It was a different time. We didn't talk about things like that. The only reason I knew about it at all was because of what my friends said. After, I went to the library to look at a few books."

"That must have been embarrassing."

"I didn't check them out!" Mom said. "I read them behind the history stacks where nobody went. That's also how I found out about the exact mechanics of sex."

"So your mom never knew?" It was so weird she had never said anything. I couldn't imagine it.

"She knew because she saw the blood on my underpants. The

next day she left me my own napkins in a brown paper bag."

"Wow."

"Not ideal," Mom agreed.

"Can I tell you when I get mine?"

"Of course," Mom said, reaching over to take my hand. "We can talk about anything Sweet Pea, anytime."

I watched Pug settle on a near shelf, returning within striking distance of the strawberries. I was certain that part of the strawberry allure was being able to steal it out from under us. Mom also tracked Pug in her peripheral vision; her eyes glinted. Pug dove; Mom, ready, snatched the strawberry plant to her chest. Foiled, Pug flashed past us, all fluttering and noise. Mom smiled, very pleased with herself. It occurred to me that she liked this game as much as he did.

"Silly bird," Mom chided.

Silly Mom, I thought. It felt good to see her silly.

41

BOB AND SUSIE

Susie was at Kennedy Airport waiting for her connecting flight back to Africa. Bob had flown from Alaska to Latin America.

"After a couple of dances, you saw us," she said, referring to our last evening together. "We went back to the booth, as if nothing special had happened. Then in Alaska, for the first two days, we barely had time for two words that weren't tanker related. But the last night, after the article was done, we went out for dinner. At my hotel door, after, I tried to kiss him. He pulled back, and told me to stop."

"Oh, God!" I groaned.

"I tried to laugh it off, and then I turned to leave as fast as I could, but I dropped my keys. We both bent to collect them, but he got there first. When we stood, my back was against the door. He put a hand on either side of me, blocking me against the wall."

I leaned forward, pressing the phone more tightly against my ear.

"If I go in that room with you, he said to me, this is going to be serious. I don't want an affair. I want a commitment."

"A commitment?" I was stunned.

"That's what I said."

"What did he say?" I didn't want any detail left out.

"He said he wanted to be immediately exclusive. He said that he had liked me from the day we met, and that if he went into my room, we wouldn't be able to come back out as just work colleagues."

"What did you say?"

"He kissed me before I could say anything."

"Oh, God!"

"I know! I mean when I opened my eyes, I was actually trembling."

"And?"

"He made me promise – 'no guys, no girls, not even flirting.'"

"He knew about Diana?"

"We *are* investigative reporters."

I laughed. It was a point.

"He also said we had to communicate every day, regardless of where we were."

"Every day?"

"And then," said Susie, "he asked me to marry him.

My jaw dropped. "Marry?"

"I know!"

"What did you say?"

"I just shook my head no. I was so shocked."

"What did he say?"

"He asked me again if I wanted him to come in."

"And?"

"It was incredible."

"Really?"

"We felt so connected, like he wasn't just touching my body, he was also touching my soul."

"Wow."

"I know! We made love two more times that night, and then he had an early plane to Florida."

"After Florida, is he coming back to Africa?"

"Not before your wedding. He has two assignments down in Peru."

"Seriously?"

"He's already called. Twice."

I leaned back against the kitchen chair, taking this in.

"I really like him."

"That's so great."

"What if he thinks it is all some mistake?"

"He won't."

"You don't know that."

"He asked you to marry him," I pointed out.

"I don't want to get married."

Her boarding call sounded; it was distinct even to me.

"I better go. I've got to pee and get some gum quick."

Sadness swept through me as it always did when Susie left.

"Be careful," I admonished.

"I miss you already," she answered.

"I'm serious."

"I'll call you when I get in."

I thought of mosquitoes, of unclean water, of an unexpected scorpion as I replaced the receiver. In Africa, life was so cheap. In Africa, it could all end so quickly. I imagined Susie before a long line of bathroom stalls looking for the green mark that indicated one was empty.

I stood, setting my empty tea cup in the sink. It was misty outside. Tonight, fog was to blanket the city. I wished our fire was wood-burning, not gas. I suddenly longed for the crackle of burning kindling, for its smoky scent. I remembered suddenly the tree costume Mom and I had made for ecology day all those years back, me searching for spare greens beads amongst her boxes. I wondered where the costume was now. It would have to be somewhere. Mom never threw away anything if it had to do with me. It was certain to be in a plastic box some place, hidden amongst my every school paper.

42

JAY

Jay was mainly here now. He never went away for more than a few weeks' at a time.

The swing rocked rhythmically beneath the bougainvillea-covered trellis. A mosaic of birds covered the porch. Laying a mosaic floor had been Jay's idea as well. He had loved stories of John Jay and the birds. Also, it had been a way to extend our work for several weeks more. Neither of us had expected the room to finish so quickly once we had started working together, and we weren't ready for its conclusion. It was strange to think that John Jay had been dead almost two years now. Was he still a baby? Or was he also older like me – a toddler running somewhere in the clouds?

Time had faded the pain, but with it John Jay's aliveness had diminished too, dulled like watercolour bleached by sun. Whole days passed now where I did not think of him – days with tests to take, track to run, friends to see, and I would go from school to activity to kitchen to desk to bed without stopping once.

Yet here, when I listened to the burble of his fountain, when I watched the birds splash, when I rocked before the open valley, it was as if I had unlocked a door through which John Jay slipped. Sometimes the pain of his memory could still catch me out. Then my heart tore open again, like stitches ripped from healing skin. I gave in to this hurt. It was entangled in his smell, in the sound of his laugh when I blew on his belly, in his warm weight that I could sometimes still remember, heavy, in my arms.

A breeze lifted – the Genie. It swirled, rose, trying to build momentum without being detected. I leaned out to look at the sky above the mountains. It was still, without cloud. Mom was also mostly better now. Like Genie today, bathed in full light, Mom's eyes were not as shadowed and hollow as before. Still, she wasn't the same; nothing was the same. Her fiery temper was quicker to flare at smaller things – a late shipment, lost papers, spilt milk, my messy room. She also still went absent, as if she had gone into a void where no one could reach her until she was ready to come out. She went a lot less now, but it still happened from time to time. We could be in the middle of a conversation, and she would just vacate; she would be right there in front of me physically, but mentally she was somewhere else. Jay would stroke her arm to call her back. I would raise my voice louder and louder and louder, until she came to with a start.

Once, I had overheard Jay talking to Mom about these times. He had asked if she was aware of them. Mom said she was with John Jay when she went, as if their spirits were crossing paths somehow. When his spirit came close, she always went to hold him, to talk to him, no matter what she was doing. When she came back, she said it felt as if an alarm were shattering a deep, deep dream; for one disorienting moment the dream felt more real than the world.

Mom told Jay she worried that something might be wrong with her, but Jay didn't think so. It was true that John Jay's death had left its scars on all of us. Once I was surprised to come upon Maria rocking one of John Jay's old teddies and singing. Fernando had found me, and we had watched together. Maria packed away the teddy when she was done, her eyes glistening. Fernando said that she sang to the teddy when she was lonely for my brother; it made her feel better. For his part, Fernando attended to the plants in John Jay's room with obsessive devotion.

Genie's dry breeze swept over the land again, brushing up the old Landslide, bending tall grasses on its way. I saw the wind's rushing an instant before I felt its stroke. Growth flourished here now. It was Susie who had pointed out it was because of the buried Bonsais. Their enchantment had made the whole area highly fertile.

The breeze continued up to tease the snow-tipped mountains. Maybe it would enrage the mountain into clouds. I would like the rain to come. It sounded good to sit in front of the fire and do a whole lot of nothing for a while. Mom had said that there was rain in the forecast. Maybe it would start tonight. Maybe I would get lucky. Maybe it would fall all night and all day.

43

MOM

My eyes drooped as I stretched out on the lounge under the Lavender Room's Olive Tree, my science book flat across my chest. Around me Michael Marmot, Red Rabbit, and Daisy Deer snuggled. Harry Hedgehog, Squirrel and Rascal Raccoon were in the tree having played a good game of climbing. Lionel perched on my head, his front paws on my forehead, surveying. It had been a long while since I had taken my animals outside. Mainly now, I played with them in the window bay, but I no longer dressed them in clothes. Instead, I only let myself play wild animal games with them, games of the darkest, deepest forest.

"Hey."

I opened my eyes. Susie leaned over me, dressed in a short jean skirt and a tight tank top. Silver hoops glistened large against her black hair which she had grown long down her back. Mascara smudged under her excited eyes. She plopped down beside me on the recliner.

"What's Lionel doing?"

Embarrassed, I quickly took him from my head to tuck him at my side. Susie hardly came to the Garden now. She was always in town, hanging out with Chad or friends when she wasn't at school doing some extra-curriculars. Now when we made plans to go shopping, just the two of us, it seemed we were forever running into her high school friends who talked about high school people I didn't know, films I hadn't seen, music I hadn't heard. It was weird the difference high school made. It made me not want to start the following year.

"Guess what?"

I looked at her. Her eyes brimmed with news.

"What?" I asked, cautiously.

She broke into a broad smile.

"What?"

"I slept with Chad."

"What do you mean?"

She widened her eyes at me, the way that she did when I was missing the obvious.

It dawned on me slowly. "You had sex?"

Susie nodded, giggling.

I couldn't believe it. "When?"

"After school today at Chad's house."

"But what if you get, you know. . .?"

"He wore a condom."

I didn't know what to say.

"You look shocked."

"I'm not," I lied.

"You are. I can see it in your face."

I looked away from her.

"Ask me how it was."

"How was it?" I asked, looking back.

"Amazing," she said, giggling again.

"I thought it was supposed to hurt."

"It did a bit at first, but after, it was amazing." Susie looked happy. "He told me he loved me."

"He did?"

"I love him, too."

My stomach tightened. I felt my cheeks flush.

"Don't be."

"What?"

"Like that."

"I'm not."

"You're the only one I have told, and the only one I'm going to tell."

I nodded. I tried to pretend that I was cool. This was just so like Susie. Why was she always rushing stuff?

"Jill. . ." Maria said, entering the room.

On her heels, came Mrs. Smith. Their faces looked wrong. Susie and I exchanged looks. Did they know about Chad? Susie's cheeks flushed. Had they just overheard us? "Mom," Susie stammered. "What are you doing here?"

Mrs. Smith dropped on her knees before me and took my hands. I looked at Susie in confusion.

"Mom?" Susie repeated.

Mrs. Smith's eyes brimmed with tears. "Your mom," she said. She choked on a sob. "Your mom. . ."

"Was killed," Maria blurted.

"In a car accident," Mrs. Smith finished, her hands tightening on mine.

This was impossible.

"She died before she reached the hospital," she tried to explain.

I swung around, sitting up so suddenly that my animals scattered across the floor.

"You're wrong."

"Oh, Niña," said Maria, the tears falling on her cheeks.

"Honey," Mrs Smith tried.

I pulled back my hands. "You're wrong," I said, standing. The science book thwacked on top of the animals. Lionel lay crushed under its weight.

"No, Niña."

It didn't make sense. I looked at Susie. Her face was white. Mom had said at breakfast this morning that she had afternoon meetings, but would be home by five. I looked at my watch. She should be back now. I pushed past them. I started moving toward the house. "Mom?" I called. I began to jog. "Mom!" Picking up pace, I searched the house, throwing open doors. In the Green House, I screamed her name with all my might.

Susie blocked the Green House door as I tried to leave.

"Move!"

"She's not here."

I knew, but I didn't want to know. I felt as if I was falling. I felt tears. I raked at my face. I would not cry. I could not do all that crying again. I couldn't. I wouldn't. Oh, God, I thought. Please, I've been so good. Please, please, please don't take my Mom.

I could hear Maria coming. They would make this real; if they caught me it would be true. It could not be true, not ever. Susie moved toward me, but I shoved her out of the way. Maria called for Fernando. He caught me before I could go down the Landslide. I tried to turn on him but his arms were strong. I started kicking him as hard as I could, driving my shoes into his shins. He grunted, but didn't release me. Instead, he sank down with me sitting on his lap, and he pinned my legs under his. I slammed my head back against his shoulder. Fast, so I couldn't evade him, he shifted so one of his arms now pinned both of mine, while the other arm locked my head against his chest. I fought to break free, but Fernando was unyielding.

"Let me go!"

"I can't Niña. Not until you calm down."

"I'll kill you."

"If that would make it better, Niña, I swear I would let you," his voice scratched, all broken. In it, I could hear his crying.

* * * *

Fernando held me still long after first gathering me in his arms. I had lost all my fight, but he still rocked me softly, trying to silence my moaning that came in place of tears.

"Remember when you were little?" he asked me. "Do you remember how I read to you?"

I didn't answer.

"You had this favourite book – *What could Newt do for Turtle?* Do you remember?"

Maria was nodding. Like me, she remembered.

"You see, I am Newt and your mom, well she is Turtle. What did Turtle do in the story?" He didn't wait for me to answer. "He freed Newt from the mud when he had got stuck. And what did Newt do?"

I remembered. Newt sat on his thinking rock, wondering how to repay Turtle for his kindness.

"And do you remember the snake? How the snake would have eaten Newt if Turtle hadn't called to him? And the bird? He would have caught Newt, but Turtle's splashing distracted the bird long enough for Newt to hide? Each time Turtle saved Newt's life, Newt considered how to repay Turtle for all he had done."

I remembered. Fernando rocked. It was as if Fernando were reading the story to me again.

"You remember what happened next?"

"Bobcat attacked Turtle and flipped him on his back," Susie whispered.

I looked at her. She had loved that book as much as I.

"He was on his back," Fernando affirmed.

"He would die that way," Susie whispered.

"Newt finally had something he could do for Turtle. Do you remember Niña? Remember how he levered him upright with the stick?"

I did.

"Well that's what it's like with your mom and me. When I met her, I had nothing. She taught me the business. Remember how Maria and I lived with you when you were little? It was because my little sister got sick, and I wouldn't have been able to send money home if I had to pay rent."

"My mama," Maria said. "She needed an operation four years ago. Becky gave me the extra money."

"You know all the things that your mom did for me," Susie cut in, tears streaming.

"If it wasn't for your mom," Susie's mom added, "I could quite possibly be dead."

"And all this time," Fernando said. "We all kept asking what can we do for Becky? Now we know," he said, his voice choking. "Now we know what she would want most of all. We will be a family for you. With Jay, we will take care of you and love you."

I looked from face to face. Fernando held me only loosely now.

"No one can be your mom," he said, his deep, Spanish-accented voice raspy with hurt. "But each of us carries her in our hearts. We hold her stories, her kindnesses. We will give these back to you, and we will give you us, too. Do you see?" Fernando asked softly.

It was so hard to see.

"This way, we will keep her alive together."

She's dead.

"This way we will all take care of you."

44

JAY

I awoke to dark night. My head pounded. "Mom!" I wanted to call again, but my head whirled with nausea.

"Jill?"

"Sick," was all I could get out.

Jay pulled me from bed, carried me to the commode. I was barely over the bowl before I began to vomit. Jay pulled the hair from my face, rubbed my back. I retched again, whimpering between heaving.

"Please," I cried to Jay. "I need Mom." I gagged.

"It's going to be all right," Jay kept repeating.

I vomited until there was only bile, and then until there was no more bile. Finally, I collapsed on the cool tiles, shaking with wet and sweat. Jay tried to lift me.

"No, please." If I could just be still awhile.

"Take your time," Jay said, patting my back. My eyes were closed, but I tightened my hand on his knee. I might have slept. I don't know. I became aware that I felt icy.

"Jill?"

"I'm so cold."

"Can I move you?" asked Jay.

I nodded.

Jay carried me to the living room, and wrapped me under blankets on the couch. I curled tight into a ball. He crumpled newspaper, arranged kindling, stacked logs. They caught quickly. He added more logs. Soon the fire's heat lapped against my skin. Jay sat next to me, his rough hand stroking my hair. I stretched out my legs a little bit, unfolding.

"Better?"

I nodded.

"Can you drink some tea?"

I nodded again.

"I won't be long, all right?"

I watched the fire's shadows dance like puppets on the wall. Leaping, illusion – a false husk of its real self. Mom was illusion now. I looked from the shadow to the wide stone mantel on which rested one her beading boxes. Never again would she bead without looking, bead like the winter rain that fell all day long.

Jay knelt at my side. Peppermint steam rose. Mom called it run-away mint, not without fondness. She would rip it up, its crisp scent released when its spidery roots tore free. Tears pricked. I will not cry, not again, not as I did all those hours. I pushed myself up. I began to rock, back-forth, forth-back. If I could just rock, rock like the wave machine, rock.

"Can you. . ." my voice caught. "The wave machine."

Jay followed my eyes.

"Turn it on?"

"Yes," I nodded. Its colours swirled, liquid soft. Again he offered tea. The sweet mint tea was hot and good. I was thirsty. As I drank, tears stung: tighten, open, tighten, open, I blinked, blinked more. Stay ahead of it: rock, rock, rock.

"Ok?"

I nodded. I could not talk.

* * * *

The logs had burnt to embers. Jay added more wood. Light would soon come. I dreaded the light. If only it wouldn't be light; if only the first bird wouldn't sing. There could still be a chance – still, before the first day without Mom; still, before the first time I would wake without her calling; still, before I would eat without her chiding my perching elbows; still, before I would climb into bed knowing there could never ever be another good night hug.

The embers were hot. Flames leapt from their coals. Panic took hold. With Mom gone, would we have no more Garden? No more House?

"What's going to happen to me?" I whispered to Jay, my voice catching. I will not cry. I dug my nails into my thighs.

"Happen?" Jay asked.

"Where will I live?" I could barely get the words out because I was afraid of the answer. "Who will look after me?"

"I will."

"But your photos."

"I'll take local jobs."

"You'll hate that."

"I won't hate being with you."

"You never wanted to before."

He flinched, but his voice was steady, "Be with you," he said gently, "always. With Mom here, I thought I could do my work too. Now, I'll be with you all the time no matter what."

"You mean you'll never ever be away again?"

"I'm sure there will have to be some times when I'll be away for a day or two, but not any time soon. Maria and Fernando will stay close by. So if I do have to go, they can take care of you."

"So we will stay in the Garden?"

"Yes."

"But you don't make much money do you?"

The firelight reflected in his sad eyes. "Why do you say that?"

"That's what Susie says. She says it is the same for writers."

"In general, Susie's right. But I have been doing it for a long time, so I do better than you might think. Besides, we will continue to run Mom's business."

"But you don't know how."

Jay smiled. "I appreciate your votes of confidence."

"But. . ." I faltered. "I mean, you don't design gardens."

"No, but we have Fernando for that. Fernando and Maria are part owners."

"What does that mean?"

"Mom gave a part of the business to both Fernando and Maria about three years ago. I was thinking about giving them each more, particularly as they will be doing most of the running of it now."

"So we won't move?"

"No."

"Never?"

"Never," he promised.

45

SAD

1:23 a.m. glowed dully on the digital clock. 33 days since my Mom died; technically, it was 32 days, 10 hours, 17 minutes. My eyes felt gritty. I was terribly tired despite being wide awake now.

Jay had asked if I wanted to miss school. I didn't. He had asked me if I wanted to build another Garden room. I didn't. What was the point? To cry, like I had with John Jay? I had done enough crying. I didn't feel like crying. What I felt was angry; angry about not being able to fucking sleep. Now, I liked to say *fuck*. Not out loud, not at school, and definitely not in front of Maria and Fernando, but I said it to myself. Like why do I even fucking try to sleep because I always wake in the middle of the night? I imagined what Mom would say if she heard me. She would be furious; no, worse – she'd be disappointed and sad. God, what I'd give for her to be angry with me right now. Now, everyone was so fucking nice all the time. It just didn't feel right.

Tears stung. If I stayed in bed any longer, I would cry. I sat up. Beside me I could feel the clock's ticking, as if it were physical. I should get rid of that clock. Minute after minute, hour after hour, I wished it would tick faster, until it was finally morning, and then, at dawn, with all my might I would will time to stop so I would not have to face another unending day. Sometime right before I had to get up, I always fell deeply asleep. The imminent alarm then shattered my dreams like breaking glass.

I considered whether to try to complete the homework I had left unfinished. My mouth felt parched. Was Mom watching me now with John Jay? I loved thinking of her with John Jay. Tears pricked. I made myself move.

In the darkened kitchen, dried dinner pots piled on the dish rack. Mom had always insisted that all the dishes were put away before bed. She liked starting the day with what she had called a clean slate. I had resented drying. I argued that if we just left them, they would dry on their own. Now I wished the kitchen could be tidy the way that Mom liked it. I began to put away the pots. The last utensil was a carving knife. I ran my finger carefully over its sharp silver blade. I turned it this way and that. It glinted in the streaming moonlight.

"Hey," said Jay.

I jumped.

Jay looked at the knife, at me. "What are you up to, night owl?" he asked gently. His eyes returned to the knife in my hand.

I blushed, stammered, "I was just . . . the dishes."

Jay looked toward the empty dish rack, and then again at the knife in my hand. He waited.

I slipped the knife into the block. There was something different in his eyes when I looked back at him.

"Thanks for putting away the dishes," he said.

I shrugged.

"Hot chocolate?" he asked.

"Sure." Jay set milk to heat on the stove, readied cups with chocolate and marshmallows.

Uncertain what else to do, I sat at the table. "Your mom always put away all the dishes at night, didn't she?" Jay asked as he set mugs and Maria's cookies on the table.

"We used to fight about it," I said. "I thought it was stupid to dry the dishes when they would just dry naturally."

I could see Jay considering. Finally, he said, "But there's also something nice starting the day off tidy."

"Maybe," I admitted.

"Maybe we should put away the dishes too?"

I nodded. Tears sprang. This time it wasn't just a few tears either. I stood up.

"Wait."

I looked at him.

"Let's go outside."

"Now?"
"Yes."
"Where?"
"Anywhere you want."

* * * *

At first, I walked down the trail toward the Genie, but the path descended steeply, and my pace naturally increased. It felt good to bounce from trail to rock to trail; my pace picked up until I ran. The running helped; the inside pain became physical. By the time I got to Vulture, I was breathing hard. Jay came quietly behind.

Without asking, I began climbing to the top of Rabbit. The top of Rabbit was quite high, but the rock was easy to scale since its one side sloped up at an angle. As the rock angled up more steeply, Jay shadowed me. He seemed to offer a false security. If I slipped now, wouldn't I just carry him down, too? At the top, I looked up at black sky, pinpricked with uncountable stars. I heard Mom's voice – sound without words. The night sky lit the park scrub, which stretched out endlessly.

Next to me, I became aware that Jay was crying. I had seen Jay cry – while making dinner, at the funeral, holding the straw hat that Mom had worn on the day when they first met. Each time I had felt I was an intruder and had slipped quietly away. With him now on the rock, there was no easy way out. I looked to see if he was embarrassed, but his tears fell naturally. Not knowing what else to do, I laid my head against his arm. He shifted so that his arm was around me. Suddenly, it felt right that Jay was crying. Mom was gone. I was heart-broken. Tears trickled. I feared that I would get lost forever if I started, swept away by the force of my grief. My tears trickled. My sadness was crushing. I began to rock. Jay tightened his arm around me, and I moved in closer – rock, rock, rock.

46

WEDDING

Susie and I sat in St. Sebastian Monastery, high in the Canadian Rockies, invited because the monks were Jay's friends. Outside the window, goats nibbled the high alpine meadow, their bells jingling. Snow-tipped peaks drew sharp lines across the deep sapphire sky.

When I had told Jay that Charlie and I were marrying, he'd asked if we would consider having our wedding here. For Jay, monastic life embodied a quintessential spirituality that went beyond the prescripts of any specific denomination. Jay found that monks, regardless of their religion, had not so much a greater knowledge of God as a better feel for Him. I sensed that Jay felt the same when he was in the Wild – mountain, sea, forest, desert. There he could push himself to the edge of his limits, so that he inhabited himself fully, with no empty space at all.

Generally, St. Sebastian shunned visitors. Yet Jay's friendship with these monks was long. When Jay was nineteen, the monks had found him struggling down a snowy trail with a fractured ankle, exhausted and in shock. They had rescued and nursed him; once well, Jay had stayed for another six months. He had been coming back periodically ever since.

The logistics of the wedding had not been without challenges. Reaching the Abbey from the nearest town meant trekking three miles up a steep trail. Susie had insisted on bringing our bouquets, tequila, and the wedding cake. I tried to argue her out of the wedding cake since there was little chance of getting the tiered pastry up undamaged. However, she had been passionate about the wedding cake being a "centerpiece of gaiety." Fortunately, when we arrived at the trailhead, the monks were already there. Susie's cake had pride of place on a specially built platform that two monks cheerfully hoisted above their shoulders.

Now I sat before a wooden desk, clad in a white lace bra, underpants and matching garter while Susie twisted up my hair. A wooden cross rested over the single bed; next to us, a fire crackled. The monks had placed a large mirror on the desk especially for me. Otherwise, the only looking glass was a small oval made obscure by its smoky crystal; it hung over a little porcelain sink tucked in the room's corner.

"Was it weird?" I asked Susie about seeing Bob again for the first time since Alaska.

"He introduced himself to Mom and Jay as my boyfriend!"

My eyes widened. "Did your Mom even know about him?"

Susie shook her head, red tinging her cheeks.

"What did they say?"

"Are you kidding? I dove inside as soon as I realized what he was doing."

"Coward," I laughed, imagining her.

"There," she said, pushing the last bobby pin in. I looked from her face back to my reflection.

"What do you think?" she asked.

I turned my head side to side. "It's perfect," I breathed.

"Wait for it." She attached the veil, spreading its luminescent material to encircle my head like a halo.

I stared, astonished, overcome by a sudden sense of the surreal. I was getting married. I just couldn't believe it. She squeezed my shoulder and I reached up to take her hand, our two bracelets touching.

"Ready for the dress?"

Yes, no, I didn't know; it was all happening so fast now.

She pressed my fingers. "It's time."

It felt oddly dreamlike as she zipped the back, and as she rearranged my long veil down the length of my back. Yet, at the same time, wearing my wedding dress made the commitment I was about to make feel sharply real.

"You look beautiful," she said, hugging me from behind.

I just stared. I couldn't get over it.

Just then, Mrs. Smith and Maria came in. I twirled to see them, and the white long dress swished around my feet.

"Oh, Jill, you look beautiful!" Mrs. Smith exclaimed.

"Like Heaven itself," Maria agreed.

"We have things for you," Mrs. Smith sing-songed excitedly.

"We do!" Maria chorused happily.

I gathered with them on the bed. From a silver cloth bag, Maria removed a small velvet box. "Something old," she told me. Inside were two antique diamond and white-gold daisy hair clips.

"Fernando and I found them at an antique market in Bogota," she told me. "It was Fernando who spotted them and said they were perfect for you."

"I love them! Maria, thank you." Susie placed them in my hair, beneath my veil. They glinted gaily.

"And something new," Mrs. Smith said, handing me a small crystal bottle wrapped with a sheer pink ribbon. "I had it made from the Garden flowers," she said as I inhaled the perfume deeply. I could detect jasmine, honeysuckle, citrus and rose. Susie dabbed the scent behind my ears, on my wrists, inner elbows, breasts. Mrs. Smith and Maria held up my dress and Susie touched my ankles, behind my knees, my groin. I was overcome.

"Something borrowed," Maria said, handing me a black pouch. From it, I pulled a necklace of tiny iridescent pearls. They had been her great-grandmother's. Her grandmother, her mama and Maria had all borrowed them for their weddings. "All our marriages have been happy and long," Maria told me. "They will bring you good luck too." They looked pretty beyond expectation when I put them on.

"And something blue," said Mrs. Smith. Unwrapping the white tissue present that Mrs Smith handed me, I found a blue silk garter. "Throw it at Susie," said Mrs. Smith, with a wink, as she slipped it on.

Susie rolled her eyes.

"And the bouquet too," Maria chimed in.

Mrs. Smith leaned in close, her voice a mock whisper. "I like that Bob."

I would have cried if Susie had not pinched me hard.

"Well, now," said Maria. "I think it is time Niña."

I looked at Susie.

"You ready?" Susie asked.

I nodded. "As ready as I am ever going to be."

Maria lowered the veil over my face. "Like an angel," Maria said. "Your mama would be so proud."

* * * *

"Wow," Jay said, as I descended the broad wooden steps. "You look exquisite."

I blushed.

"Shall we?" he asked, offering his arm. I linked mine through his and he led me across the short stone path to the chapel. Its tall wooden doors were thrown open, and late afternoon sun pooled in the chapel's foyer. Monks played flutes and a harp inside, their song soaring, exuberant.

Jay stopped before the doors, turned to me. "I'm so happy." His eyes were shining with love.

"So am I." We both laughed, astonished, overcome by wonder.

As we entered the little chapel, everyone rose. The monks changed their tune to something decidedly matrimonial. Pine boughs and meadow flowers formed a path of garlands; one linked the pews while the other lined the floor. They led to an all-glass altar. The altar was built on a glass platform extending out over the mountain cliffs. When standing before it, there was no longer any mountain underneath. It was as if we were floating on sky.

My eyes locked with Charlie's as I walked toward him. When I stood at his side, he lifted off my veil that was to have stayed down until after our vows. "I want to see your face." In his eyes, I saw love – simple, pure, perfect – in all its flaws.

"Dearly beloved," Brother Thomas began. His deep, resonant voice carried easily, his pale blue eyes gleaming against browned skin and grey-white hair. "Marriage is the union of husband and wife in heart, body, and mind."

Charlie never took his eyes from mine. When the Brother asked if Charlie would take me to be his wife, he answered fiercely, "I do." When he slipped the ring on my finger, the moment felt solemn, sacred, true. As Brother Thomas pronounced us man and wife, for the first time since John Jay's death, I felt God's presence, made real. He was all around us, once again like that yellow shaft of sunlight on the peach roses. And though he was again gone as quickly as He had arrived, He had been with me.

****

After the ceremony, we stayed outside, drinking champagne and talking until the sun went down. The mountain chill came quickly as night descended. By the time we made our way into the Great Hall, goose bumps prickled my arms. The Great Hall blazed with candles flickering across the long wooden table and in the large metal candelabras hanging down, while fires burned brightly in the Hall's two hearths. Practical pewter silverware rested on each side of sizable white porcelain bowls laid up and down the table. Little meadow flowers filled tin cups doubling as vases.

Charlie and I sat at the head of the table, looking along its length at parents, friends, and those abbots not cooking or playing music. In a corner, three brothers strummed guitars along with a flutist and a harpist. Their music was haunting, beautiful. For a moment I saw that Charlie was able to do nothing more than close his eyes. Down the table, Jay was laughing so hard with Brother Thomas that he used his napkin to dab his eyes. Then, the side doors burst open. Brown-robed friars swept in, carrying trays heaped with food. Suddenly, I was starving. All day, nerves had kept me from eating. Now my stomach rumbled hungrily.

Brother Thomas stood, and without tapping a single glass, he held our attention. "A prayer of thanks."

We bowed our heads.

"Thanks, God, for this meal, for our friends, for our great celebration today." Gratitude came at me with a rush. Charlie found my hand and squeezed it.

"Let the feast begin!" Brother Thomas boomed theatrically. Warm bread and steaming lamb stew were dished; red wine filled and refilled short, clear glasses. After the stew, leafy green salad filled the empty bowls. Bowls changed to tin plates replete with the Abbey's homemade cheese, bread and honey. My stomach groaned from overeating, but my palate remained eager.

After the cheeses, Susie stood. The *ting, ting, ting* of fork on glass silenced the talking. The Hall became still, expectant.

"When Jill and I were little, we played many games in her Garden. But," she said, pausing for effect, "the scariest was Shadow."

I was taken aback. Charlie leaned forward with interest. I had never told Charlie about Shadow. I had never told anyone.

"Shadow was scary since the game required that we reveal our deepest secrets, fears and wishes. We began the game by circling the Heaven Mirror, a Garden sculpture which reflected back both Garden and sky in this liquid, watery way that we thought was magic. Absolution finally came when we sprinkled the bird bath water held by a marble angel. "Now...," said Susie, smiling, pausing again. I could feel Charlie looking at me curiously. I blushed, bowed my head. I was going to kill Susie.

"If you know Jill, you know that she is as close to an angel as any in heaven. I, on the other hand, well...," she said, her smile wide and sly. Diana hooted. The room laughed. Susie lifted her voice to be heard over the disarray of simultaneous speaking. "Yet no matter how bad my sins, Jill never doubted me once, although there were many times when she tried to set me straight." She turned to me. "Her belief in me," she said, her voice wavering, "Is what made me believe in myself."

Then her eyes changed, twinkled. Her gaze shifted back to her audience. "Still, as angelic as Jill is she is still only human and I bet you want to know the dirt."

"You tell it Susie," Tim cried out. Others laughed. Some pounded the table encouragingly. Susie lifted her hand.

"Telling her Mom she had brushed her teeth when she had not was a recurring theme."

Laughter broke out.

"So was saying *Hell* and *Damn*. Which if you knew *my* mouth..."

"We do," several chorused.

"...was nothing compared to what I used to spout. And once, and I swear this is true, she confessed to picking her nose and eating the snot."

Horrified, I stomped my foot on hers.

"Ouch," she cried out theatrically.

Everyone was laughing. Charlie tried to pry my hands away from my face.

"But," Susie continued, holding up her hand. "While her sins may have been modest, there were times after her brother and her mom died when her fears were as black as any night." Susie's voice again grew solemn. "She faced such adversities with unwavering courage and with incredible heart. So Jill," she said, lifting her glass before me, "it is to your unconquerable spirit that I raise my glass tonight."

"Hear, hear!" everyone cried out.

"And to Charlie," Jill said, turning to him – "because you are the man who captured her heart – to your happiness!"

"Happiness," chorused the hall.

As the Great Hall quieted, Jay stood next. "To begin, thank you my friends," he said, his eyes traveling to each monk in turn. Jay then turned to me. "There isn't one day that goes by when I don't miss your Mom with every fibre of my being. She would have been so proud of the woman you have become. I see a celebration of her in everything that you do."

I was overcome, tears spilling down my cheeks.

"And Charlie," Jay said, looking at my husband, "you are everything I could have ever wished for in a son."

I looked at Charlie; his moist eyes shined.

"Let's raise our glasses!" Jay called happily. "To a lifetime of love!"

"A lifetime of love!" everyone cheered.

"An eternity even!" Father Thomas called out.

Charlie's mom took her turn. "What makes your dad and me so proud," she said to Charlie, "is that you have become the kind, hard-working, educated, honest man that we raised you to be. What has amazed us is all the other qualities you gathered along the way – your love of adventure, your resilience, your eagerness to try new things. Your enthusiasm has enabled you to follow your imagination." Then she laughed. "The failures have also been spectacular."

"I'll drink to that!" called Tim.

Laughter resonated.

"But so have been your successes. And the greatest of them is sitting beside you."

Mary turned her gaze to me, to both of us. "So on this happiest of days, I wish you both a life full of all these values – honesty and adventure, kindness and resilience, hard-work and imagination."

Charlie's dad now stood and added the Irish blessing: "May God be with you and bless you. May you see the children of your children. May you be poor in misfortune and rich in blessings. May you know nothing but happiness from this day forward."

"I agree with adventure," said Tim, standing up, even before the chorusing tables quieted. "Buddy, we have had some good ones," he said, raising his glass to Charlie.

Charlie, laughing, lifted his in return.

"Like racing gale-force winds and fifty-foot seas across the Atlantic," said Tim. "Or our first double date in eighth grade where we had a bet on who would get the first kiss. Or all those 4:45 a.m. paper routes. But weren't they worth it?"

"They were," Charlie agreed.

"So to Jill and Charlie!" Tim called out, lifting his cup. "May the adventure continue with your marriage, and may you have all the tenacity, love and laughter you need to tackle the surprises through which your adventure leads."

The applause was raucous, happy.

"Amen," intoned Brother Thomas, rising. Everyone quieted to listen. "God is joy; God is love. Here, there is great joy and love." He glanced up, smiled. "Thanks God." Turning back to us, he said, "Now, if I might, I'll ask you all to rise and stretch."

A general scraping of benches and an outburst of conversation sounded as everyone rose. Rapidly, the monks cleared the remaining dishes. As we gathered in groups, tables were rearranged to create a new seating area and a dance floor.

"No way," Charlie said. I followed his eyes. From the side doors, monks were moving in a drum kit, electric guitars and keyboards, amps, and a saxophone. Soon one of the monks was testing the amp by picking out a rock and roll riff.

"No way," Charlie repeated, his laughter mixing with incredulity. By the time the monks cranked up, Charlie and his friends were with them, Charlie on the electric key board. Cries of appreciation rocked the hall. Tim grabbed me to dance as hands clapped to the beat. Over his keys, Charlie found my eyes, his happiness bright.

After the first song, Charlie took me in his arms. With a dramatic flourish, he dipped me down, brought me up, spun me out, twirling me back to him until I pressed against him and we were dancing, and then the whole room was dancing. The tequila was out, and Susie was teasing the abbots into knocking back shots. If Charlie wasn't dancing he was playing. If I wasn't dancing with Charlie, I was twirling with Fernando, the monks, Jay, Bob, Susie, friends . . .

We celebrated until the sun broke, until the birds called. By the time we finally collapsed in bed, and I lay naked in Charlie's arms, the monks were chanting, chanting. Deep and lyrical, their voices carried to every part of the Abbey. Hours later, I woke up briefly. I could smell the yeasty scent of baking bread as sunlight spilled across our pillow. I could hear the monks still chanting, blessing, blessing the mysteries of God.

47

MOUNTAIN

The story I had to write for English was due the next day, and it lay on my desk as blank as the paper was white. It was to be a continuation of *The Light at the End of the Tunnel*, a fantasy in which a girl finds another world at the end of a sewage pipe. I had found the book beyond stupid. All evening, I had tried to write the continuation, but all I could think of were sarcastic, sick plots which would land me in the counsellor's office.

Frustrated, I pulled Lionel close, hoping his nearness might inspire. Reflexively, I glanced at the now empty window bench. In a fury last week, I had swept all my animals into a plastic bin. Michael Marmot had landed belly up, his eyes pleading as I shuttered the green lid. When I shoved the box onto a shelf in the storage shed, Daisy's little deer face was smashed tight against the box's corner. Pain ripped through me, inflaming my feelings of treason. My anguish made me even angrier. These weren't my children; I didn't even want children. They were stuffed animals, childish toys, and I wasn't a child anymore. After all, how could I be a child without a mother?

The hallway clock chimed ten, which wasn't good. Even if I blew off the rest of my homework, I had to get this story done. It was true that my teacher was certain to give me an extension if I asked, but she would also be concerned, and would want to talk. I didn't want to talk. What good was talking anyhow?

Maybe with tea, ideas would come. I moved down the hall. At its end, the fire glowed. From the living room doorway, I saw Jay staring at a thin, blue letter. Hurt broke up his face: new hurt. Something was the matter.

"Hi," I called softly.

He returned a pained smile.

"You ok?"

"Yeah."

"You don't look ok."

His eyes fell to the airmail. Jay received many blue letters like this one.

"Is it bad news?" I asked, indicating the letter.

He nodded.

"From who?"

"Nima, the wife of my Nepalese friend, Kamala. Kamala has been beaten and jailed. Nima's not even sure where he is right now."

I moved closer, coming to stand by his shoulder. "Why?"

"The government closed the Buddhist monastery in his village because its monks had been active in protesting against government corruption. Kamala joined in the protest against the closure. His voice caught; underneath I heard the anger.

I looked at the blue paper. "That's horrible."

"Unconscionable."

I felt afraid as I asked, "Shouldn't you go to help?"

Jay's smile was sad, but his voice certain. "My place is here."

I felt relief, but I also felt bad that I felt that way. "But what if you are the only one who can help?" I persisted.

Jay looked at me fully. "If Kamala knew I had left you to come to him, he would send me straight back."

"Really?"

Jay smiled. "I wouldn't even be able to get two words out."

So Kamala knew about Mom. I wondered if he also knew about John Jay.

I could see Jay retreating inside himself; I could see pain. I knew this hurt. It was black dark, as unendurable as madness. Jay shouldn't go there. We couldn't go there. I grabbed his arm.

"Come on," I said, pulling.

Jay hesitated.

"Please," I pleaded.

Outside, the night air was crisp, cold. Speckled stars threw off clear light. I went fast up the mountain. Soil, rock, water, and clean fresh pine mixed with and then overwhelmed the floral smells released by the night's dew. It wasn't long before I was sweating. I tied my fleece around my waist without breaking stride. On the last bit of the long trail, we crunched through isolated snow patches, my breath bursting in white puffs. Jay took my hand as he sat next to me. From our peak, we could see all the other mountains. They undulated northward, their peaks luminous under the full moon. In this eerie, muted moonlit night, it was easy to imagine we were close to Heaven. My mind traveled. I hoped again that Mom and John Jay were together; if only they were together, it might be all right.

"Jay?"

He was gazing across the horizon. He seemed better now for the climb.

"Do you really think Mom sees us?" It was a question I had asked Jay many times.

"That's what I feel."

I shivered once, thinking about this.

"We better not linger," said Jay, squeezing my knee. "We'll get cold quickly sitting here."

Jay led us on the descent. Suddenly, I felt tired, as if I could sleep for days. About a third of the way down, Jay led us to a little camp we had previously made. It was by a stream, well-protected from the wind. While I sat against a tree, Jay built a fire in our rock ring. It soon spat and leapt. Jay busied, cooking instant noodles taken from the backpack that was now always ready by the door. The soupy noodles heated my hands as they hugged the metal bowl. They slid warm and comforting into my stomach. I ate with appetite. Jay exchanged our emptied noodle bowls for hot chocolate mugs.

"More marshmallows for your thoughts?"

I looked up. I had been lost in the fire.

"Are you thinking about Mom?" Jay asked.

"How can you have no doubts about Mom being out there somewhere?"

"My heart just knows, just like I know I love you."

"That's not the same," I said.

"Isn't it?"

"I exist."

"Your existence certainly makes it easier," Jay agreed.

More than easier, it makes it possible, I thought. I watched the flames dance.

"I am angry with God for taking John Jay and your mom," Jay said. "Sometimes I get so angry I can't feel anything but that. Yet, out in the woods, with you, like this, my anger quiets. I find Mom inside me then."

"Isn't that just memory?"

"I don't think so. When I remember, it comes from my head – pictures I see, words I pull up. When I find your mom, there are no pictures or words. She is just here; it is like her essence is filling me up."

"Filling you up with what?"

"Mostly with what I need; it has been different things these last four months, sometimes courage, sometimes stillness, often love."

"Have you felt John Jay?"

He smiled sadly. "No."

"Why?" I asked, watching the moonlight come and go through the pine boughs as the wind moved them.

"I think it is because I only knew him through the stories you and your Mom told me."

"Does that mean that he doesn't exist?"

"Oh, I believe he exists. I am certain you could find him. It's just that in this life, it will be less easy for me."

I tossed a stray pine cone on the fire. The flames bounded to consume it. I had never felt John Jay in Heaven, and I knew him better than anyone. I blinked back tears.

"What about you?" Jay asked me for the first time. "Do you believe Mom and John Jay are somewhere?"

"I have to. Only because believing they don't exist would be so painful that I don't have the courage for it."

Jay smiled gently. "I understand that."

I rubbed my eyes with my sleeve. "I already feel I have forgotten so much about John Jay. It's like he's become blurry. It makes me feel like I have lost him twice." My voice choked. "I couldn't bear it if that happened to Mom too. If I can't have her, than at least I want to remember her as much as I do now."

"The thing is," said Jay, "We have to forget in order to live."

"Why?"

"Life constantly makes new memories. With enough time, our old memories fade because we have so many new experiences stacked in front of them."

"But I can remember some things about John Jay as clearly as if they happened today."

"Some you will; some you will your whole life. The first time I saw your mom is as sharp as if she were in front me right now. But most memories grow fainter with time."

"Then I don't want time."

Fire snapped through one of the thicker branches, and an ember jumped outside the rock circle. Jay grounded it dark with his foot. Using a spare stick, he pushed the burning wood back into a tight bunch at the rocks' center.

"The funny thing about loss is that it creates contradicting truths," Jay said, laying the stick by his feet.

"What do you mean?"

"I was gutted to lose my rancher friend at school, but if my friend hadn't left school, I probably would have never hiked as much as I did. Without hiking, I might never have discovered the beauty of nature in the same way, so I might not have become a photographer; I always thought I'd be a doctor."

I never knew Jay had thought about medicine.

"If I wasn't a photographer, I would not have been in Morocco, as the only reason I was there was to take pictures. If I hadn't been in Morocco, I wouldn't have met Mom."

"So the sadness about your friend went away?"

"Eventually."

"So sadness about Mom will go too?"

Jay grimaced. "I can tell you one thing," he said finally. "I am getting to know you in a way that I never would have if Mom had been alive."

"But wouldn't you trade knowing me for Mom?" I would make such a trade, I knew. I'd rather have Mom than Jay; I'd make that trade all day long.

"Honestly? I would give anything to have Mom back, even for

just one minute more," he said, his voice rough. "Anything."

I knew it.

"But to a fault, I spent too much time relying on Mom to take care of you. I regret that. I wouldn't trade a minute of our time together now. Not one minute of it."

His words made me feel better. "Two truths contradicting?"

Jay smiled, nodding. "Two truths."

"What happens if I make it so that Mom never fades?"

"Then you get stuck living in an endless loop."

"What if I only let the pain partly go?"

"When you love someone as deeply as we have loved Mom, it's hard to stop the pain completely. But I think we can get close enough."

"What's enough?" I challenged.

"Close enough to feel joy, to enjoy friends, to feel productive again."

"So you want to replace her?" This made me angry.

"No, never," Jay said. "But feeling better doesn't mean replacing her. I'll never have another Becky. But I believe I'll find other, different happiness. I'll believe one day I will hear you laugh again. Even without Becky, in this life there is still great meaning to be understood, important work to be done, and love to tend."

I shook my head fighting tears. "Since Mom's death, each day has been as bad as the first," I whispered. The truth was that I wanted the days to be bad because I was angry, but somewhere I was also afraid I would always be this unhappy.

"I know it's hard to see a way out right now," Jay said gently. "We have to keep chipping through the pain."

"But I don't want to forget her!"

Jay enfolded me. "Even if you tried to do nothing else for the rest of your life but hold on to her," he told me, "she would still fade. Time, and even your sadness, would still wear her into a faint memory, yet it would be a corrosive wearing. When we grieve properly, people fade like fabric bleaching in the sun; all the beautiful patterns and hues are still there; they're just lighter, softer. When we don't grieve properly, the colours still fade, but the fabric itself also erodes, becoming shredded, thread-bare."

I looked up into his face. "But how much pain will I have to endure?"

"It is such a big love," he said, his voice all cut up.

"But how much?"

"I wish I could say, sweetheart."

Sorrow overwhelmed me. It came on a wave of sobs that finally broke through the dikes I had been trying so hard to reinforce. Jay stroked my hair as I buried my wet face in his fleece. When the grief subsided, it left me both worn out and washed clean. Hiccups started; I sounded like a frog. Jay told me to drink my cool chocolate down without stopping once. Jay smiled when I hiccupped again as soon as the cup was put down. I tried another cup. We both waited, expectant. For a minute, there was nothing. Just as I was saying they had stopped, I hiccupped loudly. Jay laughed. To my surprise, I laughed with him. The laugh ended in a hiccup which made us both laugh harder. I wiped at my tearing eyes.

"Feels good to laugh, doesn't?" said Jay, sighing.

It did.

"It's going to be all right, sweetheart," he said, hugging me again. "We'll be all right. We will get through this somehow."

For this instant, I believed him. I didn't know if I would always believe him, but I did for right now.

* * * *

"Are we Christian?" I asked Jay as we began making our way back down the trail. I felt cold away from the fire; we hadn't yet been descending long enough for our movement to warm me.

"I definitely feel the greatest affinity with Christian rituals and symbols."

"Was that the same for Mom?"

"I think so."

"Then how come we never go to church?"

"We could if you like."

"But why haven't we?"

"I think your mom's and my ideas about God have changed over time. I don't believe that any one religion holds the absolute truth."

"So you don't think anyone has it right?" I asked, ducking under a low hanging pine branch.

"Not completely no. A Hindu priest told me once that God is like this immense mountain, too big ever to be climbed. Everyone sees their part of the mountain and says: *this* is God – he is rocky and sheer; he is meadows blanketed with flowers; he is snowy fields or slopes of dense green forest. Because their little bit of the mountain is all they can see, they assume it is all anyone can see. They feel right, because is it not their waterfall plainly before them? What they don't realize is that they see just part of the truth. This mountain is so large that even if you were to spend your whole life traveling from one mountainous region to another, you would never fully cover its terrain. You will always have an incomplete understanding of the mountain and of God."

That seemed right somehow. I had always thought that if you were born where Christianity did not exist, then how could God condemn you, just because you had the bad luck not to be baptised? It would be too cruel.

"Seems to me," Jay said after a bit, as we slowed to pick our way down a bit of steep trail, "that you were planning to get homework done when you came into the living room."

I was constantly taken aback at how little Jay missed. The truth was I was really tired now. There was no way I would be able to get the story done before school the next day. I had had two weeks to complete it. "I haven't even started," I confessed, my stomach constricting.

"Any ideas?" he asked after I had explained my assignment.

I shook my head.

Jay was quiet a bit, thinking. "My experience is that most fantasy is just a battle between good and evil played out in an imaginative world," he said finally. "Let's start with the world. Do you want to write about mountains? Snow? Desert? Sea?"

"I don't know."

The trail widened and Jay slowed to walk next to me. He took my hand. "What about using our mountains here, just mix the colours up."

I looked at him doubtfully. "Like purple mountains, orange skies, yellow trees, and white nights?"

"That works."

"But what could they be fighting about?"

"Why can't they be fighting, like my friend in Tibet, to save the worship of their Gods from a stronger power? Let's say that this power wants to wipe out their culture so they can take over their land to get at some special resources they have. . ."

"Tree nuts from the yellow trees which only grow in their high Alpine forests?" I tried.

"Why nuts?"

"How about because a plague wiped out most of the planet's animals, and the nuts are now one of the only sources of protein still remaining?"

"Sounds like a story," Jay said, approvingly. "When we get home, why don't you go right to bed, sleep until you can't anymore. When you wake next, you can write it. When it is done, I'll take you to school."

"What if it takes me all day?"

"Let it take all day. I'll take you in tomorrow."

"Really?"

"Very much really," Jay said, smiling.

My relief was immense. "That'd be so great," I breathed.

48

ACCIDENT

"It was my fault," Maria cried. "If it weren't for me, Becky would be alive and that poor boy would be walking."

I froze, unseen, listening.

"No Carita!" Fernando said, trying to console her.

"You know that's not true," Jay affirmed.

"But if we hadn't fought about the invoices," Maria insisted.

"It was natural for you to defend yourself," Fernando countered.

"But don't you see?" Maria's voice cracked. "The fight wasn't about the invoices. It was about losing John Jay. It was a bad day for her. I had known that."

"She had a lot of bad days," Jay said quietly.

"But that was when she got most distracted," Maria argued, her voice rising. "I should have dropped the papers off at the accountant, not her. I had even thought about offering, but I was cross that she had yelled at me."

It was too much; I had to know. "What boy?" I asked, stepping into the kitchen.

Maria blanched.

"What boy?" I insisted, my voice louder. I turned to Jay. "You said Mom's death was an accident."

"It was," Jay said. "She ran the red light by mistake." Jay's voice sounded overly controlled.

"What?"

"We don't know for sure, but we assume she lost her attention and didn't see the light."

"And she hit a boy?"

Jay nodded.

"And he can't walk now?"

Jay answered with his eyes.

"How old?"

"Ten."

I wrapped my arms tight wound myself. "That's what killed Mom? Hitting the boy?"

"She seemed to have tried to swerve around him at the last minute. After clipping him, she hit a light pole. She wasn't wearing a seatbelt," Jay said, his voice barely above a whisper.

"She wasn't wearing her seatbelt?" Never in my whole life had Mom not worn her seatbelt. "Would she have been ok if. . ." I couldn't even finish.

"Likely," Jay said, tears wetting his eyes.

"She could be alive." I couldn't believe it. She could be alive. It felt like my knees would give way. Even Fernando was crying.

* * * *

Exhausted, I went to sleep without dinner. I awoke around midnight to a pounding headache. I found Jay by the fire. His vacated, hollow eyes looked red, but he came into them again when he sensed me. "Hi," he said softly.

I sat away from him on the couch, drawing my knees close against my chest. For a bit, we kept silent; I became lost in an image of Mom stringing red beads on wire. The image morphed into a faceless black-haired boy, both his legs covered in white bandages.

"What's happening now?" I asked Jay.

"Now?"

"With the boy?"

"Our insurance provided the boy's family with a very large settlement," Jay said. "He'll have the best possible care."

"To help him walk?"

"No," Jay said, grimness edging his voice. "He'll never walk again."

The news felt like a punch in the gut. "How could she have?"

Emotion, anger even, flooded Jay's voice. "Do you think for one moment she would have wanted to hurt that child? What's worse, don't you think that it will haunt her for all of eternity?"

Oh, God. Jay was right. Mom would never forgive herself for this, not in a million years. The thought was devastating. I buried my forehead between my knees.

After a while, Jay said, "A scientist friend of mine once got caught under the water in a river; after several minutes, they got his breathing going again. When he finally awoke, he described an infinite space of joy and love. In that space, he felt completely connected to all humanity from the very beginning of time, each moment of our lives weaving into the larger picture of all life itself. He learned then that we can't always understand the reasons why some things happen to us because our events connect to events that we don't even know about."

"You mean there was a reason for Mom's accident?" I asked, my voice wobbly. "That she was supposed to hurt that boy?"

"I hope so," Jay said. "I don't know what could ever justify crippling a boy and taking Mom, but that's what I really hope."

I thought about all the people who had been alive and would ever live; about the ripple effects if one life connected to another then another then another across space and time; how it made sense that the way Mom raised me came in part from the way her Mom had taken care of her, and that the way Grandma was raised was also influenced by her community. It all made me feel very tiny.

Jay rose to stoke the fire. He added another log. When he came back, I moved close. He wrapped me in his arms. Outside, the wind was stronger. Maria had said that rain might come. It was true that the wind now chased in an unsettled way, racing through the Garden like a living thing, rattling branches, chasing the clouds that had settled on the mountain since late the previous afternoon. Right now, I hoped with all my heart that it wouldn't rain. I didn't want a Rain Day without Mom. If rain was coming, I wanted it to begin late, after school had started.

49

SURPRISE

I looked outside my gloomy office window. For days, I had felt as murky as the light, depression running like a low grade fever. Each limb felt weighted. Even simple tasks took effort.

My depression came erratically. Most times, I never knew what set it off. Sometimes, ten days into it, I might suddenly remember that it had been John Jay's birthday, or that Susie had just returned from covering a situation that was more risky than I would have liked. Usually it came around my periods, which had become as erratic as my sadness. Some months my periods came every six weeks; other months they came every three weeks for long stretches at a time. I was not suited to the birth control pill, swelling like a tomato pumped full of water when I used it, so I did not have the benefit of artificial hormones to even out my cycle. My doctor had no good theory as to why my periods had become so uneven; my pap smear and all other tests were normal. Some women were just like that, he explained. As I didn't want to have children, he assured me that my here-there-everywhere periods were just a nuisance.

Listless, I rested my chin on my crossed knuckles, my elbows propped on unattended papers. I closed my eyes sleepily.

"Busy, I see."

I jumped. "Charlie!"

"Hello, beautiful."

"What are you doing here?"

"Taking you away."

"I'm lunching in today. I already told you that."

"You do seem really busy," he teased.

"I am," I protested, beginning to collect scattered sheets.

"It's all been arranged."

"What do you mean?"

"Miguel and Lucy have got it covered."

"We do," they both said, appearing in the door frame.

"What are you talking about?"

Charlie took my hand, pulling me up. "You'll see. The car's waiting."

"I have to be back by four," I insisted. Secretly I was pleased to be leaving. "I've got a call I have to take. Lucy you told him about the call, right?"

"I told him," she confirmed.

* * * *

"Where are we going?" I asked, as we pulled into the traffic.

Charlie had a cat-got-the-milk grin. "It's a surprise."

I guessed we were going to Alfredo's. When we passed its turn, I was sure it was Windows. It had a Chinese Chicken Salad that Charlie knew I loved. Charlie chuckled. It was obvious he had been following my thoughts. I tried to read his face, but he wasn't giving anything up. As we pulled onto the freeway, I was certain. Peet's! But at Peet's exit, we sped on.

"Where are we going?"

Charlie's smugness was annoying. Two could play this game. My mind began scanning further afield. We were heading south. Loyola Gardens! I had been telling Charlie I wanted to go to Loyola for months. The chef at the Garden Spot had just been given a Michelin star. I wondered how Charlie had managed to get a reservation at such short notice. But how perfect! Even more so as, away from the water, the fog was already lifting. By the time we reached Loyola, the sun would be out. Right now, sun sounded wonderful.

"I know where we're going," I sing-sang to him.

"No you don't," he chorused back.

"Loyola Gardens."

"You're wrong," he chanted.

"No I'm . . ." The car turned off the freeway to the airport exit.

He wouldn't have, would he?

"Charlie?"

He just raised his eyebrows at me.

We were definitely going to the airport. "Charlie, this isn't funny anymore. Tell me where we are going right now!"

Charlie, though, was finding it hilarious.

"I can't go away for the night. I have way too much to do."

"We aren't going away for the night."

"Promise?"

"Promise."

When we got to the airport, however, the driver removed two suitcases from the trunk.

"Charlie. You promised!"

"We aren't going away for the night," he said cheerfully. "We are going away for nine."

I was flabbergasted.

Ignoring me, Charlie paid the driver.

"Charlie!"

Taking a suitcase handle in each hand, he briskly headed off.

I chased after him. My calendar for the next nine days flooded my thoughts. I had three different meetings with Giovanni's design team coming in from Italy. I needed to finalize the bench drawings by next week if they were to make the summer market. That was just the beginning of it.

"No, Charlie, I can't!" I said, pulling on his arm so that he would stop.

"It's all been sorted," he said. "The specs for your new lines are already waiting in the hotel. The new Home World contracts are in my briefcase. Your every meeting has been rescheduled or will be taken by Lucy or Miguel."

I was dumbfounded. Charlie again strode through the terminal.

"You couldn't have. . . " I objected, following, but again Charlie cut me off. He listed every major commitment I had in my diary by memory for the next nine days along with the accommodating arrangements. He stopped in front of British Airways, first class.

First Class? England? I had never been first class in my life.

"Where are you traveling today sir?" the man behind the counter inquired.

"India."

"We're going to India?"

The ticket agent shot me a quizzical look as he took the passports that Charlie proffered.

"Surprise!" he said, beaming.

"You're taking me to India?" I sputtered.

Brushing my hair back with his hand, Charlie leaned in so that his breath tickled my ear. "If you're lucky, I might also take you on the plane."

I blushed. My eyes darted to the check-in man. He was busy ticketing our suitcases.

"Shall we?" Charlie asked, holding out his hand after we had been given our boarding passes.

* * * *

In the first class lounge, over a glass of champagne, confusion reformed into thoughts. "India?"

"You have always wanted to visit Varanasi. That's where we're spending the last three days."

"Oh, Charlie!" Mom had told me so many stories about Varanasi.

"We've both been flat out. We need a break. To start, I've booked this amazing hotel in Goa right on the ocean."

The beach! My mind sighed inside with pleasure. How good a beach sounded.

"And there is an environmental conference in Calcutta. One of the topics is micro-credits for sustainable small plot farming for women. When my friend Rick called me about the conference, we got to talking about your Water Drip technology. They want to talk to you about helping with some of the irrigation concepts they are developing."

"I'd love to!"

Charlie smiled. "That's what I told them."

"Oh, Charlie," I repeated for what felt like the umpteenth time. "I don't know what to say. It's all so perfect."

An impish look settled on Charlie's face. He leaned in close. "Say you'll make love as soon as the seat belt sign is off."

I could feel colour pink my cheeks.

Charlie's eyes gleamed. Clearly, he had been thinking a lot about this.

I bit my lip, looked around. Fellow travelers focused on newspapers, reports, the TV football game. The only visible serving staff tidied a snack bar. As unobtrusively as possible, I slipped my hands underneath my skirt. Wiggling slightly, I pulled hooked panties from my bottom to my knee. I could feel Charlie's rapt attention despite my downward directed eyes. Bending as if to collect a dropped pen, I quickly slipped the panties off. I leaned over to press the balled, black laced underwear deep into Charlie's blazer pocket. When I looked up at my husband, an amazed, aroused smile had spread across his face.

* * * *

Charlie and I walked hand in hand as balmy, indigo water swept languidly over our feet. The late afternoon sun was warm on our bare legs and arms. I sighed with contentment.

"Happy?"

"So happy," I said.

Charlie smiled, pleased. "It is good to be away, isn't it?"

"Unimaginably good," I agreed, lifting my face to the yellow light. "Sometimes I forget how beautiful a clear sky can be."

"You did seem a little down," Charlie said gently.

I looked at him, surprised.

"I thought you might be upset about Jay going back to Antarctica."

"No," I said, but then stopped.

"You haven't been quite the same since he called you about it."

Since our wedding a year before, Jay had returned to traveling the way he had before John Jay had died, accepting extended assignments to remote places where he was hard to reach.

"I think our getting married has been really difficult for him," Charlie ventured.

"Why would you say that?"

"Caring for you filled a big gap for him. Now that you are married, it's emptied out again."

"But I've been taking care of myself for a long time now," I protested.

"I think he's really missing your mom."

What Charlie said felt right. If Mom were alive, she might have started traveling with him again. I wondered again how lonely Jay felt. He had lots of friends, but they were strewn across the world. His projects distracted him, but they always concluded, and again he faced Mom's absence. I thought too that he was affected by his getting older. I imagined there would come a time when even he would want to be still, to find some rest, but it was hard to be in one place with no one around.

I leaned toward Charlie. His arm slipped round my waist. I felt suddenly sad. I always thought of Jay as possessing a pulsating life force, yet now I saw how wearing his sadness was, how weary he was from constantly fighting its drag. I felt grateful suddenly that he was going to Antarctica where it was raw and beautiful, but I was worried too. I wondered if someday Jay might retreat to a Monastery. This unexpected thought made me sadder still, as it was likely I would then see even less of him.

"Look," said Charlie.

Up ahead on the sand, a turbaned man blew a soft tune on a thin pipe. Before him, two cobras rose from wicker baskets, their necks fanned. A small crowd gathered. I tightened my grip on Charlie's hip. I didn't like snakes.

"Want to go in for a closer look?" Charlie asked as we neared.

"No!"

Charlie laughed. "They won't hurt you."

"No way," I insisted. There had been stranger stories in this world than mesmerized cobras suddenly becoming un-mesmerized.

Past the snake charmer, three small open-air cafes sat under coconut shade as the beach cove curved to a point. The smell of curry infused the sea scent. I sniffed hungrily. It had been hours since our last meal. Suddenly, a black cat darted out of the coconut grove in front of us; just as quickly it tore back, disappearing.

"Yikes!" I exclaimed, drawing back.

Charlie laughed, shaking his head. "You and Susie both, you're as superstitious as witch doctors."

"Everyone's superstitious," I countered.

"Not me."

"Yes you are. You just don't realize it."

"Wrong," he insisted amiably.

I thought hard. It was true that Charlie had never thrown salt over his shoulder or touched wood for luck. He didn't hold his breath by cemeteries. "Magpies?"

Charlie's eyes crinkled." That's a nursery rhyme."

"Star light, star bright, first star... I wish I may, I wish I might?" Charlie shook his head.

I punched him. "What's wrong with you?"

"What's wrong with me?" he said, rubbing where I had hit him theatrically.

"You mean to tell me that you wouldn't avoid walking under a ladder?"

"Not unless something about it looked dangerous." His amusement goaded me. Then it hit me. I squared my shoulders.

"What?"

"Remember when we were in Napa and we threw coins into every fountain?"

"Yeah," he said, drawing out the word trying to see where this was going.

"When I threw in the coins, you reminded me to make wishes."

Charlie was laughing now.

"Superstition!" I triumphed.

"That was just a silly game."

"Based on superstition," I argued.

Charlie looked at me.

I jigged in the sand.

He rolled his eyes. "The making wishes was for you. I didn't make any."

"It is not my fault that because you already had me, there wasn't anything more that you could want."

"Oh, please."

"Oh, victory," I said, jigging again.

My dance took us to a narrow, rocky peninsula that jutted into the sea where the beach ended. We climbed up. The beach continued on the other side, empty except for a few fishing boats. Dense coconut forest flanked its back, unbroken by buildings. We stepped quickly across hot sand until we were back to the water line.

"It's going to be a beautiful sunset," Charlie commented, indicating the changing sky. The light was already draining yellow from its pallet.

"What would you rather watch, a sunset or a sunrise?"

"Both," answered Charlie.

"But if you had to choose?"

"Sunset," he said after a moment's thought. There's nothing better than an amazing sunset after a great day's sail." He squeezed my hand. "Or a lingering walk on beautiful beach while holding the hand of the love of my life."

I smiled up at him.

"You're sunrise."

"How do you know?"

"Think of how many times I find you watching the sun come up."

It was true that I found such promise in the breaking of a brand new day.

Before us, young children were building sand castles. The oldest dribbled wet sand into drip turrets. Sitting nearby, what looked to be a two or three-year-old girl released handful after handful of sand into bucketed sea water. Her little toy monkey was all sandy next to her. I slowed to watch, smiling.

"They're lovely children, aren't they?" I said to Charlie.

Charlie watched me watch them.

"What?" I asked.

His eyes were quizzical, masked.

"What?"

50

PREGNANT

Susie's sobbed over the long distance line.

"What's the matter?" I begged. I felt an anxiety that always lurked: Susie had been hurt, had been raped. Her mother had died, or Jay; something awful had happened to Bob. . . "Please," I pleaded. "What's wrong?"

"I'm pregnant."

"Pregnant! How?"

Susie snorted despite her distress. "How?"

"I mean when? I mean how far?" I stammered.

"About three weeks."

"Does Bob know?"

"I couldn't reach him," she said, sounding miserable. "He's in the bush shooting elephants."

"Not shooting shooting. . ."

"Don't be stupid."

"You're not thinking of . . ."

"No."

Susie had been pregnant once before, her senior year in high school. She had refused to tell Chad because he was deeply religious. I had argued that he couldn't have been that religious if he was sleeping with her in the first place. She had already gotten into Columbia. She wasn't even planning to stay together with Chad when they left for university. She wanted an abortion. She wanted me to accompany her.

My every instinct wanted to fight to protect the baby. There had already been so much death. I told her that I would care for it, that her mother, Maria and I would all raise it while she was away. Susie had ridiculed my naïveté. Never could I have imagined a situation in which I would not have been there for Susie; never, not once, had she not been there for me, but I did not want to go to the abortion appointment with her. Then the night before her appointment, she miscarried. Our relief was overwhelming.

This time, Susie said, she meant to keep the baby.

"Good," I said before I could stop myself.

"I know."

I swiveled in my office chair. "What do you think Bob will say?"

"How could I have been such a fucking idiot?"

"Maybe he'll be pleased."

"We've spent a grand total of thirty-three nights together. A baby might be a wee bit premature, don't you think?"

Since they had started dating, work had been unkind to their relationship. While Susie was traveling throughout Africa, Bob had won four extended assignments in Latin America, the last of which had earned him a Pulitzer. Susie had joked that maybe if they broke up she would see more of him. Bob, now back in Africa, had not seen the humour in that. For a laid back guy, when it came to Susie, he was remarkably serious.

"He wanted to marry you," I reminded her.

"In all the time I have worked with him, he has never once mentioned children."

"That doesn't mean anything."

"Jill." Sadness cracked her voice.

I wheeled my chair to the window with my feet. I rested my forehead against the cold glass. "You love him."

"So much."

"He loves you, too."

"He is the best thing that's ever happened to me. Now I am throwing it all away."

"You don't know that."

"Even if he sticks with me, there was so much we wanted to do."

"You still can," I insisted.

"Dragging a baby overland through Africa? Are you oblivious to reality?"

Outside, people gathered on benches in the sun.

"What are you going to do?"

Susie was silent for a long while. "I think I'll wait until he gets back to tell him," she said, finally. "That way I can watch his eyes. Bob's a good guy. I don't want him to stay with me just because he's obliged."

"What if he doesn't? I mean I am sure he will, but. . ."

"If I have to go it alone?"

"You'll never be alone," I said fiercely.

"I'm going to have to try to get myself the hell out of Africa to start."

"You'd come back here?" I asked with unmasked hope.

"I have to find work."

"But you'd try to come here?"

"Yes."

We both became quiet, lost in our own thoughts.

"A baby," Susie said in complete disbelief.

"You're having a baby," I repeated, equally astonished.

"I may still miscarry."

"You won't." I didn't know why I knew, but I did.

"I know," Susie said, with equal conviction.

"A baby."

"What have I done?"

51

MISSING MOM

Mom had been dead fifteen months now. During the time that she had been gone, my body had changed almost as much as my heart. Now, Susie, her mother, and I sat around their glass kitchen table. I hung my head, horrified, as Mrs. Smith suggested that we go together to get my first bra. Susie pressed her knees against mine for support.

"While Susie and you look around, I'll have a quiet word with the sales lady. Then you and Susie can try them on together. The sales lady can be close by if you need help."

I didn't move. I didn't say anything. My cheeks burned.

"Or my mom could help," Susie offered.

Instinctively, my hand pressed against the table, fingers splayed, as if I was trying to hold it down.

"I'll pay for everything," Mrs Smith continued.

"Jay wouldn't even have to know," Susie explained.

My eyes shot to hers.

"It will just be between us girls," Mrs. Smith encouraged.

What choice did I have?

"Shall we go now?" Mrs. Smith asked.

My eyes flew up in alarm.

"Waiting will only make it worse," Susie reasoned. "If we leave now, it can be over by dinner."

* * * *

On the drive to the store, Susie and her mother got in a fight about Susie's wanting to go for pizza with her soccer team after the game. Her mother reminded her that she'd been grounded on Saturday for not doing her chores. Susie spoke back, pointing out that pizza was technically still part of the match and she couldn't be grounded from school activities. I listened jealously as we rode up the escalator. What I would have given to be grounded by Mom.

When we reached the second floor of the department store, naked mannequins wearing black bras and undies greeted us. My cheeks seared. I wanted a hole in which I could hide.

"Why don't you girls look around," Mrs Smith suggested. "I'll see if I can find help." Susie started to follow, but I pulled her back. I was starting to cry.

Susie took my hand. "Let's go hang by the pyjamas. That way we can spy."

Her mother was speaking with the woman at the till; she turned to indicate us, but I hid behind nightgowns. Only when we knew that everything was ready did we slip into the dressing room. A large selection of bras hung on metal hooks. I stood awkwardly as Susie sorted through them.

"Try these on first," Susie suggested, holding up what resembled three half shirts. "It's what I started with. They feel about the same as wearing a camisole."

Self-consciously, I unbuttoned the over-sized short-sleeved blouse I had been wearing, then took off my t-shirt.

"Wow!" said Susie, looking at me. "You're bigger than I thought! No wonder you've been layering."

Embarrassed, I crossed my arms over my breasts.

Susie dropped the bras she held. She riffled thorough the others on the hooks. "Try this one."

I slipped it over my head and pulled it across my chest. I considered myself in the mirror. It made me look smaller, which was what I liked.

"What do you think?" Susie asked.

"What do *you* think?"

"I think it's good," she said with a nod of approval. "Get several." Susie returned to the bras. Her next selection had triangle cups. One was lacy. "What about these?"

I shook my head.

"You don't even want to try them on?"

"No."

"Take these two anyway," she said, exchanging the lacy bra for some white cotton triangles.

I protested.

"Just put them in your drawer. You'll be surprised how much they will come in handy like when you want to wear a sundress."

"How you girls doing?" The sales lady had dyed black hair and wore thick mascara. Dark maroon outlined her lipstick-darkened lips.

"I think we are all set," Susie answered.

"Your mother wanted me to check on you, dears."

"No! No! No!" I mouthed to Susie.

Collecting the bras, Susie slipped from the cubicle. I quickly locked it behind her, retreating to the bench.

"We're taking these," Susie told the sales lady, whose high-heels clicked quickly after her. Dressed, I cracked the door open to peer in both directions. I escaped back to the pyjama rack, where I hid again behind the flannels.

* * * *

On the ride home, Mrs. Smith stopped in front of Quick Mart, and Susie went in for milk. The last time Mom and I had been there, I had convinced her to try a watermelon slushie. She had loved it despite the sugar and despite the food colouring. When she had finished her small watermelon, she kept pestering me for sips of my large blueberry.

"These are for you, honey," Mrs. Smith said, handing me a paper lunch bag. I looked at it, confused. "They're tampons and pads."

I coloured.

"I thought it'd be good to have supplies just in case."

I couldn't look at her.

"Do you know how to use them?"

I nodded, even though I wasn't sure.

"You know you can ask me anything."

* * * *

In my room, I removed the brown paper bag from my backpack. I placed it on the bed next to the plastic sack of bras. Mom had been given her brown paper bag. Now I had mine. Mom had promised me it would be different for me. But it wasn't at all. I pulled out the box of tampons, opening it to remove the instructions. I hadn't realized exactly that the tampons went inside. I took the paper wrapping off a tampon and pushed the slider forward so that the cotton wad popped out. I held it up by its string.

Jay knocked. My heart seized. I shoved everything under my pillow. Jay popped his head in. "Homework almost done?"

I felt myself flush. "Just about," I said, not looking up.

I could feel his eyes consider me; it occurred to me that none of my school books were out.

"Fifteen minutes to dinner?"

"Great," I said, keeping my eyes down.

"Everything ok?"

"Yeah," I said, trying to sound normal.

"Tacos tonight."

Tacos were one of my favourites.

"I'd appreciate some help chopping."

"I'll be right there," I said quickly.

When I was sure he was gone, I put all the tampon stuff back in the brown bag and hid it in the bathroom. I stuffed the bras into the back of my drawer. Then I went back to my bed and took up Lionel. I hugged him tightly until I quieted my thumping heart.

52

BUSINESS

"Giovanni. How are you?" I asked brightly, happy to hear his voice.

"Like a fucked duck."

I laughed.

"Don't laugh. You're like a duck too."

"What are you talking about?"

"We're on strike."

I leaned forward in my chair. "But why?"

"It's not about us, if you are thinking this. My workers are union. If union says strike, they strike."

"But the shipment?"

"Won't be ready."

"Not ready?" My voice rose. I had a lot of working capital caught up in this. "But I thought you said it was done."

"*Almost* done; we were needing at least two days more before we are shipping her."

"None of it is ready?"

"No."

"But couldn't you just bring in someone else?"

"Not without making it so my factory, she might be having a terrible accident."

"But the strike could last just a day or two?"

"It could," Giovanni said. "But I am doubting this."

"Fuck."

"You see?"

"Fuck," I said again.

"I think you call Home World; otherwise he'll be fucked too."

I rubbed my fingers across my forehead. "We have to figure out Plan B." Already, in my mind I was thinking what else I could promote.

"He doesn't want to be hearing this."

"I don't want to be hearing this."

"But you don't rip off my balls."

"Would it help if I did?"

Giovanni laughed. "Not with this, no."

Before I could think, before dread overwhelmed me, I called Martin at Home World.

"Just who I was going to dial," said Martin happily. "I have good news."

"Good news?" I asked, tentatively.

"Your line is featured in the first six seconds of our May Day TV ad. I just got the clip. It cost me an arm and leg, but it is a big upgrade from our usual ad. We start running it tomorrow."

Fuck! I thought. Fuck! Fuck! Fuck! "Actually, I'm calling about the line," I started.

"Is there a problem?" The cheerfulness in his voice turned wary. Martin could smell trouble like a blood hound.

"A strike. In Italy. The factory has been shut down."

"For how long?"

"I don't know."

"My shipment?"

"At this point, I can't guarantee anything."

"Oh, shit."

"I'm so sorry. What I was thinking. . ."

Martin cut me off. "I don't want to know."

"But. . ."

"You've lost my business Jill."

"But. . ."

He hung up the phone.

I was stunned. Tears sprang to my eyes. The telephone rang. Relief flooded. We had been disconnected. I grabbed the phone without waiting for Lucy.

"You're being audited," my accountant Steve said without preamble.

"Audited? But we haven't. . ."

"Done anything wrong," he preempted. "Of course not, but it'll still be a serious time sink."

An expensive time sink, I thought, considering Steve's fees.

I ended the call, feeling utterly dejected. I tried Charlie, but just got his voice mail. My stomach felt twisted. I had to get out of the office.

* * * *

I racked my brain as I drove. Martin was angry now, but he was a good guy and he liked me. I thought about the commercial. Last time we'd lunched he had told me he felt Home World was under-advertised. He must be out on a limb if he had promoted the commercial. At least I could offer to finance a re-shoot of my part in it. Nothing like paying to advertise my competitors.

I turned onto Old Sea Road that curved and curled through pine groves. I concentrated more carefully; the descending narrow road had many hair-pins, and it had been a long time since I had driven on it. The road finally flattened into a thin valley, patchworked with small farms growing pumpkins, strawberries, and cauliflower. Scruffy greenhouses and rusty tractors rested next to squares of dark earth and flourishing vegetables. Hand-painted signs advertised pick-your-own. Occasionally, clumps of eucalyptus bunched by the road.

Around a last corner, among shaggy trees, large metal dinosaurs, giraffes and elephants reared. I slowed to take a better look. The animals had been welded from a hodgepodge of metals. Life-sized deer grazed or stood startled; pigs rutted; dogs were caught mid-wag. They were wonderful! Behind the sculptures in a shabby shed a visor-masked man bent over a white-hot blow torch.

Turning onto Coastal Highway, I pulled into the first place I could park. I slipped off my flats and stockings. Gravel pricked as I picked my way gingerly to the sand. Cold sea crashed onto the shore, rushing up frothily as I walked along its edge. It dragged at my feet as it retreated. Far out, towering container ships passed like distant ghosts.

I missed Susie. Bob had been overjoyed about the baby. He had asked her again to marry him, but she had again refused. She said it was bad enough moving from Africa. She wasn't now going to play wife. It had devastated me that they were moving to her old house by our Garden, although I understood why. Mrs. Smith had deeded them the house free and clear, as she now lived full time with her sister. Freelance again, they could live anywhere.

Already, Susie had gotten an assignment covering old growth redwood forests and another about Mark Twain and the Mississippi. She was grateful, but the stories also made her sad. In Africa, she brought famine, conflict and poverty to the world's attention. She championed Africa's successes. The U.S. stories made her miss Africa all the more. Yet already she loved her developing foetus fiercely. Whenever I called, Mozart played loudly in the background. I knew that Susie wanted this baby to have the stable, safe home that she had missed out on because of her mom's drinking.

It was late afternoon when I finally made my way back across the parking lot. While brushing sand from my feet, it hit me. What Martin needed was something unique to lure people into his stores. That's why he was keen to feature Giovanni's animal pots and statuary. What if he showcased the welded animals instead? The big animals could greet customers at the entrance. The smaller ones could be scattered between his bedding shelves. I was willing to bet they'd sell splendidly, and they'd go beautifully with my Metallics line for which I had plenty of inventory. I wondered how many animals the artist had. My excitement rose. This could work, especially since I still had inventory left from some of Giovanni's older creations. I considered calling Martin right away, but no, first I had to negotiate with the artist. Please let him be keen, I implored God, the sea, the road, the sun as I turned back on Old Ocean Road. Let him be keen, and please, please, please, let him be reasonable.

53

SAILING

Sierra cut through gentle waves on a mild wind. The breeze was just cool enough to keep sweat from breaking as I stretched out in my bikini. Charlie steered the boat with his foot while applying sunblock to his chest. Closing my eyes, I exhaled languorously. Thought fragments drifted like floating clouds as I relaxed blissfully. It had been a long, hard, exhausting week, and it was not helped by the fact I had just finished a mega-eight-day period which had made fatigue drag at me like weights.

The metal animal sculptures that I had finally convinced Martin to sell during his May Day promotion had been a huge success. Now almost six months later, Martin sold the metal animals exclusively. The problem was that their creator, Rick, had never quite transitioned from artist to professional. He now had two apprentices working with him, but he was still in the same run-down shed keeping erratic hours. I had visited three times the week before, trying to get him to finish the next shipment on time. On time meant telling him I needed the animals a full two weeks before I had promised them to Martin.

The best bit about that week was that Susie and Tabitha had visited. Tabitha was almost eight weeks old now. Watching Tabitha suckling on Susie's darkened nipple still fascinated me, and I was still caught up by the idea of Susie being a mother. I was caught up too by the way Susie and Tabitha had formed a unit unto themselves, making me the outsider. Yearning overcame me sometimes when I was with them. I did not want a child, yet there was something about Susie and Bob now belonging to something larger than themselves that made me feel oddly empty.

"Jill." Charlie was shaking me. "Jill."

"What?" I tried to make sense. I was trying to wake without even realizing I had slept.

"You're burning."

I flipped over on my stomach, my eyes already closing. I was just aware that Charlie had put a straw hat over my face turned to one side. I needed to call Giovanni, which reminded me I needed to get an insurance quote. I had asked Charlie twice to get it done the previous week, but I knew he still hadn't. Otherwise, he would have told me. He had also promised but had failed to get the car serviced. It made me really cross that in the morning he would say he'd get something done, then come home in the evening with the chore still unfinished. We fought about this. If he would just become more organized, he'd get ahead of it all instead of always trying to stamp out the fires perpetually rolling across his desk. Nine times out of ten, I did Charlie's jobs as well as mine; otherwise we would be constantly paying late charges.

I rolled on my back, blinking at the speckled light seeping through the hat's weaving. I could feel towels covering my whole body. Sweat made my skin sticky. Water moved faster underneath us. The wind had picked up.

"Good sleep?" Charlie asked.

"What time is it?"

"Almost one."

"I've been sleeping two hours?"

"Like a log."

"Gosh," I said, forcing myself up. As the towels dropped to my lap, I shivered.

"You ready for lunch?"

Just the thought of food made my stomach grumble loudly.

Charlie laughed. "Take her," he said. "I'll lay it out."

Charlie returned with plates of thick turkey and avocado sandwiches, barbeque chips, and strawberries. I scooted over to make room. I leaned into him as we ate. After my sandwich, my tongue crushed sweet strawberries against the roof of my mouth until they burst. The strawberries made me think of Pug and Pat. I promised myself to call Maria when I got home.

"A Penny?"

"Oh, just that I owe Maria a call."

"How is she?"

"I think they are both missing work." About a year earlier, Fernando had decided to stop taking new clients so that they could spend more time with their family in Mexico. "Maria says that she is happy to see more of their family, but really, I think they're bored."

"What about doing some volunteer work?" Charlie asked, eating chips.

"Fernando has been helping the church with their vegetable garden."

Charlie smiled. "I bet it's feeding half the village."

"And then some," I said, smiling with him. "Maria helps the church organize a food pantry where people can now go if they don't have enough food."

"They've always talked about retiring early," said Charlie.

"I know, but I don't think it has been what they imagined."

"That's the problem with childhood dreams," said Charlie, wiping his face with his napkin, dropping the balled napkin on his emptied plate. "Being an adult never turns out how you imagined."

I considered dreams. Susie had wanted to be a journalist. She had never talked about being a mother. For me... I thought back to the Garden. The more I thought, the more I realized that for most of my life in the Garden, I just was. Before Mom and John Jay had died, playing there had left no room for anything else. After they died, I was too busy surviving to think of the future. By the time I was healed enough to think ahead, my thoughts were no longer childhood dreams. They were the plans of a young adult. By and large, I had acted on them.

"I didn't really have any dreams," I told Charlie. "Before Mom and John Jay died, I wanted to stay in the Garden forever. I thought it was the best place in the whole world."

"None at all?" Charlie asked, surprised. After his Superman phase, I knew Charlie had wanted to be a garbage man for a long while. He had thought garbage-eating trucks were the coolest.

"I know it used to bug me when Susie talked about wanting to be a journalist and travel," I said after a bit more thought.

"She had a lot to escape."

"Maybe that's right," I agreed, although that also implied that she wanted to escape the Garden and me.

"Hey, look!" Charlie cried.

I swiveled to see where he was pointing. Two dolphins leapt and dove like children playing. Charlie came close so that his stomach was against my back, his arm around my waist. The dolphins cavorted toward us, then veered abruptly.

"Brilliant," Charlie breathed, when the dolphins had gone. I smiled. I loved how things touched Charlie so deeply. I loved how I appreciated things more just because of his enthusiasm. He made me take time to notice, to see, instead of always being bogged down in the day-to-day. I relaxed back against his chest. With my hand, I rubbed my stomach.

"How's it feeling?" Charlie asked.

"Still tender."

"Even Susie thinks you should go see an OBGYN again," Charlie said, picking up an argument he had been making all week. But I hated doctors. It felt like bad luck just going inside their offices. Besides, I wasn't the first person with an irregular menstrual cycle. The last time I'd gone, the doctor had told me that there was nothing to worry about.

"You didn't do insurance nor did you take the car in to be serviced," I deflected.

I could feel Charlie tense. "We're talking about your health, Jill. This is different."

"We're talking about having the time to get things done. You don't get your things done."

"That's not the point." Charlie's voice had lowered.

"It is the point because I end up doing your stuff as well as mine, which is why I don't have time to go to the doctor. If you'd be more organized, maybe I'd have more time."

"Can you lay off about my organization?" His voice had an edge.

"Then how about laying off me going to the doctor?"

"I can't, when it is your health." I could hear him consciously try to calm himself. "This is important."

"You aren't the only arbitrator of what is important and what is not," I said. Now I definitely wasn't going to the doctor. "You start doing what is important to me, then I'll do what is important to you."

Charlie slipped away from me. He went to the other side of the boat, tacked, and then winched the sails tightly. We were heading home. That made me even angrier. Why should he be the person to decide when we got to go in? What if I wanted to stay out longer?

"I don't want to go in," I told him.

"I still have time to get the car serviced today."

Now he was using my Saturday afternoon to get done what he should have done all week. "That's just great," I said.

"Yeah," he said, cool as ice. "Some Saturday."

54

BIRTHDAY CAKES

"Jill, wake-up!"

Jay was sitting next to me on the bed, his hand on my shoulder.

"Jay?"

"Come on."

"What happened?" I asked, trying to make sense.

"There is something I want you to see."

"What time is it?"

"Just gone midnight."

I pushed myself up, blinking. I had been dreaming deeply.

"What is it?"

"Come see." Nothing bad was in his expression. "Come on," he encouraged.

I pulled back the covers and swung my feet to the ground. Curious now, I padded after him. A fresh-baked chocolate smell drifted down the hallway. In the dark kitchen, a cake flickered with candles.

"Happy birthday!"

Tears caught in my eyes. He had iced it when it was still warm, and the top was starting to slip down the uneven slope of the bottom layer. Melted red wax puddled in spots on the chocolate top.

Jay sang happy birthday as I watched the candlelight caper. "Make a wish?" he asked.

I wished that Jay and Susie and Mrs. Smith and Maria and Fernando would not die, not for a long, long time. I blew out the fourteen candles in one go. The kitchen went dark. The scent of candle smoke swirled with the aroma of chocolate.

"Hurrah!" Jay softly cheered. I smiled as he lit the large candles we now kept on the table.

"Hot chocolate? It's all ready."

I saw the copper pan on a low blue flame. Dishes piled in the sink.

"Yes, please," I said, sitting.

"We're out of marshmallows," he said apologetically as he ladled. He handed me the knife when he joined me at the table. "You're supposed to cut."

I sliced two large pieces.

From a chair pushed under the table Jay pulled out a small pile of presents.

I was dumbfounded. Truth was, I didn't think that Jay even knew it was my birthday. He hadn't said anything and I wasn't planning to either. Having my first birthday without Mom was like having her die all over again. The last few days I had felt lonelier than ever. I fought tears. I didn't want to make Jay feel bad after everything he had done.

"I'm so sorry, sweetheart."

I looked up at him.

"It's nothing like it was with your mom."

"Nothing is like it was with Mom," I said sadly, not as criticism but as description.

"I realized as I was making your cake that I have missed your last four birthdays."

"I know. You've been gone for almost all of yours, too."

"What did you do?" he asked.

"What do you mean?"

"For your birthdays? Like what did you do for your tenth?"

I thought back. "It was a lion party. We made this amazing lion cake. That was the year you gave me the wave machine. Do you remember?"

"I remember the wave machine. What about your eleventh?"

"Bowling. We made a bowling cake with lanes of liquorice, coke-bottle gummies for the pins and gumballs for the bowling balls. You gave me the star projector, a book on constellations, and a book on using the stars to navigate."

"I was working on the piece about the Hubble Telescope."

"I'm pretty good now."

"Good?"

"At navigating. I've practiced."

"Really?"

"When I don't feel like reading, I'd play with it in bed."

"I was there for your ninth. It was a flower party. You all made painted flowers out of clay and different materials."

"You gave me Michael Marmot, Daisy Deer, and Red Squirrel."

"That was when I had been working in Yellow Stone."

"Mom made a great Garden cake. Do you remember it? How we made all those different flowers out of candy?"

Jay nodded. "Mom certainly was good at cakes."

"The best. Did you know that we even had a volcano cake that actually erupted lava icing?"

"Seriously?"

"We took it with us to the Natural History Museum when we visited the new area that had just been opened on volcanoes."

"I wish I could have seen it."

"I have a picture of it in our Cake Book Hall of Fame. Want me to show you?"

"You have a Cake Book Hall of Fame?"

"I'll show you." From the topmost cookbook shelf, I removed a blue album. Sitting next to Jay, I went through the pictures one by one. From my fifth birthday onward, for every cake made by Mom there was the matching one made for Mom by me with a little help from Maria. That's how I knew about icing warm cakes and how it takes forever for a cake to cool.

"How come you were never here for your birthdays?" I asked after we had finished looking.

"It wasn't on purpose really."

"But you're not really big on birthdays."

"I guess not," Jay admitted.

"How come?"

After a while Jay said, "I guess it was because my dad wasn't much into birthdays either. We never really celebrated them when I was little."

"You didn't have birthday parties?"

"When I was really little, I remember getting cakes. But that stopped when I was seven or eight."

"That's so sad!"

Jay smiled. "It's not sad if that's what you're used to. You can't miss what don't really know."

"But didn't you go to your friends' parties?"

"A few, especially when I was little, but we lived quite far from town. Most of the time I hung out on my own until my dad got home."

"Wasn't it lonely?"

"Not really. I always had a lot of chores and I was good at amusing myself. It never seemed long at all."

"Did you miss not having a mom?" I had always wondered about this, but had been afraid to ask. Jay's mom had left when he was two.

"Yes," he said without hesitation. "That was something I missed even though I never knew her."

I took a sip of hot chocolate thinking about this. Jay must have added extra chocolate powder, because the chocolate flavour was dense and extra sweet.

"But that doesn't mean that we won't be big into your birthday this year," he said, his voice bright. "Shall we have a party?"

"No thanks."

"But haven't you've always had a party?"

I nodded.

"I'd be happy to organize anything."

"Thanks, but I just don't want to."

"Are you sure?"

"I'd have to pretend that I was happy, and that would just make me feel miserable."

Jay nodded, but I could see he was sad. His eyes drifted back to the cake book.

"Let's put a picture of your cake in here."

"This cake?" Its top layer had continued its slide from the bottom. One edge now rested on the plate.

"It's a great cake."

Jay laughed. He tried to shove the top back on the bottom.

"Don't," I said. "I like it just as it is."

Jay looked at me doubtfully, licking icing from his fingertips. From the pantry shelf, I took out the Polaroid. I snapped Jay's picture first, and then I took several of the cake.

After I had finished photographing, we set to eating. I could taste where it had burned at the edges. "It's delicious," I told him.

"It's dry and burnt," he said ruefully.

"That's what makes it perfect."

Jay smiled. After a moment he asked, "So what are we going to do for your birthday then?"

"Just be sad," I told him plainly.

I could feel him search my face.

"It's all right," I reassured. "It is sad. That's all it really can be."

"Do you want to open your presents at least?"

Jay had given me new climbing ropes and a book on climbing techniques. Recently, Jay and I had started rock climbing more often. I liked how the harder the climb, the more I thought of just rock, my fingers reading its surfaces like braille. Often pictures without thought entered into this quiet space like silent friends. Lately, I had been seeing images of bonsais – pines twisting or maples, all leafy and lovely, dappled in sun. Thinking of our bonsais made Mom feel near.

The last present was a little box wrapped in shiny silver paper. Inside the box a silver frame glimmered. Inside the frame was a picture of Mom and me.

"I took that picture right before I left for Antarctica the last time. Do you remember?"

I looked more closely at our faces, our eyes. Despite Jay's imminent departure, we looked happy, especially Mom. Her green eyes gleamed like elves. He had captured her laughter as if it were still bouncing, alive inside the picture like a firefly in a jar.

* * * *

The next day was the schools' annual mother-daughter tea, held while the boys had an all-sports afternoon. It was a dressy affair, and Maria surprised me with a green, velvet and silk dress with a trim of white lace around the collar. It was the last thing I wanted to wear, although I didn't tell Maria. I wanted to wear something old, something that would allow me to fade away unnoticed. Especially, as in a pique of anger, I had cut my long hair short, and now was missing it terribly.

"Not the same at all, was it Niña?" Maria said as we drove home. A year earlier, Mom and I had worn matching flowery sundresses, and we had placed little vases of flowers on all the tables.

"It was good," I said, digging my nails into my palms.

"You don't have to pretend Nina," said Maria kindly, her voice catching.

Tears spilled down my cheeks, and then Maria was also crying.

"I think we should have stayed home," Maria said. "From now on, we will make our own tradition. You stay home, and we will do something fun, just the two of us, ok?"

I nodded, too sad to speak, but that was exactly what I wanted – to never attend the school tea again.

Once home, I disappeared into the Garden as soon as I had thanked Maria. I went into the deepest part of the Maze, where the paths were purposely deceptive in order to conceal the Enclaves. In my favourite of these Enclaves, the ancient Grandfather Tree twisted, casting cool, enclosing shadow. Fernando had hidden benches in the green shrubbery so I could sit comfortably under Grandfather's branches when I visited.

Here, away from everyone, I broke into huge, heart-broken sobs. All the time, through my tears, I could feel the Flamingos gather. I felt all alone, yet not alone because the Flamingos were with me. After a long time of crying, I finally quieted. I felt better, almost washed through, as if some of the pain had been swept away on the flood of my tears.

55

MARRIED

"You have to tell him," I argued with Susie. "You can't keep faking your periods."

"But I don't want to get married," she insisted.

"Then you shouldn't have said you would."

Susie wanted another baby so Tabitha wouldn't be an only child. She thought if she had the second quickly then she would be able to return to full-time work sooner. Susie continued to struggle to be fully engaged in the freelance feature pieces that were coming her way – foreign fish interlopers and their impact on Lake Michigan's ecosystems, historic theme parks of America, bayou culture in the south. She desperately missed covering international stories, but she wanted to be with Tabitha more. Their idea was that when Tabitha reached five or six, they would consider taking her abroad. Until then, Bob didn't want to have any more children without getting married first. He made Susie promise that when she got pregnant again, they would wed.

"I want to back out."

"But why?"

"You know why."

"But that was your parents, not Bob."

"I can't do it," she insisted, cutting me off.

"Then why did you say you would?"

"Because Bob wouldn't have another child until I agreed. I tried."

"Tried?"

"By not taking birth control, but he guessed. He kept pulling out until I promised."

I laughed. I had to give Bob credit.

"What am I going to do?"

The tea kettle whistled. I extinguished the gas.

"Make some tea," I said, suddenly.

"What?"

"Tea," I insisted. "I'll have some too. We'll have a cup together and figure this out."

With Susie on speaker, I made myself English Breakfast with milk and sugar the way that Susie liked so that even our tea choices made us tight.

"I know you love Bob," I said, taking it methodically once her tea was done.

"More than anything."

"You feel completely committed."

"Completely," she agreed.

I took a long sip of tea. Its atypical sweetness made me tongue curl. "You want your kids to have a dad."

"That's not in question."

"If he ever left you?"

"I'd rip out his eyeballs."

I laughed.

"I mean it," Susie insisted. "I'd get him for everything he's got, which admittedly isn't much."

"But that's all marriage. The only thing you're missing is the paper."

"I just can't." Anxiety flooded her voice. "I feel like marrying would just jinx everything. It's all so good right now. Too good, actually; it's scaring me."

"Don't say that," I reproved, but I felt my own rush of disquiet. "Maybe we have already used up all our bad."

Susie laughed. "You mean we front-loaded it?"

"Why not? We're good people, creating good karma. Things can go our way too."

"Quick," said Susie. "Salt."

Pinched salt went over my shoulder twice.

"Careful Jill."

"I know."

Quietly, we drank, both thinking. I listened to her swallows, to her soft breath muted by the distance between us.

"I don't see what choice you have," I said finally. "Even if you wanted to fake your period again this month, you can't forever. When he eventually finds out, he's going to be really angry."

"I know."

"It's better to fight it out now instead of waiting."

"I know," Susie said, without conviction.

"Or you could just get married."

"Just the thought of it. . . ," Susie protested.

"The thought of what exactly?" I cut in.

"Wearing a white dress, standing in front of all those people; it just doesn't feel right."

"So elope."

"Yeah, right."

"Seriously. Would Bob mind?"

I could feel her considering. "No," she said slowly. Possibility rippled faintly in her voice. "He wouldn't care how we married."

"So go to Vegas!"

Susie groaned.

"Or better yet," I said, my excitement growing as an idea took shape, "come here. We'll have a ceremony, just the five of us, with Charlie, Tabitha, and me as witnesses. After, you can leave Tabitha with us to go on a honeymoon."

"Honeymoon?" Susie said, surprised.

"Why not? We'd love to have Tabitha, and it would be good for you both to get away together before the next baby comes."

"If I really did this," said Susie, warming to the idea, "I would want Mom, my brother, Jay, and Bob's parents there too. But just the ten of us."

"Ten is good," I assured.

"And I would want to get married on the tide pools and then go to Peet's after for calamari."

"Anything."

"God, I wish I could get smashed after," she said longingly.

"After you finish nursing this baby, we'll have a night to remember," I promised her.

"Or not remember," Susie quipped.

* * * *

Turbulent clouds blackened the squall-ridden sky. Stinging wind whipped. Merciless waves crashed fiercely against the rocks. We huddled close as the rabbi struggled to be heard. Susie had never been more beautiful in white jeans, cream turtleneck and jacket. The tempestuous, deteriorating weather had made her ebullient, calm. It was as if the storm was the incarnation of her very worst fears, intimating all that unsettled her soul. Its stormy expression was her own exorcist, and it was that exorcism that was giving Susie courage now. Bob, dressed in black jeans, turtle neck and jacket was joyful beside her. Tabitha slept in a snuggly, completely covered by Charlie's wet weather gear. Maria and Fernando beamed. Maria had insisted outright to Susie that she and Fernando would be at her wedding, too. Around Susie's neck were Maria's great-grandmother's pearls.

* * * *

"Drinks on the house," shouted Bob as we passed the already crowded bar at Peet's to the table we had reserved. A cheer rose from the room. I heard one guy ask the barman if he could borrow the phone to call his girl. When word spread that it was a wedding and the fishermen heard that Susie had married in this storm by their sea, the party roared. At one point the owner locked the doors so he could join. They all played with Tabitha until she could stand no more, and she slumped, exhausted, in Mrs. Smith's arms. Susie even had Fernando knocking back shots. He was up on the table, dancing with Susie. Everyone was dancing. Susie was everywhere, ecstatic. Bob was proud, protective, exhilarated.

56

CHILDREN

The zoo's carousel pealed. Painted animals pranced up and down metal poles. Tabitha had chosen the flamingo. At first, she had gripped the pole fearfully, Charlie's arm wrapped protectively around her waist. Now, her third ride in a row, she waved at each sight of me, in a great game of peak-a-boo. At the playground after, I took off Tabitha's shoes. For a moment she took in the feel of the playground's sandy bottom on her bare feet, her little toes wiggling. Then she held up her small hand to me and we toddled off to the slide. At ten months she had been an early walker. Now at thirteen months, she was a little physical powerhouse.

It took Tabitha only a little practice to easily climb the slide's ladder. She crawled through the tunnels like a rocket. I clapped at each success. Now I pushed her on the swings. Her short black hair blew back as she rose and whooshed.

When she was finally tired, all three of us sat on the sand. The mid-day sun was burning off the fog. Charlie had bought colourful plastic sand toys from the concession stand, and Tabitha now contentedly used them to dig and pour. I leaned back against Charlie's chest as I watched. His stomach rumbled against my back. I smiled up at him, amused.

"It's lunch," he protested.

I checked my watch, surprised to see that it was almost one. Tabitha would be getting hungry, too.

"Are you hungry, Sweet Pea?" I asked her.

She considered me briefly, then went back to the sand and her bucket.

"She seems pretty happy," Charlie said. "Maybe you can feed her while she's playing."

It was a good idea. I removed the plastic container of pre-packed lunch from the bag strung on the stroller's back. Cleaning my hands with a diaper wipe, I unwrapped her tuna sandwich while Charlie helped himself to another. Tabitha opened her mouth as I popped in bites while she moved her car along a sand road that Charlie had steamrolled with his foot. Playing this way, she munched through all of the sandwich and half her banana. She caught sight of her bottle as Charlie rummaged for the chips. Her toys dropped. Her hands went out.

I cleaned the sand as best I could as she held the bottle first with one hand then the other, tilting her head back to suck. I quickly changed her wet diaper as she stood; and when she was dry, I buckled her into the stroller. I snuggled her blanket across her stomach and against her cheek. She nestled into it. Her eyes were closing even as we wheeled her toward the animals. I was sure she would nap. Already I was envisioning getting tea in the Zoo Café, but when we passed the screeching monkeys, her eyes popped open. Tabitha struggled against her belt as her empty bottle dropped.

"Hold on a sec," said Charlie, kneeling before her.

When he had her unbuckled, he lifted her up and her hand shot out, pointing.

"Monkeys," Charlie said.

She looked at him, all round eyes and amazement. The monkeys swung from tree to tree. Her finger shot out again.

"That's right," said Charlie as she checked his face for confirmation. "Those are monkeys," he said, pointing too. "See them swing!"

* * * *

"Charlie, we have to get her to bed," I said again, as he crawled on hands and knees, Tabitha riding him, happily. Susie had said she should be asleep by eight, and it was well past nine. She was surely exhausted, although she didn't look it. She had napped in the car, and since then she had been nothing but energy. At dinner, half her food went on the floor. During the post-dinner video, she had grown bored. For a while after that, we had had great fun with my old bead box. Now she charged around with Charlie, as if on horseback.

Charlie rolled on his back and bounced her on his knees.

"Let's try her bottle," I said.

Charlie rocked to his feet, hoisting Tabitha up in his arms. Tabitha tracked my every move as I heated her milk. She cuddled in my arms to drink it with her blanket snugly around her. I thought she was already asleep as I eased her into her portable crib, but her crying started as soon as we closed the door. Charlie and I looked at each other.

"Susie said to let her cry."

Her crying grew louder.

"It's well past her bedtime," I said. "Maybe she's over-tired."

We hovered. Her sobbing became frantic. She choked, coughed. I couldn't stand it. She clenched Charlie's shirt as he carried her back to the living room. He began rocking her, patting her back as I dimmed the overhead lights. "Oh mirror in the sky what is love?" he sang softly. "Can the child within my heart rise above?"

My heart filled as I curled on the couch to watch.

Charlie smiled at me over her head, now tucked under his chin. He was singing to me as well as to Tabitha. "But time makes you bolder, even children get older, and I'm getting older too." Tabitha's eyes were closing. Her hand gripping Charlie's shirt softened. "Oh take my love, take it down. Climb a mountain and turn around. And if you see my reflection in the snow covered hills, well the landslide brings it down." Tabitha's whole body had grown heavy. She hiccupped once. "Well a landslide brings it down." He kept swaying, softly humming. Finally, he sat next to me on the couch. Tabitha did not stir. Snuggling close to Charlie, I rested my cheek on his shoulder, as we both watched her quiet face.

57

MOM'S ROOM

It was Jay who had wished to build Mom a room, high up where our land merged into the Wild which overlooked Garden. We agreed it was to be the last room we would ever make. Jay had started it when he had received more bad news about his Nepalese friend Kamala. The government was angry about the continued protests in his village. Kamala couldn't prove anything, but his chickens had been poisoned, his bike tires slashed and then slashed again, his window broken by rocks in the middle of the night. Jay said that building the room helped take his mind off Kamala. He was worried, but he was also sad about Mom.

We made her room untamed, filling it with meadow flowers and wild roses. Inside, what remained of her ashes we buried under a statue of a mother holding a child. Three beds of mint encircled the statue like protective rings of green fire. In these beds I had put almost every known variety of mint. It had been a job tracking them down. Mom would have been proud. Another part of her lay under a tombstone next to John Jay. The rest we scattered. As he had done with John Jay, Genie had lifted her ashes high up as the dawn sky blazed.

I felt close to Mom in this room. Here, all the pretending stopped. Here, I did not have to make-believe that I was happy. Most people thought that my unhappiness should be over by now. After all, had not a year and a half gone by? Most people didn't understand that a part of me would never be quite healed.

I buried my face in the statue's mint, ruffling its leaves to release their scent. Her memory came – was indeed invoked – a soft, freckled, familiar face with her loving, warm green eyes. I could hear her reassuring voice even though it spoke no words. With my tears, I told her about my fears and about how my struggles wore me down. With my smile, I intimated to her all that was going well.

Here, I could take stock of time passing. Here, I could miss her so purely, an unadulterated, fresh, white missing which was what I now came to understand as Heaven. The whiteness had become what I felt when I thought of clouds.

Death had made me different, had separated me from my friends, no matter how hard I tried to fit in. It made me feel like part-outsider, no matter how much I was included. Because of this, I became an acute observer from afar. With my schoolmates, I pretended that nothing had changed. I went through the motions, knowing that often the motions were the best that I had going for me, knowing that the motions could morph into something real some of the time. Without the motions, black despair still dragged me down.

I lifted my face as snow-cooled air washed down from the mountain's top, hinting at coming night. It swirled the room's rose scent, then swept on down. I followed the breeze with my eyes as it rushed leaves and pushed grasses. My eyes lingered on the growing afternoon shadows. I reached out my hand to let the last sunlight pool. It was peculiar, this quality of light, weightless, formless but with real warmth. It skipped. It played. It became absent, yet even in its absence it was shadow. In Mom's room I felt her in the same way that I felt this light. Weightless, formless, Mom was here as surely as if she stood before me. Here, I felt her warmth and remembered her love.

58

CHILDREN

Sweat affixed the cotton night gown to my chest. Moist hair adhered to my face. I threw off the down quilt and twisted out from under Charlie's warm hand. I moved to the bed's edge where the untouched sheets were cool, dragging my pillow across. The clock's green light glowed 1:13 a.m. Not long after, I felt cold. I pulled the duvet back over me.

Heat surged. Its rush woke me and I kicked off the covers. Soon, the heat had gone, but my nightgown was wet. Sitting up, eyes closed, I took the nightgown off, and then threw my head back down onto the pillow, burying myself in the covers. Charlie pulled me in close.

I could see early light through my closed lids. I felt dampness moisten my skin as I pushed off the bedding, separating my leg from Charlie's thigh. Charlie reached over and grabbed me around the waist, pulling me in tight. "You're sweaty," Charlie breathed in my ear. His hand slipped over my breast. "And topless," he murmured, squeezing my nipple. "What did I miss?"

"In your dreams," I said, wiggling away.

"It's your dreams I want to be in," he said, following me.

"I'm hot," I said, pushing away from him.

"For me?" he asked, awake enough to be hopeful.

"Seriously," I said, rolling to face him. "I think I'm sick."

Charlie opened his eyes. He touched my forehead with his hand. "I don't feel any fever."

"I kept waking up hot and sweaty."

"Will you please, please, please go see the doctor?" Charlie asked.

"You know I hate the doctor."

"Nobody likes the doctor."

I pouted.

"If it was me, you'd insist, so I'm insisting," he said, kissing my nose. "I really mean it now. You would have never let me get away with this."

He was right, I wouldn't have.

"So you'll go?"

I remembered last night's thrashing. Maybe Charlie was right. Maybe it was time.

* * * *

"Excellent," the doctor said, and I saw in his grey eyes a glint of satisfaction as red blood filled the small glass vials. The paper on the examining table crinkled as I shifted on the examining room bed. On the opposite wall, a blown-up photo showed a field of red poppies. I thought of Jay, and of our poppy conversations of years ago.

"You really think it's my thyroid?" I asked, as he released the plastic tie from above my elbow.

"It seems likely," the doctor confirmed. "You've been more tired recently, which could be another symptom."

"When will you know?" I asked as he labeled the blood vials with my details.

"I'll rush the results," he promised.

* * * *

Charlie and I were in our study waiting for the roasting chicken. Charlie was flopped on the leather couch watching basketball. At my desk beside his, I paid bills, shredded junk, replied to invitations, wrote a thank-you note, and filed completed work. While another pencil whirled in the electric sharpener until its point was pin-sharp, I eyed Charlie's desk. Papers, bank statements, books, plans, maps, and reports were amassed and jumbled together in tousled piles, concealing every bit of the desk's wooden surface.

"Don't even think about it," he said, eyes on the basketball game.

"What?"

"Don't touch my desk."

Three unopened envelopes poked out from the bottom of a disheveled pile of papers. At a moment of high tension in the game, I pounced. The letter opener sliced through a sealed envelope before he could protest.

"You have three unpaid parking fines!"

"What?"

"On your desk, under your piles."

"I said not to touch them," he said, irritation tightening his voice.

"Two of the fines have doubled because of late charges!"

"Let me see that," he said, his eyes flitting to me briefly.

I concealed the other correspondence by my side as I passed him the parking letter. Swiveling so that my back was to him, I sliced open the other envelopes. The first suggested the ease of putting our newspaper bill on direct debit. I slipped it on my desk. The second stated that the quarterly marina charges had been due over a month earlier.

"Shit!" said Charlie. "I meant to pay that last Saturday when I was at the boat."

Feeling both vindicated and justified, I slid into his chair and began swiftly collecting like papers into bundles. It took him a minute to clock what I was doing, because the game was nearly finished. The sport commentator's voice was electrified with the excitement of the concluding crescendo.

"Stop it!"

"But there might be more unpaid bills," I protested, picking up the pace before Charlie could shut me down.

"Stop it!"

"He shoots. . ." screamed the announcer.

I grabbed the last loose sheets.

"He scores. . ."

"Ah ha!" Under a map was the unopened invitation to his parent's 30th anniversary party. Charlie had told his Mom it hadn't arrived.

"What a rout!" the jubilant anchorman cried. Fans hailed, and horns blared. Charlie clicked off the TV. Now that his full attention had shifted to me, annoyance hardened his face. I jumped out of the seat, tapping the last of his papers into an aligned, crisp pile.

"Better isn't it?" I said cheerfully, gesturing to the orderly papers, wooden desk gleaming beneath. He was not amused. Before he could tear into me, I waved his Mom's invite at him. "Look, here it is!" Keeping my distance, I tossed it in his direction. The kitchen buzzer sounded. I quickly moved to the door.

"You should call your Mom to tell her the invite's arrived," I said from the safety of the door well.

His eyes flashed, but as I continued to retreat, I saw him cut open the invite with my ready letter opener. While I carved chicken breast into thin, steaming slices, I heard Charlie talking to his mom. He told her how much he liked the invitation. He reassured her that she could now stop worrying about whether the other guests' invitations had arrived. "Jill's looking at it now," Charlie told her, as he held out the invitation for me to see. Simple black lettering gleamed from a tasteful cream card. At the bottom was a masterful etching of their Maine barn.

"Tell her it's beautiful, especially her etching."

"She says it's beautiful," Charlie conveyed, reaching over my shoulder to tear off golden skin glistening with fat. He popped it in his mouth. I prodded him with my carving fork when he reached to rip more off. "Stop defacing the chicken," I mouthed.

"Jill found it," he admitted. "On my desk."

I beamed.

"Yes, it was a tip," Charlie confessed.

I wiggled my shoulders triumphantly. Charlie retaliated by snatching another swath of skin. He stuffed it in his mouth before I could seize it back. Charlie's eyes gleamed cheekily. I couldn't help but laugh.

"Jill gets the blood tests tomorrow," Charlie continued.

"You told your mother?" I mouthed.

Covering the phone, Charlie said, "She asked how you were when she called about the invite this morning."

"The doctor thinks it's her thyroid," he continued. "I'll tell her you're thinking of her."

* * * *

The next morning, mixed with the scent of hyacinths was a riot of bright colours bouncing off the Garden patio. The previous fall, a sale on bulbs had seduced me, and I had bought more than I'd intended. I had started planting them in tidy patterned rows: pinks, purples, and then whites. The next day, with two sacks still to go, I convinced Charlie to help. He had sworn that he had pretty much kept to my scheme, although I should have been suspicious. When I had gone in for a business call, he had finished both bags in a surprisingly short period. It was clear now that he had planted them every which way, and every which where. The effect was chaotic colour demarcated occasionally by my ordered lines. As the full extent of his transgression had been exposed over the last few weeks, I had assumed a position of outrage countered by his cheery amusement.

My phone vibrated. I removed it from my pocket. It was the doctor.

"The results show that you have premature ovarian failure," he said briskly.

"Ovarian failure?" I repeated, setting my near empty tea cup on the closest table.

"At your age, the symptoms are quite easily managed through HRT."

"HRT?"

"Hormone replacement therapy."

"You mean I've started menopause?"

"In broad essence, yes."

"But I'm only 30. What about all the other tests? I thought you thought it was my thyroid?"

"Your other stats came out entirely normal. Otherwise, you're in perfect health. Why don't you come in and we'll talk. I'm sure there is a lot you'll want to ask. Were you planning to have children?"

"No," I said quickly. My stomach constricted.

"That makes it a lot easier. Come in on Monday. Then we can discuss everything more fully."

I clicked off the phone after making the appointment with his secretary. Next to the table, lemon balm grew. I crushed its leaves between my fingers, inhaling the citrus green scent. I had gotten used to the idea it was my thyroid, but ovarian failure – how was that possible?

I dialed Charlie's number. "I'm in menopause," I said by way of a greeting.

"You're on speaker," he answered.

"Shit." Embarrassment seared.

"You're off, but I've got six people round my desk. I thought you were Peter."

"Shit."

"Can I call you back?"

I hung up.

In Susie's time zone, it was a little before five. I twisted my turquoise bracelet around my wrist as the phone rang. It took five rings before she answered. Her voice was thick with sleep as if she were talking through cake batter. "Did I wake you?"

"Jill?"

"I *did* wake you," I said.

"What the fuck?"

I smiled, despite my agitation. "I'm in menopause."

"You're what?" Already, her voice was clearer.

"The doctor says I have unexplained premature ovarian failure."

"Are you sure?"

"The doctor did the tests yesterday. He wants me to go on HRT."

"HRT?"

"He says it will help mitigate the symptoms."

"HRT has risks."

"How do you know?"

"I wrote an article on it."

"That's what the doctor is recommending."

"Probably because you are so young."

"Why would I want to go on it if it has risks?"

"Well there are the hot flushes. Have you had any?"

"Yes," I admitted.

"Without your hormones you are at risk of experiencing loss of mental acuity, deteriorating skin elasticity, vaginal dryness and an increased likelihood of osteoporosis."

"Are you serious?

"Not pretty, is it?"

"No," I said, reeling.

"Does Charlie know?"

I told Susie about my call with Charlie.

"If Charlie is smart, you'll be getting flowers tonight."

I imagined deep purple tulips.

"I'll tell you one thing," Susie said, her voice teasing, "There are great lubrication products out there."

"How do you know?"

"Bob and I checked them out as part of my research."

"Some research."

"They even have chocolate and strawberry flavour. Bob calls those the munch and punchers."

"Punchers?"

"You know, punch it in there."

"Oh, yuck."

Susie laughed. In the background, I heard a child cry.

"Shoot! That's Antonia. She has a bug and has been up all night. I better go. Call me later?"

"All right," I told her.

Children, I thought as I clicked the phone shut. I didn't want children, yet this sudden elimination of the possibility made my stomach turn. I couldn't believe there was something actually wrong with me; I never got sick. Deep down, I hadn't even believed I had a problem with my thyroid. I'd thought it was some funky virus that would just require a couple of days rest. I had even looked forward to a movie fest, with Charlie bringing me delicious snacks on a tray thoughtfully embellished with a single rose in a cut-glass bud vase.

A bird sang *dee diddly dee diddly*. As I looked up to see, I found sun falling like stippled water through high branches. The soft wind rustled leaves like whispering music. Children – the word repeated in my head like a siren, sounding louder than the leaves. I smeared more lemon balm between my fingers. I breathed it in deeply, trying to calm my sinking heart. I was fine, I told myself. It was fine. Nothing had changed. Yet sadness flooded me unexpectedly, wholly, without reason.

59

DIDN'T KNOW

"Women in menopause are dangerous. . ." I read to Charlie that night from Christiane Northrup's *Women's Bodies, Women's Wisdom.*

"Dangerous?" Charlie asked, his eyebrows raised, amused. We were lying in bed, Charlie in t-shirt and boxers, and I wearing one of his t-shirts and blue bikini underwear. I rested my head on his stomach. His digestive tract gurgled with food while he read a science magazine.

"Dangerous," I continued dramatically. "Dangerous to any accommodations she has made that are stifling who she is now capable of becoming."

I paused meaningfully.

"Are you suggesting I am an accommodation?"

"She scrutinizes," I continued without answering, "every aspect of her life and her relationships in an effort to eradicate any dead wood that no longer serves who she will become."

"Are you telling me I'm dead wood?"

I went on. "Menopause provides the next level of initiation into the personal power of women, an opportunity to discover a freer, deeper experience of herself."

Charlie put down his magazine and read along with me.

"But our cultural bias suggests that without hormones we lose our attractiveness to men. . ."

"No danger of that," Charlie breathed, slipping his hand into my shirt through my collar hole. I swatted it away.

". . . that we'll dry up, like cracked, parched earth."

"Shall I see if you're dry?"

I hit my head against his belly. Under my head, his stomach muscles tightened.

"If we throw off these cultural biases, then we can truly prepare for the springtime of the second half of our lives."

I looked up. "That's just great," I said, feeling close to tears. "Just last week, I was in the first half of my life, and today I am in the fucking springtime of my second. And get this: 'menopause can last as long as thirteen years!'"

"Thirteen years?" A fleeting look of alarm passed across Charlie's face.

The truth was I had been a nightmare these last few days. Even the flowers that he had brought home after our telephone call didn't assuage my emotion. When he told me it was going to be all right, I told him he was belittling my feelings. When he said that he understood I needed to be sad, I answered that he was doing nothing to make me feel better.

"I'm going to be a dried-up emotional wreck for the next thirteen years."

"Give me that book," Charlie said, pulling it from my hands and dropping it on the floor. He pulled me up so that my head was now on his chest. "You are not in the second half of your life."

I took up a *Nutrition for Life*, and flipped through the pages: "Nutrition for the Puberty Years," "Young and Active," "Child Bearing," "Breast Feeding," "Life on the Go," "Menopause." I turned the page: "The Golden Years." Tears came again. "You see? I am one fucking page away from the Golden Years."

"What are you talking about?"

"I thought I was here," I said, pointing to the Young and Active page, "but instead I'm here, one page away from old age."

"Jesus, Jill," he said, taking this book from me too. "Don't be ridiculous."

"Without hormones I'm going to lose bone strength, skin elasticity, vaginal lubrication, mental acuity."

"Which book says that?"

"Susie."

He rolled his eyes.

"It's true," I insisted. "She wrote an article about it."

Charlie laughed.

"God, I feel depressed."

"Don't be depressed."

"Don't tell me not to be depressed!"

"Darling!" Charlie's laughter was tender.

"I know. It's just that. . ."

"What?"

"I can't have a baby."

Charlie shifted, raising himself up on his elbow so that he could look into my eyes. I felt suddenly uneasy about his reaction.

"You don't want a baby."

"I know, I didn't, I don't, but the fact that now I can't makes me feel as if maybe I've made a mistake."

Charlie shifted his gaze away as he processed what I had said. "Is it really too late?" he asked finally.

"I don't know, but I'd guess it's not looking too good."

Charlie was quiet, thinking.

"Would you have wanted kids?" I asked him.

After a while, he spoke carefully. "Truthfully, yes," he said.

My stomach lurched.

"Hey," he said, stroking my cheek. "I love you. When I decided I wanted to marry you, I accepted how you felt."

"Why didn't you tell me?"

"If you had had kids just for me, you might have felt trapped."

"But we could have talked about it," I whispered. My brimming tears threatening to spill.

My hurt reflected in Charlie's deep brown eyes, mixing with his own. "Did you really not know?"

Of course, Charlie would have wanted to be a dad. I closed my eyes. I saw him again, singing Tabitha to sleep. I felt horrible.

"I would have had a child for you."

Resoluteness made his sadness harden. "You can't have a child for me. We both need to want the child. A child is not a favour you do for somebody."

"It wouldn't have been a favour. That's a terrible thing to say." Tears stung. "If we'd only talked about it."

"We talked about it before we got married."

"You didn't tell me you wanted a baby."

"That's because we talked about why you never did." His voice grew tender. "When you told me you didn't want kids on the rock in the flower valley, it didn't change how I felt about you. I still wanted to marry you more than anything. I was afraid that if you knew I wanted kids, and you knew you wouldn't give them to me, you would have turned me down."

"Oh, Charlie."

Could he really have loved me so much that he'd give up being a father? What had I given up?

"I'm so sorry."

"I have you. It's more than enough."

I started to cry. Charlie held me while I sobbed and sobbed.

60

AT LEAST TRY

"What if we were to *try* to have a child?" I asked Charlie on Saturday morning. Coffee scents lingered with the smell of cheese and chive omelettes.

Charlie turned to face me, leaning back against the sink. He had gone for a long run and still wore a torn t-shirt and his favourite loose-fitting, blue sweat bottoms. "I thought we couldn't."

"There is some chance over the next few months that my FSH levels will normalize for a while. Otherwise we could try in vitro."

"You really want a baby that much?"

I set the coffee on the table, but still held it with my hands. "I do."

"Why now? Why all of a sudden?"

I bit the inside of my lip. It was so hard to explain. "I feel like something has been taken away from me. If I don't have a baby, I feel I'll regret it."

Charlie bobbed his head slightly as he did when he was really listening.

"Why didn't you tell me you wanted a baby?" I felt angry at him. His look said it all.

"But you'd be happier with a child."

"I can't promise I'd be happier with a child," he said. "What if the child were born with severe birth defects? What if a child made you unhappy? What if a child made us drift apart?"

"We'd never drift apart!"

"What if we started having a lot less sex?" he asked, eyes gleaming.

It wasn't funny. I slugged his shoulder. "I'm serious."

"I know you are, but so am I."

"What if it was the best thing that ever happened to us?"

"Then that would be great, but we can't spend life mourning paths we didn't take."

"But you want a baby."

"You can't have a baby for me."

"I wouldn't be just for you. It would be for us."

"What about your brother?"

I spoke slowly. "Spending all my life being paralyzed about what happened to him, or about what could happen to another baby is not how I want to live my life."

"Wow," Charlie said, crossing his arms across his chest. "You *have* been thinking."

"I lost my brother. Now it feels like I have lost this baby too."

"But there hasn't been a baby to lose," Charlie gently protested.

"It's not the way it feels."

"Hey," Charlie said, coming to me. He opened my palms, setting the coffee aside. He traced the brown, curved indent of my life line, riding it up the raised ridge of my vein. His whispery touch tickled as it traveled. Suddenly I yearned for him, and he felt my need. His arm arced clear a space on the table. He gently lifted me and laid me back. I wrapped my legs around his waist.

"I'd love to have a baby," he said quietly afterwards, holding my face between his hands. He added what I knew he had to say, "but it might be. . ." he hesitated.

"Too late," I finished.

His smile blended tenderness with pain.

"We could try in vitro," I said.

Charlie's every instinct was to hate the idea. "You really want to go there?"

I nodded.

He closed his eyes and when he reopened them, I knew he would say yes.

"I love you so much," I said when he assented.

"Of course you do," he said, his eyes crinkling.

I squeezed him hard, my nails digging playfully into his bare bottom.

"Vixen!" he said, sweeping me off the table and setting me back on my chair. He reached down to raise his sweat bottoms, dropped unceremoniously at his ankles.

"I'm so glad it's Saturday," I sighed, my hands curling back around my still warm cup.

"Even better, a Saturday with no plans," Charlie said, as he wandered over to his piano. He played a song composed for me for which there were no lyrics. I had many songs, some jaunty; some ditties with silly words. This soared, quieted, ascended again. Charlie worked his mouth as he played, and his head rolled from side to side, as if he listened first with one ear and then the other. I wondered what he was saying. I had little musical imagination. Charlie found this funny, but sometimes also sad.

As I listened, I thought of my hyacinths. Later I would fill vases to scatter in the house. The roses also needed tying on the trellis, and weeds choked the vegetable garden.

Charlie stopped abruptly. Discomfort pinched his face. He ran his hand over his brow and across his eyes.

"Have you made the appointment with the ophthalmologist?" I asked.

"Not yet."

I came to massage his temples and scalp. "You know you can wear contacts," I said as he relaxed under my touch. "It doesn't mean you have to wear glasses."

"It's not about the glasses."

"Mmmm…"

"Let's watch a movie," Charlie suggested suddenly.

"Now?"

"Why not?"

We never watched movies in the morning. Mornings were for doing things.

"Hitchcock," he enticed.

I loved Hitchcock. How hedonistic, I thought, and how exactly what I wanted.

61

ANNIVERSARY

I inhaled deeply and threw the tennis ball up. It hit the net, but the second serve was good. Charlie batted it back easily, forcing from me from one side of the court to the other. Worse, than that, he was smiling. I saw an opening, tapped the ball softly, drawing him forward. I returned his shot high, over his head, and as he scrambled back, he tripped.

"My point," I said. Before he was in position, I served again, narrowly missing him. "My point again," I called. My satisfaction was not diminished by the cheating. I went again, but by now he was ready, and he hit it back so fast and hard that I had no chance to get near it.

"My game," he countered cheerfully. "In fact, I think they're all my games."

I scowled.

"You played well," Charlie consoled, coming to my side of the net and draping an arm around my shoulder.

"I lost every time!"

Charlie looked fresh, his faded white polo barely moist. "Yeah, but today I played harder."

I considered him with disgust.

He laughed. "Come on, I'll buy you a drink."

"Lunch at Alfredo's. It is our anniversary."

"So it is, Mrs Eaton, so it is."

* * * *

It was hard to believe that we had been married for six years. It seemed that our wedding had just taken place. Maybe that was the problem. Time had been passing me by, and I hadn't been keeping up with it. I had been so happy, so caught up in work and Charlie that I had forgotten to look ahead. I never neglected time when it came to work. I had new product lines in design a year or more from production, yet it had not occurred to me to revisit the idea of having a baby. If Charlie had just brought it up, I would have been happy to talk about it. Why hadn't he said anything? Today, at least, we had thought to stop time.

Perhaps it was my body in charge. Babies were now accosting me everywhere. Two nights before, I had dreamed my baby had slipped under the bath water; I kept trying to reach it but I couldn't. I awoke, heart pounding. I soon realized that the dream had been based on a scene in a Chinese movie we had seen the night before. However, the terror of the dream had lingered.

"A penny for your thoughts?" Charlie asked, glancing at me as he drove.

We were passing the military cemetery. Quickly, I sucked in air to hold as I did each time we drove by it. I pointed to burial ground.

"So?" asked Charlie again, as I exhaled noisily.

I hesitated. It wasn't like me not to tell Charlie what I had been thinking, but our meeting with the doctor had not been encouraging. His description of hormone injections, of anesthetized egg removals, and of the quite slim chance of our success was enough for Charlie to reject the idea outright. I could see it in his eyes as the doctor was talking. I was afraid he might now shut down the conversation before it could get started. Charlie wasn't one to dwell on what could have been. Nor was he one to engage in a lot of artificial medical technology for something that should have happened naturally. I thought he might be more open to the idea of donor eggs, but I still wanted to try my eggs before using another's.

"Nothing much," I obfuscated.

* * * *

"What are you having?" Charlie asked.

"Pasta Carbonara," I said happily. It was a favourite and I was hungry.

"I'll have the tuna," Charlie said, returning our menus to the server.

Holding hands, we sat quietly. Around us, two tables away, a couple argued, softly, heatedly. The young woman's pinched face looked volatile with emotion. Next to them a fatigued-looking group of older women drank Bloody Marys, laughing loudly. A red-headed guy sat alone, finishing an omelette and reading the paper while a scruffy, cheerful-looking family with young children received their food from the waiter in the corner. The youngest had placed her whole fat fist into her yoghurt bowl, and now happily lapped pink goo from her fingers. The waiter soon brought our champagne. The cork popped. Bubbles fizzed festively, filling our glasses.

"Six amazing years," Charlie said, raising his champagne.

"Six perfect years," I returned, clinking against him.

"You look beautiful," Charlie said.

I rolled my eyes. Charlie said I was beautiful almost every day, often when I felt my most bedraggled. I viewed these compliments sceptically, pulling faces at each individual admiration. However, cumulatively, they had their effect, seeping in like rain into soil, and I felt prettier because of their constancy.

I selected a warm raisin and walnut roll from the woven basket and buttered it thickly as I considered the best way to discuss a baby. Finally, I just launched in. "I'd like to do IVF."

His face took on the same closed-down expression I'd seen by the end of the fertility appointment. "It's such a long shot Jill," Charlie countered.

"I think it's worth it."

"I don't know."

I waited. The best approach with Charlie was always to be patient. If I pushed too hard, Charlie would feel backed into a corner.

Our food arrived. Charlie busied himself grinding pepper over tuna. I twirled creamy pasta around my fork.

"Are you sure this is really about a baby?" he asked finally.

"As opposed to?"

"If not for this ovarian failure, you wouldn't even be thinking about having a baby right now."

"That's not true."

He looked at me steadily, head cocked. His being right annoyed me. Suddenly, his eyes crinkled.

"What?"

"Are you planning to stab me?"

I looked down to see my tightly-gripped knife pointing directly at him. I laughed, but it was a laugh which tears could quickly follow. I stabbed my knife into my pasta so that it embedded vertically.

"Me in effigy?"

It took me a moment to clock what he meant. When I laughed again, this time the tears swelled. I dabbed at my eyes with my napkin.

"Hey," he said, grabbing my hand. "I do understand."

I looked at him questioningly.

"When you thought you didn't want kids, the truth is you hadn't thought it fully through."

I nodded, but that was what was so deeply frustrating. I was 30 for God's sake. At some point, nature would have forced the issue. If my ovarian failure hadn't happened, would I have found myself in this same position at 35? At 40?

"But I have spent a lot of time thinking about what our life will be like without children, and I am really happy with it."

"Really?"

"When I imagine the future, I see lots of sex. . ."

I scowled.

He continued seriously. "Eventually, I would love it if we could sell our businesses. . ."

I looked at him, horrified.

"I'm not talking about right away or anything," Charlie said quickly. "But as it is, we have more money than we'll ever need."

That wasn't the point. I wasn't working for the money.

"What I hope is that someday we could use the skills that we have learned and the money we have earned to make a difference. We could take on the environment, AIDS, education, poverty, or even focus on children. Instead of making a difference to the one or two lives that we created, we could make a difference to thousands. That would be our shared legacy. Not having children gives us a certain flexibility and effectiveness that we wouldn't have as parents."

I was taken aback, but part of me could see what he was saying.

"If you really want to try IVF, I'll support you for a time or two," he continued. "But I don't want you to go at it stubbornly the way you get about things. Pumping yourself full of hormones and fertility drugs isn't healthy, and I'm not willing to put you at risk for some hypothetical child."

"I won't be stubborn," I promised quickly. "I just want to try at least once."

"I know you do. I'm all right with that."

I squeezed his hand. Underneath the table my feet tapped out a quiet jig.

* * * *

On the way back from Alfredo's, we stopped at the store. My phone rang as we pulled into the market parking lot. "Giovanni, hold on a moment can you?" I put him on mute.

"I'll shop," Charlie offered, opening the door.

"We're both traveling this week, so don't get a lot, just something for dinner, fruit, coffee, and milk."

"I've got it," he said, alighting.

"And paper towels and toilet paper."

"I've got it."

"But we don't need anything else."

The shutting car door cut me off.

"Sorry about that Gio," I said. "What are you doing, working on a Sunday?"

Forty minutes later, Charlie returned pushing a laden shopping cart. I jumped from the car indignantly. "What did you get?"

"How did the call go?" he answered cheerfully.

I rifled through a bag. "Why did you buy more yogurts? We have yogurt at home. And sweet and sour marinade?"

"It's for the stir fry tonight."

"You bought three bottles of it."

"Three for two sale," he said happily.

I held up a bag of corn chips as I put the next bag into the trunk.

"Don't you mess with my corn chips," he said.

"And tuna fish? We have tons of tuna fish!"

"Would you stop it," he said sharply, his good humour turning. "Instead of criticizing my every purchase, why don't you try thanking me for shopping while you made your call."

"You're supposed to be the big environmentalist," I shot back, "but your indiscriminate purchasing means that we're going to throw half of this out, as usual, because we'll never get to it before the sell-by date."

Charlie didn't answer. When he was mad, he became quiet. We loaded the rest of the bags in silence. As we drove home, he didn't even turn on music. I began to feel bad. I heard Susie in my head: "Guys are quantity shoppers. They can't help themselves. It's their hunter-gather nature. Like sex. A basic instinct."

I smiled. Charlie glanced at me.

"Thank you for shopping," I said.

"Humph," he grunted.

"Thanks for lunch, too. I'm having a great anniversary."

"Grumph," he said again, but he reached to turn on the music. Rolling Stones: *You Don't Always Get What You Want* came on. Figures, I thought, but reached over and cranked up the volume.

62

MOM

Jay sat on the floor of the bedroom he had shared with Mom, surrounded by piles of her clothes folded into tidy, exact piles. Empty black garbage bags yawned before him like gaping mouths. Pain made Jay's face raw. His eyes had a wild look. He did not sense me watching at the door.

Recently, it seemed that Jay's sadness had grown worse. Maria said that as soon as I left for school, Jay would be in the mountains, running for hours. Susie thought that Jay had put part of his hurt at bay in order to help me through Mom's death. Sometimes now I felt he went into the blackness of it willingly. The week before I had found him ripping up piles of Antarctica pictures. A great mound of shredded photographs spilled around him like confetti. That night I had led him far up into the mountains, where we walked for hours.

"Jay?"

It took his eyes a second to actually see me.

"What are you doing?"

"It's time to give away your Mom's things."

I came closer. "Why?"

"Because there are people out there who have little to wear."

I looked at the piles. I recognized every piece of clothing, even the socks. I picked up a green paisley shirt. She had worn it at my parent-teacher conference with her long, green feather earrings. After, we had gone to get Japanese food. She had been cross with herself when she spilt a little soy sauce down its front. I looked closely. The stain was still there, barely visible. I brought the shirt close to my face. Mom's vanilla scent barely clung.

I leaned my head against Jay's shoulder. He took my hand. We looked at her stacked, spilled clothes.

"You ok?" I asked gently.

"Yeah," he said.

"You don't seem ok," I said cautiously.

From my peripheral vision, I could see Jay thinking about this.

"What if the pain is just too big?" I asked him.

Jay smiled ruefully. "We have to just keep feeling it. What else can we do?"

We sat in silence. After a long while Jay asked, "Can you help me pack up?"

"Can I keep some things?"

"You keep anything you want."

Later that night, my period started. I went to call Susie but remembered she was away at a writing workshop. I thought about who else I could call, but no one else felt right – not Susie's mother, not Maria, no one. I locked the bathroom door. From its hiding place, I slipped out the brown paper bag. Following the instruction sheet, I attached a pad to my pants. On my bed, I curled up under my covers, clutching Lionel close.

63

BUSINESS

The sound of Charlie's piano greeted me at the door. I listened, trying to determine what Charlie was feeling from his sound. Sun from the stained glass skylight washed colour across the floor, and I lingered in the vivid light as I kicked off my shoes and scanned the mail. The light made me think of sprites the same way bay leaves evoked elves and soil.

A savoury smell met me as I walked with the mail down the hall. I sniffed deeply – chili! What was Charlie doing making chili on a work day? Charlie was so lost in his music that he didn't hear me come behind him. I wrapped my arms around him; he tensed, but instantly calmed, never breaking his playing. Only when I bit him on the ear did he reach around to pull me on his lap.

"How was your day?" he asked.

"More to the point, how was yours?"

"Full of news."

"Tell me."

"Over dinner. You hungry?"

"Starving."

"Chili."

"How did you have time to make chili today?"

"I came home at 1:00."

"1:00! Did you lose the Norwegian contract?"

Charlie laughed. "There's a vote of confidence."

"What's going on?"

"Come sit down," he said, pulling me by the hand toward the table. I watched as Charlie ladled steaming chili on baked potatoes.

Beefy aromas rose with the steam. A large leafy green salad rested between our plates. I sprinkled my chili amply with cheddar cheese. I had only had an apple at lunch.

Charlie sat down opposite me, also reaching for the cheese. He smiled. He was enjoying the suspense.

"Tell me."

"EnviroOptions made an offer to buy Wind Alternatives. It may be too good to refuse."

My fork suspended mid-bite. "You're kidding."

"I'm not," Charlie said, tasting a big bite of chili. "Pepper," he decided. Taking the wooden grinder from the table, he peppered both our plates.

"Are you going to sell?"

"Tim wants too. If I don't, I think I'll have to buy him out."

I studied Charlie's face. "But you don't want to sell, do you?"

"I'm conflicted," he admitted. "Giving control of Wind Alternatives to someone else seems unimaginable. On the other hand, they're offering $40 a share."

"$40!"

"Exactly," said Charlie, watching me do the mental calculations. It was too good not to consider.

"They want Tim and me to stay on for at least eighteen months, although what they really want is for us to keep running it."

"Why would you do that?"

"Exactly."

Charlie dropped a big dollop of sour cream on top of his chili.

"Selling Wind Alternatives would give me more money than I could ever want. Maybe I could use part of it to fund that charity we talked about. Maybe it's time to start giving back."

"But. . ."

Charlie reached to take my hand, stopping my protest before it started. "I'm not asking you to sell and I won't. Just because I'm thinking about a change doesn't mean you have to change too."

"I'm not ready."

"I know that."

"I might not be ready for a long time."

"I know that too."

"I might not be ready to quit ever."

Charlie laughed. "You can run that company until you're a hundred, if that's what you really want."

"I just feel a little blind-sided."

"You're telling me," Charlie said.

We looked at each other. I searched his eyes.

"You're going to do this," I said.

He nodded. "I think so."

I tried to smile, but all I had known of my life with Charlie were the rhythms that were set by our work. What would it be like when Charlie changed?

"What are you thinking?" Charlie asked.

"Nothing."

"That's a lot of nothing in your eyes."

"I'm just trying to imagining you not working," I admitted.

"My not working is at least two years away."

"What if we had a baby?"

"That'd be great," he said, taking a big bite of salad.

"But would you take care of it?"

"You mean be a stay-at-home dad?"

I blushed.

Charlie laughed. "We'll figure it out. If we are so lucky, we'll figure that part out just fine."

64

TECHNICALITY

I awoke before the alarm. Charlie breathed evenly into my ear. I stretched to press my full body against his. I started my fertility treatment that morning.

"You awake?" he mumbled, his voice still thick with sleep.

"Mmmm," I said.

"Don't go," he said, tightening his grasp.

"I've got to," I said, loosening myself from his grasp and pushing myself up. Charlie propped himself up too, rubbing his temple.

"Do you still have your headache?" I asked.

"These four-hour sleep nights are killing me," he complained as I leaned on his shoulder. I switched on the news. We both listened drowsily, he waiting for sports, I for weather. Tired, I slipped lower under the covers and rested my head on his chest. He caressed my hair with his hand, and then farted loudly.

"You're repellent," I said, yanking the pillow from under his head and turning away from him and the emerging smell. He laughed, following me to spoon.

"Do you go back to the lawyers this morning?"

"Yeah, we have to give final comments on the purchase contract."

The idea of Charlie selling his company continued to unsettle me. It was the end of an era that I didn't want it to end.

"We're getting old," I worried.

"We are not getting old. We're becoming different."

"I like the way things are."

Charlie pulled my head to him so that he could see my face. "Are you nervous about this morning?"

"A bit," I admitted.

* * * *

I entered the IVF clinic elevator bank at 7:10, intent on being the first to see the doctor. Women already filled the waiting room.

"Goodness," I told the receptionist, "I thought I'd be first."

"If you want to be first," she said plainly, "you queue before we open."

Dismayed, I looked around the packed room.

"It'll move fast," she assured me. "We process quickly."

I unfolded the morning paper. From behind its screen, I surveyed the other women. Like me, most were dressed in office wear, briefcases by their feet. Many also read the news. Some studied documents. The woman next to me surveyed her diary. She had a breakfast at 8:45, a lunch at 12:30 and two afternoon meetings, but I couldn't tell from any of it what she did exactly. Most women seemed to be older than me. The woman across was obese, her thighs bulging inside beige polyester. A low-cut clinging top revealed mounds of breast. She looked decidedly groggy; I guessed that it took several of those extra-large coffees she was drinking just to get her going in the morning. I wondered if her weight affected her ability to become pregnant.

As I waited, women continued to stream in. Soon they leaned against free spots on the wall. The receptionist was right; others moved quickly into the clinic. Those who had finished re-emerged, eyes down, hurrying to the exit door. I found the numbers depressing. The clinic felt like a factory. I wondered about their selection criterion. Surely there couldn't really be this many women who couldn't have babies naturally. Then again, I thought dejectedly, if the program had been more selective, I probably wouldn't have made the cut. Whatever their problems, I doubted many women struggled with early menopause.

"Excuse me," said a woman with a too-loud voice. All eyes turned to the door. A short, hard-faced woman spoke over her large, old-fashioned baby carriage. She had manoeuvred the stroller to the reception desk, where she asked, "Is the wait long?"

"About nineteen people ahead of you," responded the receptionist quietly.

"Maybe I should be seen earlier. The baby?" Her loud whisper rose pointedly. The receptionist was unmoved.

"Baby will have to take its turn with everyone else."

The mother's lips pursed as she signed at the bottom of the list. After, she searched for a chair. Eyes dropped, as if no one had been watching. The woman wheeled her stroller along the seats, although it was clear that no spots were available.

"Would you like my seat?" a lady diagonally across from me offered, standing up.

Once seated, the woman leaned over her stroller. "Is Mama's little girl hungry?" she cooed, lifting the completely pink-dressed bundle from the stroller. Every woman in the room looked at that baby.

"Jill."

I was slow to react.

"Jill Easton?" The nurse repeated more loudly.

Flustered, I gathered my briefcase and purse, dropping my paper as I stood.

"First day?" the nurse asked as I sat where she indicated.

"Yes."

"Until we harvest your eggs, one day's pretty much like the rest. You come here for blood work, and then go in for an internal."

I tried to smile.

"Arm please. Fist."

I put my arm up on the rest.

She pulled an elastic tight above my elbow, disinfected my vein. "Start your meds tonight?"

"Yes."

She stabbed me quickly. My arm jerked a little, but the spot was optimal, and blood began flowing into the vial. "Unclench. You're dehydrated," she said pleasantly.

"Dehydrated?"

"Your blood's running slow. Make sure you drink before you come in tomorrow."

"When?" I asked.

The nurse extracted the needle, discarding it into a red hazard bin. She plastered my puncture.

"In the morning. You can even drink in the waiting room if you like."

"It works that quickly?"

"That quick," she said, sticking pre-printed labels onto my blood vials. "Room five," she said, standing. "Undress from the waist down. There's a paper sheet for cover. Place your feet in the stirrups."

* * * *

I had just spread the paper sheet over my nakedness when a knock at the door sounded. Before I could answer, two doctors entered.

"How are you today?" my doctor said cheerfully.

"Fine," I lied.

Dr. Rogers snapped on rubber gloves as he introduced Dr. Savoy. Dr. Rogers handed him back the probe. "Little more gel on that," he said to the younger doctor. The doctor squeezed more K-Y jelly on top of the white plastic stick. "It's his first day on OB," he said to me conversationally. "Legs open wider. That's it." Dr. Savoy was now staring at my vagina.

"Just relax," Dr. Roger instructed. He began pushing the probe one way, then the other. It hurt. The picture on the sonogram changed as he moved. He stopped to click pictures. Then he retracted the probe and handed it to Dr Savoy, who removed the protective condom. "Looks good," he informed me. "Any questions?"

"When will I see a response to the drugs?"

"About a week."

"But you're sure I'll respond, right?"

"We're hoping so," he said cheerfully. "We'll take another look tomorrow."

At this comment, Dr Savoy looked again. When he looked up, I caught his eye. His expression was professional, friendly.

* * * *

"Ready?" Charlie asked, the hormone-filled syringe poised. Charlie held the syringe like a murder might grasp a knife.

Standing in a t-shirt and underwear, I considered him warily. Until the doctors harvested my eggs, I had to have these shots daily. "I guess."

Charlie swung the needle.

"Wait!" I cried, jumping back.

Charlie paused mid-plunge. "What?"

I could feel sweat on my forehead. "Go slowly!"

Charlie slowed his movement, but the needle still looked menacing.

"Don't!" I said, flinching backwards.

"Jill," Charlie comforted. "It's not going to hurt."

"Of course it'll hurt!" Irritation prickled.

"Just think when a doctor gives you a shot. Those don't really hurt."

"They do! Besides. . ." It was one unpleasant thing to have a highly trained doctor inject me; it felt a totally different, and terrifying to have Charlie do it.

"Besides what?"

"I think it would be better if I just did it myself."

"I don't know if that's a good idea."

"Give me that."

Charlie held the syringe forward. I wiped my sweaty palms on my leg before reaching to take it.

"Stop!" said Charlie severely.

"What?"

"Now we need to disinfect your leg again." Charlie went to wipe my leg again with alcohol. I grabbed the swab. "I'll do it."

"Fine," he said, his voice growing tense.

As the needle approached my re-disinfected skin, my hand began to shake. I forced myself to continue, but my hand was shaking so much that when the needle got close it scratched. "Shit," I said, jerking. The dropped needle rolled under the commode.

"Jesus, Jill," said Charlie.

"Would you just stop!" He was making this so much worse. I picked up the needle and was going to quickly plunge it in before I could change my mind, but Charlie grabbed my hand.

"Are you insane? You'll get an infection that way!" He pulled the needle from me, pouring alcohol directly on the needle as he held it over the sink. "I'm not liking this whole IVF thing," he said, his voice hardening.

"What do you have not to like? It's me doing it, not you," I shot back.

A mixture of emotions crossed Charlie's face; I could see he had a lot to say, none of which I wanted to hear.

"I'm sorry," I said, trying hard to calm down. "You're just making me more nervous. Can you go?"

"Go?" Hurt cut into his eyes.

"Please? I think it will be easier that way."

As soon as he was gone, I collapsed on the bathroom floor, supressed tears falling. "Fuck," I thought, wiping at my eyes. "Fuck, fuck, fuck."

A moment later, Charlie tapped. "It's Susie."

I opened the door just enough so that he could hand the phone in. I took the phone without looking at him, and then immediately re-locked the door.

"I'm so unhappy," I cried.

"I know."

"I have to shoot myself up with scary-sounding drugs to try for a baby that I probably have no fucking chance of getting."

"That about sums it up," said Susie matter-of-factly.

"You're comforting," I said, laughing despite my upset.

"Want to quit?"

"No."

"Then let's just do this, all right." Her voice was take-charge, reassuring. "Are all the needles full?"

"One."

"Put me on speaker and then fill the rest."

"What hurts most is breaking the skin," Susie instructed as I readied. "Once the needle is through, it doesn't sting as long as you stay still."

I looked at the phone disbelievingly. "Who told you that?"

"I just know."

"How do you know?"

"Just do it," she insisted.

"Now?"

"No, next Wednesday."

I eased the needle until it rested against my skin. I pressed.

"Hurt."

"Push."

"Hurt."

"Push!"

"Did."

"Now squeeze in the stuff."

"Did."

I could hear Susie breathe out.

"Pull it out."

"Out."

"Drop it. Grab the next."

Finally, the two syringes lay empty on the floor. I felt nauseous from strain.

"What am I doing?" I asked unhappily.

"Having a baby."

"But..."

"Don't even go there. Not right now. Go watch a Bogart."

"Bogart sounds good," I admitted.

"Bogart's always good," Susie assured me.

"I couldn't have done it without you," I told the phone, nodding even though she couldn't see me.

"You could have, but poor Charlie was so worried that I figured I'd better talk you through it just to calm him down."

"Really?"

"Where is poor Charlie?"

"Charlie?" I called.

"I'm here," he said from the other side of the door.

* * * *

Charlie was waiting, his back to the wall, facing the door. I went to him and laid my head down in his lap. "Thanks," I said, indicating the phone.

"Did you?"

"Yes."

I could hear him exhale in relief.

"I'm sorry about before."

"Nothing to be sorry about," he said, stroking my hair.

From where my head lay in his lap, I could see one of the discarded needles.

"I wish we could just make a baby the natural way."

"Oh, my love," he said. "We've made hundreds of babies; thousands of them. This is nothing but a technicality."

65

PREGNANT

The operating theatre was brightly lit. In its center, a bed with metal stirrups waited empty, flanked by a sonogram machine glowing grey. Next to it, metal instruments covered a sterile green cloth spread across a shiny metal tray.

"If you could slip your feet into the stirrups now," the nurse instructed. Examining the area between my legs, she requested, "Scoot down please." I eased down toward the end of the bed. She had another good look. "Perfect!" she said, smiling brightly. "Everything's all lined up."

I could hear the doctors entering behind me as I stared up at the bug-eyed operating lights. Masked and gloved, they chatted first between themselves, and then to me, as they readied my operation. "You might feel nauseous when you wake up after the egg harvest," the anaesthesiologist was telling me. Dr. Rogers added, "If you do, one of the attending interns will give you medication."

A plastic mask came down on my face. I felt rising panic.

"You can start counting," the anaesthetist said. I was cornered. I had to get out.

"Start counting," he repeated. I moved to lean forward, but his hand pressed on my shoulder.

"Two," he said, saying the numbers for me.

I tried to tell him to stop.

"Three. . ."

And I went under.

****

"As good a batch as we could have hoped for," Dr. Rogers informed Charlie. My harvested eggs were now fertilized with Charlie's semen and had begun to divide inside the petri dishes. Now it was time to put them back. I felt exposed despite the white sheet between my splayed legs. Having Charlie in the room made my nakedness feel less clinical, particularly as I knew that Charlie was all too aware of the two male doctors.

"We have four eight-cell and two six-cell embryos."

"You're putting six back?" Charlie asked, taken aback.

"It's not uncommon at all," said Dr. Savoy, standing in the corner.

Almost imperceptibly, Charlie stiffened.

"The number of embryos returned is your choice, but given your wife's fertility profile, we would recommend putting at least a minimum of three back."

"If Jill became pregnant with six, her health could be at risk," Charlie argued.

We had agreed to put them all back. Charlie had agreed, although we hadn't thought there would be six.

"It would be highly unlikely for them all to implant," the doctor explained.

"What if they did?"

Dr. Rogers turned to face Charlie fully. "We would council selective abortion."

My hands went to my stomach. "I wouldn't abort," I said, before I could stop myself.

"Even triplets have greater health risks for both the mother and the babies," the doctor said, his voice neutral.

"What if we don't use all the embryos now?" Charlie asked.

We had talked about all of this.

"You could freeze them."

"Charlie," I said, trying very hard to keep my voice calm. When he looked at me, I told him with my eyes it wasn't fair to re-think this now.

I could tell Charlie wasn't convinced.

"Let's do six," I pleaded, quietly.

I could see counter-arguments marshalling in his eyes.

"Please," I mouthed.

"All right," he agreed against what I knew to be his better judgement. "We'll do all six," he told the doctor.

"Thank you," I whispered when Charlie turned back to me. His brow was creased. I took his hand and squeezed it.

* * * *

"I'm pregnant," I sing-songed to Susie over the phone as I wandered the aisles of the baby store.

"What are you talking about?"

"I might not keep these embryos, but right now they are alive inside me," I told her, stopping in front of an aisle of strollers.

"I have good feeling about this," said Susie, her voice excited.

Suddenly, I was whispering, "So do I. It's like I'm already pregnant. In fact, I *am* pregnant. All the little guys need to do is hang on."

"I guess the more interesting question now is how many?"

"I want two girls."

"Really? Not a boy like John Jay?"

"I'd want two sisters first. But if I had three, then one should definitely be a boy."

"You don't seriously want triplets?"

"I don't know what I want."

"What about work?"

"What do you mean?"

"It would be pretty hard to work with triplets."

"Not necessarily."

"Oh come on Jill. You can't have it all."

"Why not?"

Susie snorted. "Why do you think? Look at me."

"You're still working."

"Not the kind of work that I want to be doing. Not the work that really matters."

"What you write is mattering."

Susie scoffed. "New ideas for school lunches?"

"Studies show that good nutrition is a key factor in securing academic success," I said, quoting roughly from what Susie had written.

"You're keeping our nation competitive by making sure that our children are educated."

"Yeah, right."

"Besides, Charlie might stay home," I proffered, feeling the texture of a pink baby blanket.

"He said that?"

"Yeah," I said.

"So you go off to work and he stays home with the babies?" Susie clarified.

"Yeah."

But I felt not wholly right about that as I said it. Would I really go to work and leave them?

"Wow! Times they are a changing," said Susie.

I shook a little baby rattle. "Yes," I answered. "I guess they really are."

"Come visit," said Susie, suddenly.

"You mean now?"

"Why not? Your goddaughters are desperate to see you, and we haven't been together in an age."

Mentally, I scanned my schedule. I couldn't that week. I had Giovanni coming in.

"What about weekend after next? I can be there just before the pregnancy test."

"We'll all get ready to celebrate together!"

"It sounds so perfect," I said.

66

GIOVANNI

"Rico is farting like a German," said Giovanni as we walked along the beach. Age had made Giovanni more handsome. His angular features had relaxed, become more magnetic, but his physique remained rock hard.

I laughed.

"This is not funny," protested Giovanni theatrically. "The stink of it. Even with the windows open."

"Can't you just put him outside?"

His expression was as if I had told him to pull out Rico's paw nails one by one.

"He has always been in the office with me. Now that he is old and farting, you are saying I am throwing him out?"

"No," I backtracked quickly.

Giovanni's eyes twinkled. He had a comic's gift of animation. "What is making it worse is that the poor dog, his hearing is going too now. He likes lying on my feet now to make sure I am not leaving him." He paused dramatically. "And they're silent. Sssssst," he hissed. "Like gas in the trenches. On his bad days I am wearing my grandpa's gas mask on my head like a hat. When he is letting one go, I am pulling down the mask until the air clears."

The image was too much. I was wiping away tears.

"What can a man do?" he asked, but he was laughing with me.

"So how are you liking married life?" I asked. He had a baby girl who was a month old. He had married in a civil ceremony about three weeks before she was born. When he told me, it had come as a complete surprise.

Giovanni looked out across the sea. It was a still warm day that felt like summer even though it was barely March. We walked the end of the Tide Pool Trail slowly now, knee deep in the cold ocean. The waves lapped like a lake, barely pulling as they withdrew. Long-legged seabirds birds dashed in their wake, seeking crustaceans.

"My baby," he said, his eyes warming. "Already she is the love of my life. Every time I see her, my heart she is filling all the way to the top."

My own heart tugged. Instinctively, my hand went to my belly and I hoped for the millionth time that my own two little girls were growing in there, healthy and strong. Giovanni's face saddened.

"But. . ."

His voice trailed off.

"Your wife?" I asked gently. It had seemed weird to me that he had never mentioned her.

"She is a good woman," he insisted. "She is kind and sweet."

"But?"

"I don't love her, not in this way."

"Then why did you. . . ?"

"The condom broke," he said, cutting me off. "As soon as it happened, I just knew. After all, it was a sin what I was doing – sleeping with her to pass time. I am caring for her yes, but she is not – what did you call it with Charlie?"

"Your soul mate?"

"Yes," he said. "The mate of my soul."

"But that could change."

He shrugged. The sadness in his eyes did not suggest hope.

"But at least now you have a baby."

His eyes immediately sparked. "She is worth it. She is worth everything."

"You are so lucky," I breathed.

"Does this mean that Miss American Businesswoman is finally thinking about being a mama?"

Unexpectedly, tears pricked.

"I am only teasing," he said, and I could already hear the apology in his voice.

I shook my head, wiping at my eyes. "It's not that. It's just. . ."

"Just?"

"I think I left it too long."

"You are only young. How is this possible?"

I told him about the ovarian failure, and the IVF. Then I told him something I had never told anyone, not even Susie.

"After Mom died, I boxed away all my toy animals. I loved those animals as if they were my own children. It hurt so badly to do that, but you see, things come in threes. In my mind I exchanged my toys and having a baby for no one else dying."

A new wave folded in, erasing the spiky footprints of the birds ahead of us on the sand.

"It's not that I still believe that putting away my animals will keep people safe, but it got me in the habit of imagining my life without children. I can't believe I was so stupid."

"But even without the stuffed animals, you are only young. Thirty, yes?"

"Almost thirty-one."

"Do you think you would be having a baby earlier, anyhow?"

I watched three seagulls bobbing gently on the rolling waves. It was a fair point, and who knew the answer?

"Maybe it is not yourself you are really angry at."

"What do you mean?"

Giovanni's smile was wry. "He is not always perfect, is He, our God?"

"No," I admitted.

Giovanni laughed, but it was without malice. "I am also thinking this, but then we are only human, and we can't always hope to be understanding everything."

Sometimes it felt that I understood nothing.

"Still," he said after a bit, "I am feeling your children."

My hand went to my stomach again. "Really?"

Giovanni's eyes went far out across the sea. They stayed there, searching, and I imagined him seeing fractured light flitting off.

"Yes," he said, his voice certain. "I am feeling your children a lot."

That evening I received his faxed sketch. It showed an adult hand holding the hand of a child.

67

GARDEN

My return to the Garden was joyful. I had visited it only once since Susie's return. Jay and Susie mostly came to visit me. The sea restored Jay. When Jay was with me, we spent hours at its shore. Similarly, when Bob traveled, Susie and the girls would often come for a week or more. It gave Susie a break from our mountain's isolation. Even Maria and Fernando were now frequently on the road. Three years earlier Maria had taken it in her mind to visit all the great gardens of Europe. Country by country, she and Fernando crisscrossed roads in rented cars, seeking even the smallest estates. Maria regularly sent pictures of vases, benches, statuary, gazebos, and window boxes she had discovered, while Fernando's Garden water colours now rivalled Mom's. Their research became vibrant inspiration for my new lines. In the course of their journeys, they spent six months in Italy close to Giovanni. His family became another extension of theirs in the way that Maria and Fernando had of adopting people. It led to working with Giovanni to get our new concepts production ready. Our expanding lines meant that there was a deluge of work when the new products were introduced each fall and spring.

While they were gone, the Garden thrived with neglect. Everywhere plants took over like jungle. One room's jasmine intertwined with another's honeysuckle. Flowers spilled across walkways. Ivy snaked up trees and covered statues. Plant debris collected in sheltered corners and under boughs.

"The Garden is beautiful this way," I said to Susie as we swung on John Jay's porch swing. "I like it wild."

"I think Jay does too," Susie told me. "But when Fernando

comes, he can't help himself. He goes mad with pruning."

I laughed, imaging him crazily attacking the overgrowth.

It was in Fernando's nature to restore order. I used to think it was in my nature as well, but realizing that I wanted children had shaken my belief in all the things I had once considered to be at my core. So much had been determined by John Jay and Mom's deaths. To survive, I had put in place all kinds of constructs, like my need for organization. What if those constructs had all been artificial? What if they had only been created because I had no other way of holding myself together? I guessed we were all a sum of our experiences and our reactions to them. In the end, maybe the trick was being able to evolve old paradigms as life went forward, not try to get them right first time out.

After Susie left, I again strolled through the Garden, this time more slowly. Its fragrances made me recall Mom's box of scents. I remembered, too, our old conversations which took on new meaning in the context of now.

Outside Mom's room, I was arrested. Maybe it was the particular way that the coming twilight had intensified all the colours right before darkness would begin draining them away; maybe it was the way that the Rose Arch was thick with flowers, and I was just underneath it, but for what was a suspended moment, I felt with every cell what Jay must have felt the day that he had seen the elk – wondrous, absolute beauty. Seeing the Garden this way made me feel life's poignant fragility, and a deep, humbling gratitude.

At times, mountaineering had also made me feel grateful in this same way. When the rock became hard, when the climb became steep, all of life's confusions and complexities seemed to shed. Chaotic thoughts stilled. I became just the pull and push of hands, just the steady step of feet. When ascending became nothing but hand and foot rhythm, emotional pain worked itself out like cramps easing. Hope eased into the void, making me feel that I would get through the deaths of Mom and Jay, that despite everything I would get out the other side. At the climb's top I always felt a brief moment of exhilaration. That was a wonder for me, especially when death was still so fresh. The feeling of happiness, of wonder – even if it came only for an instant – helped me go on.

I think Jay had found aspects of this same gratitude in the monasteries that he haunted. He had found that – regardless of their faith – some monasteries, some people were the purest manifestation of God's immense goodness. He felt that goodness in the same way that he felt the elk. I sensed that Jay's Nepalese friend Kamala embodied goodness in this way, simply, without dogma. I think it was one of the reasons that Jay felt so devoted to him, and so protective when Kamala's right action put him in the way of harm.

68

CHARLIE

Susie called just as I was drifting off to sleep. On the swing we had discussed the timing of my pregnancy test. Technically, the following morning was the first day that the pregnancy could be detected.

"Surely the test will show if you are pregnant by now, particularly if you're having twins," Susie argued again, as I shifted in bed to get more comfortable.

I had been sorely tempted. The pregnancy test beckoned.

"I feel like I'll jinx it if I go early."

"Mmmm..."

Susie was unsatisfied, but cautious. "What does Charlie say?"

"To be honest, I've barely spoken to him. He's been at the lawyers almost non-stop for the last four days, trying to finalize his company's sale. He arrives here crack of dawn tomorrow."

"Ouch."

"Both he and Tim are totally fried. Charlie's had ceaseless headaches; I think he's been taking Tylenol like candy. He said he was feeling pretty nauseous last time we spoke. He's definitely coming down with something. I think he is barely eating"

"Poor guy."

"Tim on the other hand is averaging about twelve donuts a day."

"Oh, yuck!"

I laughed. "He says the constant sugar drip keeps him thinking."

"He would say that." Tim had a notorious sweet tooth.

"They're supposed to be signing sometime tonight. Hopefully that'll make two reasons to celebrate."

"How are you feeling?"

I ran my hand over my stomach.

"Bloaty."

"And your breasts?"

I circled them with my fingers. "Swollen and tender."

"Good, good, good," said Susie. "That's exactly how they're supposed to feel. It must be twins. I'm certain of it."

"Boys? Girls?" I asked happily.

"That I can't tell you."

"No guesses at all?"

"I'd say a boy and a girl, but that bit's just guessing."

"As opposed to knowing the twin bit?"

"I'm telling you."

I laughed. "As long as it isn't four or five..."

"It won't be."

I yawned loudly. "Wow. I'm knackered."

Susie laughed. "Get used to it. You're going to be exhausted for the next twenty years."

* * * *

I awoke at first light. I caressed my stomach, my breasts. I froze. My breasts felt flat, deflated. Suddenly I was wide awake. Carefully, I eased myself out of the bed. I struggled with the pregnancy stick's plastic wrapping. As I began to urinate, I could already see blood. Still, I waited to watch the urine race from the cotton tip to the indicator box. Hope rose as the first blue line showed dark, but even after a long wait, no second line appeared. I wiped between my legs. The red gash on the toilet paper looked like a wound. Carefully, I returned to bed, slipping inside the covers.

The phone rang.

"Hi," I whispered to Charlie.

"Oh, sweetie."

I began to cry.

"I'm coming," Charlie said. "We're taxiing to the gate right now."

* * * *

"No," I whispered to Susie, curled in bed like a ball.

"No?" her voice was astonished. "But. . ."

"I know."

"I was so certain," she said. "It was as if I could feel them already."

"Me too."

"Charlie?"

"He's at the airport heading here."

"You can try again."

"I don't know if I even want to."

"You will," Susie encouraged.

"How do you know?"

"Because hard never stops you."

"And Charlie?"

"He'll let you."

"How do you know?"

"Because he wants a child as much as you do."

"But I couldn't hold on to them."

"This time. Next time will be different. Do you want me to come up?"

"No," I whispered. I curled tighter still. Cramps pinched my stomach. I could feel a gush between my legs. I felt suddenly exhausted.

"You'll call if you change your mind?"

"Yes."

"Promise?"

* * * *

I rolled over, stretched out my legs, which both felt stiff from being bent tightly. I blinked, disorientated, still partly asleep. I looked at my watch. I had fallen back asleep almost two hours before. Where was Charlie? I reached for the phone. His number rang, eventually clicking into voice mail. My anger surged. Was he really still negotiating Wind Alternative's sale, given my call? I punched the re-dial button.

"Hello?" a female voice said.

I looked at my screen to confirm that I had called Charlie.

"Hello?" the woman said again.

"Who is this?"

"Are you a friend or family of Charlie Easton?"

"Who is this?" I repeated

"I am a nurse at St. Peter's Hospital."

"What?"

"Are you a friend or family of Charlie Easton?"

"I'm his wife."

"Charlie Easton was brought here after collapsing at the airport. Is it possible for you to come here as soon as possible?"

* * * *

"I don't know," I told Susie as she drove. "They just told me that he collapsed at the airport."

"Give me your phone," she said as we bumped down the mountain's gravel road.

My hand shook as I passed it to her. She pushed redial and put it on speaker. Pretending to be me, she questioned the nurse. Charlie was currently in the ICU. They were still unsure what was wrong with him. It wasn't a heart attack. It wasn't a stroke. I began shaking. My stomach dropped. "It was because I tried to have babies."

"What are you talking about?" Susie asked.

I told Susie what I had told Giovanni. I should have left my having babies boxed safely away, cocooned with my stuffed animals in their plastic container. By trying to have a baby, I had sacrificed Charlie.

"No," said Susie.

"But he is the third," I cried out.

"This isn't because of your trying to have a baby."

Tears rolled down my cheeks.

"No!" Susie insisted again. "Sometimes good karma trumps bad luck. No one, but no one is better than you. You'll get this break. I feel it. I really do."

"You felt my babies," I accused. "You were sure of it." Despair rushed in like a storm surge.

Susie's faced looked crushed, as if she were falling within herself.

"I know. I'm so sorry."

* * * *

Almost two hours of tests later, the doctor told us, "Acute liver failure brought on by an overdose of acetaminophen or Tylenol."

"But how could that be?"

"Too easily – especially if Tylenol is combined with alcohol and too little food. About half of acute liver failure cases are caused by either intentional or unintentional overdoses of acetaminophen.

"He wasn't drinking."

"But the Swedes," Susie said. "I bet everyone was having a drink or two with dinner."

I knew he hadn't been eating much. His appetite had been off. He thought he was getting the flu.

"But he will be ok?" Oh, God please.

"We're giving him intravenous N-acetylcysteine and vitamin K. We are hoping this will stabilize him. As a precaution, however, we are alerting the liver transplant unit and putting his name on the donor list."

I grabbed Susie's hand.

"Liver transplant unit?" she asked.

"It is too early to tell," the doctor said. "But if he does need a new liver, we have one of the best programs in the country."

"He's not going to. . ." I couldn't even finish the sentence.

The doctor's eyes were kind, competent. "We are doing everything we can," he promised.

* * * *

Antiseptic odours and a hidden smell of rot pervaded the ICU. Even after seven hours of sitting by Charlie's bed, I had not grown accustomed to their scents. I held Charlie's limp hand close to my face, his Castile soap still offering its weak fragrance of lemon. When the kind nurse came and went, she brought in the fragrance of her just-washed hair. It wafted on the stir of air caused by her movement as she checked the beeping life support machines and adjusted his IV meds.

Charlie's skin had yellowed, darkening with each hour. A breathing support machine whirred as it aided his each breath. It sounded false, mechanical. Its relentlessness was wearing me down, stealing my words that should have continued to tell Charlie that I was there, that he was going to get better, that he had to keep fighting, and that I loved him more than life itself. Now all I could do was focus on the drip, drip, drip of the N-acetylcysteine and vitamin K, willing it to wash out the poison.

If he died, I wouldn't be able to bear it, but it also felt like a certain and growing reality. A shudder convulsed my whole body all at once. I felt so cold. If he died – Charlie was my life. I wouldn't survive his death, not another death again. If he died – what would be the point? To work? Sell my business and engage with a charity? That was our dream. Ours! Not without him. If he died. . . The thought of suicide left me ice cold and hopeful both at once. My mind raced – how? Car fumes? Jump out my office window? It was ten stories up – an experience of brief intense terror, and then blessed nothing. Sleeping pills! That eliminated even the terror. I'd just drift off. I could do that. I had some too, and Charlie had just stocked up on Nyquil in a three-for-one sale. We had a new bottle of tequila. I could wash down the sleeping pills with tequila shots and Nyquil chasers. Maybe I could even add Tylenol. . . Anything to join him.

"Mrs. Easton?"

I startled. I hadn't seen the nurse enter.

"Visiting hours are over."

"But. . ." My eyes filled.

"I'm sorry," she said gently.

"But. . ."

"I'm working all night," she told me. "If there is even the slightest change in his condition, I'll call you."

What if. . . what if I wasn't there?

She squeezed my shoulder. "It'll be all right," she told me. "He's very stable right now."

I wanted to know what stable meant, but I had no courage. He had turned a more sallow shade of yellow. That could only be a bad sign.

"Jill," said Susie, standing up from the chair outside the ICU door.

I became aware of the nurse's arm as it pressed against my back and Susie's touch as she took my shoulder, replacing the nurse's arm with her own.

"It's ok," Susie murmured as we walked. "Let's go home. We'll get you a shower."

"But. . ."

"We'll be back as soon as we can."

69

JAY

We saw Jay's truck as we crested Garden's drive. Susie shook her head when my eyes asked if she had spoken to him.

"I just got his voicemail saying he would be here. He has been trying to reach you."

But I had thought Jay was in Nepal.

"I talked with Charlie's parents."

Charlie's parents! I hadn't even thought!

"There's a bad blizzard in Maine. Most of the Eastern seaboard is shut down, but they are trying to get out."

I nodded.

"Tim, Fernando, and Maria are all catching the first flights they can."

It felt surreal as I walked to the house. How familiar was this surreal! This empty walk! This reality where once again the rest of the world still turned unaware of the magnitude of my cataclysm. Blood that should have been our babies poured from my insides, making my gut ache.

Jay greeted us at the door. A little black-haired girl rested in his arms. At the sight of him, I began to cry. He hugged me close, his scent as comforting as his solidity. Susie told Jay all that was going on as I buried myself in the warmth of his arms.

It was then that I felt her hand resting on my head, her touch so light it might have been a whisper. I looked up through my tears at her little face. Her almond brown eyes were large and solemn.

"Anna," Jay said. At the sound of her name, the little girl looked at Jay. "This is Jill. Jill, this is Anna."

"Who is she?"

"I'll tell you," Jay said, his arm still around my shoulder. "Come inside."

In the kitchen, after we were holding steaming mugs of tea and Anna had a bowl of strawberries, Jay explained that Anna was Kamala's daughter. The little girl sat on his lap leaning back against his chest as he talked. "Kamala and Neema were killed."

"Killed?"

"There was a protest. It was largely peaceful, but they were targeted. Kamala made me promise to take her if anything happened to him. Now she's mine."

"Yours?" I was trying to make sense.

"She wasn't safe staying in Nepal. I bribed people to get her papers, then took her out through India."

All the time that we talked, Jay softly stroked the girl's shiny shoulder-length hair, as black as ink. She watched first me and then Susie with her big eyes. "She cries most nights. During the day, she hardly makes a sound. She saw them die."

"Oh, God!"

"How old is she?" asked Susie.

"Nineteen months."

"What's her name?"

"Anna," Jay repeated.

"Anna?" It was so hard to get my mind around it.

Jay smiled. "Neema learned English by reading *Ann of Green Gables*."

My stomach cramped. I rubbed it with my fingers.

"I was coming to ask if you and Charlie would raise her," Jay said. "I would have called, but it wasn't safe until we got on the flight. When I arrived here, well, it seemed best just to come with her here."

"Charlie and me?"

"I'm an old man," Jay said, "fit to be a grandfather, yes, but too old to be her dad."

I imagined Charlie. I imagined sitting next to him now.

"But what if Charlie..." I couldn't go on.

"Jill," said Susie, grabbing my hands. "Maybe this is the baby."

My face crinkled in confusion.

"That I was feeling," she whispered. Her eyes widened purposefully. Her meaning slowly dawned on me. I looked back at Anna.

"There's a boy," Jay said, then halted. "Her brother." His voice cracked. "He's only eight weeks old." He was asking.

A smile spread on Susie's face. "Babies," she whispered. "Twins."

I looked back at Anna's little red-cheeks. Her wispy fringe was just below her eyebrows. They had killed her parents. Now, she was going to lose her brother if he stayed in Nepal.

"Get him."

"Really?" Relief and gratitude filled Jay's expression.

"Yes."

70

NOT READY

"Good news," said the nurse as I came into the pungent ICU the next morning. "Charlie's acetaminophen levels are flattening."

Charlie's skin was a deep, disturbing colour of yellow, even more yellow than when I had seen him last. His breathing machine whirred rhythmically. What looked like a new bag of N-acetylcysteine hung from his IV pole. "So, he's going to be ok?"

"It's definitely a good sign." No promises, she meant.

I sat next to Charlie, pulling the brown vinyl chair close to his bed. I gathered up his limp hand. Its smell of lemon was almost extinguished. "I should have brought herbs in with me," I told him, as I enclosed his hand in both of mine. "Lemon balm, spearmint, thyme. They would have helped you. Why wasn't I thinking?"

I knew why I hadn't been thinking. I had been up late with Jay and Anna, who both had upside down sleep schedules due to jet lag. I couldn't engage with Anna; I was too exhausted, but I lay on the couch and watched Jay play with her before the fire. She was a lovely girl. The one time that Jay got her laughing by his tickling her, Anna's whole face lit up, like Christmas lights.

What if Charlie wasn't okay with Anna? I mean I was almost certain that he would be, but I had made a decision alone that was going to affect the rest of our lives. I certainly would have wanted to be consulted first.

As the machines hummed, I started telling Charlie about Anna, starting at that long ago night when I had come in to find Jay reading that first blue airmail letter from Kamala. Detail by detail, I told Charlie all I knew about the long road that had led Anna to us. It was a story of friendship and loyalty. It was a story of a little girl left quite precarious in a very uncertain world. "Her name is Anna," I told him. "She's ours now."

* * * *

Exhaustion pulled at my bones like a heavy weight. I hunched over a cup of steaming tea at the kitchen table. My dry eyes scratched. My neck felt crunched. The kind nurse had allowed me to stay until right before morning rounds. Tim was in the waiting room, ready to visit with Charlie when the doctors had finished. I had come home to shower, brush my teeth and change my clothes.

Jay came in, carrying Anna. She wore a dress of coarsely woven fabric. He eased down next to me, shifting Anna to his lap. "I have to go now and try to bring her brother to us."

I sat up a straighter.

"The longer I wait, the less chance I'll have of getting him out."

He shook a backpack off his shoulder and put it on the table.

"Extra diapers are in here, but she'll need more soon. She'll probably be hungry, too. It's been a while since her morning bottle."

I realized that he meant to leave her all alone with me. Panic electrified my fatigue. I wasn't ready to take her. I couldn't do this, especially not right now. I was just too tired.

"This is going to be hard for her."

The intensity of his voice darkened his blue eyes. With that he handed Anna to me; she began crying instantly, throwing her arms up for Jay to take her back.

"Hold her," he said standing to leave.

Anna began to fight against me.

"Hold her," he told me more forcefully. He moved quickly across the kitchen. The further he went, the more frantic Anna became. At the door he paused. He raised one hand to us, then he was gone. Anna wailed. Her despair sounded more animal than human. Her little face look terrified.

"It's ok. It's ok," I repeated over and over, trying to calm her. I walked as I spoke, crossing and then re-crossing the kitchen floor. It seemed like forever before her sobs grew quiet, but just as I began to ease my hold, she fought against me again. Her struggle was so unexpected that I dropped her as she broke from my arms. Before I could catch her, she raced toward the just washed sliding door.

I moved fast, grabbing her just as she collided. The collision made her cry harder. "It's ok, it's ok," I whispered again and again as I paced anew, but it didn't feel ok. What was I doing? What was I possibly thinking when I said I would keep her? I needed to focus on Charlie. Charlie could die at any moment. I couldn't play at being her mother now.

About thirty minutes into my second bout of pacing, Susie came. I broke into tears as soon as I saw her. "I can't do this." I held Anna out. "You take her."

Susie shook her head. "She needs you, not me. You're her mother now."

"I'm not ready."

"Whether you are or not doesn't matter." I had rarely seen Susie look so serious. "What matters is this little girl. This is bigger than you now."

"But. . ."

"There are no buts," said Susie.

"I can't walk anymore."

"Then sit."

"She'll cry."

"She's already crying."

I crumpled to the ground, my sore back braced against the glass. Anna became more upset. I tried to get up again, but Susie held me down. "Give her a minute."

"She's so unhappy."

"Rub her back."

I stroked her hair the way Mom used to stroke mine so that my head tingled. Although she was still crying, she seemed to like it. She rested her head against my shoulder.

"That's good," Susie encouraged.

"Jay says she could be hungry."

"Have you tried to feed her?"

"She wouldn't stop crying."

"Let's try now."

After a first bite of egg, I was able to turn her so that her back was against my stomach, making it easier for Susie to feed her. The relief was enormous when she finished her egg and started on her banana.

Susie smiled. "She's got a good appetite."

I closed my eyes and smiled slightly for the first time in what seemed like days.

"She's such a sweet little girl."

When breakfast was done, Susie filled her bottle. Anna reached for it with both hands. She rested against me as she suckled. I could feel her body relaxing.

"Nothing like a good cry and a good meal to get ready for a good nap," Susie said.

Anna did seem thoroughly tired.

"Let's get her diaper changed before we lose her completely."

I looked up at her questioningly.

"We'll change it just as she is."

Anna became more alert as Susie lifted up her dress and un-snapped her undershirt but she didn't protest. Soon she shifted more comfortably in my arms. Within minutes, her breathing regularized. For a while all three of us sat silently. I felt the rise and fall of Anna's chest. Her warm breathe caressed my chin.

"If Charlie doesn't make it," I said," it'll break me."

Susie did not offer false assurances but touched my hand gently.

"She's broken too. How can she not be, having seen what she did?"

"But if Charlie doesn't make it. . . "

"If that happens, she will be the only thing that will get you through it." I took in the conviction in Susie's eyes. "And sometime, when she feels good and safe, she will need to grieve for her parents. You'll get that, really, really get that. That's why the world has led her to you. Your understanding will heal her, too."

71

LANDSLIDE

Next to me Anna stirred. She was pressed against me, her little arm thrown across my stomach. Susie had insisted that I lie down with Anna after her bottle. I had protested that I would not sleep, but Anna would not settle unless I was next to her.

"Hey," said Susie. She was sitting in the bay window working on her computer. "How're you feeling?"

"Charlie!"

"Bob and Tim are with him. Mom's with the girls. "

I asked with my eyes.

"He's good, stable. His acetaminophen levels have dropped again. In fact all his blood counts are improving."

"What time is it?"

"Almost 1:30."

1:30! I had been sleeping for almost four hours. I tried to sit up, but couldn't. It had been such a deep sleep. My head felt fuzzy, like cotton wool.

"Hey, beautiful," said Susie. I looked over. Anna's almond eyes were open. I felt her hand tighten on the fabric of my t-shirt.

"I bet you're hungry," I said. It seemed to be the voice of someone else.

Anna shifted so that her leg went over mine.

"You need to eat too," Susie said to me. "You're the pillar now."

Charlie was my pillar. I wanted him to be the pillar, not me.

"I have tuna fish sandwiches, mango, carrots, cucumbers, and a bottle waiting. If you guys are good to eat for a bit, then I'll run to the store to get more diapers. I also want to pick up a few t-shirts, shorts and dresses for her. Poor thing has almost no clothes."

I wanted to lie there forever. I felt done with doing things.

"Jill?"

From not feeling tired, now I felt I could fall right back asleep.

"Actually, maybe I'll stay for lunch," Susie said. She glanced over at Anna. "That way I can give you a hand if you need anything. What do you think, beautiful?" she asked, stretching out her hands toward Anna, who tightened her grip on my t-shirt. Her second hand clasped my shirt at its shoulder. She shuffled so that half her body was on top of my side.

I forced myself to sit. I had to get up. I had to see Charlie. Anna came with me, sliding into my lap. I could feel where wet had seeped through her diaper.

"No, go."

I could tell Susie wasn't sure.

"Seriously," I insisted.

"I'll only be 45 minutes," she promised.

* * * *

We sat in front of lunch, Anna on my lap. While she ate the sandwich, she reached for the mango hungrily. When I spooned yoghurt, she reached for cooked carrot. I hugged her protectively. Her eyes looked up at me, and I smiled encouragingly. In response, she held out a piece of cut sandwich. I shook my head no, but she touched it to my lips. I indicated no again, but she pressed it harder to my mouth so that it began to crush. As I opened my mouth to voice refusal, she slid it in – all yogurty from her fingers. I offered her another bite of sandwich and she brought a second bite to my lips. I tried to persuade her to take the bite, and she did the same with me. When I took my bite, she would take hers. This way, together, we ate everything that Susie had prepared.

I switched on the radio as I cleared the dishes to the counter. I held Anna with one hand, while loading the dishwasher with the other. She had her bottle and was tilting her head back to suck on it.

"*Took my love, took it down,*" the radio sang.

"*Climbed a mountain and I turned around.*"

I froze. It was Charlie singing. It was his voice I heard, not that of Fleetwood Mac.

And I saw my reflection in snow covered hills
Until a Landslide brought me down.

Charlie's voice was rich, melodious; I saw his face lost in the notes as it always was at his piano.

Oh mirror in the sky what is love?
Can the child within my heart rise above?
Can I sail through the changing ocean tides?
Can I handle the seasons of my life?

I gripped onto the sink. I was shattering. Mom didn't make it. John Jay didn't make it. Oh, Charlie...

Well I've been afraid of changes
Cause I've built my life around you.
But time makes you bolder,
Even children get older
And I'm getting older too.

I could see him rocking Tabitha. Then he was driving me to Betty's Café on our second date.

Oh take my love take it down.
Climb a mountain and turn around.
And if you see my reflection in the snow covered hills,
Well the landslide will bring it down.

I slumped to the floor. Terror closed its grip on my heart. All I could do was rock, rock, trying to hold it off. Anna swayed, swayed with me, sucking her milk in my trembling arms.

72

MARIA AND FERNANDO

I wasn't allowed to stay in the ICU during the night, even though Charlie's condition was improving. The kind nurse had the night off. The new nurse was nice, but procedural.

I awoke the next day at dawn to a piquant green chili scent of corn bread baking. I found Maria by the stove, removing bread from the oven. She moved quickly when she saw me, and she was hugging me before I could even get to the table. "I know, Niña, I know," she told me without my saying a word. My heart broke again because she did know, because she could catch the pieces. "We will get through this, too," she promised.

But would Charlie?

"I am praying," she told me. "Our whole church is praying."

I searched her eyes. Not promises, but she had hope. I didn't want to talk about it more. This hope she spoke of could be false.

"When did you get in?" I asked instead.

Maria was drying her eyes on her apron. "Last night. I didn't want to wake you."

"Where's Fernando?"

"In the Garden. He took his clippers out at first light."

My eyes went to the window.

"He's anxious to see you," Maria said softly. "He is very worried, Niña. He does not understand how there can be such sadness for one person." Anna shifted, releasing her arms that had tightened around my neck when Maria had come in for a hug.

"This is our Maria," I told her, looking down. Anna turned to look at Maria.

Delight melted Maria's eyes. "Hello, little Angel."

Anna stretched a little taller at Maria's attention.

"You and I, little Niña, are going to be very good friends. Did you know that?"

Anna turned back to me as if she was seeking confirmation. "It's true," I whispered.

A smile brightened every corner of Maria's face. She squeezed Anna's toe affectionately. "You are most wonderful, did you know that?"

"The best, most wonderful girl," Fernando purred. Anna's head swiveled. "The best most wonderful girl in the whole world," he continued, coming to our side. Fernando was rounder, greyer, but the agility of his movements made it seem as if he hadn't aged at all.

"How are you my Niña?" he asked.

I nodded, blinking fast.

"I am still your Newt," he promised me solemnly. "And you are a good, good Turtle."

I smiled at him through tears that I wiped on Anna's shirt.

"The very best, my Niña," he insisted. "The most very best in the whole wide world."

73

FATHER

I held Anna in my arms as I entered Charlie's room. Technically, Anna was too young to be in the ICU, but the kind nurse was back, and Anna became upset if I tried to put her down even for a moment. She seemed to have transferred to me whatever little bond she could create in an unfamiliar, changing world of unknown faces. When I had to use the toilet, I pulled down my pants with one hand while holding her with the other. When I showered after lunch, she came with me, crying at the pouring water, but more frantic still when I tried to set her on the other side of the clear glass wrapped up in a towel. Susie had said that she would take her, crying or not, but I didn't have the heart for it. Not yet anyway. It had been terrible getting her in a car seat. She cried fiercely even with me sitting next to her holding both her hands and leaning forward so she could see my face.

"The breathing tube's gone!" I exclaimed.

"It is," said the nurse. "We've also stopped the sedation that we were using to make the tube more comfortable. He's doing well."

"Really?"

She smiled warmly. "It's all good news."

"Thank God," I breathed. I moved close to his bed. His skin was very yellow, but he looked more human without the tube coming out of his mouth. I stroked his dark curls away from his face, kissing his lips.

Sitting with Anna in the brown vinyl chair, for a while I just watched him. Without the breathing tube, his yellow-grey face seemed stone still, quiet, but not peaceful. Maybe it was because he wasn't really resting, but was fighting at the molecular level. All the energy that normally animated his exterior, even in sleep, seemed to have been drained, as if it had been redirected to dispel the attack from within. His skin, his outside, had an empty, abandoned quality. Now that he was getting better, this emptiness scared me. Or maybe because he was getting better I could feel frightened, whereas before, the fear would have crushed me with its force.

Anna shifted. Her attention had been taken up by the foreign room with its humming machines attached to the strange person in front of her. Now her body was beginning to move. To engage her, I brought out a plastic bag from my purse. Inside were a variety of mints and herbs that we had collected from the Garden.

"We brought you scents," I told Charlie, trying to keep my voice steady. "Didn't we, Anna?" Anna selected lemon balm from the bag that I held open to her. I rolled the sprig between my hands. Its fresh lemony fragrance filled the area around Charlie's bed. I brought it near his face.

"It's like your lemon body wash."

Anna's hand went out. I let Anna smell it, too, as she collected it in her hand. "And this is thyme," I told her as she drew out the next sprig. "Thyme," I said again, letting her smell. "And this sleepy person in the bed is Charlie," I explained as I held the thyme close to his face, my tears brimming.

"Charlie, do you remember how you like to add thyme to your roast lamb?" I compressed rosemary next. "With rosemary and garlic?" I gave Anna a smell. "I always think rosemary smells a bit like soap," I told her. Anna took the rosemary from my hand. She added it to the other herbs she had bunched like a bouquet. I removed Garden mint, then spearmint and chocolate mint next. I crumpled each shoot gently, then waved them in the air together.

For a moment I closed my eyes and I was back in my mint hideaway. I felt the stem tug. Anna was bringing one of the chocolate mint leaves to her mouth. "Don't eat that," I said as she slipped it between her lips. Her expression crinkled as she spat it out. I laughed, my tears spilling. "It smells better than it tastes," I explained.

"Jill?"

"Charlie?" I couldn't believe it. Charlie's eyes were open.

"Hi, Charlie," the nurse said, leaning over the other side of the bed. She had entered while Anna and I were playing with our herbs. "You're in the Intensive Care Unit of St. Thomas Hospital. Your liver made you ill, but you're getting better now."

Charlie's eyes shifted from the nurse to mine. I wiped at the tears slipping down my cheek.

"You gave me quite the scare," I told him taking his hand in mine. "I was really worried."

"You've been here about four days," the nurse went on. "We have been giving you medication to clear all the Tylenol that has built up in your system. You're doing really well now."

"Really well," I confirmed.

His eyes went to Anna. I could see him wondering.

Should I tell him? Just as he was waking up? But what else could I do?

"This is Anna."

I told him the story, speaking quickly. All the while Anna and Charlie studied each other. Anna pulled another mint strand from my hand, reaching it toward Charlie. I laughed through my tears.

"We brought you Garden herbs to smell, didn't we Anna?"

"Is it ok?' I whispered to Charlie as Anna shook the mint.

He smiled, nodded, but already his eyes were closing. I looked at the nurse, alarmed.

"That's natural," the nurse assured. "He's going to be very tired for a while."

"Tired," Charlie whispered.

"That's ok, sweetheart," I said, squeezing his hand, leaning to kiss his lips. "You sleep all you need."

"And you, lovely girl," the nurse said, coming to kneel before her. "You did a good job of waking up our Charlie, didn't you?"

Anna shook the mint again. The nurse laughed.

"That's exactly right," she said.

Gratitude coursed through me; I just couldn't believe it. "He's going to be all right isn't he?" I asked the nurse.

"Yes," she said. "I'm quite sure he is."

Thank you, God, I said in my head. *Thank you, thank you, and thank you.*

74

GARDEN

Anna slept at an angle, her feet on my stomach, her silky hair dark against the corner of the white pillow, her hand curled around the rabbit that Susie had given her the day before. It was hard to believe that this was only the third day Jay had been gone. It felt as if Anna had been with me much longer. Already she had become a part of my heart.

I moved carefully from the bed so as not to wake her. I had just stood when she opened her eyes. Solemn, she looked at me. I leaned in to stroke her hair.

"Don't you want to sleep?" I whispered. "It's early."

In answer, she put both her arms out. She still smelled of the oranges she had eaten before bed.

"Shall we change your diaper?" I asked her softly, bouncing her on my hip. She played with her rabbit as I undid her nappy. She shook Rabbit, pulled at his ears, and touched her finger to his eyes.

"Rabbit," I told her. "I had a rabbit once. Jay gave him to me when I was just a little older than you are now."

She watched me as I spoke, and then she walked Rabbit across her tummy.

"I wonder if you had rabbits," I said, scooping her up in my arms, "way high up in the Himalayas? You definitely had yaks."

In the kitchen, eggs cracked against a glass bowl, strawberries slipped sliced into a dish, butter melted in a pan, and salt sprinkled on yellow white scramble.

"Yaks are one animal that you definitely won't find in the Garden," I told her, slipping her onto my lap at the table, "even way up high in the peaks above the Wild."

Back on my bed, I changed what was now a poopy diaper after I had stacked dirty dishes in the sink and washed her hands in warm water. She held very still all the while I cleaned her, her round face studying mine. It wasn't the first time I thought that her eyes looked worldly-wise. I speculated about her thoughts: Did she wonder who I was? Did she remember her parents? Did she miss her home where life was so different? Jay had told me that Anna had begun to speak before her parents were killed, but her speaking was mainly identification words: *fire, stick, pot, rock, rice, snow, goat, no! yes!* Maybe she experienced the answers to my questions as feelings to which no words were attached.

Before the mirror we brushed our teeth in the bathroom sink. In a drawer, we found a collection of my old barrettes. I clipped back her hair with two pink dogs.

"Look at you," I said.

Anna touched herself in the mirror.

"That's right. That's Anna."

She touched me. I didn't know what to say. Was I to be Jill as Jay was Jay? Mommy? What right did I have to call myself Mommy? But if not me, than who?

"Let's get me dressed now, shall we?" I asked, as I settled her on my hip.

* * * *

Outside, Anna's little hand encircled mine.

"Where to?" I asked.

She led every-which-way through the Garden. I noted work that needed to be done as we walked: prune the bonsai, dead-head the roses, cut back mint in my old hideaway. In the Maze, Anna reached out to touch each of the Flamingos, resting her fingers lightly in the space between their eyes. I wondered if she had seen her Mom do that, as it was such a particular gesture. If the Flamingos had not been of green stone, they would have stretched their tall necks down to meet her little hand; that was how much they liked her. Instead, I held her high, so she could caress each elfin bird in turn.

In the Arabian Room, I helped Anna pick ripened oranges from the tree. We ate them behind the now thread-bare curtains on the dirty divan. The fountains arches were not on, but blue-winged birds gathered at the pool's edge.

Anna held my hand more tightly in Southwest Room with its unfriendly skulls. Half way through, I picked her up. Finding the hidden latch in the Concealed Door, I carried Anna into the Forest leading to the Hidden Monastery. I moved slowly, my legs pushing back enormous leaves while I felt for the disguised stepping stones.

Inside the Monastery, early warm sun poured in. The courtyard grass had grown long and soft. I knelt, shifting Anna to my lap. I un-buckled her shoes. Her bare toes just touched the grass. I waited. At first, she was perfectly still. I followed her eyes into the gothic walkway with its alcoves of statues. She kicked her toes. The grass shushed against her feet. She slid closer and kicked again. Taking my hand, she stood up. I watched inquisitiveness take over. She circled me in the grass. I passed her from hand to hand as she went round and round. When she tugged to go further afield, I stood. We walked underneath the Gothic Arches. Goosebumps rippled my skin since it was still cool out of the sun, but Anna's arms were unruffled. At Mom's drawing table, Anna stopped. She examined the grey stone box. I eased open its lid. Inside I was surprised to find the plastic bin of Mom's paints and paper. Anna's finger shot out.

"Paints," I said, lifting the plastic box to the table. Anna looked inside.

"Paints," I said again.

Anna watched as I opened a box and set it before her. Slowly her finger came out and she touched one of the coloured circles.

"Look," I told Anna. I collected her and filled a cup with water from the small fountain in Abbey's corner. Anna watched the paints as I carried her to the water, but as water splashed into the tin cup, she turned to the sound. Back at the table, I poured a drop of water on each paint colour. Once they were wet, my brush tip twirled in the green. I drew a stripe. Anna's wide eyes looked up at my face.

I smiled. "Paint, green paint."

Anna touched the red. Green swirled in the clear water as I cleaned my brush. I made another stripe. Colour by colour I turned the blank paper into painted rainbows. When I had finished, I handed Anna the brush.

"Anna paints."

She looked up at me. I put down clean paper and guided her hand. We made a purple line. That was all the encouragement she needed. Mixing one colour with another, emptying the tin water over the paints, pouring wet paint water on to paper, she covered page after page. The cosy sun glinted off her hair, dark as onyx. I ran my fingers through it as she worked, inhaling its faint strawberry shampoo. Finally, she pushed to get down.

"All done?" I asked.

She wriggled off my lap.

"I have to tidy first," I told her. She leaned against my leg as I cleaned. When I stood, her shoes tucked into my back pockets, she felt warm and light and good all at once.

"Let's get your pictures, shall we?" I asked, gathering up her art. "And then," I said, squeezing her bottom and bouncing her a little as we moved up the stairs, "we need to change this wet, wet diaper. It's already soaked."

* * * *

"What do you think?" I asked Anna once we had finished taping her art to the cabinets. "Anna's pictures."

Anna pointed to a painting. "Here's a red line," I told her. "Purple. I see yellow. And here! Look at this dark black."

She pulled at a painting and a corner came off, along with some sticking tape. She touched the tape with her fingers, and it clung. Her eyes brightened. "Sticky," I confirmed, touching her finger to the tape and pulling it away.

She repeated the motion many times, and then she gazed at me.

"See?" I explained, taking the picture from her hands and adhering it back to the cabinet door. It was as if a light bulb had gone off. She took the water colour off. I helped her stick it back. We replicated this game many times.

Anna lunged forward. I had to catch her with both hands so she didn't fall. She was reaching for the green tape dispenser on the counter. I lowered her until she could take it in both hands.

"Tape," I said, setting her on the counter and showing her how to take a piece. She pulled out a piece the length of her arm. She looked to see my reaction. I smiled. With that, she proceeded to empty the dispenser. She worked with great concentration, not quite able to cut the tape off on its serrated edge, becoming tangled in the growing strand. When it was done, she held up the emptied dispenser.

"All gone," I confirmed.

She dropped it on the floor, looking to see where it landed. Then I watched as she struggled to get the tape off her. As soon she pulled it from her pants, it stuck to her hand. If she took it from her hand, it adhered to her arm. Her eyes grew alarmed. I rescued her from the tape, balling it up and throwing it in the trash.

"All tidy," I said, setting her down. She went to the bin and started opening the lid. She wanted her tape back.

"Dirty now."

She leaned forward toward the waste basket. I could feel her determination. I scooped her up.

"It's time to go see Charlie," I told her. "Let's get ready now."

75

MOTHER

The yellow tinge of Charlie's skin was fading. The ashen tone that now replaced it had a slight under-wash of pink. Charlie smiled at the sight of Anna.

"How are you?" I asked him.

"How is she?" Sensing that she was being spoken about, Anna held out Rabbit for Charlie to see. His smile warmed. "That's a great rabbit," he told her.

Anna bounced it up and down on her lap.

"Is he hopping?" Charlie asked.

"How are you?" I asked again.

"Better," he said, "but still wiped."

"You're going to be tired for a good while," I told him. "You almost died." The accusation in my voice could be felt even though I had not meant to accuse. Now that the poison's grip was lessening, my suspended feelings were flowing through the cracks. I blinked back tears. I had ripped off Susie's head before coming to the hospital for suggesting that I needed to eat some breakfast. Speaking with Charlie's mom on the phone the night before, I had started sobbing for no reason at all.

Charlie reached for my hand. "I'm not going anywhere."

"But you almost did." Anger surged.

"Hey." His voice was gentle, kind, soothing. "It's going to take more than a few Tylenol to knock me off. After all, we have a little girl who needs us now."

"And boy," I blurted.

"Boy?" he asked, confused.

My cheeks reddened. I hadn't told Charlie before for fear it would be too much, but today he had to know. "She has an eight-week-old brother. Jay went back to try and get him."

Surprise froze on Charlie's face like a snapshot. Before it faded, in his eyes I saw his mental landscape regrouping. Waking up from near death to find that you are all of a sudden a father of two was a lot to take in.

"She lost her parents, Charlie. I couldn't let her lose her brother too."

He nodded.

"I would have waited to decide together, but there was no time. The longer Jay waited, the greater the risk." I bit my lip, trying to gauge Charlie's expression. Usually I could read Charlie's feelings like a book.

"Are you mad?"

His face gentled. "Of course not."

"Is it really ok?'

His eyes flashed. The old Charlie sparkled, and I could see a witty reaction in his eyes, then the truth.

"It's amazing," he said.

"Really?" I breathed out in a rush.

He squeezed my hand tightly.

"How lucky are we?" he asked.

I clasped back hard, relief dashing at my heart.

"The luckiest people in the world," I told him. "And I am the luckiest wife."

"That you are, Mrs. Easton." His eyes twinkled as he did a little bed-dance. "For a *lot* of reasons."

I laughed despite myself. "Seriously?"

Charlie's grin broadened.

"There isn't even a million to one chance," I said sternly.

Charlie's sparkle re-ignited. "Didn't you just say that we are the luckiest people in the world?"

I rolled my eyes, but I was smiling. If Charlie was well enough to joke about sex, then I was definitely smiling.

"In my book, that's million-to-one lucky," he told me.

"Your little girl is sitting right here," I chastised.

"Then we're lucky she doesn't yet speak English."

"You're incorrigible."

Tenderness softened his expression. "And you're a mother."

A mother! Who could have believed it? Right then and there I vowed to Anna's parents that I would love their children with all my being. I vowed to take the very best care of them. I vowed to try to feel them in my heart, whenever a big decision needed to be made, or whenever I was not sure what to do.

One thing I was suddenly sure of was that I would build her parents a Garden room. That way they would have a home in our home, a house in our house. It hit me then that I wanted to stay in the Garden. The Garden felt right again. It felt good and safe. I looked at Charlie playing rabbit with Anna. Rabbit was now hopping on Charlie's leg. I needed to be sure this wasn't just a passing feeling. Charlie loved the city. He loved the sea. He loved the energy of constantly being surrounded by new people. I'd wait on this news. There had been enough news for today.

76

ANIMALS

The big doors of the large shed creaked then rumbled as they slid open, reaching their terminus with a clunk. A dusty musty smell emanated from the dark interior. Plastic and cardboard boxes were stacked on metal racks. In some places, overspill heaped in the narrow paths along the floor. Mom's old business records filled many of the bins. Jay's photographs jammed many more. Interspersed with these were boxes with my school work, Mom's beading, keepsakes, and John Jay's things. There seemed to be no rhyme or reason to the way that the boxes piled, although labels clearly indicated contents. There was nothing for Anna and me to do but search. John Jay's books were our treasures. We had kept every one of them.

Anna held my short bottoms as she tended to do when I needed both my hands to do something. Her other arm wrapped around Rabbit. In the center of the aisle, I began amassing boxes that I wanted to explore – Mom's beading, boxes of old garden designs, old family photographs, my old toys.

I heard Anna's little hand tap a plastic box on the other side of the aisle. I knelt to see what she was seeing. There was Daisy's little deer face pressed against the bin's corner. The accusation in Daisy's eyes that been her departing look was gone; instead, all I saw was welcome and joy. My heart panged suddenly for Lionel. He sat curled on top of our bed at home.

Anna tapped on the box again. I blinked back unexpected tears. "Hello Daisy," I whispered to her, shifting her green-lidded box on top of the one I had just found with John Jay's books and his toys. "Let's get these outside," I told Anna. "Then we can come back for more."

We walked at a toddler pace back to the Great Lawn, where a blanket was already spread under the Poplars. I eased the bins down, then sat myself. Anna plopped in my lap. She looked up at me expectantly. My heart quickened as I snapped off the lid. Anna pulled Daisy out by the ear. "That's Daisy Deer," I said. Michael Marmot lay where he had been dropped, belly exposed. "And this is Michael Marmot," I said, taking him up. I could smell his familiar well-worn scent. "I'm sorry," I whispered as I held close to my heart.

Anna plucked out Raccoon. "That's Rascal. He's always getting into scrapes. When I was little like you I spent half my time rescuing him from one escapade or another." Anna looked at me as I talked. Then she reached for Red. I introduced her Rabbit to Red Rabbit. Red Rabbit then touched her cheek with his paw. The hint of a smile lit her eyes.

She played with the animals for a long time, pressed against my legs while I laid back on the blanket stroking Daisy, who rested on my chest. I watched sun sift through the poplar leaves as I felt Anna hop first one animal and then the other up and down my leg. A kaleidoscope of animal memories came and went. It felt surreal, as if a missing piece of me had been re-slotted.

Eventually, Anna leaned back against me. I sat up so I could see her face. "I bet you're hungry," I told her. I checked my watch. Tim, Richard and Mary were with Charlie this morning. Anna and I were going right after lunch. We should start lunch right away if we didn't want to rush. Anna tried to gather up all the animals in her arms when I rose, but they were too much. I set Harry, Michael, Daisy and Rabbit on the book box that I balanced on my hip while she carried Red Rabbit, Rascal and Squirrel. I would read to her while we ate. I remembered John Jay's books well, even after all this time. They were like long ago friends I was seeing again for the first time.

77

JAY AND JAKE

Shaking disrupted a deep, far-away sleep. Shaking again, and this time I became aware. Jay – and then I saw him – a little baby wrapped in soft, cream cloth. Only his face showed with its little wisps hair.

"Can you take him?"

I looked from the baby to Jay. He looked all used up.

"Everything you need is here," Jay said, holding the baby in one hand, and sliding a tapestry bag off his shoulder with the other. I pushed myself further up the pillows. Jay opened the bag's flap. Inside were bottles, diapers, and a few clothes.

Anna stirred beside me. She threw a hand over my stomach.

Jay's face warmed. "How is she?"

A slideshow of Anna images flashed through my head: in the bath, painting, her finger pointing, eating yoghurt, playing with Rascal who had become her favourite.

"Good."

"Charlie?" he asked without saying a word.

"Really good. He's out of danger now."

A smile lit Jay's weary face, but his exhaustion soon overwhelmed the light. Darkness ringed his eyes. He slipped the baby in my arms. He was so small and light.

"He's a lovely boy," Jay said.

"Will you be ok?"

I had never seen his face look so haggard.

"Right as rain with a little sleep," Jay answered.

"Was it all right? Getting him?"

"It wasn't easy."

Questions flooded, but I held them in check. "What's his name?" was all I asked.

A funny smile traversed his face. "Little Jay."

"Little Jay?"

"I thought we might call him Jake."

"Jake," I repeated looking down at the infant. "I like it." It suited him somehow. His crisp little features went with a sharp, short name whose K reminded me of mountain tops.

* * * *

Jake awoke not long after Jay left. His eyes were large and almond-shaped like Anna's. I unwrapped the blanket. As soon as his legs were free, they began to kick. "Hello, little one," I whispered down to him.

He wiggled more.

"Well, hello, hello!"

I played all the games I remembered playing with John Jay. His favourites were having his feet pedaled first fast then slow or his leg tickled when I "spidered" my fingers up and down it. Jake watched me intently as we played. His eyes fixed on my face. After we'd played for a while, his little face rumpled. Discontent washed over him like a wave. He made sad, strange mewing sounds. I realized he was hungry. With the tapestry bag over my shoulder, I carried him into the kitchen to warm his bottle.

A cry, just once, plaintive – it was Anna.

"I'm coming," I called, sending my voice ahead.

"Anna we're coming," I called again, as we hurried toward her. From the doorway, I could see tears like fat rain drops falling down her cheeks. My heart clenched. "Look," I soothed coming to her. "Look, who I have." I held Jake low so that she could see him. "It's your brother." Her eyes went wide. "Do you remember him?" She touched his cheek, his hair, brought her face close to his, and his face became wet with her tears. His legs kicked excitedly. She beamed back. Off the bed, to the door she went, looking up and down the hall then back at me.

It took me a moment to clock, "Are you looking for your mom?"

If Jake could come why not her Mom? After all, how could death be comprehensible to a one-year-old? How is it comprehensible to anyone?

Jake again made his sweet sad mew, his hunger no longer distracted by his sister. I sat on the bed with him, my back against the pillows. He drank from his bottle hungrily. Anna came back, her smile gone. She slipped next to me and I scooped her under my arm, her head against my breast. After about half the milk was gone, I set the bottle between my legs and held Jake against my chest. I patted his back gently, remembering. Jake expelled an unexpectedly loud burp.

"Goodness," I said, bringing him down to look at his face. He bicycled, then whimpered. He latched on as soon as I offered the nipple, but he was asleep before the bottle emptied. I pulled it finally from his sleep-limp mouth. For a moment, both of us watched him. I marveled at this perfect little bundle of innocence that was our son. I couldn't wait for Charlie to see him.

"Are you ready for your Baba now, too?" I asked Anna, showing her Jake's bottle. "Shall we have bottle and books and tuck right back into bed?"

I surrounded sleeping Jake with pillows in the bed's center and changed Anna's wet diaper. She rested her head against my shoulder as I carried her to the kitchen. She didn't look around as she usually did when I warmed her milk. It occurred to me that she was sad. She wanted her mom, even if she couldn't say it in words. I hoped she was missing a mom who was cooking Anna her favourite rice, and not the mom lying dead, in an expanding pool of blood.

* * * *

"He's beautiful," I told Susie as soon as light broke. Tabitha clamoured in the background. She begged to see me. At five, she could understand that Charlie was sick, but it was harder for her to understand why I hadn't come to see her alone since I was well.

"Come now. Bring the girls." I smiled, as I heard Tabitha's cries of excitement at the news.

They found us on the Great Lawn. Anna and Jake were playing

on the quilt. We played with the trove of little toys Anna had discovered in John Jay's keepsake box. Rabbit and Rascal watched. Michael Marmot, Red Squirrel, Harry Hedgehog, and Daisy all waited back on the bed. And Lionel was already on his way, shipped special delivery. I explained to my secretary that he was for Anna, although I wasn't really going to let her have him. With Jake and Anna here now, it didn't feel right not to have him close.

I heard the girls before I saw them. Their feet pattered along the path. Tabitha reached me first. As I stood she threw her arms around me. Three-year-old Antonia came next, holding Susie's hand. As the girls approached, Anna took two steps forward, then stood uncertain. Susie knelt before Anna, letting go Antonia's hand. "Is that your brother?" Anna followed Susie's eyes to Jake.

"He's beautiful," Susie breathed to me.

"Isn't he?"

Antonia turned to take in her Mom's face and then looked again at the baby on the ground. She had Bob's red hair that fell in ringlets around her cheeks.

"Is this your new baby?" Tabitha asked.

I stretched out my arm to Anna, who came quickly, tucking in tight. "Yes," I nodded and was again taken aback by incredulity – my babies, mine.

As we all admired him, Jake had grown very still. His expression turned, almost as if he were listening inward. Then his face tightened, reddened and his bottom exploded. Tabitha burst into laughter. Antonia laughed with her and then even Susie. Jake's little face reddened again and a series of small spurts came loudly from his rear. Tabitha collapsed on the grass with mirth and copying Antonia, rolled on the grass with her. Under my hand, I could feel Anna's stomach titter. Jake made one more enormous blast, and then his face cleared, and he began bicycling his legs. All the laughing got louder, even Anna's. Her laugh sounded like pealing bells.

Jake whimpered. Poo had leaked from his diaper and was seeping through his clothes. It spread all the way up his back. From the diaper bag, I unfolded the plastic changing mat, placing Jake on top of it. As I began un-buttoning and removing his clothes, the girls gathered round to watch.

"Look!" said Tabitha when I undid his diaper, "He's got one just like daddy."

Susie laughed. "That's because he's a boy, silly."

"I have a vagina," Tabitha told me knowingly.

"So do I," I confessed.

"Vagina," sing-songed Antonia. "Vagina, vagina."

"Hush you," said Susie, tickling Antonia's tummy.

Anna leaned into me as she watched the girls watch her brother. She wasn't missing anything the girls did, not one bit.

* * * *

Charlie was resting on a lounge chair under the flecked shade of the Olive Tree in the Lavender Room. Its musky purple scent eddied gently in the warm afternoon sun. The trip from the hospital had exhausted Charlie and he had slept all morning. But now, his cheeks were already rosier for being in the Garden. Already, he had walked more strongly from the house to the Lavender Room than he had walked from the car to the house. Jake slept in his arms while Anna played between my legs, as I relaxed on the lounge next to Charlie. Rascal, Rabbit and a choice of toys had come with Anna, carried in my old purple backpack. Sweetness filled Charlie's eyes as he looked down at Jake's sleeping face.

"I want to stay in the Garden," I blurted. I bit my lip. I had promised myself that I would give Charlie time to settle in so he could see what it felt like spending time in the Garden before I brought up the idea of staying for a while, but it was hard having secrets from Charlie. So much of my thinking about Anna and Jake, about his getting better, about us becoming a family was wrapped up in the Garden and its rhythms. I had imagined transferring my office to Mom's old work space. I had imagined sharing more of the work burden with Maria and Fernando so I could continue working and be a stay-at-home mom the same way Mom had done. I wouldn't be able to do both in the city, at least not in the same way. Here, I would be close to Susie. Antonia and Anna shared almost the same age difference as Susie and I had during the early days. Maybe they would become best friends too. Stranger things had happened. Here, too, Jay was at home.

"I know."

I was astonished. "You do?"

"I've been watching the idea develop in your eyes. Every time you talk about the Garden, I can see it. I can see you making plans."

"I want them to be our plans."

"I know."

There was something about his tone. It did not bode well. If only I had been patient. If only I had given Charlie time to see how the Garden made him feel better before bringing up the idea. Now I might have ruined everything. He was still so weak. Right now he didn't need me throwing the idea of uprooting us on top of it all. Charlie sighed deeply. Tears unexpectedly stung.

His voice was gentle as he continued. "Everything else aside, the sale contract stipulates that I continue working for the next two years. If I don't keep to the contract, the whole sale could fall through."

I nodded. I knew this.

"That's everything else aside. I like the city. I like the sea. What exactly do you expect me to do here?"

"I thought you could work remotely at least part of the time."

"You mean come and go like Jay did? Is that the kind of father you want for these children?"

I could feel myself getting cross. "That's not fair. Going to the coast for a few days a week is nothing like Jay disappearing for months at a time."

Pain pinched Charlie's face. He shifted his knees up, setting sleeping Jake between them. One hand rested on his stomach, his thumb massaging a spot on his skin. The other covered Jake's feet like a warm blanket. What had I been thinking? He didn't need this right now.

"My dad was home for dinner every night."

"You're not a furniture maker, Charlie. You run a global business for God's sake. Even if we stayed in the city you'd have to travel, especially since the company now has a Swedish owner."

"What about your work?" he countered.

"I'd keep the city office going for now, but over time, I'd shift more of the operations here. Maria and Fernando could help. Fernando's itching to take on more of a role. With Maria and Fernando and Jay, I could work and be a mom."

"You can't go back, Jill. You're not a child anymore."

Irritation flared to anger, but it was more than just anger. It was all the stress and emotion of the last week uncorked. "That's what you think this is? Me re-living my childhood?" The sharpness of my voice caused Anna to look up. "You almost died Charlie," I continued in a loud whisper, tears spilling. "You were supposed to be my safe harbour, but you're a storm just like everyone else." Anna had stopped playing. Wrapping Rascal and Rabbit in her arms, she leaned her back against my chest. I tried to calm myself. "You almost died," I whispered again.

"Hey," said Charlie, taking my hand. "I'm not going anywhere."

"You can't control that," I countered. "Do you think their parents wanted to leave Anna and Jake? Do you think my mom wanted to leave me?"

"No," he said quietly.

"It's just that. . ." I trailed off. I tried to order my fragmented thoughts, to put into words my feelings that ricocheted. Mental images took on meaning like words: Genie's breath swaying the tall grasses as it swept up the old Landslide; under it, buried Bonsai healing the hurt earth. "I feel safe here," I said finally. "Not safe in the sense that nothing bad will happen, but safe in the sense that regardless of what happens, here I will have the strength to deal with it. I'm scared Charlie."

Charlie's grasp on my hand tightened. He was trying to reassure me, trying to take away my fear.

"I am scared about the awesome responsibility of taking these two children."

"You're going to be a great Mom," he said passionately.

Charlie would be an even more amazing father, but that wasn't the point.

"I need time to stop being so frightened. I need time to feel strong and solid again, and I can do that best here. I need time to make these children my family, and family doesn't mean just us. That means Jay, Susie, Maria, Fernando, Bob, Tim, and your parents too. That way if things happen to us it will be all right, because they will have many, many caring people who will love them still."

Charlie was nodding. I could see in his eyes he was beginning to understand.

"It doesn't have to be forever. We can keep our city house. The children are young and they can come and go. But for a while right now, I just need to stay here. I need to feel safe again. I need to know you are strong and well. I just need to stay put."

78

MOUNTAIN

Jake slept in a bassinet while Anna played with pots and wooden spoons on my lap and I finished my tea. I felt restless. It had rained earlier and the Garden looked fresh and clean and cool.

"You leave them with me. Go outside for a while," Maria offered.

The idea appealed, but as I stood, Anna twisted to put her hands around my neck and wrapped her legs around my waist. Maria's eyes twinkled. Humming happily, she returned to the stove where she was assembling a tray of baking ingredients. Anna and I watched as she placed a small handful of chocolate chips into a plastic measuring cup. Maria poured the chips into a small plastic bowl and then back into the cup again. Now that she had Anna's complete attention, Maria took a chocolate chip from the bowl and popped it into her mouth sighing pleasurably. Anna shifted her weight forward in my arms. Anna liked Maria and liked to watch her cook. Maria popped another chip in her mouth, closing her eyes in delight at its sweetness. Even I wanted the chocolate now. Maria placed a chip on her palm and held it out flat to Anna, whose fingers darted out. She brought the chocolate to her mouth. Her eyes lit up.

Maria laughed. "Go get me a chair," she said as she busied herself with the chips on the counter. Anna pivoted toward Maria as I carried her toward the table, her body stiffening. She relaxed again as we re-approached the stove, pulling the chair behind us.

"You put the chair next to me," Maria instructed. "Have her stand on it."

Anna willingly slipped from my arms onto the chair, although her one hand still held my shirt. Maria handed her another chip, which went right into her mouth. Maria placed an empty glass container in front of her, and handed her the chip-filled measuring cups. Anna poured.

"Muy bien, Niña!" Maria encouraged. Pleasure blazed in Anna's eyes, and I felt I was seeing a little of what Anna might have been like before her parents died. Maria nudged another bowl close, but Anna pushed it away to choose a smaller measuring cup. Using both hands now, she decanted the chips from the cup into the half cup so the excess spilled across the counter. Maria laughed. With her eyes, she told me to go. I hesitated, but she shooed me out with her chin.

* * * *

It was the first time that I had been alone since Charlie had fallen ill. I inhaled deeply the rich smell of pine as I climbed higher into the Wild. A ways up a back trail that eventually connected to the main mountain trail, I found two unfamiliar blue stepping stones. When I stopped, I saw a third. They made a path half buried under fallen leaves and needles. Only Mom could have laid this path. I wondered what she had been thinking. I envisioned the Garden below. I was above the Meadows that burgeoned with spring flowers. Maybe this path was to wind down through the flowers as a walk-about.

To my mind came images of stone animal statues and wooden climbing structures. In my imagination, these disparate images began to coalesce into a coherent playground. It would be an adventure playground where miniature climbing walls and long rope swings led to a tree house fort from which descended a circle slide. Made of all natural materials, it would blend into the forest as if it were camouflaged. The stone animal statues would be enlarged replicas of my old animal friends. Wild flowers could frame the path. Where the forest opened to a little sunny meadow, a picnic table would invite respite.

As I left the blue stone path, I began to gather speed. I pushed myself. My breath came fast. Sweat broke. My muscles burned. It felt good to go hard. The physical movement expressed some of the repressed pain still bottled up in me. At the summit Jay stood, waiting.

"How?" I stammered, trying to catch my breath.

"I felt you might come when Maria said you had gone."

I was glad to find him here. Slipping on the sweatshirt that I had tied around my waist, I sat close to him so that our shoulders touched. For a while we were quiet. Far out, a falcon circled, gliding on the mountain thermals.

"There were days after your Mom died when you were in school that I made this mountain loop three, even four times in a row," Jay said. "I'd never go farther than here in case you needed me. I carried a special satellite phone just in case, and I would push myself to see how fast I could get down."

I could see Jay circling, circling, cresting only to descend without stopping once.

"I want to stay in the Garden," I blurted. "I want to stay here with you."

Jay smiled gently. "But Charlie?"

I shook my head.

"A lot's happened to Charlie. He's hardly had a chance to keep up."

"It's happened to me, too."

"You have had time to get used to being a mother. I think Charlie deserves a bit of time as well."

"He almost died," I said, barely able to speak the words.

"I know."

"I wouldn't have been able to live if something had happened to him."

"These children will keep you going now the same way you kept me going after Becky died." Jay shifted to face me more fully. "Our time together has been one of the greatest privileges of my life."

"But if you could choose," I insisted, thinking about Mom.

"But that's the point. We didn't get to choose, did we? Over and over again, where has been your choice? Or Anna's?"

The falcon suddenly dove. When it climbed, a small rodent struggled in its talons. The falcon banked, and then flapped its wide wings, heading away to some uncertain destination.

"All we can do is make the best of what life brings us. Each hardship carries gifts no matter how disguised. We have to keep going for it, wringing out the best of each and every moment."

I knew Jay was right, but how could I go for it when I felt fear paralyzing me?

"We can't have preset notions about how our stories will play out," he insisted. "We have to be open to whatever life brings to us."

"Some people live their lives exactly as they planned them," I countered.

Jay smiled. "But we don't seem to be those people, do we?"

I laughed.

Jay's eyes teared. "When we see Becky again, I want her to be so proud of us. I want our resilience and our gratitude to be a way to her own forgiveness."

I looked at Jay questioningly.

"Every day she looks down on that crippled boy who is now a man. I want her to see by us that no matter how unexpected and hard life can be, it is still good."

The light bulb went off. If life could be good no matter what, then there would be nothing to forgive.

"I think about that a lot," he said, squeezing my hand. "I think about how that might be why we keep getting tested."

"Or maybe God is cruel and evil is real."

"Evil is real all right," said Jay with absolute certainty. "But it is only a smaller number of tiles in the greater mosaic of good."

"And God?"

"He's just trying to help us all figure it, while weaving us into one eternal cloth. We are all nothing but His threads."

A sprinkle of rain began. A large cloud greyed the sun. I shivered once. In the valley where the falcon had circled, the sun still shone. A rainbow arched. I looked at Jay. The rain pleased him, even as the sprinkle became more determined, even as my shiver became more violent.

"Get out of here?" he asked, taking my hand and pulling me to my feet.

I looked once more at the bright rainbow stretched against the discoloured sky. "Yes, let's."

As we hiked down the mountain, I remembered the mysterious blue stones.

"I know those stones," Jay told me.

"I was thinking of building a playground there."

"A playground?"

"For the children. We could build it together."

Jay's smile grew broad.

* * * *

Anna came running as soon as she saw me. When I picked her up, she held tight.

"She's missed you," said Maria. "She's been happy, but for a while now it was as if she was looking for something."

"Have you been looking?" I asked Anna, pulling back so that I could see her face. Agitation was still there, like a faded water colour. "I won't ever leave you," I whispered to her, tightening my hold. I knew it was a promise that would be impossible to keep, but I said it because I wanted to believe in certainty, until certainty vanished.

79

SKULL FIRE

A full moon and a blanket of stars cast soft light in the dark. The bonfire's flicker skipped across Southwest's walls, making the cattle skulls cast ghostly shadows. Its heat radiated in even the far corners of the small room. The smell of blistering sausages and browning marshmallows mingled with wood smoke. On stone tables around the fire, plates of chips and guacamole sat between Maria's enchiladas and cornbread. Graham crackers and chocolate were scattered next to plates of brownies and fruit.

Fernando strummed guitar and Jay played his wood flute. Charlie, Maria and Fernando sang old cowboy songs. Mary, holding the sleeping Jake wrapped in a soft blue blanket, hummed along with Mrs. Smith.

"Ansel Adams is one of my heroes," Bob was telling Richard. "I love the photo of him standing on top of his beaten-up station wagon by the east side of the Sierra Nevada Mountains.

"I like Adams' photos of the sand dunes," Mrs. Smith said. "The way he captures their rippling texture is truly exquisite."

"Those *are* good," Bob agreed.

"He has this quote," Mrs. Smith continued, "About how he felt that sometimes he got to places 'just when God was ready to have someone click the shutter'."

I listened to their conversation as I leaned forward in the lounge to eat a sausage over Anna's head, drippy with juices and sweet with ketchup and pickle relish. Anna was between my legs, playing with a set of cardboard box stacking toys that Mary and Richard had given her. She hid pine cones in their center, dumping them from one box to another. Maria sat close by, feeding Anna bites of sausage and fruit as she played. She opened her mouth like a little bird each time the fork came toward her.

To one side, Susie and Tim helped Tabitha and Antonia roast marshmallows. Susie took the marshmallows that were not immediately eaten and pressed them between graham crackers and chocolate to fill a little platter. Tim was pretending to gobble Tabitha's just-browned marshmallow. Tabitha was ringing with laughter.

Licking my fingers after finishing the sausage, I leaned back, closing my eyes. Jay was playing a Mayan tune that I remembered from my childhood. It gave thanks to the sun which grew the food and warmed the valleys. It reminded me of how I used to pretend that the fire was the sun healing in our hearth.

"We're very lucky aren't we, Niña?" said Maria, catching my eye when I bent down to retrieve several of Anna's boxes that had tumbled to the floor.

"We are," I agreed, looking around the room. "*We really are.*"

80

FAMILY

Charlie and I lay on each side of the full bed as Anna and Jake slept between us. Jay, Fernando, and I had spent a large part of the afternoon clearing the ground around Blue Path and now my arms and shoulders ached pleasantly. My eyelids felt heavy despite it only being 7:45, and when I closed my eyes, dream pictures came immediately. Blue Stone Path wandered off, far into the distance.

"Four in the bed and the little one said, 'Roll over, Roll over!'"

I opened my eyes to see Charlie's smiling face. The yellow undertone had mostly faded from his skin; his pallor had become rosy from his time resting in the sun.

"So, they all rolled over and one fell out," he continued, singing softly.

I laughed. It was true that Anna and Jake took up the lion's share of the bed.

"We definitely need to get a bigger bed," Charlie said. In the city we had a king bed. The implication was that the bigger bed we needed would be here. I smiled inwardly.

The sale of Wind Alternatives had occurred almost a month earlier. Tim had made certain that Charlie would not need to start work until September, over three months away, while Tim would continue to work throughout the transition process. When he had told Charlie this, Tim had rested his hand on Charlie's heart. I had thought it an odd gesture, until I looked at Tim's face. Like Susie and me, Charlie and Tim had been childhood friends. It occurred to me that their whole life had been lived in reference to each other. They were the context in which their destinies played out. I realized that Charlie's brush with death had frightened Tim as much as it had petrified me. Maybe his hand sought the reassurance of Charlie's beating heart. Maybe he was trying to transfer some of his own life force into Charlie – willing him to heal and gain his strength.

What was certain was that he was very protective right now. When Charlie had protested that the time off was excessive, Tim said, "Wind Alternatives doesn't matter now, buddy. What matters is that you get better, and that you take time to make these children your family. Everything else is dust. When we finish this contract, that's when we'll figure out what we want to do next. That's when it can start mattering again. Right now, you just take care of yourself."

I had taken Jay's advice not to push the idea about staying in the Garden. I was just giving Charlie time. It was only in the past week that he had grown strong enough to make moving back realistic. His previous energy was resurging and the old spring was back in his walk. Like me, he had started spending most mornings on the phone or working on the computer. In the afternoon we played with the children. Tabitha and Antonia usually joined us as soon as Tabitha was home from kindergarten. If Bob wasn't away, then all four of them would come; and often Antonia, Jake, and Anna napped together while Tabitha followed Maria like a shadow. All the children adored Maria and Fernando.

The older they got, the younger Maria and Fernando seemed to become. It wasn't uncommon, for instance, to find Maria under a table cloth with the girls, playing fort, or in the Monastery painting butterflies. Fernando transformed their butterflies into little kites and then took the girls out by the Landslide Cliff so Genie's breath would make them fly. He galloped them back on his back, often with all three clinging to him at one time.

On Friday Tim would fly in so Charlie and he could work together. The week before, they had ordered solar panels for the house. Jay, Charlie, Fernando and Tim were planning to install them together. On little scraps of paper, Charlie had begun sketching other solar ideas. He sketched them almost absently and often discarded them immediately. I collected the bits wherever I found them and put them in a shoebox. I thought them beautiful. I liked best that he seemed to draw them only on random paper scraps so each paper had a different texture and shape.

Charlie's smile softened. "I am happy here, and so are the children."

My heart leapt.

His eyes cautioned me. "In September I will have to return to the city to work, and I won't want you and the children here if I am there. I would miss you all too much."

"That's all right," I rushed. What mattered most was that he was happy here, in the Garden. What mattered most was that he wanted it to be a real part of our lives.

"But I am hoping that we can go back and forth a lot. Tim has been negotiating to allow us to work remotely for at least part of our time if we commit to extending our contract by another six months."

This was great news.

Charlie smiled. "I didn't want to tell you until I was certain. I didn't want to disappoint you if it didn't work out."

His expression changed, became more cautious. "I also thought that in the fall we could try IVF one more time."

I was completely taken aback.

He smiled down at Anna who had thrown her hand over his chest. "Now that we have these two, I want more of them. I want as many as we can get."

I laughed. There were moments with Anna and Jake when I felt the same way. A hundred thousand children would not be enough.

"I'd understand if you don't want to."

I shook my head in wonder.

"We could adopt more. We don't have to do IVF."

"I want to. I want to try."

"But if it doesn't work out?"

"Then I'd like to adopt."

Charlie reached over and took my hand.

"You're amazing, you know that?"

I smiled. "You're not half-bad yourself."

81

HACKING ALL THE SEASONS

Anna had been asleep since eight, Charlie alongside her. Jake was now resettled after his ten o'clock bottle. I turned on the taps to let steaming water pour. While the tub filled, I went into Mom's bathroom in search of a new razor. In the back of a drawer, I found her old wooden scent box. I unfastened the lock. Diminutive dusty bottles lined up in rows. Randomly, I chose a bottle in the middle and unscrewed a tiny blue top. The scent of wild strawberry lifted. Instantly, I was back in Glass House with Mom.

"Can I tell you when I get my period?" I had asked her, as Pug dive-bombed the cherries.

"We can talk about anything," she had promised.

"It's all right," I whispered to Mom as I brought the box against my heart. "You've been here with me the whole time. And the people you gave me," I said, wiping a tear from my cheek. "Jay, Maria, Fernando, Mrs. Smith, Susie. I would have never have found any of them if it hadn't been for you." I smiled at the irrationality of such a statement. Without Mom and Jay, I wouldn't even be me.

The water had filled halfway up by the time I returned to my bathroom. Undressing quickly, I slipped under the bubbles with a sigh. For a moment, I let the hot water soak my muscles and could feel them soften. Then I sat up to remove all the bottles from the box, collecting trees, flowers, and herbs into their own groups. On the bubbly surface floated fat drops of pine oil, which I mixed with cypress. I kicked my legs to disperse the oils and release more scent. I leaned close to the water to splash handful after handful across my skin.

I added jasmine drops next. They mixed with the evergreens, and I was back in my wedding dress. There was Charlie, waiting for me at the end of the flower-garlanded pews. I smiled as once more he exclaimed "No way!" when the monks brought in the electric keyboards.

There again was that yeasty warm smell of bread baking. There again was the sound of the monks chanting, as I lay newly married and entwined in my husband's arms. I lay a long time in the warm scented bath, remembering the monks' rich, certain voices; they fell and rose, rose and fell – chanting, chanting the mysteries of God.

ABOUT THE AUTHOR

Born and raised outside of San Francisco, Melissa Leet currently lives in Chicago with her husband Ken, her youngest son James, and their Golden Retriever Neo. Her older children, Christopher, Dillon, and William, are attending university. Melissa holds a BA from Smith College, an MBA from Columbia University, and an MA from the School of Oriental and African Studies (SOAS), University of London. She is founder of Chinafolio, a think tank which conducts academic research on China.

This book is set in Garamond Premier Pro, which had its genesis in 1988 when type-designer Robert Slimbach visited the Plantin-Moretus Museum in Antwerp, Belgium, to study its collection of Claude Garamond's metal punches and typefaces. During the mid-fifteen hundreds, Garamond—a Parisian punch-cutter—produced a refined array of book types that combined an unprecedented degree of balance and elegance, for centuries standing as the pinnacle of beauty and practicality in type-founding. Slimbach has created an entirely new interpretation based on Garamond's designs and on compatible italics cut by Robert Granjon, Garamond's contemporary.

To order additional copies of this book
or other Antrim House titles, contact the publisher at

Antrim House
21 Goodrich Rd., Simsbury, CT 06070
860.217.0023, AntrimHouse@comcast.net
or the house website (www.AntrimHouseBooks.com).

•

On the house website
in addition to information on books
you will find samples, upcoming events, and
a "seminar room" featuring supplemental biography,
notes, images, writings, reviews, and
writing suggestions.

CPSIA information can be obtained
at www.ICGtesting.com
Printed in the USA
LVHW04s1832070518
576287LV00013B/1199/P